WCC
7/21

D0480819

THE IRON RAVEN

Also by Julie Kagawa

The Iron Fey series
The Iron King
The Iron Daughter
The Iron Queen
The Iron Knight
The Lost Prince
The Iron Traitor
The Iron Warrior

Shadow of the Fox series
Shadow of the Fox
Soul of the Sword
Night of the Dragon

The Talon Saga
Talon
Rogue
Soldier
Legion
Inferno

Blood of Eden series
The Immortal Rules
The Eternity Cure
The Forever Song

JULIE KAGAWA

THE IRON RAVEN

ONE PLACE. MANY STORIES

This novel is entirely a work of fiction. The names, characters and incidents portrayed in it are the work of the author's imagination. Any resemblance to actual persons, living or dead, events or localities is entirely coincidental.

HQ
An imprint of HarperCollins*Publishers* Ltd
1 London Bridge Street
London SE1 9GF

www.harpercollins.co.uk

HarperCollins*Publishers*
1st Floor, Watermarque Building, Ringsend Road
Dublin 4, Ireland

This edition 2021

1
First published in Great Britain by
HQ, an imprint of HarperCollins*Publishers* Ltd 2021

Copyright © Julie Kagawa 2021

Julie Kagawa asserts the moral right to be
identified as the author of this work.
A catalogue record for this book is
available from the British Library.

ISBN: 978-1-84845-828-4

MIX
Paper from
responsible sources
FSC™ C007454

This book is produced from independently certified FSC™ paper
to ensure responsible forest management.

For more information visit: www.harpercollins.co.uk/green

Printed and bound by CPI Group (UK) Ltd, Croydon CR0 4YY

All rights reserved. No part of this publication may be reproduced,
stored in a retrieval system, or transmitted, in any form or by any means,
electronic, mechanical, photocopying, recording or otherwise,
without the prior permission of the publishers.

This book is sold subject to the condition that it shall not, by way of trade
or otherwise, be lent, re-sold, hired out or otherwise circulated without
the publisher's prior consent in any form of binding or cover other than
that in which it is published and without a similar condition including this
condition being imposed on the subsequent purchaser.

To the fans of Puck who wanted him to tell his own story.

PART

I

THE HUMAN WORLD

A long, long time ago

It was almost time.

I peeked out of the bushes and grinned. The stage was nearly set. In the tiny, sun-dappled clearing beyond the trees, the crystal-clear pool glimmered, attracting all manner of life to its sparkling waters. A herd of spotted deer bent graceful necks to the surface under the watchful eye of a great stag, standing tall at the edge of the pond. A few rabbits hopped through the bracken scattered through the clearing, and a family of squirrels scolded each other in the branches of a large gnarled oak. Birds sang, wildlife meandered, and the wind gently rustled the leaves overhead. It was a blissful, picturesque woodland scene, a perfectly peaceful day in the human realm.

Boring, boring, boring.

I smiled, reached into my shirt, and pulled the pan flute into the light. It was my own design; I'd spent several days gathering hollow reeds, cutting them, binding them together, and making sure the tone was perfect. Now I was going to see what it could do.

Drawing glamour from the forest around me, I raised the flute to my lips and blew out a single note.

The clear, high sound cut through the stillness of the woods, arcing over the grove, and all the animals clustered around the pond jerked up, eyes wide and nostrils flaring. The rabbits sat up, ears twitching back and forth. The deer raised their heads, dark eyes huge as they gazed around, ready to flee. The squirrels' tails flicked as they clung to the branches, their chittering voices silenced.

In the sudden stillness, I took a deep breath, gathering my magic, and began playing.

The melody rose into the air, cheerful and fast-paced. It swirled around the pond, into the ears of every living creature. For a moment, none of them moved.

Then, one of the rabbits began tapping its foot. The others followed, thumping their hind legs in tune to the rhythm, and the deer began tossing their heads to the music. In the branches, the squirrels bobbed, tails twitching back and forth, keeping time, and the birds added their voices to the song. I bit down a smile and played louder, faster, drawing in more glamour and releasing it into the notes trilling through the forest.

With a bugle, the ancient stag reared up, tossing his huge antlers, and bounded gracefully to the center of the clearing. His sharp hooves pawed the grass, gouging the earth, as he stepped and leaped with the music. As one, his herd joined him, cavorting to his side, and the rabbits began flinging themselves in wild arcs around the stomping deer. My glee soared; this was working better than I had hoped. It was all I could do to keep playing and not let the song drop because of the enormous grin wanting to stretch my face.

Rising from the bushes, I walked toward the grove, the pan flute moving rapidly under my lips, the song rising and the magic soaring in response. My feet itched, and I started to move them, dancing to the center of the clearing. Filling my lungs, I played as loudly as I could, my body moving almost on its own, leaping and twirling and spinning through the air. And all around me, the forest creatures danced as well, hooves and horns and furry bodies barely missing me as they bounced and cavorted in a frantic circle, hurling themselves around the grove with wild abandon. I lost myself in the music, in the excitement and ecstasy, as I danced with the forest.

I didn't know how long the melody went on; half the time my eyes were closed and I was moving on pure instinct. But at last, as the song reached a crescendo, I sensed it was time to bring it to a close. With one final, soaring note, the melody died away, the wild emotions faded, and the whirlwind of magic swirling through the grove fluttered out, returning to the earth.

Panting, I lowered my arms. Around me, my fellow dancers also came to shuddering stops, breathing hard. The great stag stood a few feet away, antlered head bowed, legs and flanks trembling. As I watched, he quivered and collapsed, white foam bubbling from his mouth and nostrils as his head struck the ground. One by one, the rest of the herd crumpled as well, some gasping wide-eyed for breath, some lying motionless in the dirt. Scattered around them, furry lumps of rabbits lay in the churned mud. I looked at the trees and saw the squirrels and birds lying at the bases of the trunks, having fallen from their perches once the music ceased.

I blinked. Well, that was unexpected. How long had I been playing, anyway? I looked at the sky through the branches and saw clouds streaked with orange, the sun hovering low on the horizon. I'd come to this grove and played the very first note early this morning. It seemed our wild revel had lasted the entire day.

Huh. I scratched the back of my head. *Well, that's disappointing. I guess I can't push these mortal beasts too aggressively, or they just collapse. Hmm.* Tapping the fingers of one hand against my arm, I gazed at the pan flute in the other. *I wonder if humans would do any better?*

"Boy."

The deep, lyrical voice came from behind me, and a ripple of magic shivered through the air. I felt a stab of annoyance that someone had been watching my revel; that was why I'd chosen to do this in the human world, after all—so I could worry less about curious eavesdroppers.

I turned and saw a procession of horses at the edge of the clearing, watching me from the trees. The mounts were fey creatures, lighter and much more graceful than their mortal counterparts, their hooves barely touching the ground. The riders atop them were sidhe knights, clad in armor of leaves, vines, and branches woven together. Part of the Summer Court, I realized. I'd seen them before, as well as the knights of the Winter Court. I'd even played with a few of them in the wyldwood, though they never realized the cause of all their small, annoying mishaps was a forest boy too insignificant to notice.

But the rider at the front of the procession had definitely noticed me, and he was impossible to miss, too. His mount was bright gold, brighter than any mortal steed, but the noble atop it outshone even his mount. He was dressed in armor of green and gold, with a cloak made of blooming vines that left flowers where he passed. Long silver hair flowed from under the huge antlered crown that rested on his brow, and the piercing green eyes beneath it were fixed solely on me.

Why was *he* here? Had he heard my music and been drawn to the sound? That was unfortunate. I tried to avoid catching the eye of the Summer Court, particularly *this* faery. I hadn't been doing anything wrong; the fey cared little as to what happened in the mortal world. The deaths of a few forest creatures meant nothing to them.

But attracting the attention of one of the most powerful faeries in the Nevernever was a dangerous game. Depending on his mood, he might demand that I "gift" him the thing I'd worked so hard on, play the pipes for him and his knights for as long as he was amused, or entertain them all by becoming the next hunt. The fey lords were notoriously unpredictable, and I treated them as I would a sleeping dragon: it was okay to tiptoe around and steal their gold, as long as they didn't see you.

But now, the dragon had spotted me.

The sidhe gentry nudged his mount, and the horse stepped into the clearing, striding across the grass until beast and rider loomed before me. I stood my ground and gazed up defiantly at the noble, who was watching me with appraising eyes.

"So young," he mused. "And such an impressive use of glamour. What is your name, boy?"

"Robin."

"And where are your parents, Robin?"

I shrugged. "I live by myself. In the wyldwood." I couldn't remember my parents, if I'd even had them. My earliest memory was the tangle of the wyldwood, foraging for food and shelter, learning the skills I needed to survive. But even though I was alone, I'd never felt like I didn't belong. The forest, the wyldwood, was my home. That was how it always had been.

"Hmm." The tall noble didn't press the question. He observed me in silence for another moment, his face giving nothing away. "Do you know who I am, boy?" he asked instead.

This time, I nodded. "You're King Oberon." It was obvious; everyone knew who the Summer King was, though I'd never seen him in person. It didn't matter. I had never seen Queen Mab, ruler of the Winter Court, either, but I was certain I would know her if I did.

"Yes," the Seelie King agreed. "I am indeed. And I could use someone of your talents in Seelie territory." He raised a hand, indicating me with long, elegant fingers. "You have power— raw, unfettered Summer magic rivaling some of my strongest allies in the court. Such a gift should not go to waste in the wyldwood. You should not be living in the forest like a beast, singing to birds and squirrels. You should be part of the greatest court in the Nevernever. What say you, Robin?" The king regarded me with eyes like pale green frost. "Would you like to become part of the Seelie Court?"

Part of the Seelie Court?

Curiosity battled defiance. I was intrigued, of course. Living by myself in the wyldwood meant I could come and go as I pleased, but it was getting a bit lonely. I wanted to talk to people, others of my kind, not just forest creatures and the occasional scatterbrained piskie. And of the two courts, Summer territory sounded much more pleasant than the frozen, hostile land of Winter.

Still, it was never a good idea to take the first offer. Even I, with my limited knowledge of bargains and deals, knew that much.

"I like it in the forest." I crossed my arms and smiled at the king. "Why should I go live at the Summer Court?"

The Seelie King smiled, as if he'd expected that answer. "Because, Robin, I am king." He spoke the phrase like it was the most important fact in the world. "And as King of the Seelie, I can give you whatever your heart desires. I can grant you power, wealth, the love of as many hearts as you wish." He paused when I wrinkled my nose. "But I can see you are not interested in these things. Perhaps, then, this would be of note. I have many enemies, Robin. Both within the court and without. From time to time, these enemies need to realize that they cannot underestimate the sovereignty of Summer. If you join me… Well, let us say you will have plenty of opportunities to practice your magic on things other than common forest beasts."

Now *that* sounded interesting. I glanced back at the pond, at the motionless bodies surrounding it. Poor dumb animals. I hadn't meant to harm them, but it seemed normal creatures were very fragile. I would love to try some of my ideas on sturdier creatures, maybe even a few fey, and Oberon was dangling that big, bright carrot in front of me. He seemed to know exactly what I wanted. The only question was, did I care?

"So, Robin of the Wyldwood," King Oberon went on, peering down at me from his horse. "What is your decision? Will you join my court? I will name you court jester, and you can play your tricks and practice your magic without boundaries. All I ask is that you do me a small service from time to time. Do we have a deal?"

Something nagged at me, a feeling that this agreement wasn't quite what I thought it was. I'd made deals before, but they were with piskies and sprites and a couple local dryads. Never with someone as important as the ruler of the Seelie Court. Was I missing something? This did seem a little too good to be true.

I hesitated a moment more, then shrugged. Then again, why not join the Summer Court? What was the worst that could happen? I was aching for something new, and if I was under the protection of King Oberon himself, think of all the pranks and tricks I could play without fear of retribution.

This was going to be fun.

"All right," I agreed, grinning up at Oberon, who raised a thin silver brow in return. "You have a deal, King. I'll join the Summer Court, as long as I get to practice my magic and play as many tricks as I want."

"Excellent." Oberon nodded and raised both hands. "Then I name you Robin Goodfellow, jester of the Summer Court," he announced in sudden, booming tones, and the branches of the trees shook, as if acknowledging his declaration. Lowering his arms, the Summer King gazed down at me with a sudden, almost proud smile. "Welcome to the Seelie Court, Robin Goodfellow. Wear your name proudly. Perhaps someday the world will come to know it as well."

1

PUCK IN THE MARKET

Present day

I love the goblin market.

I mean, don't get me wrong, the market is super sketchy and dangerous. Make the wrong deal, agree to the wrong bargain, and you'll find yourself cursed or enslaved for a thousand years. Or under contract to give away your firstborn kid (not that I have any). Or in possession of a thing that wasn't *quite* what you were expecting, in that it tries to eat your face off every now and again.

You can find anything in the goblin market. Need a potion that will make someone fall in love with you? There's a vendor on every corner that will sell you one. Want to buy a lamp with a genie inside that will grant you three wishes? The goblin market has you covered; turns out genies aren't quite as rare as everyone thinks.

What they neglect to mention is that the love potion you bought will make your target psychotically obsessed with you, and the genie will grant your wish in the most twisted and sadistic way possible, because that's just what they do. And this is *after* you've bargained away your soul or your voice or your best friend. The prices at the goblin market are high—mostly too high—for anyone to pay without massive regrets.

So yeah, the goblin market equals dangerous. Dangerous, risky…and tempting. Because that's the allure, isn't it? What's life without a little danger? And Robin Goodfellow never backs down from a challenge.

It was midnight as I strolled through the weed-covered gates of the abandoned amusement park, the grounds silver and black under the light of the full moon. Beyond the fence, I could see the rusted hull of the Ferris wheel silhouetted against the sky, looming over the trees. Straight ahead, an ancient carousel sat silently in the dirt, its once-bright horses flaking and chipped, paint and plaster scattered around the platform. An old popcorn booth rested close by, the glass shattered, all the kernels long nibbled away by rats or crows or roaches.

Pulling up the hood of my green sweatshirt I headed into the park.

The sounds and smells of the market drifted to me. Surrounding the carousel and scattered through the dusty yard, hundreds of tents, carts, booths, stalls, and tables of every size turned the flat, open space into a miniature labyrinth. Crowds of fey milled through the aisles, faeries of every shape, size, and court, from Summer to Winter to the wyldwood, as the goblin market was neutral ground and everyone was welcome as long as they could pay.

The vendors at the various booths came in every shape and size as well. A green, pointy-eared goblin stood beside a table selling dice sets of carved bone. A few tents down, a Summer gentry brushed her collection of cloaks, all made of leaves, feathers, or spiderwebs. The smell of grilled meat filled the air, coming from a spit with an entire boar spinning slowly over the flames, a lanky gray troll turning the handle. Its beady red eyes caught sight of me and widened, and its sinewy body straightened in alarm.

With a grin, I ducked my head and melted into the crowd. As fun as pissing off a troll could be, the aftermath would probably cut my visit to the market short. For once, I was just browsing, not on any official business, and I wasn't ready to leave.

The ground under my boots became packed and hard as I walked down the center fairway. Vendors called to the crowd, hawking their wares: herbs and crystals, weapons and trinkets, dragons' blood, hens' teeth, hairpins made of sculpted ice, potions, magic beans, faery dust, and everything in between. I hesitated at a table selling beads that would turn into mice if they got wet, my brain spinning with hilarious ideas, but I shook my head with a frown.

Stop it, Goodfellow. You're already in pretty hot water with Titania, I reminded myself. *Making her tub explode with rodents while she's taking a bath would get the hounds and the knights and those creepy spriggan assassins sent after you. It's* probably *not worth it.*

Pause.

Nah, it's totally worth it.

"Robin Goodfellow?"

I winced and turned. Across the aisle, a crinkle-faced gnome whose white hair looked like a miniature sheep was sleeping on her head peered at me over a long, low table. The counter before her was lined with green, longneck bottles that, even from several paces away, let off a heady sweet smell that could make a lesser faery slightly dizzy.

I grinned and stepped up to the table, putting my fingers to my lips. "Shh, Marla. Don't say my name too loudly. I'm incognito tonight."

"Incognito." The ancient gnome scowled, making her eyes nearly disappear into the folds of her face. "In a heap of trouble, more likely. What are you doing here, you terrible thing? And get away from my bottles. The last thing I need is for my wine to *somehow* make its way into the livestock tents. I can just see the nobles' carriages veering into ditches and trees because their horses are all suddenly very drunk."

"What?" I blinked at her, wide-eyed. "That happened at only one Elysium, and no one could prove what went wrong." The biannual event where the faery courts came together to discuss politics and review treaties while parading around in fancy clothes was just as boring as it sounded. For my own sanity, I made it a point to spice things up every once in a while. "Though come on, admit that watching Mab's carriage walk in circles the whole way out was hilarious."

"I will admit no such thing," the wine vendor snapped, and jabbed a withered finger in my direction. "Only that you are an incorrigible troublemaker and always up to no good. I don't know why Lord Oberon hasn't banished you permanently."

"Well, he keeps trying." I shrugged, grinning at her. "But never sticks. I guess I'm just too charming. I've been banished from the Nevernever…what, three times now? Or, is it four? Eh, it doesn't matter. Eventually, he always orders me to come back. Funny how that happens."

It happened because I was far too useful to keep away for long, and Oberon knew it. And while it was comforting, in its own twisted way, that the Summer King would never truly get rid of me, there were times when I wished I could be free, even if that would leave me homeless.

The gnome shot me a dark look, and I gave her a dreamy, overexaggerated smile. "Between us, I think Titania secretly misses me too much."

Marla snorted. "If the Summer Queen heard you say that, there'd be lightning storms for a month," she muttered, then straightened in alarm. "Wait, you were looking at Ugfrig's wares a moment ago," she exclaimed. "Don't tell me you were contemplating the mouse beads."

"Well…"

A snuffle interrupted us. I looked down to see a small, brown-and-white dog gazing up at me, stub tail wagging. It was cute, in a scraggly, ankle-biter kind of way. But I could see the copper gears, cogs, and pistons poking through its fur that marked it as a creature of the Iron Court. A clockwork hound. Or terrier, I supposed. A pair of flight goggles on its head glittered in the moonlight as the dog gazed up at me and whined.

I smiled. "Hey, pooch," I greeted. "Where did you come from?" It gave a small, hopeful yap, and I shrugged. "I don't have any gears you can munch on, sorry."

Marla gazed over the edge of the table and recoiled like I was talking to a giant cockroach. "Abomination!" she spat, and the clockwork terrier cringed at the sound of her voice. "Get out of here, monster! Shoo!"

The small creature fled, gears and pistons squeaking as it scurried away and vanished around a booth.

I frowned. "Well, it's a good thing you scared it off. It looked terribly vicious."

"It was of the Iron Realm," the gnome muttered, wrinkling her nose. "It belongs to the Iron faery that set up shop in the goblin market. Horrible creature. They shouldn't be allowed."

"Wait, there's an Iron faery here? In the market?" I was surprised. Though there was no law that barred the Iron fey from the goblin market, in the early days most of the traditional fey would not have tolerated their presence. Recently, however, it had been officially decreed that the goblin market was open to *all* fey, including the faeries of the Iron Realm. This was at the Iron Queen's insistence, because the faeries of Summer and Winter welcomed change as well as an old cat welcomed a new puppy. But this was the first I'd heard of one setting up shop.

"Where is this Iron faery?" I asked.

The gnome gave a disapproving sniff. "In a tent on the far edge of the market," she replied, stabbing a finger in that direction. "Beneath the old Ferris wheel. At least it has the good sense to keep away from the rest of us." She eyed me in a critical manner. "I guess I shouldn't be surprised that you would want to associate with those abominations."

"Nope, that's me. I love hanging around abominations." I grinned at her sour expression, though truthfully, I was surprised at the venom coming from the tiny gnome. Though the Iron fey still faced fear and distrust from the rest of the Nevernever, most residents of Faery had accepted they were here to stay. "But, uh, you are aware that we've been at peace with the Iron Court for years now, right? And that their queen is kind of a good friend of mine?"

She snorted. "I don't mind the Iron Queen," she stated. "Or the rest of them, as long as they stay within their own borders. But I don't want to have to worry about Iron fey when I'm in the goblin market. Or anywhere that isn't the Iron Realm." Marla shook a finger at me. "The next time you see the Iron Queen, you should tell her to keep her subjects within her own territory, not allow them to wander where they please, terrorizing normal fey."

"Well, this has been a riveting conversation, but I'm afraid I have to go." I stepped back from the counter, smoothly avoiding a collision with a dwarf, who grumbled at me under his beard. Tugging my hood up farther, I glanced at Marla over the bottles of wine and offered my best disarming smile. "I'm off to find this Iron vendor and send them your well wishes."

She sighed, shaking her head. "This will be ignored I'm sure, but be careful, Robin. You might be in the good graces of the Iron Queen, but none of those things can be trusted."

"Careful?" I grinned. "I'm Robin Goodfellow. When am I not careful?"

She rolled her eyes, and I left, melting back into the crowds of the goblin market.

Well, that was weird. I wonder what's up? Did a gremlin spit in her wine or something?

I wasn't naive. I knew there were those in the Nevernever that still hated and feared Meghan's subjects; I just hadn't expected to run into such blatant hostility here. In the market, you left all grudges, feuds, and personal vendettas behind. It was how a Summer sidhe and a Winter gentry could browse side by side without killing each other. Or why a halfling could walk past a motley of redcaps without fear of having their limbs ripped off. One did not tamper with the sanctity of the market, especially since many of the vendors sold some of the most dangerous, rare, and questionable items in the entire world of Faery. Make trouble here, and the least that could happen was being banned for life. Not even *I* would risk pissing off the goblin market.

Regardless, that seemed a bit extreme. It's not like the Iron fey have threatened anyone since the war with Ferrum.

I made my way through scattered booths and tents, ignoring the vendors that called to me. A persistent kobold latched on to my sleeve, squawking something about his fine tools; I turned my head and grinned at him beneath my hood, and he let go like he'd grabbed a scorpion.

Finally, the crowds thinned, and the booths and tents fell away until I stood beneath the rusted hulk of the Ferris wheel, which groaned softly as the wind blew through the metal frame.

Straight ahead, in the shadow of the derelict ride, stood a strange setup that was part carnival stall, part wagon, part junkyard. The booth sat on four rusty wheels and looked like it had been slapped together with corrugated metal and duct tape. Boxes, crates, and flimsy metal shelves surrounded it, blinking with strands of Christmas lights, and a neon pink sign flashed OPEN against the wall of the booth. Another sign, this one made of wood and iron, had been jammed into the ground near the entrance. Cricket's Collectables, it read in bold copper letters. Trinkets, Gadgets, Oddities.

A low growl echoed from the shadows as I approached the booth, and a pair of clockwork hounds, these much bigger than the brown-and-white terrier from earlier, slid from between crates and boxes to stare at me. They looked like rottweilers, the gears and cogs in their fur spinning lazily as they came forward.

"Oh hey, guys." I stopped, raising a hand to the dogs, who eyed me with flat, unfriendly gazes. "I come in peace. I'm not going to snitch your stuff." They continued to shoot me baleful looks, and I offered a weak smile. "Um… I'll trade you safe passage for a squeaky bone."

"Ooh, a customer." The door of the stall opened, and a figure emerged, the small brown-and-white dog at her heels. The two clockwork hounds immediately turned and trotted back into the shadows, becoming one with the piles of junk surrounding the stall.

"Howdy, stranger." The figure strode toward me, beaming a bright, toothy smile. She was small and willowy, with long pointed ears and bright copper hair that seemed metallic. She wore a brown leather corset, leather gloves, and knee-high leather boots, all trimmed in gold, iron, and copper gears. Her skin was circuit-board green, and the pair of leather-and-gold goggles perched on her head were almost identical to the dog's.

Yep, this was definitely an Iron faery. Just the amount of metal studs and loops in her long ears would be enough to give a traditional faery heart palpitations.

"Welcome, welcome!" the Iron faery said. "What can Cricket find for you this fine evening? Have you come to browse my wares, or are you looking for something in particular? Waaaaaaait a second," she added before I could answer, and shiny black eyes peered at me beneath the goggles. "I've seen you before. You're Robin Goodfellow, aren't you?"

I grinned. "Guilty as charged."

"Oh wow." The faery grinned back with excitement. "I hear the stories they tell. You're famous! Is it true you stormed Ferrum's moving fortress with Queen Meghan and helped her defeat the false king? And went to the End of the World with the prince consort? And ventured into the Between to fight the entire army of Forgotten by yourself?"

"All true." I smiled. "Well, most of it, more or less." She sighed dreamily, and I gestured to the booth behind us. "But what about you? Can't imagine you get many customers, even in the goblin market."

"Not yet," Cricket admitted cheerfully. "But setting up shop in the Iron Realm sounded so boring. There's huge potential to be had in the market! Just think of the profit that will come from being the first Iron faery to run a successful trade alongside the other courts."

"Right," I said. "But there is that small, nagging problem of regular fey being deathly allergic to iron. Kinda hard to sell someone a product that melts their fingers off."

Cricket shrugged. "All great treasures come with a certain amount of risk," she said. "And not all of my wares are from the Iron Realm. Some come from the mortal realm, from the places I've seen and traveled to." She waved an airy hand. "Besides, I'm confident that the regular fey will find a way to deal with their iron intolerance. They'll adapt and evolve, I'm sure of it. It might take a while, but hey, I've got time. Eventually, Cricket's Collectables will be a household name through all of Faery."

"Yeah...sure," I said, because I didn't want to dampen her enthusiasm. "Well...good luck with that."

She gave me an appraising look. "And what about you? Do you need anything special tonight, Robin Goodfellow? A pocket watch with a heartbeat? A mechanical bird that sings? A handkerchief embroidered with the fur of a silver-metal fox?"

"Um..."

Deep, low growls cut through our conversation. Both clockwork hounds had stepped forward again, only this time, their hackles were raised and their iron teeth were bared to the gums.

Cricket turned on them with a frown. "Ballpeen! Springtrap! That's not nice. I'm with a customer."

"Excuse me."

The quiet voice echoed behind us, and my stomach lurched. Even before we turned around, I knew who it was.

A figure stood at the edge of the yard, cloaked and nearly invisible, blending seamlessly into the night. The cloak was ragged at the edges, fraying into wisps of shadow that writhed into the air like a formless black cloud. The hood was drawn up, hiding the face, but I caught the flash of an ice-blue eye in the darkness of the cowl, the only spot of color I could see.

Ballpeen and Springtrap exploded into a chorus of loud warning barks. I was going to say something, but my voice was drowned out in the cacophony of doggy fury.

Cricket whirled around, clapping her hands sharply. "Boys! Stop that right now!" she ordered, and amazingly, the hounds ceased their frenzied barking, giving her betrayed looks, which she ignored. "Bad doggos, what is wrong with you? We don't bark at customers. If I lose this transaction, I will be very cross." She stamped her foot and pointed dramatically. "Go to your beds."

The hounds slunk off, melting back into the junk piles surrounding the stall. Cricket took a deep breath, smoothed back her coppery hair, and turned, beaming smile in place once more.

"Hello there!" she greeted the cloaked figure, still hovering silently at the edge of the yard. "Please excuse my security—they can be overambitious at times. What can Cricket's Collectables find you today? I have a fantastic deal on living spark plugs, if you're looking for something truly useful."

"I'm not looking for anything." The mysterious figure edged into the dim light. "I would like a message delivered," he went, his voice low and soft. "To Mag Tuiredh, please. To the court of the Iron Queen herself."

Cricket blinked. "That's...not really a service I provide," she said uncertainly. "I wasn't planning on returning to the Iron Realm anytime soon, sorry." She chewed her lip, then brightened. "Perhaps you would like a lovely mechanical pigeon to carry a note where it needs to go?"

I stepped forward. "Since when do you have to rely on the goblin market to send messages to the Iron Realm, kid?" I asked loudly. "Did something happen that we don't know about? Or are you in trouble again? Or both?" I shrugged. "Both is always an option, I've learned."

The cowl moved, the hood lifting slightly, as if its wearer had just realized I was there. His icy blue gaze seemed dangerous for a split second, hard and cold, just like another faery I knew, before recognition dawned and he relaxed.

"Puck? What are you doing here?"

"Oh, you know. Mostly looking for trouble." I waggled my brows. "But I could ask you the same. What are you doing in the goblin market? Don't you have more important places to be?"

Cricket gazed at both of us, lips pursed in a puzzled frown.

The figure hesitated, giving the vendor a brief glance before turning back to me. He didn't want the Iron faery to know who he was. "Perhaps we can talk somewhere in private," he suggested, taking a smooth step back. "I will wait for you on the other side of the Ferris wheel. Please find me when your business here is complete."

With that he spun gracefully and walked away, vanishing into the darkness as silently as he'd appeared. When he was gone, Cricket turned on me. "Who was that?" she wanted to know. "He seemed...familiar, for some reason."

"Just the kid of a friend of mine." I shrugged, very casually. "Tends to get himself into trouble if we don't keep an eye on him. Speaking of which, this has all been very interesting, but I should really be going."

"Hold on, Robin Goodfellow." The Iron faery held up a hand. "You cannot leave Cricket's Collectables empty-handed. There must be something here that you'd find interesting. Hmm, let me think, let me think…"

"I don't really need—"

"Oh, I got it!" She snapped her fingers, then pulled something from a leather satchel and thrust it at me.

It was a playing card—the Joker, to be exact—with a grinning black-and-white jester in the center. Ordinary looking at first glance. But a glamour aura clung to it, pulsing with magic and making my brows shoot up. A Token. A mortal object that had been so loved, cherished, feared, or hated by its owner that it had developed a magic all its own. Like a never-ending glamour battery. Tokens were rare, and the magic coming off this one was strange. It felt almost defiant, like it was daring the world to do its worst.

"This," Cricket announced, waving the card back and forth in my face, "was a famous gambler's lucky Joker. He believed that as long as he had this card up his sleeve, he could never lose a poker game. Apparently, it was lucky in other ways, too. According to the stories, lots of mortals tried to kill the gambler by shooting, hanging, even burying him alive, but it never took. Somehow, the bullets missed anything vital, the ropes snapped, or he miraculously escaped." She pulled the card back, watching me over the rim with a smile. "That luck could be yours, if you just do me once teensy-tiny itty-bitty favor."

"Always a catch," I sighed, and crossed my arms. "Let's hear it."

"Just this. If someone asks where you got such a treasure, tell them you found it at Cricket's Collectables, your one stop for the most unique items in the Iron Realm and beyond."

"That's it?" I said, dubious and surprised. Tokens were valuable, and the bargain to get one was usually a lot more than that. "No, seriously. I was expecting at least a lock of hair. It's never that easy. What's in it for you?"

"Lock of hair?" She gave a high-pitched giggle. "Oh, you old-bloods are *so* old-fashioned. It's called word of mouth, silly. Free marketing! If the famous Robin Goodfellow, friend of queens and hero of the Nevernever, recommends my shop to anyone, that alone is worth a dozen bargains. No strings, no fine print, this is just business. So…" She held the Joker out once again, waggling the card in an enticing manner. "Do we have a deal? You know you want it."

Oh, what the heck? She seemed nice enough, if a bit unhinged. And you only live once.

"Deal," I said, and snatched the card out of her fingers before she could add anything else. "Not that I need the luck, but more is always good, right?"

She beamed. "Pleasure doing business with you, Robin Goodfellow," she exclaimed, and took a step back. "Don't forget, if anyone asks about that Token, point them to Cricket's Collectables. You have a good night now." She lifted a hand in a wave, then turned and walked back to her stall, followed by the little terrier and eventually the two big dogs.

Man, easiest goblin market deal I've made yet. Free word of mouth, huh? Maybe she's onto something, after all.

I grinned, stuck the card in a pocket, and went looking for a cloaked faery king.

He waited for me on the other side of the massive wheel as he'd promised, hood pushed back, face no longer hidden in shadow. The moonlight caught in his silver hair, which was longer than I'd seen it last and pulled into a tail behind him. Tall and lean, he stood motionless, watching me approach, and though his face was young, the set of his jaw and the grimness in his eyes made him appear much older. He was dressed completely in black, down to his boots and gloves, the shadowy cloak rippling around him. Except for his pointed ears, he would've given a vampire a run for its money.

And though I hated to admit it, it suited him.

I wished it didn't. I remembered a time when he had smiled easily, when that bright blue gaze could charm a manticore, when he would listen, wide-eyed, as I told him stories about my greatest adventures in the Nevernever and beyond. I'd watched him grow up, watched as he developed the best, and worst, parts of both his parents—his mother's kindness and empathy, his father's courage and warrior spirit. And the mile-wide stubborn streak of them both. But I'd also seen that hint of darkness within that not even his parents had noticed, had watched it grow and fester until, eventually, it had swallowed him whole, and he'd turned into something no one recognized. A threat to the entire Nevernever.

Thankfully, with the help of his family and a certain infamous trickster, he had been able to drag himself out of the darkness, back into the light. But as was always the case when one returned from the void, he wasn't quite the same. Tragedy had marked him, and the taint lingered. For his crimes against Faery, he'd been banished from the Nevernever and forbidden to return to the place of his birth. Now, he lived in a place called the Between, the veil between Faery and the mortal world, with the shadowy fey called the Forgotten.

I worried for him. Despite everything he'd done, he was still a good kid, wanting to redeem himself for the crimes of his past. But I saw that hint of darkness in the shadows that clung to his skin and curled around him like grasping claws. He reminded me of another faery who, at a time when rage and despair had driven his every decision, had turned on his former best friend and tried to destroy him. I saw hints of that grief in the faery before me now. He was very much like his father.

Keirran, son of the Iron Queen, former prince of the Iron Court and King of the Forgotten, faced me calmly in the shadows cast by the Ferris wheel.

"Princeling," I greeted as I sauntered up. "Fancy meeting you here. Aren't you supposed to be in the Between ruling a court or something? Are the Forgotten driving you crazy, or did you just get bored?"

"I've been trying to get a message to Mag Tuiredh," Keirran replied, all businesslike and serious. "But the normal ways haven't been working. The gremlin messengers disappear—they never make it to the Iron Realm."

"Gremlins are flighty and easily distracted at the best of times," I pointed out. "You sure they didn't just see a chicken or a rock and forget what they were doing?"

Keirran frowned. "I've always been able to get the gremlins to listen to me, even before I became the Forgotten King," he replied. "There's no shortage of them in the mortal world, and they've always obeyed me before. At least one of them should have made it."

"What about Furball?"

"I sent out a request for Grimalkin, but he hasn't answered." Keirran shook his head with another frown. "Of course, Grimalkin will come only if he feels like it, and he's decided not to show. I'm running out of options. Since I can't go into the Nevernever myself, I figured I would come here to try to get a message to the Iron Court."

I narrowed my eyes. It wasn't that I didn't trust Keirran. I believed he was trying his best to do right, to make up for his past. But he ruled a creepy land shrouded in mist and darkness, with faeries that sucked the glamour out of other fey because they had none of their own. That would put a strain on even the most levelheaded faery, and with his amount of power, a stressed-out Keirran was no good for anyone.

"Is there something going on we should know about, princeling?" I asked. "Are you in trouble again?"

"No. *I'm* not in any trouble, but…" Keirran hesitated, a slight furrow creasing his brow. "Something strange is happening in the Between," he admitted. "There have been…incidents, with the Forgotten. Violent incidents, which is not like them at all. And the Between itself is… It doesn't feel right, if that makes any sense." He sighed, sounding frustrated and, for a moment, looking years younger. "I don't know what's going on, and that worries me," he muttered. "I was hoping Mom or someone from the Iron Court would be able to help. I certainly can't bring my concerns to Summer or Winter."

"Yeah, that would probably be a bad idea."

While the rulers of the Seelie and Unseelie courts didn't exactly hate Keirran—well, except Titania, but she hated everyone—they were old-fashioned and stuck in their ways, and if a problem didn't affect their own territories, they were content to do nothing about it. And if it *did* affect their own territories, their answer was usually to eradicate the problem, swiftly and with lots of pointy, stabby things, before it could become a threat. Though Keirran was very begrudgingly accepted as a ruler of a court, the fey tended to fear and despise anything new. Both the Forgotten and Meghan's own subjects, the Iron fey, had struggled with that.

The Forgotten King scrubbed a hand over his hair in an eerily familiar way. He was so much like a mini Ash it almost hurt. "I don't know if I'm being paranoid," he said. "It's my realm, I should be able to take care of this myself. I don't want to bother the monarchs of the other courts if it's not important. But..." His eyes narrowed. "I guess you should know the real reason I came. The Forgotten aren't acting normal, and...there is this *thing* out there, stalking them through the Between."

"A 'thing'?" I blinked. "Uh, can you be a little more specific, princeling? What type of thing? Are we talking haunted toothbrush, evil mushroom person, carnivorous house? Maybe a sadistic potted plant? Tell me if I'm getting close."

"I don't know." Keirran's eyes went unfocused. "It was like a living shadow, almost insubstantial, but the way it moved was just wrong. Maybe it's a new type of Forgotten, but it was like nothing I'd seen before. And it emanated...pure loathing." He shuddered, looking grim. "I could *feel* this thing's hatred. As if it despised everything and wanted all of us dead. Not just me and the Forgotten—everyone. All living creatures, in the Between, the Nevernever, and the mortal world."

"Well, that isn't very nice. It doesn't even know me."

Keirran shook his head. "I encountered it once before, after I returned from Ethan and Kenzie's wedding," he went on, naming the Iron Queen's recently married brother and his princess. "I thought I killed it, but either it's back, or there's more than one." He hesitated, then continued in a grim voice, "I think it's the reason the Forgotten have been acting strangely. This thing, whatever it is, *radiates* loathing. And the Forgotten have no glamour of their own, so..."

"They suck it up like a sponge." I whistled softly. That did sound serious. Definitely something that needed checking out. "Well, I'm no monarch of Mag Tuiredh," I went on, "but I *have* been lots of places, all over the world, really. And I've seen *a lot* of weird stuff, both in Faery and the mortal realm. So, here's a solution—why don't I go back with you to the Between? We'll just have a quick lookie-loo, see if we can't find this 'I hate everyone and their dog' thing, and determine if it's something Meghan and the courts need to worry about. But I doubt it. I mean, you're the Forgotten King, and I'm the one and only Robin Goodfellow. Between the two of us, we should be able to handle anything."

There was a tiny prickle of warning in the back of my mind. How many times had I said those exact words to Ash, back when the two of us thought we could take on the entire Nevernever? How many times had we ended up in way over our heads, facing dragons and monster swarms and ancient, powerful guardians trying to crush us as we struggled to survive and escape? More times than I could count. Now I was saying it to Ash's son, who had already turned the Nevernever upside down with his antics. Who was very much like his father, but without the centuries of fighting skills and lived experience to back him up.

I wondered if it was destiny or a very bad omen that we'd both come here tonight.

Ah, it'll be fine. This is Meghan and Ash's kid, after all. What's the worst that could happen?

The Forgotten King considered it. "Maybe that's for the best," he mused. "If the two of us can keep this contained, it would be better not to involve the rest of the courts. And if it is something we can't handle, at least you can go back to warn everyone. All right." He nodded decisively. "It's settled, then. Puck, if you would accompany me back to the Between, I would appreciate it."

"No problem, princeling." I grinned, rubbing my hands together. "It's been a while since I've been on a decent adventure. A trek into the Between sounds fun."

Keirran lifted his chin, looking like he was going to comment on that. But before he could say anything, a scream echoed beyond the Ferris wheel, and angry voices rose into the night.

2

NYX

Keirran and I exchanged a glance. In the shadows of the Ferris wheel, the Forgotten King's expression was impassive.

"Uh, you didn't come here with a mob of angry trolls on your heels, did you, princeling?" I asked.

The shadow of a smirk crossed his face. "I was about to ask you the same," he said dryly. "Apparently, there are rumors that a few thousand wild geese *somehow* appearing in Queen Titania's throne room this summer was not entirely a fluke of nature."

"Touché." I grinned back at him. "Not that I would confess to anything about that incident, but man, geese are *loud*. You could hear them honking for miles. Well, then." I dusted imaginary dirt from my hands and turned toward the direction of the shouting. "I guess we should go see what's up."

Together, we walked across the fairgrounds toward the distant hubbub. As we drew closer, the voices got louder and angrier, though any actual words were blown away on the breeze. Whoever they were, I hoped it wasn't an angry mob looking for Keirran, or me. Hard as it was to believe, there were creatures out there who didn't like me that much. Titania herself sicced her hounds on me at least once a year. You couldn't be the World's Greatest Prankster and not have people wanting to kill you all the time.

We were nearly to the carousel, tents and booths lining the walkway again, when the tenor of the voices changed. A blood-thirsty howl rose into the night, indicating something had gotten tired of words and switched to violence. More voices echoed the call for blood as rushing footsteps and snarls of rage indicated the fight had finally broken out.

Keirran and I sprinted the final paces around the carousel and found the ruckus.

A crowd of a couple dozen fey, eyes hard and lips curled in shouts or snarls, clustered in a loose half circle around a wagon. Most of them were Unseelie: redcaps, goblins, and a few Winter sidhe that held themselves apart from the "lesser" fey. But I saw a handful of Seelie scattered throughout the throng as well. Marla, the gnome, stood at the edge of the mob, her wrinkled face pulled into an ugly scowl as she shook a fist at what was happening in the center of the circle.

A group of four redcaps—think evil gnomes with jagged shark teeth and a hat drenched in the blood of their victims—surrounded a figure a few paces from the wagon steps. The figure's back was to us, so I couldn't see its face, and a hooded gray cloak hid the rest of its body, but each of its hands, slightly raised from its sides, gripped a curved, shining blade. My eyes were drawn to those blades. They glowed silver-white in the darkness and didn't appear quite solid, as if the figure was brandishing two razor-thin shafts of moonlight.

Whatever they were made of, they were definitely sharp enough to do the job. A pair of redcaps lay writhing in the dust at the stranger's feet, blood streaming from identical hair-thin gashes across their throats. As I watched, the bodies rippled, then dissolved into piles of squirming slugs and worms as the bloodthirsty faeries died in the manner of all fey and simply ceased to exist.

The rest of the motley snarled, baring their fangs, but seemed reluctant to fling themselves on the stranger's blades of light. Around them, the crowd roared, perched on the edge of devolving into utter pandemonium.

"Enough!"

I jumped as the booming voice rang in my ear and shook the struts of the carousel. Startled, I paused, and Keirran strode past me toward the mob, power snapping around him like a cloak. Overhead, lightning flickered, and ice spread out from his boots as he walked, coating the ground with tiny crystal daggers.

Eyes wide with fear and recognition, the throng cringed away from the Forgotten King as he stopped in the center of the circle. The redcaps hissed and scuttled back into the crowd, and the rest of the mob shuffled nervously, averting their gazes. Keirran might be the newest ruler of Faery, a mere child to most, but he possessed a special talent that none in the Nevernever could boast: the ability to wield all three glamours, Summer, Winter, and Iron.

"What is the meaning of this?" Keirran's voice was back to its normal calm, but there was no mistaking the steely edge beneath. "Have you all lost your minds? The goblin market is neutral ground. All fey are welcome here, even those of the Iron Court. Explain yourselves."

"Forgotten King." A Winter sidhe, tall and draped in a robe adorned in colored icicles, stepped forward. The icicles jingled like chimes as he raised an arm, pointing a long finger at the cloaked figure. "This creature came into the market and was clearly dangerous," he accused, his voice high and haughty. "We thought the threat should be eliminated."

"It attacked every one of you?" Keirran's voice was just the right mix of skeptical and mocking. "It came to the goblin market with the sole purpose of starting a war? How very ambitious. Perhaps we should ask how it intended to accomplish such a thing." He shot a glance at the figure standing motionless beside him. "What say you, stranger? This lot accuses you of single-handedly trying to slaughter them all. What is your side of things?"

"Nothing quite so interesting, Your Majesty." I blinked at the voice. Lilting, confident, and as wryly amused as Keirran. Also, definitely female. "I came to the goblin market searching for someone. Apparently, stopping to ask for directions is a crime worthy of death in this era, though it turned out to be a blessing in disguise. At least I found whom I was looking for."

She raised her head, gazing directly at the Forgotten King, and Keirran stiffened. Not noticeably; he hid his surprise quite well. But I saw the flash of recognition and shock in his eyes, and my own curiosity flared.

"Well, then." I stepped from the carousel's shadow and strode to the middle of the circle, beaming my brightest smile at the crowd of fearful, angry faces. "Obviously this has been a giant misunderstanding," I said loudly, "one we can all put behind us and forget about. I'm sure that's what we want, right? I'm sure nobody here wants to explain to the courts why the entire goblin market suddenly exploded in a rain of fire, blood, lightning, and frogs. Why frogs, you ask? Well, that's what happened the last time the goblin market tried to put an end to a certain Summer jester. Nothing but frogs as far as the eye could see." I found the gazes of the redcaps and the Winter sidhe. "It was so epic, the humans in the mortal world still talk about it. But I don't see any reason that it should happen again, right?"

"Robin Goodfellow is here, too?"

I didn't see the speaker, but at least half the crowd cringed back even farther. The Winter sidhe with the tinkling coat shot me a glare of absolute loathing, but I saw fear on that pale, haughty face as well. The redcap motley peeking out of the crowd cast furious gazes between me and the cloaked stranger, but this mob was done. No faery in their right mind would pick a fight with the Forgotten King *and* Robin Goodfellow, and after a tense silence, the Winter sidhe gathered up his robe and stalked off in a huff, cheerful jingles following his exit. The rest of the throng dissipated quickly, with only Marla giving me a pinched, disappointed look, before she, too, vanished into the market, leaving Keirran and me alone with the stranger.

"Well, that was fun." I laced my hands behind my head and grinned at Keirran. "Nothing screams 'exciting evening' like cowing a bloodthirsty mob and sending them scurrying back into the dark. Though you went right to the fire-and-light show there, princeling. I could've handled it in a less…direct manner, you know."

"A rain of frogs is not subtle, Puck," Keirran replied, but he wasn't looking at me. His attention was riveted to the stranger, who had dropped to a knee before him and bowed its cowled head. "Nyx," Keirran said matter-of-factly. "What are you doing here?"

"Looking for you, Your Majesty," came the reply from under the cloak. "My apologies for causing such a disturbance. I forgot the fey of this era have not seen my kind before. Apparently, I startled the faery with the blood-soaked hat, and it acted on instinct. I did not mean to draw blood in the market."

Keirran frowned. "No one should have faulted you for defending yourself. And I told you before, you don't have to bow to me every time we meet. Get up."

Gracefully, the figure rose and brushed back the hood, and the comment about Keirran and proper fey protocol died on my lips.

I'm a pretty old faery, and don't take that the wrong way—it's not like I'm some toothless hunchback in a rocking chair waving a cane and shouting, "Git off my lawn!" at neighborhood hooligans. What I mean is, I've been around awhile. When humans feared the dark and the things lurking in it, I was one of those things they feared. I have ballads and poems written about me. I made some writer dude named Shakespeare famous. Or maybe that was the other way around. The point is, I'm no spring chicken, and I've seen a lot. I've battled creatures from storybooks and had tea with legends. I know my faeries, myths, and monsters.

I had never seen this type of fey before.

She was sidhe, I could tell that much. Commonly referred to as high elves in more modern speak—thanks, Tolkien. Generally, there were two types of sidhe: the Seelie of the Summer Court, and the Unseelie hailing from Winter. Over the centuries, a few splinter branches had cropped up: dark elves lived underground, hated the sunlight, and had an unnatural obsession with spiders; wood elves kept to the forests and were of a more primal nature; and there were a couple clans of snow elves that rarely came down from their icy mountain peaks. But with a few differences in clothing and mannerisms, whether they would make you dance until you died from exhaustion or just stab you in the face, most sidhe were the same: slender, beautiful, otherworldly, and pointy-eared.

This faery was all of those, right down to the knifelike pointed ears, but she was still something I had never seen before. And that made her the most intriguing faery I had met in centuries.

She was shorter than most sidhe; I had several inches on her, and I'm not exactly tall. Her skin had a bluish-gray tint to it, not ghastly or corpselike but almost translucent, and tiny, star-shaped markings hovered under her eyes and spread across her nose like silver freckles. Beneath the cloak, she was clad in what looked like black leather armor, formfitting and leaving little to the imagination. Though I didn't see any scabbards for the pair of glowing blades she had wielded; they seemed to have dissolved into thin air. Her long hair was silver-white, even brighter than Keirran's, and cast a faint halo of light around her head. When she looked at me, I expected her eyes to be pale blue or black, or even silvery white with no pupils. But they were a luminous gold, like two glowing moons, and, looking into them, I felt my stomach drop.

She was…old. Older than me. Maybe older than the courts. She didn't *look* old, of course; her face had an almost childlike innocence that was quite jarring as she stared at me with the gaze of an ancient dragon. Age meant nothing to us, some of the oldest fey I knew looked and sounded like they were twelve, but… holy crap. Who was this faery, and where had Keirran found her?

The stunned amazement must've shown on my face when I glanced at him, for he offered a grim smile. "Puck," he began, indicating the faery before him, "this is Nyx. She's a Forgotten. I met her when I was first investigating the incidents in the Between. She comes from a place called Phaed."

"Phaed?" I blinked in shock. I'd heard that name before, remembered it from an adventure with a certain Winter prince. "That creepy town in the Deep Wyld?"

"It's not entirely in the Deep Wyld," Nyx said quietly. "Its borders touch the Between, so it drifts in and out of the Nevernever, manifesting itself only briefly." She cocked her head, giving me an appraising look. "Although, I'm surprised that you've seen Phaed. Usually only the Forgotten, or faeries close to death, can find their way to the Town that Isn't There."

"Ah, well." I grinned at her. "You know me. The impossible has a nasty habit of landing right in my lap. Same goes with any type of curse, disaster, bad luck, or calamity. I'm a trouble magnet—one of the perks of being me."

"I see." Nyx gave me that cocked-head, scrutinizing look again. "And you are?"

"Robin Goodfellow. I'm sure you've heard of me."

She pondered that a moment, then shook her head. "No," she said clearly. "I don't think I have."

"What?"

I almost choked on the word. Nyx continued to watch me, completely serious and straight-faced. I waved a hand at an imaginary me off to the side. "Robin Goodfellow. Puck? The famous trickster from stories, poems, and *A Midsummer Night's Dream*? The one who gave Nick Bottom a donkey head and made Queen Titania fall in love with him? Everyone knows who I am."

"Robin Goodfellow." She made a point of thinking it over for another moment, then firmly shook her head again. "No, I'm afraid it's not a name I've heard before."

A coughing sound echoed beside us. Keirran's face was red, one fist pressed against his mouth, as he clearly tried very hard to hold in his laughter. I scowled at him, and he immediately took a quick breath and sobered, though his mouth still curled at the edges. "Sorry, Puck. Let me introduce you properly. Nyx, this is Robin Goodfellow, also known as Puck, personal servant to King Oberon of the Summer Court. He is…rather well-known, in Faery and the mortal world. That part isn't exaggerated."

"My apologies." Nyx gave a graceful, formal bow. "I meant no offense, Robin Goodfellow, but I have not been back in the world very long. My memories are fragmented, and I fear I have lost a great deal. Keirran has attempted to explain what has happened in the time I was gone, but the mortal realm has changed so much. Even Faery is unrecognizable." Nyx shook her head, a haunted look going through her golden eyes. "Everything is so different now," she murmured. "The last thing I remember is being with my kin in the Lady's service."

"The Lady?"

"The Queen of the Forgotten," Keirran said.

"Then…" My brows shot into my hair. "Wait, you're telling me she was around when the Lady ruled the Nevernever?" I asked incredulously. "As in, before the courts? Before Summer and Winter even existed?"

Keirran nodded gravely, and I let out a breath in a rush. Nyx wasn't just old, she was primordial. True, I had seen the mortal world change, and Faery with it, but I had been awake through the whole process. I'd seen the great forests cut down and replaced with cities. I'd seen humans' belief in magic fade away as they turned to science, computers, and technology. I'd adapted, as had all fey—the ones who'd survived. I couldn't imagine waking up and finding everything and everyone I knew gone, and the world a vastly different place than the one I left.

Honestly, she was handling it far better than I ever would.

Though, her being a servant of the Lady, the Forgotten Faery Queen who had tried to take over the Nevernever a few years back, was mildly concerning. If Nyx was a Forgotten, Keirran would be her king now, but only because he'd killed the Lady in the war with the Forgotten several years back. That was probably another shock: waking up and finding that not only had the world changed, but the queen you served was gone and three new courts had taken her place. I know I'd be shocked if one day I woke up and Oberon was no longer king. If Titania was gone, I'd be devastated; who would I play all my hilarious pranks on then? I didn't have to worry about her, though. That basilisk would live forever on spite alone.

"Nyx," Keirran said, interrupting my musings. "Why are you here? Last I heard, you were going back to Phaed to check on things. Did something happen?"

"Yes." The faery turned to Keirran with a grim expression. "You must come with me to the Between, Your Majesty," she implored. "Something terrible has happened. The town, the fey there…they're gone."

3

HOUNDS IN THE MIST

Keirran straightened. "Gone?" he repeated. "Did they all Fade away?"

I repressed a shudder. *Fading* was the term for a faery who was slowly ceasing to exist. It happened sometimes to fey exiled from the Nevernever, as the magic and glamour they needed to survive was cut off. But it could also happen if mortals simply stopped believing in us, when our stories and tales were replaced with shiny new distractions, when our names faded from memory. The Forgotten were faeries no one remembered anymore, and before Keirran had become their king, they'd been in danger of quietly vanishing from existence, with no one the wiser.

It was a pretty sucky situation, but at least with Keirran as their king, the process seemed to have slowed, if not halted completely. *He* remembered them. The Forgotten King made sure to know each and every one of his subjects, making sure they did not Fade away through sheer force of will. And maybe because he was partly human, or because he was just as stubborn and willful as his parents, it seemed to be enough. For now.

"I don't know," Nyx replied, her voice somber. "Perhaps? Most of the Forgotten left town with the Lady when she woke up, but a few remained. The Fade has always been a slow, inevitable decline—many of us linger and drift in and out of existence for years. I find it difficult to believe they all vanished so quickly, and at the same time. Please." She took a step toward Keirran, imploring. "You're our king now. The Lady is gone, and the other courts won't help. We can depend only on you. Will you return with us to Phaed?"

"Yes." Keirran raked a hand over his scalp. "Of course."

"Wait wait wait." I held up a hand. "*Us?* Are you using the royal we or did someone else come with you?"

A loud, despairing sigh echoed behind us.

"How very typical," said a slow, contemptuous voice that could belong to only one creature in the entire Nevernever. "I was hoping that, were I not present, a decision could be made quickly and we could get underway. But even in dire circumstances, it seems nothing can ever be decided without having to talk it to death. I will never understand."

I saw Keirran wince, and even I stifled a groan as we turned around. "Oh hey, Furball," I said, meeting a pair of slitted golden eyes watching us from the shadows. "So, you're here, too, huh? Fancy that. Well, if *you* decided to show, then things must be serious."

The eyes blinked, and a large gray cat materialized on a fence post where nothing had been before. "I am uncertain you know what that word means, Goodfellow," Grimalkin said, plumed tail twitching behind him as he met my gaze. "The Nevernever could be crumbling under our feet, and you would make a joke about it."

"Well, duh. It would be my last chance to. If I have to stare Death in the face, I'm gonna do it laughing at him."

"Grimalkin." Keirran stepped forward. "I take it you came here with Nyx?"

The cat yawned. "She was looking for you," he said lazily. "I happened to know where you were, or where you would be going." His gaze slid to me. "I *suppose* it is fortunate that Robin Goodfellow is here as well. The journey will be entertaining, if nothing else."

I crossed my arms. "How did you even know where to find us?"

Grimalkin blinked. "I am a cat."

Well, I should've seen that one coming.

Grimalkin sniffed, waved his tail, and turned, gazing at us over his shoulder. "Are we finished here, then?" he asked in a voice of exaggerated patience. "The night is waning, and it is not a short journey to Phaed. If one of you could open the Between, we can get this endeavor started. That is, if you are done talking incessantly at one another."

I smirked at him. "But I like hearing myself talk. It's one of my best qualities."

"I think perhaps you are confusing *quality* with *quantity*. In any case, we are wasting time. Which is another thing you are so very good at."

"I'm sorry, Furball, but who's wasting time sitting here arguing with me?"

I could feel the gaze of the Forgotten on me as I spoke. This faery who didn't know my name or anything about me. It was such a mind-blowing notion: everyone knew who I was. Even humans in the mortal world had at least heard the name Robin Goodfellow or Puck, thanks to a certain famous wordsmith. She probably thought I was a buffoon, but that wasn't unusual; most people did. Because that's what I wanted them to think.

"A waste of time, indeed." The cat thumped his tail. He glanced at Keirran, who didn't seem to be listening to us, his eyes shadowed and worried as he stood there with his arms crossed. "Shall we go then, Forgotten King? You know the way to the Between, do you not?"

"Yes." Keirran shook himself and turned, suddenly all business as he gazed over the fairgrounds. "The Veil is thin over by the fun house," he said, indicating the way with a quick gesture. "We should be able to cross into the Between from there."

"We follow you, Your Majesty." Nyx drew up the hood of her cloak, hiding her hair and star-speckled face from sight. "Lead on."

No one bothered us as we walked back through the goblin market, though we caught several fearful, wary, and downright hostile glances from the surrounding fey. Whether they were reacting to the Forgotten King, the Great Prankster, or the unknown faery beside us, I didn't know. Maybe all three of us together. But the crowds seemed to melt away before us, until we were standing at the doors to the fun house, which were set into the laughing mouth of a giant clown head at the entrance.

I grimaced and looked at Keirran. "Oh, that's great. Nothing screams *fun* like walking into the jaws of a maniacal killer clown. Bet they gave a lot of kids nightmares with this thing."

"I don't choose where the Veil is thin," the Forgotten King replied, as Nyx gazed at the doors in open wonder. "The Veil is constantly shifting. Crossing into the Between can be challenging, because the places where one can enter never stay accessible for long. On the other hand, you can almost always find a way in, if you're willing to search. Or wait."

"And miss out on the wonders that await us through the jaws of death?" I grinned and made a grand gesture through the gaping lips. "After you, princeling."

We walked through the clown jaws, which emptied into one of those giant tubes that would spin slowly if the place had power. Beyond the tube, we walked through a maze of dark, twisting corridors that would've been pitch-black had Keirran not lit the way with a globe of faery fire. The bobbing orb of bluish light cast eerie luminance over slanted walls decorated with clown heads, porcelain dolls, and other things that made you generally uncomfortable.

Beside me, Nyx moved quietly, with a grace that went beyond the innate elegance of her kind. But her eyes were wide beneath the hood, gazing at everything with a mix of awe and utter confusion. When we turned a corner and came upon a clown mannequin hiding in an alcove, she jumped, and two curved glowing blades appeared in her hands like magic.

"Easy there." I reached out and rapped the dummy's forehead with a knuckle. "Not real. No need to slice and dice yet. Though trust me, that reaction is probably why weapons are not allowed in these kinds of places. Lots of stabbed mannequins, I'd wager."

"What is this place?" The faery lowered her arms, the blades vanishing like they were made of starlight. "What purpose does it serve?"

"Purpose?" I shrugged. "To scare the pants off people? Humans like being scared nowadays. In a totally safe, nonlethal environment, of course. That's where the 'fun' in fun house comes in."

She looked completely poleaxed. "Mortals *want* to be frightened now?" she almost whispered. "When I served the Lady, humans didn't dare venture out alone at night. They didn't need to invent terrors to frighten them—*we* did that."

"Yeah, I know." I gave her a sympathetic smile. "Unfortunately, the days where mortals feared the dark and the things lurking in it are gone. True, there are still some forgotten places where humans remember and respect us, but for the most part…" I gestured to the mannequin and the things hanging from the walls around us. "Their world is so tame, they invent things that will frighten them, and pay for the experience of being scared."

The faery shook her head in disbelief. "So, this is why we're Fading away," she murmured, almost to herself. "They've forgotten everything about us."

That seemed to be a sensitive subject for the Forgotten, so I left it alone.

We left the maze and stepped into a long hallway with mirrors on either wall. Not normal mirrors, but the ones that showed grossly distorted images where you looked like a bean pole or you had a bathtub for a butt. Nyx caught sight of her warped reflection and gasped, flinching back from the image staring through the frame.

"What...what has happened to me?" She held out a hand, staring first at her delicate normal fingers, then at the distorted view in the glass. "Is this a curse? Some kind of strange human magic?"

"Nope, just their idea of entertainment." I stepped behind her and grinned at my balloon-headed reflection, waving a sausage-fingered hand at us both. "The mirrors are bent in such a way that they distort the reflection. Humans like the grotesque and monstrous, as long as it isn't real."

She took a calming breath. "This world is very strange," she remarked with a frown. "I used to know a hag who could curse someone to look like this always." Raising her other hand, she waggled thumb-like fingers in seemingly morbid fascination. "Now it is merely a trick, a momentary distraction."

"Well, if it makes you feel better, I know a couple witches who have threatened to curse me if they ever saw my face again." She raised a silver brow at me, and I grinned. "I know, can you believe it? I mean, who would want to curse this innocent, angelic face? I would make a terrible frog."

"Puck, Nyx." Keirran's voice came from ahead before she could answer. "This is it."

We joined the Forgotten King and the cat in front of another mirror, this one making our heads look like watermelons. I looked down and saw that, for whatever reason, Grimalkin's reflection didn't seem distorted at all. Maybe he was too short.

Or maybe the cat refused to look ridiculous in any fashion. It wouldn't surprise me.

"The Veil is thinnest at this spot," Keirran murmured, gazing into the depths of the mirror, as if he could see something beyond the warped glass. "We should be able to enter the Between right through…here."

Stepping close, he raised a hand and pushed his fingers through the mirrored surface, like he was dipping them into water. Casually, he swept his arm aside, and the glass parted like it was a pair of drapes, revealing utter darkness beyond. A few tendrils of mist writhed from the opening and coiled around his feet.

I sighed and shook my head. "It always creeps me out when he does that."

"After you," Keirran told us. Grimalkin was already through the frame, vanishing into the black with his tail held high. Nyx gave me a look and slipped through the opening after him, her cloak fluttering behind her.

A cold breeze wafted through the opening, and I grimaced. "You know," I told Keirran, "I was just thinking I haven't jumped through a spooky, mysterious crack in a while. Always a fun time with you around, princeling."

"That's what I'm here for," Keirran responded dryly.

I snorted. "Stop acting like your dad. One broody, sarcastic dark prince is enough."

He just smirked at that. I gave him a return grin and ducked through the opening, into the cold, misty spaces of the Between.

The Between, also known as the Veil, is quite literally the shroud between Faery and the human world. It keeps mortals ignorant of the fey, and if you cross into the Nevernever from the human realm, you very briefly pass through the Between, as the edges touch both worlds. It is also the realm of the Forgotten, and don't ask me how Keirran and an entire race of fey can exist in a place supposedly the width of a bedsheet. It's Faery; things don't make sense, and that's just how it is.

"Okay, here we are." My voice echoed weirdly in the emptiness that now surrounded us. Most of the Between was full of nothing, a void that went on forever. The only thing as far as the eye could see was the eerie gray mist that hung in the air and writhed along the ground. "I forgot what a cheerful place this is. Don't you Forgotten ever miss the sun?"

Keirran smiled, but a strange look crossed Nyx's face, a shadow of fear that she couldn't quite conceal beneath the hood. "Not everything looks like this now," the Forgotten King said, seeming unaware of the brief flash of dread in the faery beside him. "The Between isn't quite so empty anymore. I've given some of the Forgotten leave to build their own towns and villages, provided they can find an anchor."

"A whatsit?"

"An anchor, Goodfellow," answered Grimalkin in a bored voice. "A thing that exists both in the real world and the Between. Typically, you can imagine anything into existence within the Veil—an entire kingdom if you like—but it never stays for long. It's not real, you see. Unless you have an anchor to hold it in place."

"Okay, sure. I'll just nod and pretend I know what the heck you're talking about."

Keirran lifted his head, as if sensing something invisible. "The Between feels strange," he murmured, his brow furrowing slightly. "Chaotic. Fearful." He shook his head with a frown. "I haven't felt anything like this since the war with the Lady."

Nyx stepped forward. "We should move, Your Majesty," she said in a soft voice. "We don't want to linger here. If something spawns now, it might be very dangerous."

I raised my hand. "Um, hi. Yeah, for all you Forgotten types and know-it-all Furballs, can we pretend that there is someone here who doesn't know all the weird intricacies of the Between and the Veil? What's this about spawning? Are we very close to a frog pond?"

Keirran took a deep breath. "The Between," he began, glancing at me, "is constantly changing. It is…well, it is almost alive, in that it will latch on to any strong sentiment or emotion and manifest that thought into a reality. If your will is powerful enough, you can create almost anything in the Between. But without an anchor, those manifestations fade almost as soon as they are created. Without that keystone, nothing here is real."

"But things can still spawn in the mist." This from Nyx, her moon-colored eyes seeming to glow in the shadows of her hood. "Emotions like fear, anger, confusion… The Between can create things simply based on what you are feeling at the time. And if you are experiencing a particular emotion, say, the memory of how terrifying it was to be chased by a pack of rabid wolves through a twisted forest—"

"We might find ourselves running from said pack of rabid wolves. Got it." I tapped my knuckles to the side of my head. "Sometimes I need a good clubbing with the ol' clue bat, but I get it eventually."

"There is a ruin close by," Grimalkin put in, sounding bored and impatient at the same time. "And I believe we must pass through it on the way to Phaed." He rose, arching his back in a catlike stretch before he turned, fuzzy tail waving behind him. "I suggest we head in that direction, before something comes swooping out of the mist at us."

"Swooping is bad," I agreed. "After you, Furball."

We walked in silence for a bit, the only sounds the hollow shuffle of our feet in the mist and fog. I didn't even know what I was walking on; the ground was completely swallowed by a carpet of white, and the dim nonlight made it impossible to see anything in detail. If you have ever been on a lonely road where the fog was so thick you could barely see the shapes of the trees at the edge of the pavement, that was what the Between was like. Only there were no trees. Or sun. Or ground, as far as I could tell. Everything looked exactly the same, and if I didn't know the mighty Furball always knew where he was going, I would've been a teensy bit concerned that we were walking in circles.

"So. Your name is Robin Goodfellow." Nyx's comment startled me; I'd been about to start pestering Grimalkin, just to hear the sound of someone's voice in the dead silence. I glanced over and found her watching me, an appraising look in her golden eyes. "You've been around a long time?"

"A bit." I shot her my best cheeky grin. "Not as long as you, apparently. But I know my way around the Nevernever. I'm no Furball, but within the courts and the surrounding territories at least, I've seen all there is to see."

"You're part of this...Summer Court, yes? What is it like?"

"Loud," I told her. "Busy. The Seelie fey love dancing and music and parties, getting drunk on faery wine, getting naked under the full moon. Don't let that fool you, though—they're not a nice bunch. None of the Seelie are. Oh, I suppose they're not as violent as the Winter Court. *Their* idea of a good time is to rip your limbs off and beat you to death with them. But Summer fey will turn you into a rosebush for the fun of it, or feed you faery cake until you die because you can't stop eating it, or sic their hounds on you for something as small as 'borrowing' their favorite hairbrush. I might just be talking about Titania now."

"Titania?"

"Oberon's wife. Queen of the Summer Court." I made a face. "Mistress of Spite, Lady of Pettiness, and Monarch of Temper Tantrums."

"I see." She seemed to ponder that a moment, brow furrowed. "So, not that different from the Lady's kingdom."

"Well, I don't know if I'd go *that* far."

She gave me another scrutinizing look. "Keirran said you were Lord Oberon's servant. What is it you do for him?"

"Me? I'm his jester." I struck a dramatic pose with my arms in the air. "Just a humble jester that he keeps around to entertain him. Also, his gopher, confidant, deliverer of love potions, and all-around flunky."

She looked momentarily confused, as if she didn't quite understand some of those words. I guessed language had been very different back when she had first come into being, and slang was probably nonexistent.

"What about you?" I asked. "What was life like in the court of the illustrious First Queen of Faery?"

She hesitated. "I was…"

Before she could answer, my foot kicked something hard and unyielding in the fog, making me yelp. Abruptly, the wall of mist drew back to reveal a half circle of decaying walls and crumbling stone, rising like broken teeth out of the fog. Overhead, the skies cleared, and a full silver moon peered out from behind the clouds, making me blink in shock.

"Um, okay. That's not normal, I'm guessing."

A howl echoed somewhere in the darkness, and everyone froze. Except Grimalkin, who flattened his ears as a corner of mist curled around him, and then he was gone.

I glanced at Keirran and Nyx, saw the look on both their faces, and quickly pulled my daggers with a sigh. "Oh good. And here I thought this journey was too dull."

The howl came again, a raspy, chilling sound, like the wind moving through the trees on its way to murder you. Nyx raised her arms, the glowing silver blades appearing in her hands, and Keirran pulled free the iron sword on his back. Around us, the wall of mist began to swirl.

Something pale and ragged exploded through the tendrils of white, lunging at my face. Instinctively, I leaped back, slashing with my blade, and felt the edge rip through thin cloth, as the thing whirled around to face us.

It was… How to describe something I'd never seen before? It was like the merging of a wraith and some kind of monstrous dog. The body was covered in ragged strips of cloth that fluttered and snapped with every movement, but the face emerging from the bundle of rags was definitely canine. A slimy, disgusting tongue lolled from its narrow jaws, its eyes blazed green fire, and four bony paws barely touched the ground as it spun, the claws on the end of its feet like velociraptor talons.

It wailed as it flew at me, and I dove out of the way, lashing out with my blades as it passed overhead. Again, there was that tearing and ripping of cloth, but nothing solid beneath.

With eerie howls, more wraith-dog things emerged from the mist, a half-dozen ragged monsters swirling around us. Their wails set my teeth on edge and made my vision sway, and the ground under my feet didn't feel quite solid. I staggered, and a dog instantly lunged at me, jaws gaping unreasonably wide to snap off my head.

There was a blur of black and silver, and a shining blade stabbed up into the monster's chin, impaling it through the throat. The dog screamed and flopped to the ground, rags falling away to reveal nothing but a canid skeleton beneath. Wide-eyed, I looked up as Nyx pulled back, a grim smile on her pale face. Her hood had fallen off, and her hair gleamed in the darkness as she spun toward the rest of the pack, glowing blades raised in defiance.

"Don't bother trying to cut their bodies," she told me without turning around. "There's nothing substantial beneath the rags. You have to go for their heads."

"Oh, so they're zombie dogs." I dodged and thrust as a hound flew past, stabbing my blade through one blazing green eye. The dog yelped and tumbled away into the mist. "Stab them in the brain and they go down, good to know."

I glanced over at Keirran to see if he needed help, but the King of the Forgotten was doing just fine. He whirled his blade over his head, then brought it smashing down on a wraith dog, crushing the thing's skull. As another lunged at him from the side, he turned and threw out a hand, fire igniting in his palm, and the dog's ragged body burst into flame. It howled, swirling in a frantic circle and igniting another hound that passed too close. Now there were two screeching, snapping bonfires bouncing around the rest of the pack, which threw everything into even more pandemonium.

One burning hound reared into the air and howled, a sound that seemed to echo in the nothingness and carry for miles in every direction. I didn't need to know what these things were to realize what was happening: that was a call for aid, summoning even more allies to the fight.

I dodged a hound and stabbed it through the eye, and it collapsed to the ground in a pile of rags and bones. But answering howls echoed out of the mist, coming from every direction. I grinned and raised my daggers as the bays and snarls grew deafening.

"Heads up, you two! More puppies incoming. Anyone got a squeaky bone?"

Nyx stepped in front of Keirran, her twin blades raised before her. "Please step back, Your Majesty," she said in a calm, matter-of-fact voice. "Allow me to do my job."

Keirran frowned. "I've told you before, Nyx. I know how to fight. I don't need to be protected."

The Forgotten closed her eyes. A hazy light appeared around her, and glowing runes crept up her arms, pulsing with the same energy as her blades. She took a step back, sinking into a crouch, her swords held ready at her sides. "I know, Your Majesty," she said in that same cool voice. "But you are my king, and this is my duty. Let me be your shield and your dagger, as I was the Lady's."

The hounds exploded through the mist, nearly a dozen of them, their bays and howls ringing in my ears as they swept in. Nyx opened her eyes and flung her blades at the approaching pack. They spun through the air, turning into crescents of light and scything into the hounds like twin buzz saws.

Ragged bodies split apart, heads and skull separating and dropping to the ground. Half the dogs were dead as the crescent blades spun around and returned to Nyx. She caught them as if they were a pair of Frisbees and immediately sprang forward to face the rest of the pack. I was too stunned to respond, but it was okay, because the Forgotten didn't need my help. She was a dancing, spinning whirlwind of death, leaping and twirling through the air as her blades cut the life from every dog that sprang at her.

In a few seconds, the fight was done. The sounds of battle faded. The clouds covered the moon, and the fog returned once more, shrouding everything in gray.

Keirran exhaled and lowered his sword. "Is everyone all right? Nyx? Puck?"

I was still staring at Nyx. She stood over the rag-and-bone pile of dogs she had killed, her blades shining in the nonlight, her hair and cloak fluttering behind her. As the moonlight faded, the runes on her arms disappeared, and the hazy glow around her vanished as well. She straightened, the curved weapons shimmering into nothingness, and gave a satisfied nod.

"Yes, my king," she replied. "We're done here."

I blinked hard. "Uh, okay. I think the only comment appropriate after that little display is wow. And possibly yikes." I received another slightly bewildered look from the Forgotten, and I gestured to my arms where Nyx's glowing runes had appeared across her skin. "I take it those shiny tattoos are not fashion statements."

"I...receive my power from the moon," the Forgotten replied, her brow furrowed. "When it waxes, I grow stronger and my magic becomes more powerful. I'm at my strongest when the full moon is directly overhead."

"Ah, so you're like a werewolf, fair enough. A very beautiful, nonhairy werewolf," I added as she frowned. "I'm not even going to ask how the moon can appear in the Between, because

I figure it's just one of those things. Moving on." I glanced down at a skeleton wrapped in a pile of rags and wrinkled my nose. "Can anyone clue me in on what *these* things were?"

"Manifestations of the Between," came Grimalkin's voice, as the cait sith appeared, sitting a few feet away as if he had always been there. Casually, he licked a paw, then put it down and stared at me. "You were warned what would happen if you let your emotions get away from you here," he said. "The Between will latch on to any strong emotion or memory and create a temporary representation of that thought. If you cannot control your emotions, you will very likely see them as manifestations of real things while we are here."

"Really? Does it also twist your thoughts into even more horrible versions of themselves? Because I've never seen these things before."

"No," said Nyx, stepping away from the carcasses. "My apologies. These are mine." She offered a rueful smile. "The Wild Hunt is a very old tradition. The Lady also had her hounds, and she would send them after those who angered her." She paused, rubbing her eyes, and a faintly frustrated look crossed her face. "Though I can't remember what they're called anymore."

Grimalkin sniffed. "Moonwraith hounds, I believe. Though they Faded and went extinct ages ago. Shall we continue, before more unpleasant things show up?"

He didn't, I noticed, make any catty comments about Nyx's sudden and unexpected transformation. Of course, after that whirling dance of death, I wouldn't, either. As we continued into the fog, I looked back and saw the bodies of the dogs, the moonhounds or whatever they were, shiver into mist and writhe away into nothing.

4

TROUBLE IN PHAED

I remembered when I first set foot in Phaed. It was several years ago, when Ash was just starting his quest to find a way to be with Meghan in the Iron Realm. Being a true-blooded fey, he couldn't exist in the Iron Kingdom without being poisoned and dying, so logically, he made a binding vow that he would find a way to return to his love and be with her, no matter how long it took, no matter what he had to do.

I went with him of course, because it sounded like an adventure, and there was no way the love-struck idiot would've survived without me.

We'd been following our guide through the Deep Wyld, the darkest and most dangerous part of the wyldwood, when a thick fog had rolled in, and we'd stumbled upon this ramshackle little town in the middle of nowhere. The residents of said town were strange, faeries I'd never seen before, who seemed to drift in and out of existence at random. Back then, I didn't know anything about the Forgotten, or Phaed, or what our presence would ultimately do. That first night, we discovered the Forgotten could drain the glamour of traditional fey like creepy faery vampires, and we had to beat a hasty retreat out of town before they sucked us dry.

But the Forgotten weren't the only creatures in Phaed, and our, um…disturbance through town woke up something far older and far more dangerous than we could have realized.

The Lady. The ruler of the Nevernever before the existence of the courts. She had been sleeping in Phaed, forgotten by everyone, and was none too happy when she woke up and discovered everything had changed.

Of course, that led to the war with the Forgotten, the Lady's rise to power as she tried to take back the Nevernever, and the whole mess with Keirran and his betrayal, but that was water under the bridge. As far as I was concerned, Ash and Meghan's son was all right. He'd made some stupid mistakes, but hell, we all had. I certainly wasn't one to talk.

Still, as the mist rolled back and we abruptly found ourselves at the edge of an ancient, run-down village, I caught the haunted look in his eyes as he gazed around. For him, this was the place where it all started.

"Strange," he said quietly. "I don't see anyone, but I can feel *something* out there."

I gazed into the town. It looked the same to me; wooden shacks abandoned and falling apart, sitting in the mud and fog. On the nearest porch, an old rocking chair creaked back and forth, swaying eerily in the breeze.

"It's quiet," I observed, and lowered my voice ominously. "*Too* quiet." Both Keirran and Grimalkin shot me exasperated looks, and I grinned. "Oh, come on, someone had to say it."

The Forgotten King sighed and stepped gracefully onto the path, avoiding the worst of the mud. "Let's go," he ordered. "Everyone stay close, and keep your eyes open. If something *is* still here, we don't want it to catch us by surprise."

"Right," I agreed. "Surprises are bad. No one likes surprises.

Unless it's your birthday and everyone is throwing you a party, but I don't think we're going to turn a corner and have the town scream *Surprise!* while showering us with confetti."

"Do people do that for fun now?" Nyx frowned, looking puzzled. "That sounds like a good way to be stabbed."

"Um, yeah. Remind me never to throw you a surprise party."

We headed toward the center of town, picking our way between puddles while trying to keep an eye on the houses lining the road. Nothing moved in the mist and shadows, no silhouettes appeared in windows and doorways, no eyes peered at us just beyond the light, but my skin started to crawl the moment we started down the path. It felt like we were being watched.

And there was something else. Something heavy in the air, making the hairs on my neck stand up and my fingers twitch for my weapons. It felt…angry. Not just angry. Hateful. Murderous. And it was getting stronger the closer we got to the center of town.

"Does anyone else feel that?" Nyx whispered, sounding strained.

Keirran nodded grimly. "It's him."

I frowned. "Him?"

"The thing we were chasing before," Nyx clarified. Her voice was slightly ragged, as if she was fighting to keep her emotions at bay. I couldn't tell if it was fear, anger, or both. "It's some kind of…monster. Not a faery, not a Forgotten. I don't know what it is, but wherever it goes, it leaves a trail of corruption behind it."

"Corruption?" I echoed. "What, like the Iron fey?" Meghan's subjects, though they were peaceful and mostly kept to themselves, still had a faint damaging effect on the Nevernever if they ventured outside of the Iron Realm. This caused some concern to the courts of Summer and Winter, who required that the Iron fey get permission from the court rulers if they wished to set foot in the territories other than the wyldwood. Fortunately, the Iron fey seemed pretty content to remain in the Iron Realm or the real world, where the corrupting influence of their glamour had no effect.

Nyx looked confused, and I remembered that she probably didn't know anything about the Iron fey or their kingdom, having never seen them before. But Keirran shook his head.

"Not exactly," he told me. "It's similar, but an Iron faery poisons the land with the Iron glamour they leave behind. The corruption is weak, but the effects are physical—withered leaves, dead grasses, that sort of thing. This is more of an emotional corruption. You can't see it, but it can be felt. And the Forgotten, since they have no glamour of their own, feel it more intensely than other fey."

"Oh, that's good. And here I thought the lovely atmosphere was making me twitchy." Glancing behind me, I winced. "Also, not to freak anyone out, but Furball has disappeared."

Nyx gave me a puzzled look. "What does that mean?"

Keirran sighed and drew his sword. "It means something is coming."

We had reached the center of town, which was a large open square with a dusty fountain crumbling to pebbles in the middle. I recognized it from the last time I was in Phaed, as well as the two-story, ominous-looking building ahead that, if I remembered correctly, served as an inn or hotel of sorts. Though, now that I thought about it, why would this town even need a hotel? No one came through Phaed except faeries on their way to die. And us, of course. Which was a rather morbid realization, and one that I hoped was not a sign.

As we drew closer to the open square, that feeling of simmering anger grew stronger, deeper, almost pulsing from the ground like it was alive. Abruptly, Nyx staggered, putting a hand on a crooked lamppost to steady herself. I hesitated, and Keirran stepped toward her, his expression tight with concern.

"Nyx. What is it?"

"The square," she whispered, and pointed with a shaking hand. "The creature. It's…here."

I saw it then. Or, rather, I *felt* it. The square was pulsing with negative energy: anger, madness, fear, hate, swirling around in a toxic mist of murky glamour. As I watched, shadowy tendrils began emerging from the ground, writhing about like inky snakes. Dark forms pushed through the surface, clawing their way aboveground, like zombies rising from the grave.

A chill slid up my spine. They were weird, spindly things, their bodies featureless, like a horde of shadows had broken away from their hosts to move about on their own. But their heads were clearly visible; bleached animal skulls crowned with antler-like horns, each one more disturbing than the last. Tendrils of darkness writhed on their backs and shoulders, whipping about in a frenzy as the things pushed their way out of the ground.

I drew my daggers, feeling like someone had dropped a bucket of ice cubes down the back of my shirt. I'd seen a lot of weird crap, but for some reason, these ghouls were on another level of the creepy scale. The hairs on the back of my neck stood up, as my stomach took one look at the creatures and recoiled violently. "Okay, what the hell are those? Keirran?"

The Forgotten King shook his head, his face grim as he raised his sword. "I don't know," he said, and his voice sounded a bit strained. "But I think…they might be Forgotten."

"What? How?"

Straightening, the horde of nightmare things turned, empty eye sockets black and cold as they fastened on us. I felt an almost physical hatred radiating from them, waves of icy contempt slapping me in the face. With each pulse, I could feel their thoughts, and they weren't anything nice.

Intruders. Outsiders. Not like us. Destroy.

Silent as death, the things glided forward.

I gave a yell and leaped backward, dodging the first nightmare thing as it swept in, seeming to float over the ground rather than walk. It didn't claw or reach for me with its thin, bony talons; rather, the tentacles on its shoulders flailed, lashing out like whips. I sliced at one that came toward me, cutting it in two, and the tendril spasmed like a severed worm as the thing recoiled. That cold, droning voice echoed in my head again.

Hate. Hate. Hate you. Kill.

"These things aren't really the friendly type, are they?" I quipped, dancing back as the monster hissed and pressed forward, raking with its claws now as well. "I'd hate to see the welcoming committee."

Keirran dodged a swipe from a tentacle, leaped back to avoid a slashing claw, and ducked around a tree to put distance between himself and his attacker. He was not, I noticed, attacking back or using his weapon in anything but defense. His last words rang in my head, grim and terrible as he realized what these monsters could be.

They might be Forgotten.

Keirran was reluctant to harm his people, reluctant to use his power on the Forgotten he'd sworn to protect. Which was all well and good normally, but now, when said Forgotten were trying to shove their tentacles up our backsides, it was less than ideal.

Nyx, on the other hand, had no such compulsion, especially when it came to protecting her king. She spun and danced around Keirran with that deadly grace I'd seen before, her moonblades flashing in lethal arcs that left silver tracers in the air. One blade sliced through the arm of a creature reaching for Keirran, and the thing hissed, clutching the shadowy stump of a limb.

I dodged an onslaught of flailing, thrashing tentacles, as a pair of skull-head things came at me from two directions. I ducked, but a reaching tentacle brushed the side of my head, and the stab of cold that came with it was instant and breathtaking. It was like being jabbed in the ear with an icicle that went straight into your brain.

For a moment, rage flared. Dancing back, I glared at the thing that had stabbed me, suddenly hating it, wanting to knock its ugly, disturbing head from its shoulders. Two of them followed my retreat, chasing me across the square, and I felt my lips curl in an evil grin.

"All right, ghouls. You wanna play with Robin Goodfellow? Let's play, then."

Still backing away, I sheathed one dagger, reached into my hair, and pulled out a raven feather, the short black quill barely visible in the darkness. I didn't do this little trick often, but these guys had pissed me off, and I was mad now. I felt the surge of glamour to my fingertips, the darker side of Summer magic: chaotic and wild and uncontrolled. The energy of lightning storms, wildfires, tornados, and hurricanes.

I called it to me and released it into the feather, and as the shadow things continued to press forward, I raised my hand and opened my fingers, letting it spiral up into the sky.

For a heartbeat, nothing happened. The shadows continued to pursue me around the square, swiping with long talons or flailing with their tentacles. From the corner of my eye, I could see Keirran and Nyx surrounded by three skull creatures. Keirran was finally using some of his power, but it was still to keep the ghouls at bay, not to hurt any of them. He gestured, and a barrier of ice spears thrust out of the ground between him and the monsters. I glanced just in time to see Nyx spring over the ice wall, do a midair flip, and slam her foot into the back of a ghoul's head as she came down. The ghoul staggered forward, impaling itself on a spear of ice, and Nyx continued her deadly dance into the next two.

Thrashing tentacles filled my vision, as one of the monsters chasing me around the edges of the square lunged, swiping with a claw. I threw myself backward, rolled to avoid the writhing tendrils, and came up on my feet, smiling viciously. The two shadow things paused, watching me with cold, dead eyes.

A harsh, guttural caw rang out somewhere overhead, and

a single black bird swooped out of the darkness. It circled the shadow things, then fluttered up to perch on my shoulder, digging tiny but sharp claws into my shirt. The raven cocked its head, eyed the monsters with a beady black eye, and ruffled its feathers with another croaking caw.

Another answered it. And another. The flutter of wings filled the air as dozens of black forms began swooping from the sky and circling overhead. The shadow things paused, staring at the birds filling the air, but after a moment their gazes fell to me again, and they pressed forward once more.

A raven darted from the sky, zipping past the creature's bleached skull, making it flinch. A second swooped in and sank its talons into the side of its head, cawing and beating its wings. The ghoul slapped it away, only to have another take its place, and a second and third, until half a dozen ravens clung to it, all shrieking and flapping wildly, pecking with sharp beaks. The raven on my shoulder left its perch to join its brethren, and for a moment, the scene was almost comical: a mob of creepy, shadowlike monsters with bleached skulls for heads, flailing wildly as they were beset on all sides by ravens. Claws slashed and tentacles flailed, swatting birds from the air. Ravens fell like flies, but this was just the preliminaries.

With a cacophony too loud for words, a massive cloud of shrieking, flapping ravens descended on the creatures from above. They swarmed like a horde of locusts on a cornfield, and the shadow things stood no chance. In seconds, the two vanished into a swirling mass of wings, feathers, beaks, and talons, and whatever sounds they made were drowned in a torrent of caws and guttural screams.

It lasted only seconds, though the noise made it feel a lot longer. The cloud of ravens broke apart, and the flock dispersed as the birds flew off in different directions, vanishing into the night once more. Of the shadow things, nothing physical remained, not even their skulls, just a few ragged wisps of darkness dissolving in the breeze.

I shuddered, then looked to where Keirran and Nyx had been fighting shadow monsters of their own, only to see that the fight was over. Nyx, surrounded by fading tentacles, gave her blades a final flourish before they vanished into mist in her hands. Keirran, however, was staring at me, the look on his face one of astonishment and concern.

"I've never seen you do that before," he said, in a voice that teetered on the edge of disapproval.

I shrugged. Now that the battle was over and my adrenaline was going down to acceptable levels, I felt...almost ashamed of myself. What the heck was I thinking, using that technique? That type of glamour use—that wild, furious, terrifying magic, the glamour of fear and utter chaos—wasn't me. At least, not anymore. A very long time ago, back when the world was younger and much less civilized, the name Robin Goodfellow had inspired as much fear as any demon or devil today, but it wasn't anything I'd want to go back to.

Keirran was still watching me, his eyes shadowed. With a sigh, I sheathed my remaining dagger and turned to face him fully. "It's not a trick I pull out of my hat often, princeling," I confessed. "Tends to freak people out when they see it."

"Those were Forgotten that you killed. Both of you." He looked at Nyx as well, an edge of anger in his voice now. "I could feel it. I don't know what happened to them, but they were definitely Forgotten. We might have reasoned with them."

"Yeah, maybe." I crossed my arms. "But they were trying to kill us first. And that violated my most important rule—don't die. Also, don't get stabbed, another very important rule. If something is trying to shove unpleasant things through my insides, I'm not gonna stand there and let them do it."

"I have to agree with Puck, Your Majesty," echoed Nyx. "Those may have been Forgotten once, but they were attempting to do you harm. As I served the Lady, I now serve you, and my oath remains."

"We could have talked to them. Those were your people, Nyx."

The silver-haired faery regarded him calmly, her eyes unyielding. "I am not a diplomat, my king," she said. And her voice was not bitter or angry or prideful; she was simply and quietly stating a fact. "My skills are not of charm and voice and turn of phrase. I do not have the talent or the inclination to persuade anyone. I am one thing only, and that is a trained killer. My past is hazy, but I do remember that. The purpose of my existence is to protect my liege and to eliminate those they command me to eliminate."

"And if I order you not to eliminate anyone?"

"Then I will obey to the best of my ability, but if someone threatens your life, I am honor bound to kill them. I do not know any other way."

Keirran sighed. He didn't seem pleased, but he wasn't going to argue, either.

I took the opportunity to change the subject. "So, you said those were Forgotten. Are you sure about that, princeling?" He glanced my way, frowning, and I shrugged. "I don't recall any Forgotten having an affinity for wearing skulls on their faces. Or being so very, very angry."

"I'm sure," Keirran replied firmly. "There's no doubt in my mind. Those were Forgotten." A pained look crossed his face, and he shook his head. "I don't know what happened to them, or what caused them to attack, but it's something we need to get to the bottom of, quickly."

"That I do agree with," I said. "Because those guys were not friendly at all. Any idea what caused them to hulk out on us?"

"Something changed them," Nyx said. "Those Forgotten weren't like that before. What has happened to Phaed and everyone?" She closed her eyes momentarily. "This anger... It's unnatural. I can sense the hatred of this place, pulsing from the ground. It makes me want to hurt something." She glanced at me, and for a split second, a flash of cold rage in those golden eyes made me want to reach for my daggers. But then she winced, and her expression returned to normal, as did my heartbeat.

"Nyx," Keirran said suddenly, "that creature we were tracking—do you think it could have caused this?"

"Perhaps," Nyx replied. "With the amount of negative glamour it sheds, if the creature stayed in one place, it very well could have tainted the land around it. Many of the Forgotten are extremely susceptible to outside glamour. They would not have been able to resist."

"I was afraid of that." The Forgotten King nodded. "In any event, we need to find this thing. Quickly."

"Good plan," I said. "Except, I have no idea what this mysterious creature you keep talking about is, or even what it looks like. Where the hell is Furball? He has all the answers, or pretends that he has all the answers. The fight is over... He usually pops up when it's safe again—"

A tremor went through the ground. I froze, as did everyone else, and glanced around warily.

"Perhaps we are not safe yet, after all," Nyx commented softly.

Keirran drew his sword, glamour flaring to life around him. His eyes were dangerous as he gazed toward the sky. "It's still here."

A rumble went through the ground under my feet, and a shadow fell over us. Slowly, I looked up, past the wall of the inn, and saw something massive, a dark blotch against the sky, perched on the roof. I didn't know *what* it was, but one thing was for certain—it was definitely a monster.

For starters, even hunched over, it was probably close to twelve feet tall. *Not* counting the enormous pair of jagged horns sprouting from its head like tree branches. Its upper body was thick and apelike, with long, muscular forearms ending in claw-tipped hands, and the skin was hairless except for a shaggy, matted mane that bristled from its shoulders and ran down its back. A twisted face—equal parts wolf, monkey, and bearded goat—curled its muzzle back to reveal yellow fangs the size of my fingers, and the eyes that peered down at us were empty and white. Like the tainted Forgotten of earlier, shadowy tendrils writhed and flailed around it, tentacles of dark glamour curling off its body to dissolve in the air.

It was possibly the most disturbing, terrifying thing I'd ever seen, and not just because it was one ugly mofo. In both the human and the faery world, there was a lot of weird, scary shit, so I was no stranger to the grotesque and horrible. But seeing that twisted form looming over us, silhouetted against the yellow moon, filled me with a dread I'd never experienced before. I could feel the hatred pulsing from it, the absolute rage and loathing in those blank white eyes as it gazed down at us. As if I was looking at the End of All Things, brought to horrid, twisted life.

Beside me, Keirran let out a slow, shaky breath as we stared up at the thing. "It's…a lot bigger than when I saw it last," he commented, and there was something new in his voice. An understanding not yet fully realized, but his grim tone made it clear that when that understanding did come, it was going to be horrible.

The thing threw back its head and howled, an ear-piercing wail that set my teeth on edge and threatened to blow my eardrums from my skull.

Keirran winced, and Nyx clapped her hands to the sides of her head.

The monster leaped from the roof of the building, seemed to float in the air for a split second, then plummeted toward us, landing with a crash that shook the ground and toppled a couple nearby trees. Looming to its full, terrifying height, it lurched toward us.

5

THE MONSTER

I tensed as the monster stomped forward, but beside me, Keirran was already in motion. Raising his sword, he knelt and drove it point first into the ground, in a move I had seen from his father sometimes. I felt a pulse of frigid glamour go through the air. There was a flash of bright blue, and the ground was suddenly encased in a layer of ice several inches thick.

The monster bearing down on us stumbled as ice crawled up its legs, spread over its chest, and climbed toward its face, seeking to cocoon its whole body in crystallized water. Its furious roar was cut off as the ice flowed over its head, filled its jaws, and sealed it completely.

"Hurry," Keirran urged, glancing up at me and Nyx. His expression was tight, his voice strained as he continued to grip the hilt of his blade. "Kill it quickly before it breaks loose. I don't know how long this will hold—"

With a shattering of crystal that sounded like breaking lamps, the thing reared its head up with a howl, sending ice shards flying in every direction. Keirran staggered, and Nyx shot into motion, her moonlight blades appearing in her hand as she raced toward it. Pulling my daggers, I sprinted after her.

Tentacles flailing, the creature shook itself, shattering the ice prison with a roar. Ice shards went flying, and I ducked as one went spinning past my head and embedded itself in a nearby tree trunk. Thankfully, I had lots and lots of practice dodging frozen projectiles, particularly ice daggers. As the beast turned toward us, Nyx leaped forward, the moonlight gleaming off her blades.

The creature's arm lashed out, faster than I would have thought possible, and curved black claws slammed into Nyx. Her body seemed to ripple and fray apart, like shafts of moonlight dissolving into shadow, leaving nothing behind. I didn't have time to be surprised when she appeared from another angle, nearly behind the monster, and drove her blade deep into its thigh. It roared and spun, swatting at her with a tentacle, but she was already dancing away.

Not to be outdone, I drew on my glamour and leaped into the air, feeling my body shrink in seconds, growing wings, feathers, and beady bird eyes. Flapping my wings, I flew straight for the creature with a defiant caw, seeing Nyx dodge another swipe from the monster's razor claws that raked deep gashes in the earth. Damn, she was fast. I didn't normally stop to admire another faery's fighting style, but this girl's skill might rival the best swordsman I knew, and that was saying something. Even so, between the creature's ferocity and the flailing tentacles, she was having trouble landing another blow. She could use a little help, or at least a good distraction.

I was very good at distractions.

Directly over the creature's head, I released my bird form and dropped from the air in an explosion of feathers. With a whoop, I landed on the thing's skull, between the huge, sweeping antlers of a monster.

"Hey, ugly. Let's give you something else to think about. Bet you can't get me off without ramming your face into something."

The creature tossed its head with a roar. I, of course, had been expecting that and grabbed one of those sharp antler points to keep my balance. You ride one giant angry creature that wants to kill you, you've ridden them all. It was just a matter of timing, really. The only thing to watch out for was if it decided to headbutt a tree.

"Oh, come on," I mocked as it hunched its shoulders and shook its head like a dog. "Is that your best attempt? I've piggybacked on giants and Minotaurs and once rode a very angry wild Pegasus without a saddle. You're gonna have to do better than that."

As I spoke, Keirran's Summer glamour filled the air, and the ground under the monster's feet erupted with vines, roots, and brambles. The creature halted, snarling as the vegetation wrapped around its limbs, coiling over its arms and dragging it toward the ground. The monster braced itself, fighting the inevitable pull. It was strong, but it wasn't paying attention to us any longer.

I caught a streak of shadow as Nyx darted toward the monster, vaulted off a tree trunk, and slashed her blade through the creature's thick neck. A very precise, deadly shot that would sever the jugular and bleed the thing out in seconds were it a normal beast.

I hoped it was a normal beast. Kneeling, I drove my daggers into the base of its skull, sinking them to the hilt. I wasn't usually this ruthless, and I didn't enjoy killing this way, but Keirran was right. Whatever this monster was, it had to die. No games, no playing around. Best get it over with quickly.

The creature staggered, falling to all fours. The vines and roots coiled around its body tightened even further, bringing its skull close to the ground. I saw Nyx emerge from the darkness again, both blades in hand as she rushed toward the monster's head. Probably aiming to take it off this time, which was a good move, I thought. With very few exceptions, no matter how tough something was, it needed its head to stay alive. I took a quick step back, not wanting to be in the way when those blades of light came slashing down.

Under my feet, the monster stirred. I saw it lift its head, a chilling gleam in its blank white eyes as they fastened on Nyx, and I realized our mistake. It was baiting us.

"Nyx!" I yelled, just as the faery sprang toward it for the killing blow. "Don't—!"

A massive claw shot out, tearing free of vines and roots as if they weren't there, smashing into the Forgotten and pinning her to the ground. Curling its talons around her, the monster rose easily, vegetation ripping and tearing. Bringing a dazed, unresponsive Nyx close to its muzzle, it snarled, slavering jaws gaping wide as if to bite off her head.

Rage shot through me, and I threw myself forward, plunging my dagger into one blazing white eye.

With a shriek, the monster convulsed, shaking its head and stumbling back. It hurled the Forgotten away as the tendrils on the creature's back and shoulders came to life, surging up like maddened snakes. They lashed out, and for a second, I could see nothing but black, shadowy tentacles swarming around me. I dodged one, slashed through two more, and then felt something cold and thin slam into the back of my head. I felt myself falling, saw the ground racing up at me. And then, something weird happened.

Images flared to life. Memories long forgotten flashed through my mind like a strobe light, blips of fleeting emotion and thought. A former best friend turning on me, his eyes cold with hate as he tried to end my life. The unyielding expression of the Summer King as he banished me from the Nevernever for some stupid, imagined offense. The woman I loved rejecting me, choosing instead my most bitter rival, the prince who'd tried to kill me many times over. The face of their son, a constant reminder of what I had lost, what would never be mine.

I didn't remember landing. I opened my eyes and found myself lying on my back, the last of the images flickering through my head. Glancing up, I saw the monster looming over me, tentacles flailing. Its cold, hostile gaze met mine, and for just a moment, I understood its anger, its hate and loathing for all living things. I got it. People were the worst. Selfish, arrogant, destructive, evil. The ones you cared about would only betray you in the end. Why care for anything, if they were just going to put a knife in your back?

Then the creature's talons came slamming down, and I barely rolled out of the way as they struck the log behind me, splitting it in two. Grabbing a handful of leaves, I scrambled upright, then flung out a hand with a pulse of magic. Two more Pucks joined the fray, whooping as they lunged toward the monster.

The creature's tentacles lashed out in all directions and caught the Puck duplicates, popping them into small clouds of smoke and leaves. But it allowed me to get close, beneath the monster's rib cage where its heart would lie. Smiling viciously, I drew back to stab the evil bastard, but as I did, something flickered through my head: the image of Meghan turning away from me, her gaze only for the figure behind her, a figure in black with an icy sword at his side. I faltered, my anger shifting targets, as the memory burned bright and painful through my mind.

With frightening speed, the monster spun, backhanding me as it did, and it felt like my rib cage imploded. I was hurled away and rolled several feet before I finally came to a painful stop, gasping, my entire chest on fire.

I felt its presence before I saw it, in the way the ground trembled as it loped toward me, in the noxious glamour radiating from its body. Anger, rage, fear, hatred, and loathing. The emotions swirled around me in a choking fog as I rolled onto my back and struggled to sit, feeling like a spear had been jammed through my lungs.

Pushing myself to my elbows, I looked up.

The monster loomed over me, just a lunge away. I felt its hot breath, smelled the sickening odor coming off its twisted hide. A flippant comment about someone needing a breath mint sprang to mind, but I couldn't quite get my voice to work. The creature stared at me, blank white eyes boring into mine. As I gazed at it, I thought I could feel…something else. Another presence, maybe, peering out at me from the monster's eyes. Just for a heartbeat, the space of a blink, and then it was gone. But cold spread from my heart and rushed into my veins. I felt like I had been perched at the edge of the abyss, staring into the void… and something had stared back.

"Puck, get down!"

There was a pulse of glamour, and a streak of lightning descended from the clear night sky, striking the thing directly in the skull. It roared, stumbling back as electricity coursed through it, filling the air with the acrid tang of ozone and singed fur.

His face tight, Keirran raised an arm and zotted it again, calling lightning out of the sky like a damn Norse god. But this time, though the monster shuddered as the bolt struck home, its lip curled up in a baleful snarl. Lowering its head, it charged the Forgotten King, ignoring the white-hot strands still raining around it, its thunderous footsteps shaking the ground.

I leaped to my feet, knowing it was probably too late to reach the kid or the monster barreling down on him. Keirran was strong, with the glamour of all three courts at his fingertips, but this thing was either immune to the effects of fey magic or was too angry to die. As I turned myself into a raven and flapped toward the creature once again, I wondered if I were about to watch Meghan and Ash's son get smeared to paste right in front of me.

Why did I feel almost gleeful at the thought?

Keirran stood his ground, raising an arm and sending a storm of ice daggers into its face. Though most shattered on the monster's thick antlers, the flurry was enough to make it flinch. Swooping in, I sank my talons into the monster's flesh and drove my beak into one of those bulging white eyeballs. The one I had already stabbed earlier, I noted. It howled, shaking its head, but it did not slow down or change course.

Darkness rippled under Keirran's feet, and Nyx rose out of the shadows behind him. Grabbing the Forgotten King around the waist, she vanished back into the ground, and I released my hold on the monster's face just as it plowed into that spot, churning the earth and smashing through a tree. I dodged a flailing tentacle as it spun, roaring and lashing out at everything around it, snapping branches and churning the ground to mud in its rage.

Wheeling in the air, I saw Nyx emerge a safe distance from the raging monster, Keirran's arm slung over her shoulders, and glided toward them. Nyx released the Forgotten King, who slumped against a tree trunk, breathing hard, as I swooped in to land on an overhead branch. The female faery's eyes were concerned as she stared at Keirran, who was pale and trembling with the exertion of using so much magic at once.

"Are you hurt, my king?"

"It's strong," Keirran panted. "I blasted it with everything I had and barely slowed it down." He ran a shaking hand through his hair, then cast a worried look at Nyx, not seeing me in the branches overhead. "Are you all right? I lost you when it went after Puck the second time."

"I'm fine," Nyx answered. But her voice was tight, and by the press of Keirran's lips, he knew she wasn't as fine as she claimed. "But we need to stop that thing. I don't know where Goodfellow is, if he's even conscious, so it might just be us now."

Keirran nodded, though even he looked exhausted as he pushed himself off the trunk.

The monster had stopped its rampage and was now waiting

for us in the circle of destruction it had created. I dug my talons into the branch beneath me. We weren't in good shape, any of us. I ached, I was pretty sure Nyx was badly injured, and Keirran was barely on his feet. And we hadn't even put a scratch on the thing. The odds didn't look great.

In that second, I made a decision. The monster's attention was solely on Keirran and Nyx. It hadn't noticed me, a jet-black bird, in the branches of the tree. If I could surprise attack it, strike hard when it wasn't expecting me, I might be able to take it down. Cut the big bastard's head clean off from above. Yeah, that sounded doable.

The slightly tricky part was I couldn't let Keirran or Nyx know the plan, in case the monster noticed and I lost the element of surprise. But that was fine; by the time they realized I was still in the fight, it would be over.

Nyx rose with grim determination, silvery blades appearing in her hands. "Stay back a moment, Your Majesty," she told Keirran. "Let me engage the creature. I will try to distract it, and then you can finish it off."

But Keirran gave his head a firm shake and drew his sword. "I'm not letting you fight that thing alone," he stated. "As it happens, I can swing a sword pretty well, too." He glanced to where the monster waited and narrowed his eyes. "Besides, glamour doesn't seem to work on it. Maybe the answer is three feet of steel shoved through its heart." He paused, a worried, frustrated look going through his eyes as he looked around. "Where is Puck? We could really use his help now. I hope nothing's happened to him."

Nyx didn't say anything to that, but I saw her jaw tighten as if she disagreed with Keirran's statement. I smiled to myself. *Keep watching, nonbeliever. I'll show you why Robin Goodfellow is famous round these parts.*

In the center of the clearing, the monster reared up and bellowed a challenge but didn't move forward. Lowering its head, it dug long talons into the churned mud and hunched its shoulders, as if bracing itself against something. The tendrils on its back and shoulders flared, coiling like serpents into the air, before they stabbed down, sinking into the earth around it.

Now.

Pushing off the branch, I flapped into the air, soaring toward the clearing and the creature in the center. Catching a current, I glided up until I was directly overhead the monstrous form, then tucked my wings and dove right for it. With a pulse of glamour and feathers, I shed my bird form and dropped toward its head, daggers raised to end this fight once and for all.

"Surprise, ugly!" I called, right before the ground beneath it came to life.

Shadowy tentacles exploded from the earth, surging into the air like an enraged kraken, hissing and flailing about. I yelped, twisting wildly to avoid them as they shot toward me, and managed to avoid two as they slithered by. Then something cold and sharp slammed into my ribs, driving the air from my lungs. I gave a breathless yell, instantly driving my blade into it, but the thing coiled around like a snake, pinning my arms even as it had me impaled through the middle.

Shockingly, there was no pain. But more images flashed through my mind like a strobe light, blips of thought and emotion, too fast to see. I felt something inside me pushing to get out, like a long-buried memory being dragged into the light. I was being torn in half from within, and my strangled yell caught halfway in my throat as I felt that other presence shuffling around in my head.

I see you.

There was a streak of light, and a spinning crescent shot beneath me, severing the tentacle as it passed. I fell, and it was a good thing I already had no air in my lungs, or I would've lost it all right then as I smashed face-first into the ground. The tentacles pinning my arms dissolved to shadow, and I pushed myself upright to see I was surrounded by a forest of flailing tendrils, and the monster looming overhead, blank white eyes fixed on me as it raised a claw.

A lightning bolt streaked overhead, slamming into the monster's chest, causing it to stagger back with a roar. At the same time, something grabbed the back of my hoodie, yanked me upright, and slung my arm around their shoulders.

"Dammit, Goodfellow," Nyx hissed in my ear. "Keep those things off us for a second. I need a shadow, and the only one big enough is the creature's."

"I have no idea what that means," I wheezed. "But whatever you say—"

The tentacles flailed at us. I slashed at them one-armed, gritting my teeth, as Nyx dodged and yanked us out of the way. Overhead, the monster recovered with a snarl. Gazing down at us, its muzzle curled balefully, it took a thunderous step forward, raising its talons again. Nyx's fingers tightened on my arm, and I felt a shiver go through me as a bit of my glamour was siphoned away.

"Hold on," Nyx muttered and sprang forward, darting into the monster's shadow as its talons scythed down at us. For a second, there was absolute darkness.

And then we were stumbling from the shadow of a tree into the open, collapsing to the ground as soon as we were clear. A few yards away, Keirran turned, eyes widening in relief as he spotted us.

Breathing hard, the Forgotten King jogged up to us, his face pale. "Nyx. Puck. Are you two all right?"

Something shifted in my head, like a worm oozing through a crack that hadn't been there before. Disgust flickered, and I sneered at him, my tone cutting. "Oh sure, princeling. I just love getting my face kicked in for shits and giggles, don't you?"

"It wouldn't have happened," Nyx said, her own voice cold, "if you hadn't decided to attack the monster by yourself."

"Stop it, both of you," Keirran ordered, and the Forgotten immediately fell silent, bowing her head. "We don't have time to argue. That thing is still coming."

A rumbling growl punctuated his words. I glanced up to see the monster stalking toward us, surrounded by tentacles that sprouted from the earth and lashed the air around it. Its blank, dead white eyes were fixed on me.

I felt its absolute hatred and loathing for all living things, and for the first time in ages, a shiver of fear crawled down my back. This wasn't the first time I had faced a creature that was seemingly invulnerable; there were many times in my life where a tactical retreat had been the only option. I knew, suddenly, that we couldn't beat this thing. Even with the Forgotten King's triple glamour on our side, the bastard was too strong. But there was no retreat this night, no discretion being the better part of valor. Keirran would never abandon the fight when his people were in danger, and the assassin sworn to protect him wouldn't, either. They would die fighting this thing, and there was no way I was running away, only to tell Meghan and Ash I let their kid get torn apart by a monster that couldn't be killed.

I shot a sideways glance at my companions. Keirran stared at the creature, his face pale but determined as he raised his weapon, the faint tremble of the sword betraying how tired he was. Nyx pushed herself upright, calling her blades to her hands, but I had seen that look on her face before. The one that said you knew you couldn't win, but you were going to give it everything you had before you died, dammit.

I sighed, but drew my daggers and struggled to my feet. My chest hurt, my face felt like a Jeep had bounced over it a few times, and the persistent throbbing pain in my ribs and lungs was making it hard to breathe. But Keirran and Nyx weren't going to run, and I'd be damned if I let them be heroically tragic without me.

All righty, then. This is gonna hurt.

The monster stalked closer, its silhouette blocking out the sky, the huge antlers crowning its skull stabbing up like tree branches. The tentacles on its back hissed and writhed, mirroring the ones sprouting from the earth. The monster reared up and roared, making the ground shake, then dropped to all fours with a crash, bristling and ready to charge.

I drew in a deep, painful breath, gathering what was left of my glamour to me, and felt a vicious grin cross my face. If Death had finally caught up, that was fine, but I was going to go out laughing at him, as I'd promised.

Suddenly, the creature paused. A ripple went through the air, the faintest tremor on the wind, making my skin prickle. The night darkened, and a ragged mist began creeping toward us, coiling along the ground and swirling around the field of tentacles.

The monster straightened and turned to gaze over its shoulder, as if sensing something we could not. Its nostrils flared, its breath writhing into the air as it huffed.

"What is it doing?" Nyx muttered, her voice strained. "Why doesn't it attack?"

"I dunno," I whispered. "Maybe there's a hot dog joint nearby?"

The monster snarled. Its head swung toward us again but it hesitated, obviously torn between attacking and going toward whatever had caught its attention. Abruptly, it spun and loped into the trees, the fog curling around its body as it disappeared.

"Follow it." Keirran raised a hand, frost and glamour sparkling from his fingertips. "We can't let it escape. I'll clear the way."

He knelt and pressed his palm to the earth, releasing a pulse of icy glamour that caused the ground to freeze over. The carpet of flailing tentacles didn't turn to ice and shatter like I was hoping, but they did dissolve into wisps of shadow and curl away into nothing. Keirran slumped, breathing hard, but then raised his head to glare at us.

"Go," he ordered. "Find it. I think it's headed for the River of Dreams."

"Keirran..."

"Go! Don't worry about me, I'll catch up in a second. Just stop that thing before we lose it completely."

Nyx looked reluctant but turned and sprinted into the trees, heading in the direction the monster had disappeared.

I groaned. "Right, chase down the unkillable monster instead of letting it walk away and leave us unmauled," I said, and followed the Forgotten into the mist. "I love this plan."

We came out of the trees, and the bank of the enormous River of Dreams stretched before us, its dark waters shrouded in the thick fog creeping up the bank. The largest body of water in Faery, the massive river wound its way through the Nevernever, into the Deep Wyld, and flowed all the way to the literal End of the World, where its waters cascaded off the edge into empty space. Very few had ever seen the End of the World (yours truly being one of them), but everyone in Faery knew about the River of Dreams, carrying the glamour of billions of snoozing humans through the Nevernever, infusing it with the magic of dreams and nightmares.

And speaking of nightmares.

It was standing at the edge of the river, a hulking, twisted form against the fog rolling up the bank. The tendrils on its back writhed as it turned and regarded us with those empty, baleful eyes that seemed to both chill and burn right though you. A section of fog curled away behind it, revealing a long, rickety dock extending out over the water and vanishing into the wall of mist.

The creature stared at us. For a moment, it seemed we would have another fight on our hands. Its lip curled up, showing jagged fangs, and its tentacles snapped eagerly as we sprinted toward the riverbank. Then it whirled and bounded onto the dock, its long, gangly limbs carrying it toward the river. Toward the wall of mist hovering on the water's surface. It thundered down the dock and hurled itself off the edge. An enormous splash followed as the massive creature plunged headfirst into the River of Dreams.

I slid down the bank and sprinted to the end of the dock, searching for the monster as my boots thumped against the rickety planks. I caught a glimpse of the creature's twisted body just as it vanished beneath the surface. In seconds, fog coiled around the hole left behind, the rippling waters stilled, and the monster was gone.

6

BRINGING IN THE BIG GUNS

"You caused this."

The accusation came from behind me, hanging in the air as I watched the mist curl around the spot where the creature had disappeared. Nyx stood at the top of the bank, swords in hand, glaring at me with narrowed golden eyes.

"Why didn't you wait for us?" she demanded. "If we had worked together, we might've been able to kill it. Why did you decide you could attack it on your own? Now we have to track it down again, because you thought you could be a hero."

Her words stung for a second, because she was right. I *might've* been a tad overconfident back there, and as the saying went: pride goeth before a nasty tentacle thing stabbing you in the chest and body-slamming you to the ground.

But then anger flickered as something ugly uncoiled from a hidden place deep inside, spreading through me like an oily stain.

"Funny." I turned to face the other faery, feeling an evil smirk cross my face. "I don't remember having to answer to you. Are you a queen now? Did you and Keirran elope and have a secret marriage ceremony no one knows about?"

For some reason, the thought of Keirran with Nyx annoyed the crap out of me. I had the urge to slip the Forgotten King a potion that would give him permanent donkey ears. Then he would look the part, too.

"I don't answer to anyone, my good assassin," I told her. "Every king and queen of Faery will tell you, Robin Goodfellow does what he pleases, whenever he pleases. Even Oberon can't do anything about that, and believe me, he's tried. If you think *you* change that now, well, I welcome the challenge."

What the hell are you doing, Goodfellow? Deep down, part of myself looked on, appalled. This wasn't me. Or it was, but it was a side of me that I'd buried long ago, when Robin Goodfellow was still the incorrigible prankster, but his pranks were sadistic and cruel, especially toward humans and those who had insulted him. Ice-boy wasn't the only faery with a bloody past. Once, I had been Puck of the woods, Puck the nature sprite; wild, carefree, dangerous...and kind of an asshole.

I pushed that tiny voice down as Nyx took a step back, golden eyes widening. Her look of anger was swallowed by alarm, and her arms came up, putting her blades between us. "What is wrong with you, Goodfellow?" she demanded. "You're different."

"Am I?" I grinned toothily. "Or am I just who I was all along?"

"No." She shook her head. "You *look* different."

"Are you two all right?"

Keirran came striding up, his expression, too, one of alarm, though his lacked the shadow of anger on Nyx's face. My eyes narrowed, and I felt the dangerous smile creep farther up my face. The spitefulness in me flared. Suddenly, I wanted to hurt him. This kid who represented my greatest loss, the rejection that still cut to my heart, even to this day. If he happened to disappear, then those responsible would know the same pain I was feeling. Why should they get their happily-ever-after? When would it be my turn to come out on top?

"Puck." Keirran's face paled as I turned toward him. "Are you all right? What happened? Did the monster escape?"

"Yep." For some reason, my daggers were in my hands, and I continued to grin as I stepped forward. "It did. But you know, I don't really care about that right now. How much glamour did you use up fighting that thing, princeling? I'm curious."

Like a ripple of shadow, Nyx placed herself between me and her king, both swords in hand as she faced me. "Another step, Goodfellow, and you'll have to deal with me."

"Aw, so loyal." I smirked at her, relishing the thought of fighting this amazingly fast, lethal killer. From what I had seen, she would be a challenge for certain. And I hadn't had a decent one-on-one duel since ice-boy. "What a good little assassin. I'm almost amused that you think you stand a chance."

"Puck." Keirran's tone was quietly horrified, his expression pained. "Listen to yourself. Whatever that thing did, whatever it brought out, this isn't you, and you know it."

"Not me?" I sneered at him as, deep inside, the ugliness spread. "I've always known who I am, princeling. I'm the guy no one takes seriously. The guy everyone laughs at, who has a joke for everything, because the world is screwed up and the only way to deal with it is to look it in the eyes and smile. I smile, because it's either that or get vindictive. And no one likes me when I'm vindictive." I sneered at him again, challenging and defiant. "So, there you go, prince. The hidden side of Robin Goodfellow. How do you know this isn't who I've been all along?"

The Forgotten King narrowed his eyes, and glamour swirled around him as he raised an arm. "Then take a look at yourself now, Puck, and tell me if this is who you want to be."

My breath curled in front of my face as the air around us turned frigid. Sparkling motes danced in the moonlight, drawing together with crinkling sounds as something large and rectangular began forming in ice. When it stopped, a full-length mirror sat on the frozen ground, mist writhing off the crystallized surface to coil into the air. Keirran looked at me and took a step back, gesturing to the frozen creation. Nyx followed suit but kept her blades out and her gaze trained on me, ready to defend her king if needed.

"Oh fine." I crossed my arms. "I know I'm handsome and all, you don't have to prove it to me. But if you think I'm going to see something I don't like—"

My stomach dropped, the rest of that sentence hanging in the air as I stared in the mirror. The figure in the reflection still looked like me: worn hoodie, green eyes, red hair that stuck out like I'd been struck by lightning. All very familiar.

Except…I hadn't had horns this morning.

I blinked, looking again to make sure it wasn't a trick of the moonlight or the mirror itself. Nope, I definitely had a couple protuberances that I hadn't had earlier. Small goat horns poked out of my hair, right above my forehead. I raised my arm and prodded them, feeling the short, rough edges against my skin. Further proof that they weren't an illusion.

And if I had horns…

I grabbed the sides of my pants and yanked them up, revealing the shiny cloven hooves where my feet should've been. Shaggy brown fur clung to my ankles, and I could suddenly feel the hair rubbing the inside of my pants, all the way up to my waist.

Okay, that's…not good.

My insides felt sour as that dark, spiteful part of me shriveled up and died. This was bad. This was definitely bad. When had this happened? When the monster thing stabbed me? Or had it infected me so much with its ugly, hateful glamour that I'd turned into *this*?

"Well…shit." I straightened and glanced at Keirran, who gave me a grim, understanding look and motioned Nyx to sheathe her weapons. She did so reluctantly but seemed a bit less hostile now.

"I take it this form is not normal for you," she ventured.

"Do I look like I enjoy prancing around in fuzzy pants?" I curled a lip at her. "Not that I'd recommend it, but you look up *Robin Goodfellow* or *Puck* on any computer, and chances are you'll stumble across this ugly mug. Or versions of him." I raised both arms in a shrug. "This is what the humans thought I looked like, a few centuries ago, anyway."

"An evil satyr?"

"Not a satyr." I held up a finger. "Satyrs are Greek. And they have no impulse control. I might be obnoxious, but I don't go around at permanent full mast, if you know what I mean. And if you insult me by calling me a faun, I'll spit in your drink. I'm Puck, and there's only one of me, as far as I know."

"Thank goodness for that," Keirran muttered.

I gave him a very evil smile. "Oh, trust me, princeling. You and the entire Nevernever should be thankful there's only one."

Nyx shook her head. "Yes, but *why* did you change into… that?" she wondered. "We know that creature had something to do with it, but for what purpose? Why did it choose this form?"

"Got me." I shrugged. "Maybe to piss me off? To spread the rage around a bit? I can tell you now, that thing had plenty to spare."

"It did not choose that form," came a new voice. With a ripple of moonlight, a furry gray cat appeared on a nearby stone. Grimalkin gave my new form a lazy sniff and curled his whiskers. "The creature was far too enraged, beyond logical thought, to make any intelligent decisions. As I saw it, you reverted to that yourself."

"Oh, and the fuzzy coward returns. Fabulous." I rolled my eyes. "At least we know that monster isn't coming back."

The cait sith made a point of yawning, seemingly unfazed by my hostility. "The creature is not coming back," he agreed, "because it has achieved its goal. I would be worrying about the repercussions of that, were I you." He gave me a stare of bored disdain that only a cat could accomplish, then twitched his tail. "You do not even know what I speak of, do you? The reason why the creature came here, to Phaed specifically?"

"No, but I can't wait for you to impart your wisdom upon us poor unknowing slobs."

"Phaed exists in the Between," Grimalkin went on, unruffled by my sarcasm, "but from time to time, its edges also touch the borders of the Nevernever. That is how you and the Winter prince were able to find it the first time you came here."

"Uh, you were there, too, Furball. Don't forget that part."

"I never forget, Goodfellow." He tilted his head, regarding me with superior cat eyes. "But you continue to miss the point. If you were able to travel *into* Phaed through the wyldwood, then it stands to reason that the opposite is also true."

"Which means..." Keirran jerked up with a gasp. "That thing is loose in the Nevernever," he said darkly. "That's probably the entire reason it was here, in Phaed. Once it crossed the river, it reached the wyldwood, and from there it could go anywhere it wanted."

"Indeed," Grimalkin said. "At least one of you is aware of the situation."

Nyx, who had been watching the conversation in silence, turned her attention to Keirran. "What do we do now, Your Majesty?"

Keirran raked a hand through his hair. "I think we need help," he said reluctantly. "Whatever this monster is, it's too powerful to take on by ourselves. The rulers of the other courts have to know about this new threat. If it can change someone like Puck just by touching him..." His worried gaze went to me, and I smirked in reply.

"Don't worry about me, princeling. This isn't the first time I've been slapped with a curse. You think this is bad?" I made a dismissive gesture. "Try having carrots for fingers. Bunnies become the most terrifying things in the world."

"The other courts must be warned," Grimalkin agreed, ignoring me. "The rulers of Summer, Winter, and Iron are perhaps the only ones with the power to defeat this creature, as your glamour seemed to have little effect. I will go to Arcadia and warn Oberon. The Seelie King will listen to me, as he seems to be rather annoyed with you right now, Goodfellow. It appears Titania is pressuring him to exile you from the Nevernever again, and if you show up looking like *that*, you will remind him of everything you have ever done as Robin Goodfellow. I would avoid them both, were I you."

I shrugged. "Don't need to tell me twice, Furball. I was planning to do that, anyway. I guess I could sneak into Winter and try to warn Mab. That's always a fun time."

"No," Keirran said. "I need you and Nyx to go to Mag Tuiredh and warn the Iron Queen. I'm still banished from the Nevernever," the Forgotten King went on at my surprised look. "I can't go into Faery myself, but my parents need to know what's happening. Go to the Iron Realm. Find the queen and tell her what you saw here. She'll know what to do, or at least, she has more resources to deal with this threat. But she needs to be made aware of it first."

Nyx's golden eyes narrowed. "I am your hidden blade," she told the Forgotten King in a quiet voice. "I am sworn to protect you, as I did the Lady long ago."

"I'm perfectly fine in the Between, Nyx," Keirran answered. "You won't help anyone by staying here with me. Go with Puck. Watch his back. If that monster attacks again, one of you needs to make it to the Iron Realm."

The Forgotten thinned her lips, obviously not relishing the idea of leaving Keirran alone. Or traveling with me. But she gave a stiff nod and a bow. "As you say, my king. It will be done."

"Uh, that's great and all," I broke in. "But there is one teensy problem."

Reaching into my shirt, I pulled out an amulet on a silver

chain, holding it up for all to see. It was a stylized metal raven, wings spread in flight, its eyes tiny green gems that glinted as the bird spun on its chain. "She doesn't have one of these," I announced, as Nyx flinched back from the pendant like it was a poisonous snake. "And without one, it's going to be a very short, unpleasant trip that will probably end with someone's face melting off."

"That talisman…" The Forgotten's voice was caught between horror and wonder as she stared at it. "It's made of iron. How is it not burning you?"

"It is a protection amulet." This from Grimalkin, sounding bored even as his gaze followed the pendant as it swayed back and forth. "The Iron Queen desired a way for traditional faeries to be able to survive the Iron Realm without harm. There was already a technique in place to craft such amulets, but that method was deemed undesirable."

"Because for it to work, you had to kill an Iron faery and seal their essence within the amulet," Keirran broke in, sounding angry. "That technique has been forbidden for years. I'm told Mab slaughtered dozens of gremlins to make the first protection talismans. Obviously, that didn't sit well with the rulers of the Iron Realm. So, the queen had her smiths and inventors figure out another way, one that didn't involve killing."

"Yep, and guess who was the first faery to get their hands on one." I grinned and tucked the pendant back into my shirt. "But these babies are rarer than hens' teeth. You can't just order them off Amazon. If you're going to be traveling through the Iron Realm, you're going to need your own shiny to survive. Lucky for you…" I grinned as Nyx's face darkened "…I happen to know where to get one."

The Forgotten regarded me for a moment, gold eyes assessing. "And what is the price for such knowledge, Goodfellow?" she asked. "What would you have me do?"

Typical faery response; nothing was free, and everything came with a price. I was about to shock her entire world. "Nothing."

Her brows arched, but she did a fair job of hiding her amazement. "Nothing?"

"Nothing, tra-la-la." I smirked at the impatient glare Keirran was shooting me. He wanted us to get moving, but first I had to convince this deadly, beautiful killer I wasn't pulling her chain. "I'm not like Furball," I told the Forgotten. "I've made enough deals and bargains to last me several lifetimes, and the novelty has sort of faded. I figure I *could* make you sing and dance and jump through hoops, but that would take forever, and we don't have a lot of time. So, here's the deal—I get you one of these babies…" I hooked the chain under my shirt "…and you help us send that monster back to whatever hole it crawled out of. Deal?"

Which she was already going to do, so it wasn't much of a bargain. But it did make her nod in agreement. "Yes. Agreed."

Keirran nodded as well. "I'll return to Touchstone and rally the Forgotten," he said, referring to his own capital in the Between. His gaze flickered to me. "Maybe one of them will know what this creature actually is, and how to reverse whatever happened to you."

"Doubtful." I shrugged. "If Furball doesn't even know what we're dealing with, none of the courts will, either. But I do agree with one thing—that monster needs to die. No one makes me shaggy and horny without my permission."

7

IN THE HEALER'S HOUSE

Well, today sucked on all kinds of levels.

"Goblins," Nyx muttered as we peeked around a tree, watching the not-tiny group of green, bat-eared fey squabble and laugh around a campfire. "I guess some things never change. If it is all the same to you, I'd rather avoid them."

"What? And miss out on their lovely welcoming tactics, like biting off your kneecaps and trying to shove a spear up your ass? No trip through the wyldwood is complete without it." I made a grand gesture toward the goblins, being sure to keep out of their line of sight. "And hey, if we hang around long enough, they might start singing about dismembered babies—that's always an experience."

"I've heard it." Nyx wrinkled her nose. "It's comforting to know some things never change." She turned away, but not fast enough to hide a grimace of pain. "But I'm not feeling up to taking on a whole tribe of goblins at the moment, so I suggest we go around if we can."

"Yeah." Truthfully, I wasn't feeling the greatest, either. My everything ached, and the spot where those tentacles had stabbed me burned with an icy cold that still hadn't faded. I felt like a used punching bag, and was grimly aware that, if the thing hadn't left on its own, we might all be dead. Add the sudden acquisition of hooves and goat horns to the mix, and I was feeling...very not right. *Tainted* would be a good word for it. *Pissed off* and *vengeful* would be a few more. Normally, I didn't hold grudges, but if that thing wanted to bring out the old Robin Goodfellow, then so be it. It was going to see exactly what that meant.

And who knew? Maybe if I focused all my thoughts on anger, revenge, and bringing the monster down, I could forget that, for the first time in centuries, something had scared the crap out of me.

Sneaking past the goblins was easy; most of them were drunk, the others were too busy fighting among themselves to notice anything. Nyx moved like a shadow, blending so seamlessly into the background that I felt I would lose her if I blinked. Once we were past the goblins, I took the lead and turned us in the direction of Mag Tuiredh.

The Iron Court. At the end of this road were the rulers of Iron: the former Winter prince and the extremely powerful Iron Queen. Well, to everyone else, anyway. To me, they were my good friends Meghan Chase and Ash-also-known-as-ice-boy. Hopefully they weren't in the middle of a crisis with Summer or Winter and could be convinced to leave their kingdom long enough to help track down a terrifying abomination that didn't seem phased by glamour or stab wounds or anything, really.

But it didn't matter if the monster was invincible. I didn't care how strong or special or unstoppable something was; when the three of us were together, we could take down anything.

"The wyldwood hasn't changed much, at least," Nyx mused, her voice barely a murmur in the eternal twilight. Around us, the tangle of trees and branches were decked out in shades of gray, except for a few shocking bursts of color among the gloom. Neon blue flowers and poison green toadstools glowed against the otherwise colorless landscape. "Though it does seem a little less dangerous than I remember."

"How is *that* possible?" I wondered.

The massive forest sprawled between the courts of Faery, and there were a few things to remember about it. One: it was alive. Literally. Though not exactly sentient, like a dragon sitting in a lair scheming against you, the wyldwood had its own quirks, foibles, and personality. Take your eyes off the path for a second, and it could disappear. That nice dry cave you found earlier in the day? Probably gone when you returned. Or if it wasn't, you shouldn't count on it being empty. In fact, best to avoid poking your head into strange caves in the wyldwood in the first place if you didn't want it bitten off. What did you expect? It was part of Faery, after all.

Luckily, I'd been around almost as long as the wyldwood, so we were very well acquainted. I knew all of its tricks, which berries to avoid eating (all of them), which ponds to give a wide berth, what seemingly peaceful meadows would sprout flesh-eating butterflies that tried to eat your face off. After so many years of playing, hunting, and tramping through and beneath the tangled canopy, there was nothing about the wyldwood that could surprise me.

Or so I thought.

Nyx gave me a sidelong glance, then turned her gaze to the forest around us. "It feels...tamer," she mused. "Not quite as malicious as before. Venturing into the wyldwood used to mean faeries just vanished sometimes. Without a trace." Her brow furrowed, and she shook her head. "That doesn't happen anymore, I suppose."

"Only if someone is being careless and not paying attention," I scoffed. "Don't get me wrong, it's still plenty dangerous out here if you don't know what you're doing. Fortunately, I'm an expert."

Nyx raised a skeptical eyebrow and seemed about to say something, but clenched her jaw instead, sinking to a knee in the grass.

Alarm made my stomach jump. "Hey, you okay?"

"I'll live." Her words were tight, but she raised her head, schooling her expression into a blank mask. "It's just a scratch. I've suffered worse."

Abruptly, I remembered the monster's claws smacking her from the air, the sick feeling in my gut when she crashed into a tree. We hadn't had time to bind wounds and properly heal before plunging headlong into Faery; she might be bleeding out beneath that cloak, and I wouldn't know until it was too late.

"Here," I said, taking a step toward her and earning a wary look. "Let me see." Her eyes narrowed, and I smirked. "I don't bite. Hard."

She glared a moment more, then sighed and turned her head away. I took that as agreement not to stab me and knelt beside her, carefully brushing the cloak aside to see how badly she was wounded.

My stomach dropped. Beneath the cloth, her black armor conformed snugly to her body, but three long, nasty-looking gouges had torn their way across her ribs, ripping through the material like it wasn't there. The dark armor hid it well, but the area around the wounds was slick with blood.

I blew out a breath and looked at Nyx, who continued to stare into the distance, giving no indication that there were four giant holes in her body. "Okay, clearly we need to define 'just a scratch,'" I said in disbelief. "Backing a car into a mailbox? Just a scratch. Angry kitten, just a scratch." My voice shook. I didn't know why I was suddenly angry. "This is not 'just a scratch,' Miss Stoic Assassin. We need to take care of this now."

"No." Nyx stubbornly shook her head, attempting to pull

away from me. "There's no time," she argued. "We have to get to the Iron Queen as soon as we can. That monster could be anywhere now."

I grabbed her arm. "And if we trip over it in this condition, it's going to stomp us into pudding for sure," I countered. "Not to mention, you're bleeding. In the wyldwood. And it's almost night."

She winced. Tramping through the wyldwood while wounded, announcing that you were easy prey to anything that wanted a quick snack, was a bad idea. Pushing on through the night, when all the really nasty things came out, was a surefire way to get yourself eaten or dead.

"Look, we're in pretty bad shape," I admitted with a shrug. "I have bruises on top of bruises in places I didn't know *could* bruise. Trust me, I'm all for finding and kicking this thing back to the hole it crawled out of, but if it came at us right now, I don't think I could stop it. At the moment, I'm not sure I could stop an irritated piskie."

That earned the hint of a smile from Nyx, which somehow made things a bit better.

"So yeah, we want to reach the Iron Queen as soon as we can, but we have to get to Mag Tuiredh first. Preferably alive. We're not helping anyone if we get ourselves torn apart by a Grendel in the middle of the wyldwood."

"What do you propose we do?"

I gazed around to get my bearings, then nodded. "There's a healer not far from here." I gestured through the trees in the general direction of the Summer Court. "She owes me a favor. Or, do I owe her a favor? One of those is true. Maybe they both are. Anyway, if we go now, we can get there before nightfall. Her bedside manner is awful, but her potions work miracles. With any luck, we'll be on the road to Mag Tuiredh before dawn."

Nyx sighed. "I suppose it would be reckless to continue like this," she muttered, gingerly touching the wound beneath her cloak. The barest flicker of pain went through her eyes, almost too fast to be seen. "And the king is counting on us. I can't fail." She gave a decisive nod and glanced up at me, her expression resolved. "All right then, Goodfellow, I'll trust you for now. Where is this healer of yours?"

I held out a hand. After a moment, she took it and let me gently draw her upright. I gazed down at her, smiling faintly, and she stared right back, unafraid of me, my name, or my reputation. I could see my reflection in her gaze, the horns jutting out of my hair, the slightly feral look that seemed normal for me now, but Nyx's expression didn't falter. My heartbeat picked up, and my mouth went dry as this deadly, confident, beautiful assassin held my gaze without fear.

Clearing my throat, I turned away, breaking eye contact. "Come on," I said, feeling her gaze on me as I stepped back. If she noticed the flush on my face, I hoped she wouldn't mention it. "As the great and impatient Furball would say, we're not getting anywhere standing around. And if we wake the healer up, we'll certainly be in for an earful."

"Do you have any idea what time of night it is?"

I put on my most contrite, charming smile as the wrinkled face of a gnome glared at me through the crack in the cottage door. Beady eyes flashed behind her gold spectacles, and the white bun atop her head bounced indignantly as she shook her head. "No, Robin!" she snapped. "Not this time. You cannot simply show up in the middle of the night needing aid from one of your fool pranks and expect me to drop everything to heal you."

"Aw, Miss Stacey, that's what you said last time. You know you don't mean it. I'm your favorite customer."

"Out!" the gnome demanded, trying to shove the door shut again, though I had my fingers jammed into the space. "Unless you are on Death's doorstep, which I can see you are clearly not,

I am not getting involved in whatever scrape you have gotten yourself into now."

The door pinched my fingers, sending a brief but sharp pain through my hand, and deep inside, something flared. Something...not nice. "Really?" I sneered. "Is that what you believe?" Crouching down to the gnome's level, I brought my face to the crack and bared my teeth in a vicious smile. "Take a good look now and tell me what you think."

The gnome's furious gaze met mine, and her face paled. Stumbling away, losing her grip on the door, one hand went to her chest as she stared at me. "Robin," she whispered as I stood slowly, pushing the door back. "You've reverted to *that*? What's gotten into you?" She faltered, then pursed her lips and stood firm, glaring up at me. "What can I do for you, Robin Goodfellow?" she asked coldly.

The flash of genuine fear in the gnome's eyes stabbed me in the heart, and the flare of nastiness faded. Guiltily, I raked a hand through my hair, wincing as my fingers brushed the rough ridge of a horn. Just another reminder that, once upon a time, I was not a good person.

"Apologies for barging in on you so late," I muttered, being sure to wait in the doorframe and not step over the threshold. "But this is kinda important, Stacilla. I wouldn't have come if I didn't need your help."

The gnome sighed. "You and everyone else who gets themselves stabbed, slashed, gored, poisoned, or bitten in the Nevernever." But she relaxed a bit, beckoning to me with a withered hand. "Well, come on in, don't just hover in the door letting in flies. But if you expect me to do anything about...this situation," she went on, glancing at my horns again, "I'm honestly not sure how much I can help. I don't do curses, you know. If that is even a curse."

"It's not for me," I told her, and stepped into the room, ducking to avoid the ceiling. Even though the quaint stone cottage wasn't exactly gnome-size, it was still smaller than a normal house. "A friend of mine got pretty torn up recently, and we didn't want to stomp through the wyldwood bleeding at night. We were hoping you could do the whole patch-em-up thing you do so well."

"What have you and the Winter prince gotten yourselves into this time?" The gnome rolled her eyes. "Doesn't he have healers in the Iron Realm that can aid whatever is wrong with him? Or would you get him into trouble with the queen if she found out?"

"Ah ha ha. You know us so well. But, it's not about ice-boy this time," I said, and stepped aside, letting Nyx into the cottage behind me. "It's for her."

Nyx lowered her head as the gnome's gaze turned on her. "Please excuse this intrusion into your home," she said politely. "I apologize for any trouble this has caused you."

The gnome's bushy eyebrows arched as she stared at the other faery, who waited calmly with her head slightly bowed. "What in the Nevernever…" she began, before rousing herself with a shake. "I'm sorry, but who is this, Goodfellow? I don't believe I've ever seen her kind before, and I have seen nearly everything in the entire realm of Faery at some point."

"She's a friend," I said firmly. "And she's hurt. Can you help her? We sort of got into a scuffle with something big and toothy."

Stacilla let out another long-suffering sigh and turned, shoulders hunched in resignation. "Through the hallway," she said without looking back. "Take the first door on the right. I'll be with you in a moment."

We did as she instructed, finding a small room with a bed, a chair, and a cabinet containing all manner of colorful bottles, flasks, and vials within. Curiosity flared; in a less dire situation I would be sorely tempted to fiddle, but at the moment I was more concerned with the faery at my back.

Nyx perched gingerly on the edge of the cot, moving a bit

more stiffly now, her jaw rigid as she tried to conceal how much her wounds hurt. My stomach clenched in sympathy. All that time, through the whole fight, she had been badly injured, and it had never showed on her face.

Just like another stubborn fool I know. Is it me? Maybe I just attract that type.

Nyx was certainly an enigma. I wondered where Keirran had found her, or how she had found herself in the Nevernever in the first place. She was different than the others, the Forgotten that had fought in the war with the Lady. And not just in ideals or personality; she *looked* very different. To stay alive and not Fade away, these Forgotten had been forced to subsist on a nasty glamour made from the fears and nightmares of children. And yeah, it was just as creepy as it sounded. Those Forgotten had survived, but the glamour had changed them into eerie shadow fey, living silhouettes without form or features except for their glowing eyes. The monsters that lived in a child's closet or under their beds.

If Nyx had arrived in the Nevernever after the war, then it would make sense that she had avoided the glamour that had changed her kin into nightmares. But that didn't explain how she had "woken up," or her fanatical loyalty to Keirran. From what they had said, I figured she was some kind of assassin who had served the Lady. An extremely lethal, efficient assassin. One who turned into Sailor Moon when said moon was full, and who would stand in front of a horrific, invincible nightmare beast for her king without batting an eyelash.

Nyx saw me watching her and raised a silver eyebrow. "Something on your mind, Goodfellow?" she asked.

I shrugged. "Just wondering how long you and Keirran have known each other. One normally doesn't go throwing themselves in front of massive killer death machines for total strangers."

Her lips twitched into a resigned smile. "I don't remember much of my past life," she said. "But I do remember my duty was to protect the ruler of Faery with my entire existence. Even if it meant throwing myself in front of...massive killer death machines." She stumbled a bit over the phrase, then shrugged. "I no longer have a Lady to serve, so my loyalty goes to the King of the Forgotten."

"Was it a shock? Coming back to find everything had changed?"

"A bit." A furrow creased her brow. "When Keirran and I first met, I had just woken up, or returned to existence—whatever happens to Forgotten who come back. I didn't know how much time had passed, what had happened in the human world, or anything about the rise of the new courts. I didn't believe him when he told me the Lady was dead."

"Oh, let me guess. You tried to kill him."

She winced. "I couldn't believe this half-mortal boy had defeated the ruler I had been serving for centuries," she said in disbelief. "The Lady was the most powerful faery in the Nevernever. How could this slip of a human even challenge her?"

I snorted. "Yeah, Keirran isn't exactly a normal human. Or faery. Or...anything that even comes close to normal, really. I'm betting he surprised you right quick."

"You could say that." The edge of a smile crossed her face, though it faded in a blink. "Though I still refused to believe the Lady was really dead. Even when we came to an understanding, I held out hope. I thought she might be slumbering, somewhere deep within Phaed or the Deep Wyld." A pained look crossed her face, and she shook her head. "I left to find her, but it was as Keirran had said. The Lady was gone, her existence erased from the Nevernever. Nothing remains but memory, and even that is fading."

For a moment, she looked melancholy, then took a quick breath and raised her head. "So be it. The Lady is no more, and Keirran is my liege now. I should be at his side, protecting him." Her lips tightened, and her gaze strayed toward the door. "I've already failed the Lady. I can't fail him, too."

"Keirran can take care of himself," I assured her. "Trust me, he's not too keen on someone throwing themself in harm's way for him. Worry not, though. I'm sure we'll get into plenty of life-threatening situations before this is done."

"Yes, well." Nyx wrinkled her nose, that hint of a smile creeping through again. "Don't expect me to throw myself in front of a charging death machine for you, Goodfellow."

"Aw, why not? Is Keirran the only one with that privilege? Am I not handsome enough to die for?"

"I didn't say that."

"Goodfellow." Miss Stacey swooshed through the door before I could ask what *that* meant, and shoved a bowl into my hands. "If you're going to be here, make yourself useful and go boil some water. Otherwise, kindly stay out of my way. Now…" She turned to the faery on the bed, climbing onto a stool to better see her patient. "What was your name, again, dearie?"

"Nyx."

"Well, Nyx. Since I can expect everything from cockatrice bites to being kicked by an irate unicorn with this one—" she jerked a thumb at me "—please show me what I'm dealing with today. Where are you hurt?"

Nyx pulled aside her cloak, and the gnome's lips tightened.

"Oh my." Putting down her glasses, she leaned forward and peered at the wounds. "Three lacerations, fairly deep, made by something quite large. They look clean, though." She eyed the Forgotten over her glasses, pursing her lips. "What were you and Goodfellow fighting, anyway?"

Nyx shifted on the cot. "Why do you want to know?"

"Well, if I'm going to save your life from a basilisk's poisoned claws, it would be helpful to know such things," the gnome replied. "The same goes if you've been stung by a manticore, bitten by a lycanthrope, stared at by a Medusa, or stabbed by a goblin. The more information you give me, the less time I waste guessing and the quicker I can prevent your insides turning to mush or your flesh becoming stone." She gave Nyx a stern glare. "So, I don't care how ridiculous or dangerous a stunt Goodfellow convinced you to try. If you want me to help you, I need to know what I'm dealing with. Including the type of creature that attacked you."

"I…don't know what it was," Nyx said evasively. "I've never seen the likes of it before."

Stacey turned in my direction.

I shrugged. "Don't look at me. I've never seen it before, either."

"That I find *very* difficult to believe, Goodfellow."

"Hey, you know me, Stacilla." I flashed a grin at her. "I can't lie, remember? I *will* say it was a big ugly bastard with antlers and claws and tentacles growing in places tentacles shouldn't be. And it had a really bad attitude."

And it had done something to me. Something I didn't want to mention or think about, because I was fairly certain the healer couldn't help. It wasn't the horns and hooves that bothered me (though I wasn't exactly *pleased* about them; fur in summer was just a pain), it was what this sudden transformation meant. Robin Goodfellow, the Puck of the woods, was back. Evil ideas flitted through my mind, pranks and schemes against all those who had insulted, threatened, or cheated me in the past. Pranks that, while I knew they were cruel and spiteful and just downright mean, still sounded hilarious.

I didn't like those thoughts, but I couldn't drag others into my plight. Whatever this was, whatever had happened to me, I had to deal with it myself. I knew how these things worked. A simple potion or healing salve wouldn't cut it. Maybe the only way to break this curse was to destroy the creature that gave it to me. All the more reason to bring in the big guns.

The gnome sighed. "I see," she muttered. "Well, that tells me nothing, but so be it. I will work with what I have. Now…" That dire glare turned in my direction again. "Where's that water, Goodfellow?" she demanded. "If you want me to help your friend, I suggest you make yourself useful."

Giving Nyx a sympathetic grin, I scampered out and did what I was told.

Later, having been banished to the living room, I leaned back against a floral, gnome-size couch and waited for the hallway door to open again. The cottage was still, the faint scuttle of a rodent or brownie in the kitchen the only sound in the darkness.

In the sudden quiet, I ached, the beating I'd taken earlier becoming more apparent with new bruises and twinges I continued to discover by shifting around. Despite the constant, low-grade throbbing, I felt my eyelids getting heavier, my chin falling to my chest as I slumped against the sofa.

I dozed.

And though it was impossible for the fey, I dreamed.

"You killed her."

That voice. I knew that voice. Cold. Merciless. Unforgiving.

I turned and saw him behind me, felt the chill from his presence spreading over the ground. His features were cloaked in shadow, hidden from sight, but I knew him as surely as I knew my own reflection. Even if I hadn't, two things would've been a dead giveaway: the ice sword, unsheathed at his side, that glowed like a neon icicle, throwing off waves of mist and cold that writhed into the air; and the lethal silver eyes that glittered like the edge of a blade, glaring at me with utter hate.

"Ash." My voice came out flippant, and those silver eyes narrowed to slits. I could feel a dangerous grin creeping across my face, and the hilts of my daggers pressed into my palms as I turned to face him fully, raising my weapons. "Haven't seen you in a while. Still going on about that, are you? I told you it was an accident. When are you going to forget?"

"I will never forget," the shadow said quietly. "You killed her. It's your fault Ariella died. Because you are nothing but a force of mayhem, Goodfellow. Your pranks consume whatever you touch, and you care nothing about the aftermath left behind. I will put you down, once and for all, and the rest of the Nevernever will rejoice that Robin Goodfellow is gone at last."

Deep inside, I felt a ripple of disquiet, the feeling that this scene wasn't right. The accident... I knew what Ash was talking about, of course. How could I forget? The day when I'd unknowingly led my two best friends into a monster's lair, and one of us hadn't survived the encounter. Ariella had been struck down and killed by a giant wyvern, and Ash had never forgiven me for her death.

I knew the incident Ash was referring to, of course. But...it hadn't happened this way. Or had it? I couldn't remember, and after a moment, it didn't matter.

The shadow took a step toward me, raising his glowing sword, and the flicker of unease disappeared.

"Put me down?" I snickered and tensed to spring into action. "We'll see about that. Come on then, ice-boy," I mocked. "You want to get rid of me? You and the entire Nevernever. Let's see if you get any luckier than the last faery who tried."

The shadow lunged at me, sword raised high. I sprang forward, and around us, the seasons changed as we fought. Winter to Spring, Summer to Autumn, our blades clashed against one another as lightning flickered and snow fell from the clouds. Back and forth we went, neither giving an inch, sword and daggers seeking to end the other's life. A cycle that would never end. And all the while, his words echoed around us, flat and accusing, filled with hate.

You killed her.

She's dead because of you.

No one wants you alive.

I was a fool to ever trust you.

Snarling, I leaped into the air, coming down with a flurry of vicious blows, and drove the shadow back a few paces, though he parried every one of them. Panting, we broke apart and circled one another like wolves, looking for an opening.

"She never loved you."

My steps faltered, a cold lance going through my stomach. Ash wasn't talking about Ariella now. Lowering my arms, I stared at him, hating the Winter prince for bringing it up. For throwing that cold truth in my face.

"In fact," the shadow went on, "she barely tolerated you. The only thing you were good for was keeping her alive those first days in the Nevernever. As soon as she found out who she really was, that she was the daughter of the Summer King, she knew you weren't good enough for her. That's why she chose me."

I bared my teeth in a grin, gripping my daggers so hard my knuckles throbbed. "Don't tell me things I already know, iceboy," I snarled, and lunged at him.

"Robin!"

I jerked awake with a start, the swirling battle, the raging emotions, and Ash's voice fading into the ether as I opened my eyes. The wrinkled face of the gnome peered up at me, the look on her face one of exasperation and concern. She held a clay mug in one hand, tendrils of steam coiling from the top and fading into the darkness.

"Back with us, then?" she asked as I blinked the last of the sleep from my eyes. For some reason, my heart was pounding against my ribs, making me frown. Had I been dreaming? That was weird; the fey didn't normally dream unless some kind of magic was in effect, a spell or a curse of some kind. What had I even been dreaming about? Everything was flashes, blips, and images I couldn't quite remember.

Something hot slid down my cheek, stinging my eyes.

"Robin," the gnome said again. "Did you hear me?"

"Huh?"

"Hmph, as I thought," the gnome went on. "You're exhausted. Don't think I didn't see those nasty bruises across your face. Something really kicked you around, didn't it? Here." She pushed the mug at me. "Drink this. It'll help with the pain."

"Appreciate it," I muttered, taking the offered mug. The steam burned my nostrils, smelling of herbs and lavender as I took a sip. "How's our good Forgotten?"

"Resting at the moment." Stacey shook her head. "Nasty business, those wounds. Deeper than I first thought. Whatever you ran afoul of, it's not something I'd want to see around here. So…" She gave me a hard stare from behind her glasses. "Answer me this, Robin. Whatever that creature was, whatever monstrosity you ran into, was it also responsible for the return of the old Goodfellow?"

I choked a bit on the hot liquid, snorting it up my nose. "Ow. What? What are you talking about?"

"Don't play me for a fool, Robin." Stacey sighed, waiting until my eyes had stopped watering and I could give her my full attention. "I've known you a long time. I remember the old days, the days when the name Goodfellow was a curse among mortals and fey alike. I know this…" she twirled a stubby finger at my forehead "…isn't who you want to be any longer. Or if it is, then *that* Robin Goodfellow is someone I really don't want to see in my clinic. Or anywhere in the Nevernever. So, what happened?"

It was my turn to sigh. "I don't know," I muttered, setting the mug down. "I didn't choose to be like this. Trust me, I did not wake up this morning thinking, 'You know what would be fun? Being an evil asshole again, that would be fun.' When we were fighting that creature, it got in a lucky shot and stabbed me. The next thing I knew… Well, I'd say I was horny, but I've already made that joke."

"So, the monster did this to you."

"Yeah, but here's the scary part." I paused, mulling over my next words carefully. "It's not like I've changed into something

I'm not. I mean, obviously it's been a while. I didn't have horns this afternoon, so there's that. But what I'm feeling now…it's like I'm turning back into who I used to be. The part that was buried."

"Mmm." Stacey looked grave. "Well, whatever you do, be careful, Robin. There are many in the Nevernever who would not be pleased to see the old you return. And many who would be quite terrified. Enough to wish you harm."

"Yeah, I get that. But you wanna know the really scary part?" I felt a grin cross my face, one of my old ones, wide and vicious and completely without humor. "I'm struggling with whether or not I should care."

"About what?" asked a new voice.

We looked up. Nyx stood at the edge of the living room, watching us without expression. Seeing her, I felt a huge bubble of relief swell up from the pit of my stomach. She was all right. I mean, I'd known she'd be fine; she was one of the toughest faeries I'd come across, not to mention stubborn, stoic, impassive, refusing to acknowledge when she was hurt…

Wait, had I just described a female version of ice-boy?

Miss Stacey, however, gave a huff and whirled around to glare daggers at her former patient. "Another one!" she exclaimed, throwing up her wrinkled hands. "Why is this a trend with all your friends, Robin? You are not supposed to be on your feet yet, young lady. I did not spend the wee hours of the dawn stitching those wounds shut for you to go tromping off into the wyldwood with Robin to fight more monsters and undo all my hard work."

She gave a dramatic sigh, and her shoulders slumped in resignation. "But that's exactly what you're going to do, isn't it? I shouldn't waste my breath. It's not like I haven't been through this exact same argument with Robin and company before. So, go on." She raised an arm, waving her hand like she was shooing a fly. "Go ahead and get yourself torn open again. I'm sure I'll see you back here before long."

I was rolling my eyes through Stacey's long-winded but familiar rant when Nyx surprised us both by stepping forward and sinking to one knee before the gnome.

"I am grateful for your assistance," she said, holding out a hand. A small, crescent shaped coin glimmered against her fingertips, and she held it out to the healer. "Our mission is urgent, and I apologize for not heeding your wishes, but we must go. I'm afraid I have nothing to offer in payment except my skills. If you ever need me or my blade, hold on to this and speak my name. I will hear it and come immediately, if I am able."

"Oh." The gnome deflated, losing most of her fury, and shook her head. "You don't have to do that, dear," she said, gently pushing the hand away. "Robin is an old friend of mine, despite all his idiocy. I am happy to help." She shot me a glance. "I just wish my charges would take better care of themselves. Robin will continue to *think* he's unkillable, until the day he's not."

"I have yet to be proven otherwise." I grinned.

Stacey snorted.

Nyx rose gracefully to her feet, pulling her hood up. "I'm ready," she told me. "We should go."

"Yep," I grunted, climbing to my feet as well. Unfortunately, I'd forgotten about the half-full mug and bumped it with a knee, sloshing hot liquid over the hardwood floor. "Oops. Uh, you go ahead and wait for me outside," I told Nyx, feeling Stacey's glare on my back. "I'll just be a second."

The Forgotten gave me a slight nod and glided out, making no sound. I started looking around for a cloth or napkin to soak up the mess, but Stacey sighed and waved a hand at me.

"Get out of here, Robin," she said in a half-resigned, half-exasperated voice. "Before you cause any other mishaps. But before you go, answer me this. That girl… Does she know who you really were, the old Goodfellow?"

"No." I shook my head. "She doesn't know anything about me. Before today, she hadn't even heard the name Robin Goodfellow, shocking as that is."

"Hmm." The gnome pursed her lips. "Then perhaps you should consider this rare opportunity, Robin. For once, your reputation does not precede you. Maybe try to make a good first impression, before she hears too many tales?"

I raised a brow. "I always make a great first impression, Stacilla. Not always a good one, but it's definitely memorable."

She rolled her eyes in defeat. I took that as my leave and slipped out, joining Nyx in the cool twilight of the wyldwood.

"Okay, that's done," I announced, dusting my hands together. "Ready to head out?"

"Are we truly free to go?" Nyx asked, tilting her head at me. "I feel strange, leaving this debt unsettled. By rights, I should at least owe her a favor."

"Don't worry about it." I waved it off. "Stacey and I have helped each other so many times we've lost count of who owes whom." Crossing my arms, I gave her an appraising look. "I gotta say, though, that turnaround was awfully quick. You sure you're okay?"

"I am fine," Nyx assured me. "I won't impede our progress or slow us down. This isn't the first time I've been wounded while on a mission." For just a moment, a haunted look passed through her eyes but was gone in the next breath. "If I was given a task, the Lady expected me to complete it, no matter what."

"That sounds familiar," I sighed. "Sucks, doesn't it?"

She blinked. "What?"

"Knowing that you're just a pawn in someone's game," I went on, "and they don't see you as anything but the means to an end. I get it. I've been there. Oberon isn't as bad as some of the other rulers—he's no Queen Mab, at least—but he is still a faery king. They tend not to take no for an answer. Of course, once you realize this, you have one of two choices. Continue on to the best of your ability, knowing your place is to serve and not ask questions, or rebel and make life very difficult for yourself." I paused, then shot her a toothy grin. "Guess which path I always choose?"

Nyx frowned, looking confused. "And your king doesn't punish your disobedience?"

"Oh, all the time. If he can catch me, that is. Turns out you can't punish what you can't see, and I've learned to avoid Lord Pointy Ears when he's in one of his moods. Eventually Oberon calms down and remembers I'm much too valuable to banish forever. He actually does have a level head on his shoulders when he's not being all high and mighty. Titania, on the other hand, has absolutely no patience for anything, and her hissy fits are legendary. She's so much fun to piss off."

"Piss off?" Nyx frowned. "I don't know that expression. And what is a…hissy fit?"

"Ah. Basically I make her so mad she throws a massive temper tantrum and I have to avoid the Summer Court for a few months until Oberon calms her down. Or she finds a shiny new plaything to distract her. Lucky for me, she's very distractible."

"You deliberately make your queen angry." Nyx's confusion now held an edge of disbelief as she shook her head. "The Nevernever is a very different place now," she mused. "If I even hesitated when answering the Lady, she might order the rest of my kin to hunt me down for treason. And she did not forget."

I blinked. "Your kin? There are more of you?"

"Not anymore, it seems." For a moment, Nyx looked melancholy, a shadow crossing her face for just a moment. "But yes, at one point, I was part of a family. My clan—my Order—was a group dedicated to serving the Lady, no matter what she asked of us."

"Yeah, she must've been all kinds of fun to work for."

"I knew what I was," Nyx said softly. "Even if I disagreed with her, my loyalty would never come into question. Even if she ordered me to kill my own blood…" She shook herself. "Anyway, it doesn't matter," she said. "We still have to get to the Iron Realm. That creature could be anywhere by now."

"Right," I agreed. "And we will. But first, we have to get *you* something so that your face doesn't melt off while we're in Mag Tuiredh. Fortunately, I'm in good with the border guards, so it shouldn't take long. Then, it's off to see the queen. And ice-boy, of course. I'm sure he'll be especially thrilled that I've come to visit."

"What is she like?" Nyx asked as we headed into the perpetual murk of the wyldwood. "The Iron Queen. Are there protocols that I should follow? I don't want to offend anyone while I'm in her court."

"Don't worry." I gave her a reassuring smile. "Meghan isn't like Mab, and she's definitely not like Titania. She's not going to turn you into a rosebush or freeze you inside a block of ice for saying the wrong thing. Meghan is half-human, and she was born in the mortal realm. So, she knows about not fitting in, probably more than anyone. My advice is to just…be yourself. Trust me, you don't have anything to be afraid of."

Golden eyes regarded me curiously. I realized I had been speaking about the Iron Queen, one of the most powerful faeries in the Nevernever, in a very casual manner. "Besides…" I grinned and jerked a thumb at myself "…you'll be with me, and I'm at least in her top three favorite faeries in the entire Nevernever, so you'll be fine."

"Really."

"Can't say it if it's not true."

"Yes, but all fey are masters at bending the truth, Robin Goodfellow," Nyx said, giving me a pointed look. "I might be new to this era, but I was not born yesterday."

"Well." I shrugged. "Then I guess you're going to have to trust me."

"I guess I will," Nyx agreed in a quiet voice that, for some odd reason, made my stomach squirm. With a faint smile, she gestured to the surrounding trees. "Lead on, then. I'll follow you to the Iron Realm, and then I'll see what the Iron Queen is like myself."

8

THE BORDER

Well, I would've liked to say that we made it to the border with no further incidents, but that would be a lie. It was the Nevernever, after all. Couldn't walk a mile without something jumping out trying to scare, eat, rob, or have their way with you. Thankfully, the goblin party that attempted to ambush us on the trail underestimated how very lethal the "snow-hair elf" really was. I didn't even have to lift a finger as Nyx decimated the half-dozen squat green creatures with no effort at all. The last goblin, a runty thing with the tip of an ear missing, squealed in terror as Nyx turned on him, the rest of his troop scattered around her in small goblin pieces.

"No kill!" Dropping his spear, he cringed back, looking like an ugly green dog that was about to get kicked. "No kill! Mercy, snow-hair, mercy. Pooga leave. Leave now, see? No kill Pooga."

I rolled my eyes, but Nyx lowered her arms, the shining crescent blades fading to moonlight in her hands. "Get out of here," she told the last goblin, who immediately leaped to his feet and scampered into the bushes. Nyx watched until the sound of rustling branches faded into the distance, then turned to me with a wry grin.

"Nice to know some things never change. No matter how many goblins you exterminate, there are always more somewhere."

"Goblins, the cockroaches of the Nevernever," I agreed. "Though I was sure you would skewer that last one. You know he's just going to scurry back and tell the rest of his friends about us, and then we'll have to deal with the whole tribe."

Nyx gave a shrug that was somehow elegant and careless at the same time. "I've lost count of how many I've killed," she murmured, "how many lives the Lady ordered me to cut short. If I can avoid it, I try not to add to that number."

"An assassin with a conscience," I remarked, surprised. "That must suck. How'd you end up with one of those?"

Faeries have no souls. It's one of the key things that separates the fey from mortals. Well, besides the pointy ears, wings, hooves, horns, et cetera. It's how, after centuries of murder, scheming and debauchery, a faery can continue its merry life without succumbing to the guilt of what it had done. No soul equals no conscience. Throw immortality into the mix, and you have a bunch of bored, capricious beings who are constantly looking for their next form of entertainment and don't care about the mess they leave behind. I know of only one true fey who managed to earn a soul, and the whole process nearly killed him. It was only his love for a certain half human that kept him sane and alive through the whole terrible ordeal.

However, there are a few of us who, though it happens very rarely, develop something that passes for a conscience. Sometimes, a faery is cursed with one, though this is one of the most terrifying things that can happen to a fey, and the poor sap who finds himself saddled with a conscience usually gets himself killed trying to undo it. But occasionally—and no one knows how it happens—a conscience develops on its own.

Some say humans are to blame, that the more time you spend with mortals, the more in danger you are of being infected with their "human morality." Some suggest that the more famous you are, the more stories, songs, and poems people tell about you, the more you start to take on aspects of the character in those tales. However it happens, slowly or all at once, it's life changing. A faery can suddenly find himself feeling guilty about actions that meant nothing to him in the past. The games he found hilarious before now make him cringe.

When this happens, there are really only two choices a faery can make: continue on as before until the guilt eventually drives him to end his existence once and for all, or adapt. Find a way to deal with it, to make up for past mistakes, and do better. Though the rest of Faery will never, ever let him forget.

Nyx hesitated, a haunted look briefly crossing her face. "It did...suck...sometimes," she admitted. "Being the Lady's assassin... I had to accept that part of me, the part that was a killer, the me that reveled in the hunt and the blood and the fear. I had to come to terms with that shadow self, otherwise, it would've destroyed me." She shot me an exasperated look, then sighed. "It's a long, morbid story," she finished. "And one I really don't want to get into at this moment. Ask me again some other time?"

I nodded. "Fair enough. Then I suggest we move before we're drowning in a few dozen vengeful goblins. We're not far from the border now."

The Crossing, as it was oh so creatively called, sat at the edge of the wyldwood, right before you crossed into the Iron Realm. It was a massive stone bridge spanning a gulf that stretched for miles in either direction, separating the Iron Realm from the rest of Faery. A squadron of Iron knights were stationed here, and a pair of them stood on either side of the enormous copper-and-iron gate, blocking the way into the Iron Realm.

Upon seeing the guards, Nyx stopped walking and drew in

a slow breath, her moon-colored eyes wider than I'd ever seen. "Those are…the Iron fey you mentioned?" she said in a near whisper. Her awe was understandable; she had never seen an Iron faery before, and the knights were decked out in their shiny metal plate armor, a torturous death sentence for any traditional fey. Even the iron-tipped spears they carried would make a traditional faery cringe.

I nodded. "Yep, and those guys aren't even the weirdest of the lot. Wait'll you get to Tinkerport, the town on the other side of the chasm. Pro tip—gremlins are the goblins of the Iron Realm. They're everywhere and unavoidable, so it's best to ignore them. Give them any attention and you'll have a whole swarm trailing you."

"Hmm." Now that the initial shock was over, Nyx regarded the knights. "There aren't very many guards," she stated as she scanned the bridge entrance. "I could probably sneak past the lot of them if I wanted to."

"I have no doubt you could," I said truthfully. "I could, too, now that you mention it. But the problem isn't getting past the guards. See that bridge?" I pointed. "Once you cross to the other side, you're in the Iron Realm proper, and without a protection amulet, any traditional faery will start feeling the effects of the iron sickness immediately."

"Is it really that bad?" Nyx wondered, and I remembered she came from a time where modernization wasn't a thing yet. Not like today, with cars and computers and technology everywhere you turned. She had never experienced the nausea of riding in a mortal vehicle, felt the fear of having a gun pointed at her, or recoiled whenever some human tried handing her a phone, a can of soda, a pocket knife, anything of metal and technology.

I imagined she had faced swords and holy symbols, fire and protection charms to keep our kind at bay. But her world had been simpler and more primal, not suffused with the iron of mankind's progress.

I offered a smile that was mostly grimace. "Okay, so imagine the most sick you've ever been," I told her, "vomiting, nausea, the works—and then imagine someone pouring acid directly down your lungs." Her noise wrinkled, and I shuddered at the memory. "Trust me, it's not fun."

"It does not sound very fun."

"Which is why you need one of these things," I went on, pulling the amulet from under my shirt again. The stylized raven glittered as it spun on its cord, pulsing with a faint green light. "And why we are going to get you one, right now. It's the only way you can survive the Iron Realm without throwing up your insides."

Nyx watched the iron raven spin on its cord a moment. "I am guessing they are fairly difficult to procure," she said, "since the Iron Realm has the best border defense simply by existing. If no traditional fey can survive the realm, the Iron Queen does not have to worry about war with the other courts. She and her people can simply retreat within their territory, and no one else can follow."

"Right on both counts." I tucked the amulet into my shirt again. "These babies are very regulated and extremely difficult to get ahold of. The rulers of the courts each have one, because they'd all be super offended if they didn't. But beyond them, only trusted allies and friends of the Iron Realm are given these amulets. So, they're fairly rare, and you need the queen's permission to have one made for you." I grinned. "Luckily, I happen to be the queen's best friend."

"Is there no other way to survive the realm?" Nyx wanted to know.

"Well, there was the old way, but sacrificing an Iron faery and trapping its essence inside a protection amulet didn't sit too well with the queen," I said. "But she wanted a way for normal faeries to travel safely through the Iron Realm without harm." I scratched the back of my head. "Also, there might've been some whining from a certain Summer faery about never getting to see her and ice-boy unless they left Mag Tuiredh. So, she had her tinkers and smiths come up with something that didn't require killing to make."

Apparently it hadn't been easy; our reaction to iron was so ancient and primeval, baked into our very nature, that it was hard to overcome.

"It took a while," I went on, "and there were lots of failed experiments with magic and tech, but eventually, they did come up with something."

A strange expression crossed Nyx's face, making me pause. "Interesting," she murmured. "The Iron Queen already had the means available to make the amulets, and yet she chose an alternative way to spare her subjects. The Lady would not have done the same."

"Yup, like I said, Meghan isn't like the other queens. She won't even stomp an iron cockroach without good cause." I wrinkled my nose. "It's a cockroach. That's cause enough, I say."

"And you believe *I* am going to be granted one of these special amulets." Nyx sounded dubious, eyeing the guards at the bridge entrance. "A Forgotten assassin who used to work for the Lady, being granted an amulet that will let her travel anywhere in the Iron Realm. And were you planning to just stroll up and ask for one?"

"Pretty much, yeah."

She sighed, shaking her head, as we left the woods and started toward the edge of the chasm. "I think we need to have a discussion about proper planning, Goodfellow."

"Planning?" I grinned back at her. "*Plan* is a four-letter word. I do my best work on the fly. Besides..." I shrugged "...my best laid plans always seem to backfire on me, so better not to have any to begin with."

The knights straightened as we came out of the trees and made our way down the road toward the bridge. I raised my arm in a cheerful wave, letting them know it was me and everything was fine. But the knights didn't respond; I didn't get a return wave or even an eye roll. And as we drew closer, I began to sense something was wrong.

"They're on high alert," Nyx observed, sounding wary herself. "Are they normally like this, or is the Iron Realm having conflicts with the other courts?"

"Not that I'm aware of," I muttered back. "And no, normally they'd see me coming and I'd at least get a salute. Wonder what's got everyone so cranky? Is the first lieutenant on the warpath again? Maybe he dressed down the whole squad, and they're still sulky about it."

"We're about to find out," Nyx mused as we approached the first pair of guards, who had stepped forward to meet us. Like the faeries of Summer and Winter, they were tall and slender, with pointed ears and the aristocratic features of all sidhe. These two were nearly twins, with dark hair, pointed chins, and steel-gray eyes that were currently narrowed with suspicion, glaring between me and Nyx.

"Hey, boys," I greeted cheerfully. "Why the long faces? Glitch working you too hard? Or are the piskies being obnoxious again? Need me to convince the piskie population that it really isn't cool to fly by and drop things on your heads when you're trying to do your job?"

"Goodfellow." The guard on the left spoke calmly, his voice flat. "Why are you here?"

"Oh, you know, I was in the area and thought I'd pay a visit to my *good friend* Queen Meghan." I waved my hand in the general direction of the Iron Realm. "You know, the one who granted me an open invitation to the palace, whenever I want?"

The knight's expression didn't change. His gaze swung to Nyx, standing quietly beside me, and those steel-colored eyes narrowed even farther. "And who is this?"

"This is my good friend Nyx," I introduced, still attempting to be polite. Beside me, Nyx gave a solemn bob of her head. "She would also like to go see the queen."

"Where's her amulet?"

"Ah, well, that's the thing." I offered a sheepish, disarming grin. "She...uh...doesn't have one—"

"Then she doesn't get in."

"—but we were hoping to procure one before we went to Mag Tuiredh," I finished, and frowned at the knight. "Okay, what's going on here? You guys know me. What's with the third degree?"

"We know you, Goodfellow," the Iron faery agreed, then glanced at Nyx again, his jaw set. "We don't know her. She's not from Summer or Winter. I've never seen her type before. What kind of fey is she?"

"My apologies," Nyx said calmly, taking a step up to stand beside me. "I'm a Forgotten, and I serve King Keirran in the Between. He asked me to deliver an important message to the Iron Queen, since he cannot be present himself."

"A Forgotten?" The other knight gripped his spear in both hands, not exactly pointing it at Nyx, but definitely ready to. I scowled at him and stepped between him and Nyx.

"Oy, bucket head, the Forgotten aren't our enemies," I said, staring him down. "They're part of the Nevernever, and they're included in the peace treaties, same as the rest of the courts. Incidentally, their king is the son of your queen, so maybe you can point that spear somewhere else."

"The Forgotten served the Lady," the first knight accused, glaring at Nyx. "As did Prince Keirran. We are of Iron, but we do not forget."

"Funny, I seem to remember a time when you guys once served a guy called the Iron King. Remember that? Remember how he was trying to destroy the Nevernever, way back when?" The Iron faery shot me a poisonous look, and I smirked. "Strange how everyone only remembers what's convenient."

The knight set his jaw. "She's a Forgotten," he said flatly. "Our orders are clear. I am sorry, Goodfellow, but we cannot let a strange faery into the realm without an invitation."

Well, this was an unexpected hiccup. I didn't think it would be this hard to get Nyx into the Iron Realm. The knights usually trusted me, or at the very least they knew I wasn't going to go on a wild murder spree once I was past the border. Granted, I didn't normally bring strange friends with me, but this level of suspicion was weird. Keirran had been part of the Iron Court, and I knew most of the Iron fey still considered him their prince, even though he couldn't return. But it seemed these two weren't going to budge, even if I asked nicely.

Then maybe it's time for some not-so-nice tactics.

I smiled, letting my Summer magic rise up within, feeling the heat of the glamour collect in my palms. Let's see how well these two guarded a gate if they were suddenly turned into fat little pigs in armor.

"What's going on here?"

The familiar voice interrupted my thoughts. A faery came striding up, causing the guards to straighten immediately. He wasn't dressed like a knight, and certainly didn't look like one. With his dark jeans, leather jacket, and iron-studded bracers, he resembled a punk rocker more than anything else. His spiky black hair looked like he'd jammed a finger in an electrical outlet, and the neon purple lightning strands flickering through it only added to the effect.

"Sir!" Both knights saluted as Glitch, first lieutenant and commander of the Iron fey army, came striding up in his combat boots.

I relaxed, shooting Nyx a reassuring grin, though a part of me was disappointed. It would have been fun seeing these stiff-necked knights bounce around on all fours and squeal like skinned pigs.

Glitch spotted me, and the severe look on his face dissolved, replaced by amused exasperation. "Oh," he commented, as if nothing out of the ordinary was happening. "It's you. There's a ruckus at my gates and the guards are suddenly whispering about an intruder. Of *course* it's you."

I grinned. Meghan's first lieutenant and I went way back—well, as far back as the Iron fey war, when he'd helped us defeat the false king. "Hey, socket-head," I greeted. "Still terrorizing the tin cans, I see."

He smirked and appeared about to say something, but faltered, purple eyes widening as he stared at me. "You...seem a little different, Goodfellow," he stated, his suddenly wary gaze on my forehead. "Are those new, or did you get yourself cursed somehow?"

"Oh, the horns." I stifled a grimace. "Yeah, that's part of the reason we need to see Meghan. There's sort of a new threat running around that could put all the courts in danger and destroy life as we know it, you know, the typical stuff. Unfortunately, your tin cans are making it very difficult to cross over."

Glitch shot a questioning look at the knights, who paled under that glare.

"Sir," one protested, stepping forward. "We were not trying to prevent Robin Goodfellow from entering the Iron Realm. He is, of course, free to come and go as he pleases. But his companion has no amulet and has not been authorized to cross the border. We did not think it prudent to allow her the means to enter the kingdom."

"She is a Forgotten, First Lieutenant," the second guard chimed in. "And she claims to have served the Lady."

I expected Glitch to smile and put them in their place; for being an Iron faery and the commander of the knights, he could snark almost as well as me, which I appreciated. But the faery's violet eyes shifted to Nyx and narrowed in suspicion.

"You served the Lady?" he asked.

"Once," Nyx replied without hesitation. "A long time ago,

before the rise of the courts, before Summer and Winter were even imagined, I was at the Lady's side."

"And what did you do for the Lady?"

"I killed for her." Again, without any hesitation, though I thought I could hear a hint of regret in her quiet voice. "I killed for her, and I protected her with my life. I cannot tell you more, because that is all I remember."

Glitch's jaw tightened, and he turned to me. "And you expect me to let a Forgotten assassin into the Iron Realm?" he asked. "To give her free rein, and the means of traveling wherever she wants within the kingdom?"

"Okay, did someone slip manticore piss into your canteens this morning?" I demanded, waving my arms at the whole trio. "What is wrong with you? All of you? It's *me*, socket-head. Do you really think I would let anything bad happen to Meghan, or put her in danger in any way? You know me better than that."

"I *don't* know," Glitch said, completely serious. "I haven't seen you in a while, Goodfellow, and now you show up with horns and a strange Forgotten who was an assassin for our greatest enemy. Shouldn't I be a little cautious?"

"I serve Keirran now," Nyx added before I could reply. "The Lady is gone, and the Forgotten King is my liege. I bring a message from the king to his mother, the Iron Queen, and I must deliver it." She hesitated a moment, then sighed. "If you wish me to swear a binding oath that I will harm no one while within the borders of the Iron Realm, I will do so. But I must reach Mag Tuiredh to see the queen before my mission is complete."

"An oath." Glitch pondered that a moment, then nodded. "Yes," he mused. "Perhaps that would be for the best."

"Uh, no. You shouldn't have to swear anything," I said angrily. Oaths and promises were a very serious business in the Nevernever. Once a faery gave their word, they couldn't break it. Even if it meant their death. Nyx had done nothing to warrant this amount of suspicion, and it was pissing me off that

Glitch, of all faeries, was the obstacle preventing us from getting to Meghan.

"No one is going to make any oaths," I protested. "It shouldn't be this hard to get a freaking amulet." The urge to unleash my glamour, to turn this peaceful little outpost into a hub of chaos and pandemonium, rose up again. If the gates were suddenly overrun with rabid monkeys, I bet no one would notice two faeries sneaking into the Iron Realm.

I tried one more time to be diplomatic. "Glitch, you know this isn't going to make the queen happy. If Meghan were here, right now, what would she say?"

The first lieutenant of the Iron fey glared at me a moment, before he sighed, and the lightning in his hair changed from neon purple to blue. "Fine," he said. "I trust *you* well enough, Goodfellow." He pointed a slim finger at Nyx, frowning. "But if that Forgotten causes any grief while she's here, she can try surviving the Iron Realm with no protection amulet. My job is to keep this realm and the Iron Queen safe, from any threat, no matter who or what it is. Even if it comes from the queen's own kin."

Ouch. He was still sore about that, then. Glitch had taken Keirran's betrayal exceptionally hard, and even though the normally reasonable lieutenant was part of the Iron Court, he was still a full-blooded faery, with all the quirks and pitfalls of the gentry. Including the ability to hold a grudge forever. I guess he hadn't quite forgiven the former Iron Prince for what he'd put them through.

Glitch shook his head and turned to the pair of knights. "Send a message to the Tinkerer," he ordered. "Tell him we have need of his services, right now. Tell him Glitch sent you."

One knight saluted, then pivoted on a heel and strode away. The first lieutenant watched him stride across the bridge until he was lost from sight, then turned to us again.

"You'll have to wait here until the Tinkerer arrives," he told me. "The protection amulets aren't something we can hand out to just anyone. They have to be specifically crafted to each faery. But he's done this sort of work before, so it shouldn't take long."

"Appreciate it, socket-head." I smirked and crossed my arms. "Though, next time, a little faster would be nice. We've just got to deliver a vital message to the queen, nothing important. Don't let us interrupt your busy day."

His brow furrowed, the strands in his hair going purple again. "Care to fill me in, Goodfellow? If there's a danger to the realm, I think I should know about it."

I gave him a nasty smile. "I would," I said cheerfully, "if my friend hadn't been treated with such disrespect at the border." I held his gaze, a challenging smile stretching my lips. "I don't know if I want to share my news with you, socket-head. Maybe if there was more trust between us."

For a second, I wondered what I was doing. Glitch was a long-time ally, and Meghan trusted him completely with the safety of her realm. We had fought side by side against all kinds of enemies, and he was one of the first Iron fey I had considered a friend. But something bitter and spiteful was stirring in me, egged on by the hostility and fear in the air around us. And right now, despite years of camaraderie with Glitch, the friendly insults, and being on the same side since the day Meghan became queen, I suddenly didn't feel like playing nice.

The Iron faery's eyes narrowed to violet slits, and the lightning in his hair glowed red. For a second, I thought he might draw the sword at his waist and swing it at me. Part of me hoped he would, but after a taut moment in which I could feel the tension in the fey surrounding us, Glitch stepped back, an air of dismissal surrounding him.

The knights relaxed, and Nyx discreetly lowered her arms under her cloak where, I was certain, two very lethal moonblades had appeared in her hands.

"Very well, Goodfellow." The first lieutenant's voice was

cold. Not ice-boy levels of cold, but definitely chilly. Turning, he pointed to a stone bench beneath a willow tree a few yards away. "You and the Forgotten can wait over there until the Tinkerer arrives," he continued, sounding impatient. "It shouldn't be long. And, Goodfellow," he warned, "don't try anything funny while you're here. I'll be watching you both."

Turning on a heel, Glitch stalked off, the strands in his hair snapping angrily as he left.

"Well," I commented as we moved toward the bench, a nice safe distance from the guards and the border. "That was... interesting."

"It seems they still do not trust the Forgotten after the war with the Lady," Nyx said. "And Keirran." She paused, frowning thoughtfully, then glanced at me. "This lieutenant. Glitch. Have you always been at odds with him?"

"Not really." I shrugged. "I mean, Glitch is a pretty cool guy most of the time. We fought together against the false king, and aside from his terrible fashion taste, I haven't had a problem with him since."

She tilted her head. "That was not the impression I got," she said in a soft voice. "I saw the way he looked at me, him and the knights both. I heard what he said about Keirran. If you hadn't been there, they might've tried to detain me. Or worse."

I grinned evilly, as several nasty ideas sprang to mind once more. "That would've been a bad day for them."

But Nyx shook her head. "I am not here to start a fight with my king's former kith," she said. "This was once his home. And they are right to be suspicious of me. I was once a servant of their greatest enemy, the Lady who stole away their prince."

She raised her head, watching the knight who still glowered at us from a distance. "Keirran told me that much of the Nevernever was still furious at him," she said quietly, "and that they would never forgive what he did. I suppose that extends to all of us. It seems I'm going to be as welcome in the Iron Realm as he is."

I was simultaneously annoyed that she was talking so much about Keirran and angry at the thought of Nyx being targeted simply because she was a Forgotten. A Forgotten assassin who once was the right hand of the Lady, yeah, who was as skilled and dangerous as she was beautiful, but she wasn't even part of the last war.

"Ah, don't stress too much about it." I plopped beside her on the bench, and she glanced at me with calm, moon-colored eyes. "Nothing's going to happen to you in the Iron Court. Anyone wants to start shit, they're gonna have to go through me."

Her mouth twitched in a wry smirk of her own. "You don't think I can handle myself?"

"Oh, believe me, I am fully aware that you can slice and dice your way through pretty much anything." I held up my hands as she watched me, still smiling. "No question about your murder capabilities, please don't stab me. But if we're in the Iron Realm and we do have to make trouble, better for the blame to land on me than you. One, you're a Forgotten, and it seems that everyone's panties are in a twist over that. Best if you lie low for now. And two, I'm good friends with the Iron Queen, and I will be playing *that* card every chance I get." One silver brow arched, and I shot her a grin. "Besides, I'm Robin Goodfellow. If things blow up, collapse, explode, or turn into frogs around me, well, that's just to be expected."

She snorted. "Is *subtle* also a four-letter word in your world?"

"Nope, but *tact* is. Also, *meek, mild, calm, care, plot, plan, mind, quit, stop, test*... I could go on if you want me to."

A creaking, jingling sound interrupted me. I turned to look at the gate and saw the top of a covered wagon making its way over the bridge toward us. At first, it looked like it belonged to a snake oil salesman in an old Western, until it drew closer and I saw it clearly.

Instead of wheels, four segmented legs jutted from the sides like those of a huge metal insect, picking their way over the ground as the wagon crawled forward. The sides were tall and banded with copper, and a pair of lanterns flickered at the back and front, swaying in the breeze. The painted sign on the side of the wagon read Tinkerer's Workshop. Repairs, Adjustments, Custom Pieces.

I groaned. "Oh yeah," I muttered as Nyx rose beside me, watching the wagon lurch toward us on jointed metal legs. "Forgot to mention... Lots of things in the Iron Realm have a really disturbing fascination with insects. Just a heads-up, in case you loathe spiders and all their ilk and believe anything with more than four legs should be cleansed from the world with fire. Except octopi—they get a pass 'cause they're cool and can squeeze their bodies through pretty much anything. Everything else, kill it with fire. Spiders, scorpions, centipedes..."

"Butterflies?"

"Have you seen a butterfly's face up close? It's terrifying." I grimaced. "Besides, the amount of times I've been swarmed by carnivorous butterflies in the Nevernever is more than once. So, yep, kill 'em with fire."

Nyx chuckled, and it sent a strange little flutter through my insides. "Well, hopefully there will be no killer butterflies inside," she said, and together, we walked toward the bridge and the Tinkerer's wagon, crouched like a giant cricket at the edge of the chasm.

9

BUG WAGONS AND KILLER BEE FEY

The things I do to deliver a message.

My skin crawled as we approached the Tinkerer's wagon. Maybe it was my own paranoia, but it felt like the wagon was watching me, patient and unmoving, like a spider ready to scuttle toward me as I got close. And it had legs. Creepy insect legs, when four nice normal wheels would have been just fine.

Squashing down my reluctance, I walked around the back of the cart and found the steps that led to a single, bright green door covered in brass cogs and wheels. A doorbell rested beside the frame, glinting bright copper in the wood, and I pressed it firmly. Something within buzzed, but there was no answer.

"Hellooooo?" Standing on tiptoes, I peered in the single frosted-glass window next to the door, but all I could see were blurry shapes against hazy orange light. "Anyone here? Are you open?"

The door clicked, then swung open a crack, and a trio of very long, very thin fingers curled from the opening. I peered into the gap and was met with a pale gray eye in an equally pale face.

"Hey." I raised a hand as the eye blinked at me slowly. "Did anyone order a pizza with extra olives?"

"Robin Goodfellow." The voice was soft and rusty, and the door creaked open a bit farther as a head emerged on a long, skinny neck. A nose like a beak narrowly missed my chin as the head rose to stare me in the face. A jewelry loupe, jutting from one pale eye, glinted as it fixed on me. I suddenly felt like I was being studied like an uncut diamond. "You are the one the first lieutenant told me about. Can I help you?"

"Yeah, actually, you can." I leaned back from the giant honker before I was impaled. "I heard you were the faery to see about getting a certain trinket? Something small and stylish, that prevents your face from melting off if you go into the Iron Kingdom?"

"That is true. I am the crafter of the protection amulets used by the regular fey to survive the Iron Realm. However…" The withered head pulled back a few inches. "I have already crafted your amulet, Robin Goodfellow," he said. "I remember each and every piece I create, and yours was commissioned by the Iron Queen herself. You do not need another amulet." His open eye narrowed sharply. "Unless of course you have lost it."

"What? *Moi?* Lose something so important? What gave you that idea?" I smirked at his unamused expression, then motioned behind me. "I don't need one. This amulet is for my friend. She needs to get into the Iron Realm to see the queen and would like to do so without imploding from iron sickness. That would be very inconvenient. Also messy."

The Tinkerer's gaze slid past me to Nyx, hovering at the bottom of the step. Two extremely long fingers came up to twirl and adjust the loupe, before the faery drew in a slow breath.

"A Forgotten? Well, now, what an interesting request. So that is the reason the knight seemed rather agitated when he delivered the message." He observed Nyx a moment longer, then frowned. "Her kind is not well received by some residents of the Iron Kingdom."

"Yeah, we got that. So, can you make her one, or not?"

He sighed. "Come in and shut the door, and please do not touch anything." He drew back, disappearing from sight, and the door creaked on its hinges as it swung open.

We stepped through the frame, shut the door behind us, then turned around.

I expected to see the interior of the wagon, cramped and crowded, with lots of items on shelves and barely enough room to stand up, much less move around. Instead, I stood in the doorway of a large room, soft orange light glowing from several lamps on the ceiling. Shelves lined three of the four walls, filled with all manner of doodads and thingamabobs, and heaps of what looked like junk lay piled in every corner. Gears, levers, springs, wires, and other metallic parts glittered under the lamps, and a faint hum filled the air from some machine in the back.

It looked part workshop, part storefront, and the faint smells of iron, copper, and various other metals were making my nose hairs tingle. Worriedly, I glanced at Nyx, knowing the presence of so much iron was probably making her insides squirm.

The Forgotten's jaw was set, her twilight-gray skin looking a bit washed-out, and her eyes were hard.

"Nyx." Stepping close, I put a hand on her elbow and felt her muscles contract under my fingers. "You okay? Hanging in there?"

The Forgotten gave a grim smile. "I will admit, I've felt better."

"Hang on." Reaching back, I pulled the protection amulet from around my neck and held it up, the metal raven glittering at it spun in a slow circle between us. Instantly, I could feel what Nyx was feeling, the nausea flooding my insides, the acidic burn in the back of my throat. "Ugh, wow, that is unpleasant, isn't it? Here, take this. At least until you have your own."

I went to drape it around her neck, but she placed a hand on my arm, stopping me. "I'm fine, Puck," she said. "One of us has to endure this. Better that I know what I'm walking into. I assume it will be worse in the Iron Realm itself."

"Besides, your amulet would not work on her, Robin Good-fellow."

The Tinkerer's voice, calm and matter-of-fact, drifted across the room. I turned to see him behind a counter, reaching a *really* long arm up to one of the shelves on the wall. And when I say a really long arm, it was twice the length of a normal arm and very thin, like a pool noodle with fingers. Also, now that I could see him clearly, he seemed to have *four* of them. Four creepy long arms, with four creepy spiderlike fingers on each hand, for maximum creep effect.

Okay, it was official. I really didn't like this place.

"That amulet will not shield her from the iron sickness," the Iron faery went on, pulling a box off the top shelf and peering into it. "It was crafted specifically for you, Robin Goodfellow, and only you can receive its protection. No one else. Now..." He put the box on the counter while simultaneously reaching up with two more arms to feel around the shelves. "Let us see what we can do for your friend."

Reluctantly, I returned the amulet to its place under my shirt, feeling both relieved and guilty when the sickness faded to almost nothing. Nyx still looked miserable, but she gave me a reassuring nod, and I had no choice but to follow her across the room to where the Tinkerer was still feeling around the top shelves with his creepy long arms. As he moved a box aside, there was sudden a buzz of wings, and a swarm of small, glittery things flew out from the row of boxes, zipping into the air.

"Confounded sparks!" exclaimed the Tinkerer, as the tiny creatures swarmed frantically around him. "I keep telling you not to sleep in the supply boxes."

The creatures buzzed back and forth, sounding irritated,

before they seemed to notice the two strangers by the door and immediately zipped over to investigate.

I tensed. Up close, they looked like piskies with copper skin, though they were half the size of regular piskies, which was to say, really tiny. This did nothing for my wariness. Piskies were what humans typically thought of when they heard the word *faery*. Cute little Tinker Bells with gossamer wings and magic dust. Trust me, there was nothing cute about them. Don't let their size fool you; piskies had incredibly sharp teeth and the swarming instincts of a school of piranhas. If they were hungry, a horde of them could strip a horse down to the bone in minutes.

The piskie swarm surrounded me, blips of frantic movement and glittering skin. The air around them buzzed with electricity, and each time they moved, there was a faint popping sound, like a static shock. If my hair didn't already have that tousled, *I just rolled out of bed but I still look good* look, it would be standing straight up.

"Um…hi?" I attempted a smile, despite being more than slightly creeped out by their spindly little arms and huge, multifaceted eyes, like those of enormous bees or hornets. Did I mention that I had a thing about bugs? Don't get me wrong, I'd seen a lot of scary things: living dolls and clowns with sharp teeth and all sorts of monsters from your worst nightmares. But everyone has that one thing that makes their skin crawl, makes them get up and flee the room if that thing pops in and says hi. If you haven't guessed by now, mine happens to be bugs.

And an Iron faery with arms like a freaking giant cricket living in a giant spider wagon with a swarm of killer wasp fey was ticking all of my *oh hell no* boxes.

"Enough, sparks," the Tinkerer called, making the swarm draw back slightly. "You are making the customers uncomfortable again. Please shoo for now."

The piskie swarm drew back, rising up to buzz around the ceiling, as Nyx and I crossed the floor to the counter.

The Tinkerer waited for us, tapping long fingers against the glass. It made his hand look like a spider in its death throes, and I repressed a shudder. "I have never crafted an amulet for a Forgotten before," he mused. "How very interesting. This could be tricky."

"Why is that?" Nyx wondered.

"Because to assemble the amulet, I must take a bit of the bearer's own glamour to craft it," the Tinkerer explained. "That is why Robin Goodfellow's amulet will not work on anyone but him—it has a piece of his essence inside it, and the amulet will not recognize anyone else."

I remembered when Meghan first mentioned the amulet to me; she had asked for a lock of hair or something similar, and had rolled her eyes when I gleefully asked why she wanted it. After explaining it was for an experiment to help traditional faeries survive the Iron Realm, I'd given her a jet-black feather, and a few days later was presented with the amulet I was wearing now.

"So?" I shrugged. "I don't see the problem here. It's not like she doesn't have hair. She has very nice hair, in fact."

"You are missing the point, Robin Goodfellow." That pale eye glared at me. "If I needed only hair, or blood, or feathers to craft the amulet, I could do so for any monkey that knocks on my door. That is not the issue."

"It's because the Forgotten have no glamour of our own," Nyx guessed. "We have to steal it from other fey, or the Nevernever itself."

"That is correct." The Tinkerer nodded. "A faery's personal glamour must be woven into the amulet for it to work properly. It is why I cannot simply mass produce these items. Each one must be specifically crafted for the bearer alone. I do not even know the final form the amulet will take—it all depends on the essence of the faery I am making it for." He eyed Nyx shrewdly. "But you, like all Forgotten, have lost your glamour along with your name. I do not know if I can make you an amulet without that magic to anchor it in place."

"Is there no other way?" Nyx wondered. "No other source of magic that can be used to craft an amulet for someone?"

"I do not know," the Tinkerer mused. Steepling long, spider-like fingers under his chin, he regarded Nyx intently. The jewelry loupe on his right eye gleamed as he turned it on her. "I can sense the emptiness inside you, my dear," he said softly. "The struggle simply to exist, to not fade away. Even now, you are subconsciously siphoning a bit of glamour from everything around you, including Master Goodfellow."

Nyx winced at that, and I straightened. I'd known about the Forgotten's glamour draining abilities, of course, but I hadn't realized it was something they couldn't control. I thought back to the battle with the monster, remembering the exhaustion and sluggishness I'd felt when it was over. Had Nyx been draining my magic while we were fighting, using it to power those cool abilities of hers?

I looked at her, and she met my gaze apologetically. "I am sorry, Goodfellow," she said. "I overextended myself in the last battle, and when that thing attacked…I reached for whatever magic I could." A brief look of frustration crossed her face, and one fist clenched at her side. "I'm not used to this, to having no glamour of my own, but that's not an excuse. I should have told you before."

"Hey." I shrugged. "I'll take being tired over being dead any day of the week. Or being squished into magic paste by ugly monsters. You need my glamour, for anything, it's yours."

"Be that as it may," the Tinkerer interrupted, reminding us of the present problem, "you cannot depend on Goodfellow's magic if you want to safely travel to Mag Tuiredh. The effect of the Iron Realm is powerful, and without proper protection, you will die even faster than the traditional fey. You are going to need a very strong, continuous source of glamour if you want to survive past the border."

"What about a Token?" I asked.

The jewelry loupe swiveled around to me. "A Token," he repeated, and those spider fingers drummed against each other. "Hmm," he mused. "That *might* work. Yes, I might be able to substitute a Token for the glamour essence of the bearer, provided I had something of hers to weave into it. I do not, unfortunately, have a Token with me, and they are relatively difficult to come by. If you know where you can find one—"

I drew the playing card from my pocket and flourished it dramatically. "Ta-daaah!" I announced loudly. "From Cricket's Collectables, your one stop for the most interesting treasures and curios this side of the goblin market. Drop on by, and find the thing you never knew you needed."

The words tumbled out of my mouth almost without thought; a side effect of the bargain I'd made with a cheerful, enterprising Iron faery. I sounded like a shifty used-car salesman, but as deals went, it wasn't too bad. I just hoped Nyx wouldn't have to announce the wonders of Cricket's merchandise to every faery who noticed her amulet.

Wait… On second thought, that would be hilarious.

Both Nyx and the Tinkerer blinked as my "announcement" came to an end. I grinned and tossed the card onto the counter. "So, will this work or not?"

"Perhaps. Let us see what we have here." The Tinkerer reached out, curling long fingers around the piece of cardboard, like a spider consuming an insect, before bringing it up to the jewelry loupe. "Fortune," he murmured after a moment. "Luck and destiny. And a bit of a passion for playing the odds. Hmm." He pulled the card away to stare at Nyx for a long moment, as if comparing the two in his mind. "I think I can make this work," he finally said. "If the bearer can give me a small piece of herself? It doesn't have to be a lot, a single strand of hair or drop of blood will work for this purpose."

Nyx reached back and plucked a strand of her silvery white hair before holding it out to the Iron faery, whose long fingers curled around it in the same slow, spiderlike manner.

"Excellent," he said, nodding. "This will do nicely." Both items vanished in the folds of his apron before he turned back to us, clasping his long fingers together. "And now, all that is left is to discuss matters of payment."

"Payment?" Though I wasn't really surprised, part of me winced, anyway.

The Tinkerer glanced my way with a raised eyebrow. "Well, of course, Goodfellow. You did not think you were going to get it for free, did you?"

"I was kind of hoping, yeah."

"Last time the queen herself commissioned the amulet. You do not have that luxury. However..." The Tinkerer paused, then sighed. "There is something wrong within Faery," he went on in a grave voice. "Not just in the Iron Realm, but the entire Nevernever itself. I cannot say what it is, but I sense a malignance in my clients, in the fey passing me on the streets. I hear whispers that chill me to my bones." He shivered, then turned his loupe on me fully, peering at me with an enormous, magnified eye. "Something is coming, Goodfellow. Something that might threaten us all. And the Iron Queen will need allies in the coming days, those she can trust with her life. I want your promise that you will aid her however you can, that when the time comes, you will be at her side. That is my price for the amulet. Swear this to me, and the talisman is yours."

"What?" I frowned, going over the deal in my head, word for word. It didn't sound nefarious or raise the usual red flags, but... "That's all? Help Meghan if she needs it? I mean, I was planning to do that, anyway. What's the catch?"

"You are Robin Goodfellow," the Tinkerer said. "The Puck.

The infamous trickster, and one of the most well-known faeries in existence. You, the cait sith, and the Winter prince are the guardians, the trio of power that surrounds the Iron Queen. I do not want you to forget. I want your promise that if the Iron Queen ever needs you, or if she ever calls on you for aid, you will be there."

"I've known Meghan a long time," I said. "I was looking out for her before she ever became the Iron Queen. You don't have to wrestle a promise out of me. I swear that if she's in trouble and needs my help, for any reason, I'd show up in Mag Tuiredh, talisman or no."

The old faery bobbed his head. "That will have to be sufficient." He drew back, one long arm moving to the door behind the counter and pushing it open with a creak. A couple sparks zipped out with high-pitched buzzes, making me wince, but the Tinkerer ignored them. "Give me a few minutes," the faery told us. "I have not crafted an amulet using a Token before. I will have to experiment with how to make this work. But it will be an enjoyable challenge, I am certain. I will call for you when it is ready."

He slipped out of the room, and the door closed behind him with a creak, leaving Nyx and me alone except for a few sparks buzzing around near the ceiling.

I glanced at the Forgotten and winced at how pale she looked. "I say we wait outside."

"I second that," Nyx agreed, and we fled the room, back to the stone bench beneath the willow tree, away from the stink of metal and the corruption of the Iron faery's domain.

I leaned back on the bench, breathing in the clean, untainted air. Nyx perched beside me, a bit of color returning to her cheeks now that we were in the open. "That was...an experience," she mused, gazing down at her hands as if she expected her skin to be peeling off. "Is this tingling sensation normal?"

"Yeah, don't worry about it." I shrugged. "That's just the

first physical sign of iron poisoning. The burning, sickness, and wanting to die comes later."

"Oh good." Nyx lowered her hands. "Something to look forward to."

I chuckled. "Ah, it's not so bad, really. Once you get past the sickness and the dying and the puking-your-guts-out part, some regions of the Iron Realm are actually quite nice. Mag Tuiredh is pretty impressive. And now that I can move through the realm freely, I get to really explore the place. Last time I was there, I stumbled onto this forest that had mirrors everywhere, growing right out of the ground or hanging from the trees, as far as the eye could see." I snorted and wrinkled my nose. "Trust me, that was the most confusing place to get out of, and the locals were no help at all. You'd try to talk to one, and the second it noticed its reflection, it would forget all about you and preen."

Nyx smiled, but the smile had a wistful edge to it. "Sounds like you've been a lot of places."

"A few. I definitely have stories. What about you?" I asked, curious now. "With how long you've lived, I'm sure you've seen *all* the crazy the Nevernever has to offer."

But the Forgotten shook her head. "I never left the wyldwood," she said solemnly. "The Summer and Winter courts didn't exist back then, and the mortal world was closer to Faery than it is today. There was no reason for me to venture beyond the Lady's domain, and she didn't like us to leave her unprotected, so I stayed."

"What? You've never been out of the wyldwood?" The thought was mind-boggling. The wyldwood was huge, and you could certainly spend your whole life there without seeing it all, but who would *want* to? There were so many other places in the Nevernever, not to mention the human world, that begged you to visit and get into trouble. "Okay, we are going to fix that," I told Nyx. "When this is over, I'm going to take you on a tour of the Nevernever. Keirran certainly doesn't need you to hang around him twenty-four-seven. He's a big boy, he can take care of himself. And after this many centuries, I say you've earned a vacation."

A wry smile played over the Forgotten's lips. "Just the two of us?"

I ignored the weird turning of my stomach and shrugged. "Well, I'd ask ice-boy to join us, but he's so busy now, what with ruling the Iron Realm with Meghan. He rarely gets to go on adventures anymore. Pity, really. Those were the days." For a second, I felt a twinge of nostalgia, regret, and the tiniest bit of resentment. Once upon a time, the Winter prince of the Unseelie Court and Robin Goodfellow were the dynamic duo of the Nevernever, seeking out adventure and getting into more trouble than we had a right to get out of alive. I'd even gone to the End of the World with him, helped him earn a soul so he could be with Meghan in the Iron Realm. Now, Ash had no time for anything but his queen. The queen he had stolen away from me.

Whoa, where'd that come from, Goodfellow? Obsessive much? It's been years. We are way *past that, remember?*

Faeries don't forget, a deeper, more malicious side of me whispered. *Or forgive. Maybe we're not.*

I shuddered and pushed that voice away. "So, yeah." I turned to Nyx. "Just the two of us. First up, we head to Arcadia. The politics are ugly, but if we stay away from the court and the queen, we should be fine. For some reason, Titania is always so cranky when I come home."

"I can't imagine why," Nyx commented, still with that faint smile.

"It's a mystery," I agreed. "But this time of year, I think we should first pay a visit to the Orchard. Best apples in all the Nevernever, and I'm an expert on the subject. Totally worth the experience, if you don't mind dodging a couple greedy giants that refuse to share. But if you go when the sun is directly overhead, they're usually asleep..."

I trailed off. For just a moment, a flicker of alarm passed over Nyx's face, making me stumble to a halt. "Or maybe not," I said. "I guess not everyone likes apples. Or giants."

"No, it's not that." The hint of alarm was replaced by confusion; her brows drew together, frustration coloring her voice. "Something you said," she muttered, "something about that scene, it felt wrong. I didn't want to be there. Not because of the giants or Titania or anything about the Seelie Court. But for just a moment, I felt deeply unsettled, and I don't remember why."

A buzzing sound interrupted us. I looked up and saw a trio of the Tinkerer's killer bee piskies hovering a few feet away, their large black eyes and copper skin glittering in the moonlight as they stared at me.

Between them, something dangled from a silver chain, throwing off shimmers of light as it swayed and twisted in the air. Glamour pulsed from it, an aura of hazy color and emotion, throbbing like a real heartbeat.

"Huh, that was fast," I commented. "You know, if you guys opened up a sandwich shop, you'd be the most popular place in the Nevernever."

The piskies ignored me. Buzzing, they floated closer and dropped the amulet into Nyx's hands, where it flickered like a lost firefly. Carefully, she rose and draped the amulet around her neck. It gleamed brightly against the darkness of her leather armor, a silver heart with a crescent moon-shaped hole in the center. Pretty fitting, I thought.

The third piskie zipped up, closer to my face than I was comfortable with, and thrust a folded bit of paper at me, shaking it rapidly. I snatched it from the air before I suffered a paper cut to my eyeballs and flipped it open.

It was, as far as I could tell, a receipt for services rendered, with a large Paid in Full message scrawled near the bottom in red ink. I didn't know if I was supposed to keep it, or if it was simply a formality, but I crumpled it and stuck it in my hoodie pocket. I'd worry about what the Tinkerer had said, and what I'd promised him, later. For now, we had what we came for.

Finally.

"Well," I said brightly, glancing at Nyx. "Now that that's out of the way, and we don't have to worry about your skin melting off in the Iron Realm, are you ready to meet the queen?"

Nyx smoothly tucked the pendant beneath her armor and drew her cloak around herself as she rose. A breeze tossed her hair, making it flutter in the wind, and the moon emerging from behind a cloud cast a hazy circle of light around her as she gazed at me with a smile. "I believe the correct expression for the times is *yesterday*."

I chuckled, feeling that odd twisting sensation in my gut again. "You know, for someone as ancient as you are, you certainly don't sound like any Wise Old One I ever met," I said as we started walking toward the bridge once more. "Shouldn't you have more thees and thous in your vocabulary?"

Nyx offered a smirk that was entirely too familiar and pulled up her hood. "I'm a fast learner."

PART

II

THE SUMMER COURT

Several years ago

I was in the middle of an elaborate scheme involving Titania and a dozen porcupines when the summons came.

"Message from His Majesty, King Oberon," a nervous-looking satyr announced, handing me a rolled-up scroll. "He requests that you meet him in the throne room as soon as you receive this. You are required to stop whatever prank, plan, or plot you are currently involved in and obey the summons now. Any delay will be punished, as will any retaliation against the messenger."

The satyr stiffened as a porcupine shuffled forward, curiously sniffing his hooves. "His M-Majesty cordially awaits your response," the satyr went on, backing away as the rest waddled toward him with jumbled squeaking sounds. "If you do not respond by the time the sun sets this evening, Lord Oberon will assume you have deliberately disobeyed him and will take appropriate actions. Have a pleasant day, Robin Goodfellow."

The satyr fled, causing the porcupine horde to chirp disappointedly and return to chewing on twigs.

I let out a sigh, feeling both amused and annoyed with the Seelie King. We had done this dance many times before, and his summonses had gradually become more and more specific as I continuously found loopholes to avoid having to do whatever he commanded. I peeked at the scroll and found that it basically said the same thing, with even more specifics and threats of retribution if I did not answer.

With a snort, I crumpled the scroll into a ball and gave it to the nearest porcupine, who happily began nibbling it to nothing. If I thought about it, I could probably find a way to get around the summons, but truth be told, I was looking for a reason to leave the Summer Court for a while. Lately, tensions had been high, as rumors surrounding Oberon's recent trip to the mortal world had swirled through the court, incensing Titania and causing her to be even more unbearable. I hadn't seen the queen so worked up in a long time, not since the famous Nick Bottom incident, and several of the common fey had already suffered her wrath and infamous petty temper.

Naturally I, being the good little Summer Court jester, had been planning something special to take her mind off her husband's actions and turn her ire directly on me. This wasn't for Oberon's benefit; Titania could do nothing to him, but if she had another target for her loathing (and boy, did she loathe me with the passion of a thousand suns), she wouldn't be such a terror to the rest of the court. Including those unfortunate enough to serve her directly.

I also suspected the Seelie King knew I was about to do something. Being one of the Erlking's favorite lackeys, I was somewhat shielded from the queen's retribution, but constantly explaining that he would not exile me for yet another fiasco was probably becoming tiring. Though, if the rumors flying around the court were true, Oberon had brought this on himself. Titania was famous for being a jealous shrew, but Oberon wasn't exactly pure like the new fallen snow, either. This time, her anger might be justified.

Fair enough; I would go see what the Summer King wanted. Maybe this assignment would take me out of Faery for a bit, into the mortal realm. It had been a while since I'd seen the real world; a trip to the Alps or to a sun-drenched island across the sea sounded enticing.

Oberon was in the throne room, sitting on one of the living thrones growing from the center of the grove. Unsurprisingly, the identical seat beside him was empty. The Summer Queen was not speaking to Oberon at the moment, and while some might think this would be a pleasant thing, faeries did not take well to being ignored. The Seelie King would tolerate his wife's cold shoulder for a little while, but he was even worse than Titania when it came to his wife paying more attention to things other than him. Eventually, he would become offended and force a confrontation, and that would not end well for anyone.

And yeah, it was super hypocritical, but try explaining that to a faery lord. They didn't do irony.

The Erlking sat rigidly on his throne, observing the court scattered before him. He looked tired, I thought, passing through a cluster of Summer gentry gossiping among themselves. They gave a start when they realized who it was, and I felt their suspicious gazes on my back as I continued across the grove. I ignored them; typical day in the Seelie Court, when Robin Goodfellow arrives, everyone gets nervous.

I reached the foot of the throne and paused, gazing up at the Summer King. I didn't bow or kneel or do anything deferential, and he didn't rebuke me for it. We knew each other too well for any of that.

"Goodfellow." Oberon's voice was impassive. "I see you've actually decided to heed my call for once. Has the court become boring?"

"Oh extremely," I replied, grinning up at him. "In fact, I was just in the middle of making things a bit more exciting around here. Although, I don't think a career in porcupine herding is in my future, sadly enough. So, if you've got something for me to do, my wandering king, I'd love to hear it."

He winced before he could catch himself, which showed just how stressed he was feeling. Rising, he gazed past my head, at the rest of the court spread before him, and narrowed his eyes.

"Leave us," he commanded, his voice booming above all other noise and conversations. Some of the nobles jumped, their expressions startled, and he swept a hand toward the exit. "Depart my presence, all of you," he ordered. "I wish to speak to the court jester alone."

They gave him, and me, knowing looks, but immediately turned and left the throne room, slipping out through the tunnel of briars that marked the entrance to the grove.

Oberon sat down again, rubbing his forehead as if he found all of us wearisome. "I have a task for you, Goodfellow," he began, lowering his arm to stare me down with ancient green eyes. "It is one I would not ask anyone but you to undertake. Of all my subjects in Summer, you know the most about the mortal realm. You travel there more often than anyone in the Seelie Court."

"Ooh, so I'm going to the human world, then." I grinned, rubbing my hands together. "Sounds like fun. So, is it to spy on a servant of Winter, remind a disobedient faery why he shouldn't defy his king, or fetch something ancient and fun from one of those human collectors?"

"None of those," said Oberon. "And I would not get too excited yet, Goodfellow. You see…" He paused, steepling his fingers under his pointed chin. "This task will require you not only to go to the mortal realm, but to live there."

I blinked at him. "What?" I exclaimed. "Are you exiling me, then? I haven't even done anything yet."

"No." Oberon shook his head. "This is not a punishment,

Robin," he assured me. "You are not being exiled or banished from Faery. But I do require you to go to the human world and not return to the Nevernever for...a while."

"How long?"

"I do not know. Possibly years." The Seelie King sighed, either oblivious or uncaring of my dismay. "I need you to find a particular mortal," he went on. "A human child. If my enemies discover her, they will use her against me. You must go to the mortal realm, find this girl, and protect her from the danger around her. You must also keep her oblivious to the world of the fey—she must never learn of her heritage, and she must never cross the Veil into Faery. Do you understand?"

"Uggghhh," I groaned. Suddenly everything made sense. So, the rumors surrounding the Seelie King's trip to the mortal world were entirely true. "You want me to become a glorified babysitter for this human?" I asked, watching Oberon's gaze narrow. "How long is she going to need someone watching over her?"

"Until I deem otherwise," the Seelie King said in that final, uncompromising way of his. "At the very least, until I believe she is in no danger and is not a threat herself."

I groaned again, and his voice became a bit more soothing.

"Do not fret, Robin Goodfellow," he cajoled. "If the girl never comes into Faery, she will have a perfectly normal human lifespan, and mortals do not live very long. At the very worst, you will have to stay in the mortal realm only until she dies."

"Guess I really don't have a say in this, do I?" I muttered, and the Erlking didn't bother to answer that question. "Fine. I'll do it, but I won't like it. Where is this remarkable human, and how will I know I've found her?"

"The child was born of a human mother," Oberon said, sounding wistful for the barest of seconds. "As of right now, they are living in a place called Louisiana. The child's name, or the name her mother gave her, is Meghan Chase."

10

INTO THE IRON REALM. FINALLY

This time, there was no trouble. Though the knights did glare daggers at Nyx as we walked by, they didn't attempt to speak or stop us as we strolled past the gates onto the bridge. I didn't see Glitch again, either, and once past the gates, the presence of the guards disappeared. We had a clear shot to the Iron Kingdom with no opposition whatsoever.

Honestly, I was kind of disappointed. That spiteful, vindictive part of me I was trying to ignore still wanted to enact a bit of gleeful revenge against the stiff-necked Iron faeries, and the thought of the tin cans rolling around in the mud like pigs made me snicker. Maybe later, when we had finished our business in Mag Tuiredh, I would pay Glitch and the knights a little visit. Remind them why the rest of Faery didn't screw around with Robin Goodfellow.

"You have that evil smile on your face again," Nyx remarked as we continued across the bridge. She hopped easily onto the railing and strolled along the edge as the wind howling up from the chasm tossed her hair and made her cloak snap around her.

"If you're plotting your revenge, I hope you plan to wait until *after* we've seen the queen. I get the feeling your vengeance plans are rather extensive."

"Revenge? Me?" I echoed, grinning up at her. "Revenge is such a petty pastime, my good Forgotten. Is this the face of someone obsessed with vengeance?"

"You have horns, hooves, and are smiling like a fox who just discovered the chicken coop was left open," Nyx replied without hesitation. Abruptly, she jumped from the railing and landed in my path with a challenging smirk, her face inches from mine and the moonlight blazing down on her. "You tell me, Robin Goodfellow."

In that moment, I almost kissed her. An instinctive reaction, really. I was Robin Goodfellow, the infamous Puck; I had kissed countless pretty girls, human and fey alike. Graceful nymphs, flirtatious satyrs, ethereal sidhe, and naive human females in the mortal world, none could resist my charm once I'd turned it on. I'd kissed a few boys as well, along with a mermaid, a trio of plant creatures that had no discernible gender, and one very disillusioned frog that thought it was a princess.

Kissing, and all the activities that came with it, was so common an occurrence in the Nevernever it was almost expected. Love was never an option, or even an afterthought. While some fey did grow quite attached to each other, even to the point of developing real affection, true love required work, sacrifice, and putting the other person before yourself, something few faeries understood. So while I had done a lot of kissing in my long years as Robin Goodfellow, very little of it meant anything to me.

With a couple exceptions, of course. The most notable was the queen we were on our way to see, right now. The princess I'd lost, who had chosen my greatest rival instead of me.

Nyx wasn't Meghan. In fact, the two were so different it was laughable. But she was beautiful, dangerous, and the most intriguing faery I'd met in a long time. I wondered what would happen if I did kiss her. Would she put a knife to my throat? Stab me in the delicates? Or...would she return it?

Did I dare take that chance again?

A squeaking, clanking, jingling sound interrupted us before I could make a decision. Looking back, I saw the Tinkerer's wagon coming toward us on its segmented insect legs, looking so much like a massive metal spider I nearly leaped over the railing to avoid it. As the wagon's girth nearly took up the middle of the bridge, Nyx hopped smoothly onto a post, and I pressed myself back against the wood as the structure lurched by, hissing, smoking, and leaving a trail of oil behind it, and continued toward the Iron Realm.

"Sure, don't mind us, we'll just get out of your way, then," I called after it, and glanced at Nyx. "Well, he was in an awful hurry. Maybe there's a long-armed-faery soiree he can't be late for. Or maybe he was avenging all those times I stepped on an ant nest."

Nyx didn't answer. She stood tall on the post, perfectly balanced with the wind ruffling her hair, staring after the wagon with a faintly awed look in her eyes.

"I can see the Iron Realm," she murmured.

I smiled grimly, remembering the first time I'd been to the capital city of the Iron fey, and the feeling of amazement, excitement, and unease it brought. "Yeah," I acknowledged, wondering how Nyx would react when she saw it up close and personal. "Almost there."

Tinkerport, the hilariously named town on the other side of the bridge, was your first introduction to the Iron Realm once you crossed over from the wyldwood. As towns went, it wasn't very large; while the grand capital of Mag Tuiredh was home to thousands of Iron fey (most of them gremlins, but still), Tinkerport had only a few hundred. But once you crossed the bridge and stepped onto the cobbled streets beyond the gates, your first thought probably went along the lines of, *Toto, we ain't in Kansas anymore.*

Or maybe more accurately, *holy shit.*

That was the look on Nyx's face as we stepped through the brass gates of Tinkerport and onto the main street through the center of town.

It was hard to describe Tinkerport. It was like a scatterbrained inventor took his entire collection of bits, bobs, and metal parts, upended it on the floor, and somehow made a city. Buildings lined the cobblestone roads, but not your regular stone, wood, and straw configurations. Walls glimmered in the fading moonlight, gears and cogs spun as they opened doors, weather panes twirled, and lengths of seemingly useless pipe stuck out at random intervals. Streetlamps sprouted right out of the ground, sometimes bent at odd angles or twisted around a tree, as if it had just grown that way. Steam hissed from vents and random pipes, curling into the air or drifting into the gutters, giving the town a hazy look.

Then, of course, there were the Iron fey. Hacker elves, cog dwarves, clockwork hounds, wire nymphs, and rust eaters were only a few of the creatures walking the roads or hovering in the shadows. And those were the faeries whose names I knew. Other, even stranger fey wandered the hazy streets. Despite their weirdness, they had one thing in common: they were all immediately recognizable as Iron fey. They had a name, and someone who knew them. Unlike Nyx, whom no one had a name for at all.

I had to give the Forgotten credit. Despite being surrounded by—quite literally—nightmares of the fey world, she remained remarkably calm. I remembered my first venture into the Iron Realm; it had involved a lot of exclamations like *eeeew* and *creeeeeepy* and *oh-crap-get-it-away.* This might've had something to do with the prevalence of bug-like things in the Iron Kingdom, but still. Just the fact that Nyx hadn't gone for her weapons was impressive, though she had drawn deep into her cloak and tugged the hood up to cover her face.

"So, whadya think?" I asked, giving her a sideways look. "It's your first trip to the Iron Realm… How are you going to describe it to everyone when you get home?"

"Shiny," Nyx muttered, and I snorted a laugh. "Truthfully, I've never seen anything like it," she went on, her voice sounding awed but trying not to let it show. "These fey…how can they exist? Is this what the humans dream of now?"

"Pretty much," I told her. "The Iron fey came from mankind's obsession with progress and technology. That's why they're so comfortable in the mortal world, and why they don't Fade away when cut off from the Nevernever. Iron and the banal effects of nonbelief don't have any effect on them."

"I see." Nyx observed the town, golden eyes taking everything in. "It doesn't seem large enough for a court, however," she mused. "I take it the Iron Queen does not reside here?"

"Sadly not." I shook my head. "Meghan lives in the capital, Mag Tuiredh, which is still quite a ways from the border. Don't worry, though. I don't plan on hoofing it to Mag Tuiredh, not when there are other, much more convenient ways of travel through the Iron Realm."

"Like the carriages? I saw a few of them earlier."

"Ugh, definitely not." I shuddered. "Did you not notice their wheels, or rather the lack of them? They have legs. Spider legs. I am not riding to Mag Tuiredh on the back of some creepy-ass spider wagon." My skin itched, and I brushed at imaginary bugs crawling up my arms. "Seriously, what *is* it with all the insect-themed rides in the Iron Realm? It's like the world's creepiest amusement park. Nope, no spider taxi to the capital."

Nyx raised a brow in that amused way of hers but chose not to comment on my perfectly reasonable spider phobia. "Then what do you suggest?"

"I thought we'd take the train."

Nyx furrowed her brow. "I am unfamiliar with this...train," she said. "Is it like a carriage?"

"Oh, I could tell you," I said, grinning. "But why ruin the surprise?" She frowned at me, and I stepped back. "Come on, it's something you really need to see for yourself."

The train station sat on the outskirts of Tinkerport, a raised wooden platform resting beside the railroad tracks that stretched away into the distance. When Meghan had become queen, one of the first things she did was build the extensive rail system so that it reached all corners of the Iron Realm. I'd ridden the train a couple times before, and I had to say, I wouldn't mind having something like it in the wyldwood or Arcadia. Tromping through the wyldwood on foot, fighting weather and vegetation and everything that wanted to eat you, got so tedious sometimes.

Only a few Iron fey waited on the platform beside the railroad tracks, mostly siting on the benches scattered about. One spindly fellow, wearing a crooked top hat that was twice as tall as normal, perched on the very edge of the platform, gazing down the tracks for the engine that had yet to appear. I caught a few strange looks from the faeries waiting for the train; I supposed that even with easier access to the Iron Realm, not many traditional fey considered it a great vacation spot. And as Nyx and I seemed to be the only non-Iron faeries in the entire town, we kind of stood out. A trio of fey that sort of resembled gnomes, but with jaws like steel traps, eyed us from a corner of the platform, whispering among themselves.

"I'm starting to feel like a satyr in a redcap den," Nyx murmured beside me, having also caught sight of our toothy observers. "I hope they don't decide to cause trouble while we're on this train."

"Oh, I dunno." I grinned, feeling the gleeful spitefulness stirring in me again. "It might be fun. They'd certainly find that they bit off more than they could chew."

"If it's all the same, I'd rather not have anything bitten off."

I chuckled, but with a piercing whistle and a billow of black smoke, a rusty, black iron engine pulled into the station and came to a heaving, panting halt beside the platform, leaking steam and puffing like an out-of-breath dragon. Nyx flinched and darted behind me, then peered over my shoulder as the train wheezed and hacked and coughed, sending smoke and bits of soot everywhere.

"What is that?" she muttered, staring at the huge, huffing engine in both wariness and awe. "Some kind of iron monster? Is it alive?"

"That," I announced, glancing back to grin at her, "is our ride to Mag Tuiredh."

"*That's* the train? Why didn't you tell me it was..." Her eyes narrowed. "You just wanted to see my reaction, didn't you?"

"It would've been funny if you tried to stab it—ow." I winced as she punched me in the ribs. "Still worth it."

The inside of the train wasn't exactly crowded, but it wasn't empty, either. It seemed Mag Tuiredh was a popular destination in the Iron Realm. Iron fey sat alone or in small groups. Curious, wary, and faintly hostile gazes followed us down the aisles, which I did my best to ignore. Finding a relatively quiet corner, I slouched onto a bench with a sigh and put my feet up on the seat across from me. My hooves clattered against the edge of the bench, and I winced. "Oof, that's going to take some getting used to again. I hope Meghan doesn't see me and freak out. Hell, I hope *ice-boy* doesn't see me and freak out." I paused. "Wait. No, that would actually be hilarious."

Nyx, leaning against the window with her arms crossed, glanced down at me. "Who is this 'ice-boy' you keep mentioning?"

"The Iron Queen's husband." I laced my hands behind my head, affecting a pose of lazy nonchalance, a stark contrast to the sudden bitterness that prickled inside. "Third son of Mab,

Queen of the Winter Court. His real name is Ash, but ice-boy fits him so much better. You'll see when we meet them."

The train chugged into motion, and soon the lights of Tinkerport faded behind us. As we picked up speed, moving away from the town, a vast, rocky expanse could be seen through the window, jagged cliffs silhouetted against a navy blue sky. The moon hung very low over one of the peaks, and the stars were beginning to disappear. Dawn would soon break over the Iron Kingdom, for which I was glad. After the darkness of the Between and the eternal twilight of the wyldwood, I was ready to see the sun.

I yawned, stretching out on the bench. "Might as well get comfortable," I told the faery standing at the window. "I'm not sure how long it'll take us to reach the capital, but Mag Tuiredh is near the center of the Iron Realm, so it could take a while. This might be a good time for a nap."

"Sleep?" The Forgotten gave me a strange look, lowering her voice. "We're in the Iron Realm, in a metal box surrounded by dozens of Iron fey. There's no way I'll be able to sleep."

"Suit yourself." I slouched farther on the bench with a yawn. "But I have the feeling we're not going to get much rest once we actually get to Mag Tuiredh, so I'm going to relax while we have the chance. Yell if something tries to eat my face off."

Nyx shook her head but turned away, staring out the window again with her arms crossed.

I leaned back and let my eyes close, shutting out the rest of the world. I wasn't *really* that tired, but I could feel the mire of resentment stir when Nyx mentioned Ash, and I didn't want to continue talking about it. For the first time in a long time, I felt it was better that I not say anything at all. Hopefully the memories would fade and take these feelings of anger and hostility with them.

The train chugged on into the night. None of the other passengers bothered us; it seemed the rest of the train had either fallen asleep or were keeping to themselves. I dozed, but was aware enough to know Nyx did not sit down the entire time, continuing her silent vigil at the window until dawn.

I felt the moment the sun broke over the distant mountains, the light warming my face and pressing against my eyelids.

A strangled sound made my blood chill. I opened my eyes just in time to see Nyx stagger back from the window. Her face was pale, her eyes glassy and pained. One hand clutched at her chest, then she swayed and fell to her knees on the wooden floor.

"Nyx." I swung my hooves off the bench and dropped beside her, putting a hand on her arm. The Forgotten shuddered, her skin cold in the faint rays of sunlight streaming through the window, and my alarm grew. "Hey, talk to me. What's going on?"

"I…I don't know." Her voice was a breath, a whisper, as if she couldn't summon the strength for anything louder. "I feel strange. Weak." She trembled and pressed a hand to the floor as if the room was spinning. "What is happening to me? Is this… iron sickness?"

My senses prickled. I glanced around to see we weren't going unnoticed. The faeries on the train who, a few seconds ago, had been dozing or gazing out the window, minding their own business, were starting to stare at us. Eyes turned, heads swung around, and gazes rose to watch us with more than a passing fascination. Glowing, curious, hungry eyes stared at Nyx, making me tense. The denizens of the Iron Realm, though they claimed to be more civilized than Summer or Winter, were still fey. And faeries could sense weakness like a shark smelled blood. I could see that predatory nature awakening in the calculating stares sizing us up, wondering how easy it would be to take us apart. The three steel-trap gnomes sitting toward the end of the car peered over a seat back, their eyes glowing and intense as they watched us.

Okay, it was a good idea to not be here now. "Nyx," I said, turning back to the Forgotten. Was it my imagination, or did she seem paler than before? Even less substantial than she had been? "Not to alarm you or anything, but we need to get out of here. Can you stand?"

Her jaw clenched, but she nodded jerkily and pushed herself to her feet, swaying a little as she did. "Go," she told me. "I'm right behind you."

I stepped into the aisle, smiling dangerously at any Iron faery who met my gaze, daring them to try something. They stayed where they were, though their eyes glittered as they shifted past me to the Forgotten at my back, making my fingers itch for my daggers.

"Don't look now," Nyx muttered, her voice low and strained. "But we're being followed."

I glanced back and saw that the trio of steel-trap gnomes had slid out of their seat and were trailing us down the aisle like dogs following a wounded cougar, scenting blood but knowing not to get too close. Annoyance flickered, dangerously close to turning into something deadly. At this rate, they were just begging to meet the old Robin Goodfellow, who in his current mood was not inclined to be nice. Unfortunately, if I responded to this threat in any way, it might trigger the rest of the faeries in this car to attack. And in such tight quarters, that could get really messy really fast. If Nyx was at her best, I wouldn't be concerned. But the Forgotten was clearly suffering from some mysterious affliction, and I was more worried about getting her to safety than giving a bunch of razor-tooth gnomes a permanent case of lockjaw.

I slid open the doors of one car and stepped into the next, which was just as crowded as the first. More faeries looked up from their seats, their attention turning curious and predatory as soon as Nyx stepped through the door.

I kept the vicious smile on my face, my gaze hard and challenging as we continued down the aisle. *Go ahead and try something*, it said. *Give me a reason to cut loose.*

As we neared the back of the second car, a large faery slid out of a booth, stepping into the aisle to block our path. He was enormous and muscular, with steely tendons underneath his dark skin and shoulders that filled his leather jacket. Thick dreadlocks hung around his shoulders like a mane, but they were made of twisted cables instead of hair. His eyes were hidden behind reflective sunglasses, but I could feel an intense, searing gaze settle on me.

I stopped and smirked up at him. "Oh hi," I greeted, feeling Summer glamour surge to my fingertips. "You wouldn't want to get out of the way, would you?"

"Robin Goodfellow." The faery's voice was deep, making the ground rumble under my hooves. "Don't you recognize me?"

"Um…" I hesitated. I did know of one faery that reminded me of this behemoth. But he was dead, having sacrificed himself to save Meghan in the war with the false king. Though they looked similar, this certainly wasn't him. "Can't say that I do. Have we met before?"

The faery sighed, and a jet of steam shot from his nostrils, coiling into the air. He took off his shades to regard me with eyes as red as burning embers. "Coaleater," he said, and my brain finally gave a jolt of recognition. "We met on the Obsidian Plains, in the war with the false king. My herd and I carried the Iron Queen and her comrades into battle. I was wearing a different form at that time."

"Oh right." I snapped my fingers. "I remember. You were much horsier then."

He gave a very equine snort, releasing another curl of smoke into the air over our heads. "I was wondering what the commotion was about," he stated, gazing around at the train car of restless fey, still watching us with curious, hungry eyes. "Of course it would be you, Goodfellow. What trouble are you causing this time?"

"Hey, this is not my fault." I held up a finger. "I was perfectly happy to have a nice, peaceful ride to Mag Tuiredh." I glanced back at Nyx, my jaw tightening at how pale she looked, her eyes glazed with discomfort but trying not to show it. "But my friend isn't feeling the greatest, and some of the passengers here thought that was an invitation to be assholes. I'm trying to get her to a quiet spot, away from the sharp teeth."

"Hmm." The Iron faery's crimson gaze went to Nyx, assessing. "You *are* aware that she is a Forgotten," he stated in a not-a-question voice.

"Really?" I gasped, one hand going to my heart. "You don't say. You mean she was a Forgotten this whole time? Well, don't I feel silly." He snorted again, and I rolled my eyes. "So, now that we've established the obvious, maybe you could move so that I can interrogate this devious Forgotten in a nice, safe, quiet spot?"

Coaleater grunted, turning his huge body aside for us to pass. "Take the booth in the corner," he said, eyeing the faeries hovering behind us. "I'll make sure no one bothers you. On one condition, Goodfellow." He raised a meaty finger of his own. "When we get to the capital, you tell me what's going on, why you're really here. Deal?"

Normally, the word *deal* would raise all kinds of red flags. I avoided making deals or bargains, unless I was really, *really* sure I wasn't being screwed over. But the Iron horses had a reputation for being righteous and honorable, upholding the values of their progenitor, Ironhorse, who happened to be a friend of mine before his noble sacrifice. Besides, having Rusty 2.0 take care of our little predator problem was a blessing in disguise. He would get the gnomes off our backs, and I wouldn't have to turn this train inside out before we got to the capital.

"Deal," I agreed, and the Iron faery nodded. Stepping back, he waited for us to pass, then planted himself in the center of the aisle, crossing his arms and glowering at the gnome trio. I retreated to the booth with Nyx, and she slumped to one of the seats, covering her eyes as if the room was far too bright.

"Nyx." I sat in front of her, taking one pale hand. It was cold to the touch, and I squeezed it worriedly. "Hey. Talk to me. You okay?"

The Forgotten gave a weary nod. "As well as can be expected," she said in a near whisper. Dropping her arm, she opened her eyes as a shudder went through her, making her brow furrow. "I remember now. I know what's happening to me."

Her faded gold gaze rose to the window, to the sun coming up over the distant mountains. "My kin and I were faeries of the darkness," she began. "The phases of the moon gave us our strength. When the Lady sent us to kill, that contract would last a single night. One night for our prey to avoid us. To have a chance at living. When the sun came up, we would lose our power, and the contract would end. If the target had survived to see the sunrise, they would be free." She paused, a haunted look going through her eyes, then shook her head. "In all my years of serving the Lady, that happened only once."

"So, you can't go into the sun? Like a vampire?"

"It's not that it hurts me," Nyx continued. "And I have no idea what a vampire is. But I get weaker and lose all my glamour when the sun comes up." She hesitated again, frowning. "Honestly, I don't exactly know what will happen if I stay in direct sunlight for any length of time. The wyldwood is eternal twilight, and I rarely went into the mortal realm." Her gaze grew unfocused, and she put one hand against the glass window, her jaw tightening as the light spilled over her fingers. "Maybe it will burn me to dust. Or I could just Fade to nothing." Her voice dropped, becoming nearly inaudible, though it still sent an icy lance through my middle. "I don't belong here, anyway," she murmured. "Maybe that would be for the best."

"Nope, that's not going to happen," I told her, making her blink. "If it comes to that, I'll make you a flipping parasol to keep the sun off. You're not allowed to Fade away on me, here or anytime in the future, got it?"

She blinked, and I gave her a fierce smile, continuing to hold her hand in both of mine.

"I knew someone like you, once," I went on, wondering why I was telling her this. "Had a troubled past, didn't think much of himself, thought that no one would miss him if he was ever gone. But he was wrong. Even in Faery, there were those who would miss him, whose lives he had changed. And if you think I'm going to let you poof into nothingness without a fight, then you don't know me very well."

Nyx held my gaze for a heart-pounding moment. Then, without warning, she leaned down, and her cool lips were pressed against mine.

I stiffened in shock, but only for a second. Turns out, I'd wanted this for a while. I just didn't think Nyx would be the one to initiate anything. Closing my eyes, I kissed her back, feeling the pit of my stomach twist itself into a pretzel knot.

It didn't last long. I'd rather it had continued until we pulled into the station at Mag Tuiredh, but Nyx drew back slightly, leaving me reeling on the floor of the train. Opening my eyes, I met her gaze, watching as one corner of her lip pulled up in a half smile.

"Don't read too much into it," she warned softly. "I just wanted to... I'm grateful, that's all. For everything you've done to get me here."

"So, that was just a thank-you without saying thank you?"

She winced. That phrase, even those words, was rather taboo among the fey. Saying thank you in Faery was the same as putting yourself into that person's debt. But being around humans, who used that phrase liberally, for so long had sort of deadened my reaction to it. Reaching up, I tangled my fingers in her long silver hair, smiling. "You're welcome," I told her. "And if you ever get the urge to thank me again, I am always willing to listen."

"Don't get cocky, Goodfellow." Nyx rose, pulling her hood

up. "And don't think you're safe. The sun sets in just a few hours."

I pushed myself upright and realized that, except for Coaleater still standing in the center of the aisle with his arms crossed, we were now alone in the car. The rest of the crowd, probably under the not-so-subtle glare of the huge Iron faery, had vacated the area. I could see a few of them peeking through the door to the adjacent car, but they weren't coming any closer. Coaleater, standing rigid with his back to us, gave a snort, a fleeting cloud of steam writhing around his head.

"Are you two quite finished?"

I couldn't be positive, but Nyx might've blushed in the shadow of her hood. I gave a wide grin and laced my hands behind my skull.

"Jealous, tin can?" I drawled. "What's the rush, anyway? It's not like we can get to the capital any faster."

"No," Coaleater agreed, turning around. "But we are approaching a rather significant landmark in the Iron Realm. As someone who fought the original Iron King, the very first of his name, I thought you might want to see it."

"Aw, are you playing tour guide, Rusty? That's so nice of you. Do you have any brochures?"

Coaleater ignored my comment. His attention was suddenly riveted to the window, to something beyond the glass. The Iron fey had removed his glasses, and the look in his burning red eyes was one of solemn respect. I followed his gaze and immediately shut up.

Across a flat, dusty plain, a tower sat in the center of the plateau, jagged metal walls catching the light of the sun. Most of the tower lay in ruins, shattered and broken around the roots and trunk of an enormous tree that soared into the air, rising above the crumbling walls to brush the sky. The tree itself, a massive oak with enormous, gnarled branches and broad leaves, glimmered and flashed in the sun, as if it was made of liquid metal. Even after all these years, it still caused a shiver to run down my spine.

Nyx gazed out the window as well, drawing in a quiet breath as she observed the ruins and the giant tree. "That is a place of power," she said softly. "I can feel it from here."

Coaleater said nothing, his silence one of somber reverence, so she turned to me.

"What is it?" she asked in a whisper.

"Machina's tower," I muttered, as memories from a darker age came back to me. "Where it all began."

11

MAG TUIREDH

Mag Tuiredh was just as wacky as I remembered. And I've seen some pretty bizarre things. The wyldwood is ever changing, but in the Summer and Winter courts at least, things were odd but expected. For example, you can expect Tir Na Nog to be cold enough to freeze your chin hairs off, and for the Summer Court to be full of frolicking Seelie fey that will either turn you into a rosebush or dance you into an early grave. Pretty standard, really. After so many years of visiting both territories, not much surprised me anymore.

The capital of the Iron Realm could still cause a shiver of anticipation to run up my spine.

It was a massive city that was a blend of old and new, medieval and modern. Or maybe medieval and steampunk would be a better description. Cobblestone roads lined with lampposts ran alongside buildings that were a hodgepodge of every building material you could think of. Stone and brick huts sat next to buildings straight out of a Victorian steampunk novel, with copper pipes and weather vanes sticking haphazardly out of the roof. Iron fey crowded the streets and sidewalks, on foot or in carriages, and you couldn't walk ten feet without seeing a gremlin, the tiny, bat-eared nuisances of the fey world, hanging on a wall or perched on a lamppost.

"So," Coaleater commented as the train began to slow, huffing and shedding steam. "Now that we've arrived in Mag Tuiredh, you going to tell me why you're here, Goodfellow?"

I shrugged. "Eventually. That was part of the deal, after all. Only..." I grinned up at him. "You didn't say exactly *when* I had to tell you. Now, later, ten years from now?" Lacing my hands behind my head, I smirked. "Gotta watch those word choices, my friend. Someone with less scruples than me could really screw you over."

He glowered. "I have neither the time nor the inclination to play word games with oldbloods," he growled. "You were one of the queen's closest companions in the war, you and the Winter prince. We fought on the same side, and the queen's lieutenant spoke of you highly." He sniffed, raising his head to peer down with a haughty look. "I thought Robin Goodfellow was the honorable sort, that he would not stoop to conniving faery loopholes like a scheming phouka."

"Oh, chill out, Rusty." I raised both hands. "I didn't say I *wouldn't* tell you. It's just a rather sensitive subject, and I wouldn't want some eavesdropping gremlin spreading rumors through the city." I jerked my head to the great castle looming over everything. "You want the details? Come with us to the palace. You can hear the whole story then."

He blew out a long, exasperated whicker in a cloud of steam. "Very well," he rumbled. "I was going to seek an audience with the Iron Queen, anyway. I suppose we will go to the palace together."

Nyx, staring out the window at the glittering city and the crowds of Iron fey milling through it, took a deep breath as if steeling herself for what was to come.

I glanced at her worriedly. "You gonna be all right?"

She nodded, one hand going to the amulet beneath her cloak. "Here's hoping I don't turn into mist or burst into flames."

I reached down and took her other hand, squeezing once. "Just stick close to me and the tin can. Anyone gives you more than a funny look, I'll put a badger down their pants."

The crowds of fey parted for Coaleater as he stepped from the train car onto the cobblestone streets of Mag Tuiredh. Just his size was enough to send most stumbling back a few paces. He really did remind me a lot of Ironhorse. A quieter, less socially awkward Ironhorse. The original leader of the herd was big, clompy, and had a voice like a tuba being played through a megaphone three inches from your ear. But he had that same noble attitude, that same proud, almost overbearing gallantry. I guessed most, if not all, of the Iron horses were like their progenitor in that respect.

"Hmph." Coaleater snorted a puff of smoke as he looked around, his gaze landing on the distant palace just visible over the city roofs. "It has been a while since I have been to Mag Tuiredh," he murmured. Which was another difference. Ironhorse couldn't murmur if his life depended on it. Everything he had said was a bellow. "It's so crowded here," Coaleater went on, raising an arm as a small, rodent-like faery ducked around him and vanished down an alley. "How do fey live with the buildings right on top of them? I much prefer the openness of the Obsidian Plains." He shook his head, then turned back to us, narrowing his burning eyes. "Your Forgotten isn't casting a shadow, Goodfellow," Coaleater observed. "That is most likely not a good thing."

Alarmed, I glanced at Nyx and saw he was right. She stood silently in her cloak and hood, the sunlight beating down on her between buildings. I could see my shadow on the ground, right next to Coaleater's massive one, but the road under Nyx was empty. As if the light was going right through her.

"Dammit," I growled. "She needs to get out of the sun. We need to get to the palace quickly. Dammit again, that means I'm probably going to have to ride in one of the creepy spider carriages."

Coaleater sighed, wreathing us all in smoke. "Wait here," he ordered, taking a step back. "I will return momentarily. Don't go anywhere without me." He turned, ducked into the mouth of the alley behind us, and vanished behind the falling curtains of steam.

Nyx shivered, then slid down the wall until she was sitting against the building, knees drawn to her chest and hood covering her face. Trying not to be overbearing, I stepped in front of her, shielding her from the sunlight with my own body, trying to bring her some relief. A soft, rueful chuckle came from beneath the cowl, though she didn't raise her head.

"Who would have thought," she murmured, "the iron wouldn't be the thing that killed me in the Iron Realm." She sighed, and there was the gleam of a golden eye beneath the shadows of the hood. "It appears I won't be going to see the Summer Court with you after all, Goodfellow."

"Eh, it's not the most exciting place in the world." I crouched down next to her, putting a hand on her arm just to assure myself that she was still there. "We'll go to Tir Na Nog instead. How do you feel about ice wyrms and blizzards and snow up to the inside of your nostrils?"

"Sounds cold." Nyx blinked at me, a furrow creasing her pale brow. "But isn't the Winter Court ruled by Mab? Won't she dislike a Summer faery trespassing into Unseelie territory?"

"And that, my good assassin, is what makes it *so* enticing."

A clanking sound interrupted us. I turned just as a huge, black Iron horse walked calmly through the falling steam in front of the alley. Pistons hissed and cylinders spun as the great Iron creature came to a halt a few steps away, looming over us. Burning red eyes peered down at me, and tongues of flame flickered through the gaps and chinks in its belly, making the air around it shimmer. It flicked its tail, iron cables clattering against its hide, and tossed its head with a snort.

"Well?" Coaleater's voice was impatient. He raised a hoof and pawed the sidewalk, releasing a tiny cloud of sparks. "Are you two going to sit and stare at me, or are you going to get on?"

I winced, remembering the last time I'd ridden on the Iron horse's back. It had been several years ago, in the battle with the false king, and we had kicked ass, but parts of me were not happy after the battle. And Nyx, in her condition, couldn't afford to get any weaker. "You know, maybe we should just walk."

"I thought you wished to get to the palace quickly." Coaleater's gaze fell on Nyx, still slumped against the wall, and he swished his tail again. "It is either this, or take your chances with the spider carriage."

"I'm all right." Nyx pushed herself to her feet, gazing up at the Iron faery. "If you can get us to the palace quickly, I can endure. Let's go."

Coaleater nodded, then bent his front legs and lowered himself to his knees, making it easier to climb aboard his back. Even weakened and not feeling the best, Nyx hopped behind his shoulders with easy grace. Glancing at me, she held out her hand with a faint smile.

"Coming, Goodfellow?"

I rolled my eyes. "Revenge of the rash, part two," I sighed, and took her hand, letting her swing me up behind her. Coaleater lurched to his feet with a snort, and I yelped as tongues of flame clawed at the bottom of my feet. "Ow, hey, Rusty, could you maybe not breathe so hard? I could probably go the rest of my life without having my toes barbecued."

Coaleater tossed his head, powerful muscles coiling beneath his iron skin as he gazed toward the distant palace. "Hang on," he said absently.

I frowned. "Hang on? On to what? I'm not seeing a saddle horn back here."

Nyx shook her head. "Just grab on to me, Goodfellow," she said, and with a deep whinny, Coaleater half reared and sprang forward, nearly dumping me from my seat. I lunged and wrapped my arms around the Forgotten's waist, feeling her slim body against mine. My stomach twisted, and my heartbeat sped up as Coaleater's stride lengthened and Nyx pressed low over his back. Her hood fell back, strands of silvery hair brushing my face, cool and softer than silk.

"Oh yeah, this definitely better than a saddle horn," I grinned, resting my chin on her shoulder. "I could get used to this—" She pinched my leg. "Ow. Okay, shutting up now."

The ride to the palace was short but very rough. Coaleater appeared to have unlimited endurance; his iron hooves clattered against the road as he cantered through the streets of Mag Tuiredh, dodging faeries, carts, vendors, and carriages. He was like a New York City cab driver, where vehicle lanes were merely suggestions and the sidewalk was a viable avenue for getting around traffic. After a few close calls, we finally found ourselves on a mostly clear road up a steep hill, where the Iron Queen's palace resided at the top.

Our valiant steed skidded to a halt a short distance from the palace gates, huffing and wheezing like the train pulling into the station, steam spewing off him like a geyser. At the end of the road, Iron knights guarded the entrance to the palace in their super shiny armor, metal swords and breastplates glimmering in the sun.

I slid from our billowing ride's back and hit the cobblestones with a grunt, relieved to be on solid ground again. The steam and humidity had made my hair stand on end like a dandelion poof. Nyx swung a graceful leg over the horse's back and dropped to the ground without so much as a stumble.

"Well," I remarked, putting my hands on my hips as we stared up at the soaring palace of stone, glass, and steel, "we're here."

I felt a ripple of Iron glamour behind me, as Coaleater shed his equine form for his more human one. The skin on his arms and shoulders still steamed, though, giving him the impression of being on fire. "I take it you and the Forgotten are expected, Goodfellow?"

"Nope," I said cheerfully. "Not in the slightest."

The Iron faery frowned. "Then how do you expect to get in to see the Iron Queen?"

Nyx gave a resigned chuckle. "We're going to walk through the front gates again, aren't we?" she sighed.

"Wow, it's like you've done this with me before."

"Yes, and it worked out so well for us last time."

"Robin Goodfellow?"

We looked up. A guard was striding toward us, not aggressive or hostile, but definitely with some purpose. I felt Coaleater stiffen, and Nyx drew farther into her hood as the knight approached, but the faery's attention was solely on me.

"Robin Goodfellow," he said again, stopping with a quick salute. "You've arrived. If you and your friends would please follow me. The queen has been expecting you."

I blinked, then turned to lift a brow at the other two, both looking stunned as the knight bowed and strode back toward the gates. "See, what did I tell you?" I said, falling into step behind the knight. "Everything works out for Puck in the end. I don't know how you could have doubted me."

12

OLD FRIENDS, OLD ENEMIES

The knight didn't take us all the way to the throne room. Once we were past the enormous courtyard, up the flight of stone steps, and through the massive double doors, a small, squat faery waited for us in the main foyer.

He wore a pair of gold-rimmed glasses on his wrinkled nose and carried an enormous pile of junk on his back. Kitchen utensils, broken appliances, several clocks, and a few shattered phones all balanced precariously between his hunched shoulders. He was a packrat and, like his name implied, hoarded all kinds of junk that, somehow, he was able to carry on his back. The larger the junk pile, the more respected the packrat. By other packrats, anyway. This one had a truly impressive hoard, reaching past the top of my head. In fact, I was pretty sure it was bigger than when I'd seen him last.

"Robin Goodfellow," the packrat wheezed, waddling forward. His enormous junk pile swayed and clanked as he walked, and from the corner of my eye I saw Nyx watching it dubiously, ready to leap back should it topple. "You have finally arrived."

I grinned. "Hey, Fix. I didn't know Meghan was expecting me. I'm guessing socket-head let her know I was coming?"

"I am not privy to the decisions of the first lieutenant," Fix replied, ignoring the rather casual nickname for the commander of the Iron Queen's army. "Nor do I question the ways of my queen. I am certain you can ask her yourself. Now then…" He paused, squinting up at me with bleary eyes.

I crossed my arms, waiting for him to say something about the pair of protuberances that hadn't been there before.

The packrat hesitated, then took off his glasses, polished them with a rag, and stuck them back on his face with a sniff. "If you would kindly introduce me to your companions," he said, as I got the impression that the glasses were purely for show. "I must at least know their names so that I can announce them to the queen before going in."

Nyx bowed, formal and graceful, even in her condition. "I am called Nyx," she said, as the packrat turned his beady gaze on her. "I am here as a messenger from His Majesty Keirran, King of the Forgotten."

Fix sobered immediately at the name. "Keirran," he repeated, almost a whisper. For a moment, he looked wistful, almost sad, before shaking himself and glancing up at Nyx again. "Well met, Nyx of the Forgotten," he said formally. "Tell me, how is our former prince these days?"

"Keirran is a fair and just king," Nyx replied, and she was being completely honest. "He puts the safety of the Forgotten before anything else. He misses the Nevernever, but he doesn't let that stand in the way of his duty."

"I see," the packrat murmured. "Well, I am sure the queen will be happy to hear it. And what of you?" he went on, gazing up, and up, at the hulking Coaleater behind me. "You are one of the Iron herd, am I correct? From the Obsidian Plains. You have come far… Do you also wish an audience with the queen?"

"I do," the huge Iron faery replied, and put a fist over his heart with a clank. "I am Coaleater, second in command of the Iron herd. I am here at the request of our leader, Spikerail. There is something the Iron Queen must be made aware of."

Fix bobbed his head. "Of course. Any of the Iron herd is welcome here. Well, then…" He stepped back, beaming placidly at us all. "If you would follow me. The Iron Queen is waiting for you."

The Iron Palace had always amazed me. It was like taking a medieval castle from King Arthur days, dropping it into a blender with an H. G. Wells novel, and hitting Puree. The ancient and the modern intertwined seamlessly throughout the halls and corridors of the palace, with more than a few hints of Victorian steampunk scattered throughout, just like the city. Gears, cogs, and wires were common decorations, and the corridors were filled with a soft but constant ticking. Sometimes gothic stone passages gave way to giant arched windows where the sun streamed through the glass, but then we would turn a corner to see a pair of ivy-covered statues sitting under a streetlamp.

Bizarre was a good word for the Iron Palace, and that was coming from yours truly; I practically invented the word. Iron fey roamed the halls and corridors of the queen's castle, seeming perfectly at home here, more than any other place in the Nevernever: Iron knights, clockwork hounds, hacker elves, cog dwarves, and the ever-present gremlins, trailing us down the hallways like cackling, bat-eared spiders. Even the massive Coaleater looked almost normal against the backdrop of the palace, blending into the surroundings like he'd been born here.

Nyx and I definitely stood out.

I had been to the palace a few times before, so for the most part, the Iron fey knew me. Still, the amount of stares I was receiving was disquieting. Maybe it was the horns. Or maybe it was the cloaked Forgotten walking beside me and making no more noise than a shadow. In any case, it was a little unnerving. When a faery with the body of a metallic centipede stares at you in abject fear and then goes scurrying around a corner, that's kind of a hard pill to swallow.

"Here we are," Fix announced at last, coming to a stop before a pair of double doors. Not the throne room, I noted, which would be full of Iron fey all demanding the queen's attention. This was probably a private meeting room, as indicated by the pair of Iron knights standing guard at the entrance. They nodded to Fix, then reached out and opened each of the doors, granting us access to whatever lay beyond.

Fix smiled at us and waddled through the doors. We followed him into a bright, well-lit room with glass doors that led to a marble balcony and a stunning view of the courtyard below. The doors were open, and a figure could be seen at the railing with her back to us, gazing out over the palace grounds.

Her long, silver-blond hair rippled behind her, held back by the thin iron circlet atop her skull. Per usual she was dressed in modern, human clothes, though over the years I'd noticed she had abandoned the faded jeans and T-shirt look for something a bit less casual and more businesslike. At least in public. You'd never catch her in a gown outside of Elysium, but the scruffy, awkward teenager who'd claimed she would rather be comfortable than popular had vanished, and the Iron Queen was all that remained.

"Your Majesty," Fix announced as we stepped through the frame, the guards pulling the doors shut behind us. "Robin Goodfellow and his companions, Nyx of the Forgotten and Coaleater of the Iron herd, have arrived."

The figure on the balcony turned, and my stupid traitor heart still gave a weird little flutter whenever I saw my former princess.

Meghan Chase, the Iron Queen, met my gaze through the balcony doors and broke into a relieved, genuine smile. Without hesitation, she strode forward, stepped into the room, and threw her arms around me in a hug.

Standard greeting, really. And one that had made my heart soar whenever it happened. But this time, something sour flared to life at her touch. I remembered, suddenly, the image of her turning away, of following another through the portal to the human world and leaving me behind. A kiss, shared in a secret bedroom, that meant the world to me and nothing to her. The agonized confession that she did love me, just not as much as *him*.

All those memories flickered through my head like a strobe light, and in the next blink, they were gone. It happened so quickly, I didn't know what to think. Or feel. Though I could sense the stunned gazes of both Nyx and Coaleater at my back, their eyes wide and staring. A queen hugging a jester was definitely something they did not see every day.

"Hey, princess," I whispered, as I always did. "Did you miss me?"

"Puck." Meghan pulled back, gripping my upper arms. Her sapphire-blue gaze was intense, which made my instincts bristle a warning. This definitely wasn't normal. "Keirran," she asked, her voice threaded with worry. "What happened? Is he all right?"

I relaxed, though at the same time, that strange bitterness trickled through my thoughts. Of course, Meghan would want to know about Keirran; he was her kid, after all, and just like she had been. Stubborn, defiant, with no concept of self-preservation.

I smirked. "He's fine, Meghan. Last I saw, he was blasting a big bad with enough glamour to shred a cement truck."

Meghan relaxed. She seemed about to say something else, when her gaze suddenly went to my forehead, and her eyes widened. "Puck," she whispered, as her hand rose to my hair. "What...?"

"Ah, right." I took a step back, wincing a little. "These things. Well, that's part of what we came to discuss. Well, this and the big ugly that caused it. So, did Glitch already tell you we were coming?" I went on, changing the subject as Meghan's worried gaze lingered on my forehead. "Keirran sent us here with a message to warn you about this nasty new threat that's popped up, but you already seem in the loop."

"My doing," sighed a familiar voice, as a large gray cat sauntered in from the balcony, his tail held up behind him. "You certainly took your sweet time getting here," Grimalkin said, hopping lightly onto a table and regarding us with disdainful cat eyes. "I had already been to Arcadia to warn Oberon before making my way to the Iron Realm. I thought you would be here already and have warned the queen, but apparently, my expectations were too high, again."

"Grimalkin was telling me about the creature you saw in the Between," Meghan went on, as the cat gave a yawn and began washing a front paw. I wondered what he would do if his fur suddenly burst into flame. "He said that it seemed immune to glamour, and that it could change faeries into monsters just by touching them. Do you know anything more about that, Puck?"

"If I may, Your Majesty." Nyx stepped forward, bowing deeply as Meghan turned to her. "Keirran and I have hunted this creature before. We first encountered it in the Between, though later it moved into Phaed and eventually fled to the Nevernever itself. I believe it came here for a specific reason. When we were battling the creature, none of us could really hurt it. It might have killed us had we kept fighting, but as soon as the way into the Nevernever opened, it abandoned the fight to cross the River of Dreams into Faery. As to why it's here…" Nyx offered an apologetic shrug. "That I cannot tell you."

"You are Forgotten," Meghan said, and Nyx gave a single nod. "How is it you look different from the rest of them?"

"I was not present during the last war, Your Majesty," Nyx replied. "I did not partake in the method used to change them into what they are today. I have been returned to the Nevernever only recently. As I once served the Lady, I now serve the Forgotten King. He is the one who sent me to warn you about this creature."

"Grimalkin has told me a little," the Iron Queen said, sounding thoughtful. "But even he cannot say what it is, or why it's here in the Nevernever. But you all seem to agree on one thing—it's a threat to everyone it comes across." She looked up at me, that worried look going through her eyes once more. "Puck, are you sure you're all right? This curse or condition or whatever it is… It's not hurting you, is it?"

Only my sanity a little. "What, this?" I pointed to my forehead and smirked. "Don't worry about me, princess. I'm just a little horny."

She frowned, unamused, and Nyx rolled her eyes. I knew the situation was serious, but I suddenly felt very immature.

"Oh, and check this out," I announced, pulling up my pant leg, where a cloven hoof could be seen beneath the cuff. "Horny *and* shaggy. Like your favorite taxidermy."

"Let's hope you don't end up on someone's wall," said a deep voice behind us. Like the echo of a dream, one that was eerily familiar. I knew that voice instantly.

And something inside me snapped.

Rage flooded me, like a smoldering geyser or volcano that finally burst into eruption. Images flashed through my head, memories and emotions long buried, springing to life again. I remembered a dream with his voice, cold and full of hate, saying Meghan never loved me, that it was my fault that Ariella had died, that the world would be better if I was gone. I remembered the endless fighting, those years when we almost killed each other, the anger and resentment that cut deeper than any sword. All of that came bubbling to the surface, hot and volatile, spilling poison into my veins.

And suddenly, I wanted to hurt him. Not just hurt him—stabbing him with my daggers would be too quick. Besides, Ash had been poked, speared, impaled, slashed, kicked, clawed, and cut open enough times that such injuries were almost commonplace now. No, I wanted to make him suffer, as only Robin Goodfellow could. To devise a prank so devious and hilarious, ice-boy would feel it for years, and all the Nevernever would never let him forget.

In that moment, I felt Puck truly die, as Robin Goodfellow of the woods rose up and took his place.

I smiled broadly as I turned to face the owner of the voice. Ash. Ice-boy. Son of Mab. Former prince of the Unseelie Court. Lots of names, but they all belonged to my greatest friend, and greatest rival, in all of Faery. He swept through the doorway in his long black coat, icy blade glittering blue at his side. Like his broody kid, he was dressed in stark black, from his shirt to his pants to his boots, but his dark hair and silver eyes gave him a dangerous edge that even Keirran could not match. I saw Coal-eater take a step back and Nyx staring at him with a mix of curiosity and wary awe. I snorted under my breath. Ice-boy did have that effect on pretty much everyone. After the kings and queens, he was one of the strongest faeries in the entire Nevernever, and he had that *presence* that turned people into slack-jawed zombies for a moment or two.

Except me. I was pretty much immune to the ice-boy effect. In fact, I'd made it my personal vendetta to get under his icy cold skin as much as possible, just to remind him that his natural awe didn't work on everyone.

"Well, look who decided to join the party," I drawled as Ash strode to Meghan's side. Anger and resentment still simmered, but I tamped them down. Now was not the time for a Good-fellow prank, not in the middle of the Iron Palace, surrounded by Iron knights, with the Iron Queen in the very same room. The best laid pranks always took a little time. "Always appearing at the most dramatic moment, ice-boy. Tell me, were you just lurking outside the door waiting for the perfect setup?"

"If I was, any discussion about mounting your head on a wall would certainly get my attention." Ash stopped just a bit shy of Meghan, giving her a brief, genuine smile before turning to the rest of us. His silvery gaze went to my horns and narrowed. "It seems I've missed a few developments," he went on, and the flicker of worry that crossed his face was lost to everyone but me. "Would you like to fill me in, Goodfellow? Is this a curse, an evil potion, or something else entirely?"

I smirked. Ash didn't know the original Robin Goodfellow, not really. He hadn't been around back then, though his two brothers had been. Maybe he'd heard the stories, but he'd never asked me about the time before we met. Too bad for him. He really should have paid attention.

"The short version?" I shrugged. "Some big nasty monster showed up in the Between, kicked our butts to the curb, gave me a few new appendages, and took a swan dive into the River of Dreams. Oh, and it's in the Nevernever now, by the way. No idea where, exactly. But it's here."

"That's why Keirran sent us," Nyx broke in as Ash frowned. "We can't seem to kill it ourselves. We were hoping you would be able to help us track this monster down and end the threat it represents to everything."

Meghan nodded gravely. "Grimalkin was saying the same," she mused, and looked at Ash. "This is definitely something we should look into. The realm is stable enough right now... I'll send for Glitch and bring him back to the capital to keep an eye on things while we're away."

"I can go with them, if you want," Ash suggested. "If you're worried about leaving the kingdom, you don't have to do this. Puck and I can probably track this thing down and put an end to it."

Just the two of us, ice-boy? I bit down an evil grin. *I think I would like that, though it wouldn't go so well for you. What kind of bizarre accidents would happen to you while we're tracking this thing down, I wonder?*

But Meghan shook her head. "No, Keirran sent them to us for a reason. Besides, I want to see this thing for myself. I don't like the idea of some creature rampaging through the Nevernever, turning my closest friends...um..." She hesitated.

"Horny?" I supplied, and grinned when Ash shot me a look. "Yeah, that's not ever gonna get old. Don't worry about me, princess. I'm fine, just gotta be careful on polished floors. What we do have to worry about is where this big bastard is. 'Cause I have no idea where it disappeared to when it crossed the River of Dreams. It could be anywhere by now, turning the local rabbits into vicious horned dinosaur bunnies."

"Not to mention," came Grimalkin's slow, superior voice, "none of you have any idea of what this creature is. And as you saw in Phaed, if you do not know what it is, you will not know how to defeat it. Rushing headlong into a battle without any sort of preparation is doomed to failure."

I crossed my arms. "You got a better idea, Furball?"

"Indeed." Grimalkin raised a hind leg and gave it three excruciatingly slow licks before he deigned to answer. "There is one who might know the identity of this creature," he said. "One whose visions, on occasion, have shown her the future, the past, and everything in between. She knows much about the Nevernever, more than she wishes to at times. She would be the one to help you decipher this new threat to Faery."

"Another oracle?" Meghan frowned. Her confusion was understandable. The original oracle, an ancient faery who could see into the future, had recently been killed by the Forgotten in the last war. "I didn't realize there was more than one."

"There is not," Grimalkin answered, confusing me now as well. "When one oracle dies, another is reborn into Faery not long after the first one's death. Or, should I say, her visions and the memories of them are reborn into another. Her name is different, as she is a different person, but she retains the memories of all the oracles before her. I believe this new oracle will have insight into the beast we are hunting."

"A new oracle," Meghan breathed. "I had no idea. Where can we find her, Grim?"

"Currently, I believe the new oracle is residing somewhere in the wyldwood."

"Oh, well, it'll be easy to find her, then," I broke in. "'Cause nothing lost in the wyldwood stays lost. Oh wait…"

The cat's ears flattened to his skull, but he ignored me. "I suppose I can lead you to where the new oracle is staying," he told Meghan. "If I do not, I have little hope you will ever find it on your own." He thumped his tail against the table surface. "But there will be a favor due for this, Iron Queen. I have already been across the Between, Phaed, Arcadia, and the Iron Realm. If I am to go gallivanting across the Nevernever with you and the rest of this circus once more, I expect to be properly compensated."

"I wouldn't expect any less, Grim," Meghan replied, and the cat yawned.

"Very well," he sighed. "I suppose as I am the only competent guide here, I will endeavor to show you the way to the oracle. When do you wish to leave?"

Meghan and Ash shared a glance. "Soon," Ash said. "Tonight. We'll need to make some arrangements, get some things in order within the palace, and then we'll be ready to go."

"Yes," Meghan agreed. "This sounds important. I don't want to put it off any longer than we have to. Puck…" Her blue eyes found mine. "Will you be ready to go tonight?"

"You know me. I was born ready, princess."

A sudden grinding sound filled the air, like hundreds of rocks being scraped against knives. At first I thought something in the room had malfunctioned, until I realized it was Coaleater, clearing his throat.

"Forgive me, Your Highness," the huge Iron faery rumbled, making me blink in surprise. For as large and imposing as he was, I'd completely forgotten he was in the room with us. "But I have traveled far from the Obsidian Plains at the behest of our leader, Spikerail. Will you hear what I have come to say? I can wait, if that is what you wish."

"Coaleater." Meghan shook her head, as if annoyed with herself. "Of course. I'm sorry, I didn't realize you wanted an audience. Any of the Iron herd is welcome here; you have my full attention."

The Iron faery bowed. "You have our gratitude, Iron Queen." Rising, he paused to collect himself, then continued in a straightforward voice. "Your Majesty, we of the Iron herd have noticed a change in the Obsidian Plains. We have always been the guardians of our territory, protecting the land around the magma pools, and recently we have felt…the only way to describe it is an unsoundness, deep in the earth. The creatures who call the plains their home have also felt it, and we have noticed some of them becoming restless and agitated, when before they have always been peaceful. It is deeply concerning, so much so that Spikerail made the decision to bring this to the Iron Queen's attention. But now, as I hear the report that Goodfellow and his companion gave, I cannot help but wonder if they are connected.

"I would not presume anything," the Iron faery went on, "but I wish to join you on this quest, Your Majesty. If anything, I can take what I've learned back to the herd. Spikerail will certainly be interested in this. And of course, I would protect you and your companions with my life. This is the Iron herd's promise."

Meghan considered, her brow creased in a slight frown. "I was unaware there was trouble in the Obsidian Plains," she murmured. "That is disturbing news. When we are done here, I will have to pay a visit to Spikerail and see if there is anything that can be done." She pondered a moment more, then glanced at the waiting Iron horse. "You are welcome to join us, Coaleater," she said. "I will not force you. This quest could be dangerous. But I would welcome your strength, if you wish to come along."

"Nothing would bring me greater honor, Your Majesty," Coaleater said with a decisive nod. "I will not disappoint you. I happily serve the queen and the realm, as Ironhorse did before me."

Throughout all this, Nyx had remained silent, drawn deep into her hood. Now, as Coaleater made his announcement, she raised her head, her skin pale in the bright sunlight streaming through the glass. A strange look crossed her face, confusion and fear...before she flickered out like a snuffed candle.

Alarm jolted my entire insides, but before I could say anything, she reappeared in a blink, though the expression in her eyes was now one of weary resignation, as if she knew what was happening.

The Fade was taking her. Right in front of me.

13

WE DO NOT FORGET

"Nyx!" I lunged, catching her as she collapsed to her knees, winking out again for a fraction of a second. Coaleater snorted in alarm, and Meghan and Ash came forward, their gazes somber, as the Forgotten flickered and sputtered in my arms like a dying flashlight.

"Nyx. Hey, look at me." I gripped her forearms, feeling helpless and terrified as she slumped against me, going transparent for a heartbeat. Golden eyes met my own, her expression solemn but calm. "Focus," I urged in a whisper. "Talk to me, assassin. You can't leave us yet. If you Fade out now, I'm going to have to tell Keirran that the Iron Realm was too much for you to handle after all, and having to say 'I told you so' for the next hundred years would be exhausting."

A faint smile crossed her face, even as she wavered at the edges for a moment. "Are you...trying to annoy me into staying, Goodfellow?"

"I play to my strengths. Is it working?"

"Well, you have succeeded in making me want to stab you,"

Nyx whispered, but she had stopped flickering like a weak candle and was slowly regaining color. Or at least not looking like a transparent wraith. She took a deep, careful breath and straightened, gripping my arms for balance, testing her range of motion. "It's over," she told me. "I think...I'm all right now. Whatever happened, it seems to have passed."

"You didn't tell us you were Fading," came Ash's voice over my shoulder, and part of me bristled at the proximity. "We could have helped you, had we known."

"The Iron Realm has some of the most advanced healers in the Nevernever," Meghan added, stepping forward. "They can't stop the Fade, but they might be able to slow it for a time."

But Nyx gave her head a stubborn shake and rose, drawing me up with her. "There's no need," she insisted. "I'm grateful, Your Majesty, but I think I just need to rest. My apologies, I didn't know I was that close to Fading, but it's done. I've always been fairly certain my time here was limited."

"Screw that," I said, angry now. "If you're so close to Fading, chasing down some big monster who nearly killed us before can't be great for your health."

But Nyx met my gaze, calm and unruffled, and she gave a wry smile. "I am fine, Puck. Whatever that was, it must have been a fluke, or a reaction to the sun and the Iron Realm at the same time. I know my duty, and this will not stop me from continuing the mission. I am in no danger of disappearing, at least not for a while." I took a breath to argue, but she overrode me. "And even if I was, what could you do about it? Some things are beyond anyone's reach."

I crossed my arms. "You'd be surprised."

"Regardless." She raised her chin. "I'm coming with you. I don't plan to return to Keirran until I'm certain the creature is dead."

I snorted. And that would be the end of it. Unless I wanted to physically restrain her, which would probably result in a knife to the ribs, she would go chasing down the monster—the monster that had nearly killed us—with the rest of the group. Weakened, possibly Fading away, but as stubbornly persistent as the most stubborn faery I knew.

Me.

"If you are certain," Meghan said, and gave a decisive nod, gazing around at us all. "Tonight, then. We'll meet in the courtyard when the moon rises. And we'll get to the bottom of what is happening in the Nevernever once and for all. Fix, if you would please show Nyx and Coaleater to the guest chambers. Puck…" She glanced at me with a warm smile. "You know the way. Now, if you would all excuse us," she went on, and looked to Ash, who nodded grimly, "we have a few things to take care of before this evening."

And with that, the rulers of the Iron Realm strode from the room, closing the doors behind them as they left.

Fix waddled forward, looking troubled as he turned to Nyx and Coaleater. "If you would both please follow me," he said. "I will show you where you can rest until this evening."

Nyx gave me a brief glance, and I shrugged. Stubborn assassin would do what she pleased, regardless of consequences. I would just have to make sure she didn't Fade away on me, even if I had to risk getting stabbed to do it. "Don't worry about me," I told her as she still hesitated. "I know this place like the back of my hand. I'll see you tonight."

She nodded once. "Tonight," she murmured, almost a promise. And then she and Coaleater followed the waiting packrat out the double doors. I watched them leave, watched Nyx until she had turned a corner and was out of sight, and told myself that this was not the last time I would see her.

"Well, then," I muttered as the doors slowly swung shut, leaving me alone in the room. The stillness was suddenly resounding. "Guess I'll go see what kind of trouble I can get myself into."

"You're falling for her."

It was early evening in the Iron Realm. The sun hung low

in the sky above the Iron Palace, and the clouds were streaked with pink. I had wandered down to the palace gardens because, one: they were the closest thing to a forest I could find in Mag Tuiredh. And two: I was bored and trying to avoid the temptation to start a gremlin riot in the castle. Meghan had not been amused the last time.

So, I was leaning against a metal trunk in the sprawling palace gardens, watching a flock of tiny blue birds flit around a steel fountain, when a deep, familiar voice echoed behind me. I glanced up to see the Ice Prince himself at the edge of the walk, watching me with a look of wry amusement.

"The Forgotten," Ash said, as if there were any question as to who he meant. "Nyx. I've seen that look before, Goodfellow. Not often, but enough. You always seem to go for the ones that can kill you." He shook his head with a faint smile. "She'll be fine, by the way. There are no further signs of Fading. I spoke to a healer, and he believes that as long as she stays out of the sun, she should be all right. So, you can stop worrying and tell me how you two met."

Relief for Nyx flared, but it was drowned in the flood of memories that roared through me as soon as I heard his voice. "Is that why you came out here, ice-boy?" I drawled, pushing myself off the tree trunk. I felt Robin Goodfellow's evil smile tugging at the corners of my mouth, the demonic, toothy grin that made kings blanch and dragons hesitate, and forced it back. *Not yet, Goodfellow. Not here. Patience.* "Was castle gossip not juicy enough today?" I went on, smirking at the former Ice Prince across the courtyard. "Or were you just curious about my new lady friend?"

"You're avoiding the question," Ash said, frowning. "But yes, as a matter of fact, I was curious. About a lot of things." Abruptly serious, he took a few steps toward me, his expression grave. "Meghan is worried about you," he went on. "We both are. You're not acting like yourself."

"Is that so?" I challenged. "And how do you think I'm acting, ice-boy?"

"I've heard the stories, Puck. My brothers would sometimes tell me about the Puck of the woods, the Robin Goodfellow that caused so much chaos and pandemonium, even they were hesitant to face him. For a long time, I thought they were exaggerating, that they were simply trying to scare me. Because the Puck I knew wasn't like that."

Ash hesitated. He had stopped a few feet away, those bright silver eyes boring into me. His posture wasn't overly cautious or suspicious, but an aura of wary concern surrounded him.

I snorted and turned away, gazing out over the gardens, because if I kept looking at him, I might be tempted to start another feud right here.

Ash didn't come any closer, either. Though I could still feel that intense gaze on the back of my neck. "But then," he went on, "the more I got to know you, the more I realized those stories weren't exaggerations. Because I've seen that side of you, Puck. Not often. And never without cause. But every once in a while, when you're truly angry and think I don't notice, I see the Goodfellow everyone was afraid of."

"Observant of you, ice-boy," I said without turning around. Anger was stirring, not vindictiveness or spite, but real anger, and I clenched a fist to shove it back. "What exactly is your point?"

"My point is that I see him right now," the Ice Prince finished in a somber voice. "More than I ever have before. He showed up today, in the middle of the Iron Palace, with horns and hooves and that look in his eyes, and he hasn't left yet. And that worries me. Meghan doesn't know this side of him, she hasn't been around long enough, but I've seen what this Robin Goodfellow can do, and I know what he's capable of. So my question to you is, what exactly did that creature do to you, and when do we get the real Goodfellow back?"

"How do you know this *isn't* the real me?" I turned, smiling broadly, and saw Ash stiffen for the barest second. "Maybe I've been playing a huge, elaborate prank on you for years. Or maybe this is who I always was, I just never showed anyone."

Ash didn't smile. "If that were true," he said, in an almost pained voice, "then we would still be enemies. The journeys we had, the times before Ariella, where we traveled to all corners of the Nevernever, those years would have never happened."

"Yeah," I husked out, and suddenly, both daggers were in my hands. I didn't know what I was doing; I didn't know where this rage was coming from, but now that I'd started down this path, I couldn't seem to stop. "Here's a notion, Your Highness," I said, pointing at him with one dagger. "Did you ever think that *maybe* I never quite forgave you for stealing her away from me all those years ago?"

"We are way past that, Puck." Ash's voice was soft; he hadn't drawn his weapon or even put a hand on his blade, but his whole posture was stiff.

"Really?" I sneered. "How long did you try to kill me after Ariella died, Ash? How many years?" I swept my other weapon up, pointing at the towers of the Iron Palace looming overhead. "More than the years you've spent with Meghan, that's for damn sure. And for what?"

Reaching up, I hooked two fingers in my collar and yanked it down, revealing a thin white gash across my collarbone. "This is yours, ice-boy," I spat at him. "Remember that? I have more than a few scars from the times you almost killed me, because you swore an oath of vengeance over a girl. Do you ever think about that? Do you ever think that maybe I was just as angry as you when I lost the one *I* loved? So, don't tell me we're past it, Your Highness. You know as well as I do, we're fey. Grudges last a lifetime with us."

"So, what do you want to do, Goodfellow?" Ash wondered quietly. He raised his arms in a resigned motion, watching me with bleak silver eyes. "Enact your own oath? Swear vengeance on me, right here?"

"No." I gave him a vicious smile. "Not my style, ice-boy. You know my general dislike of obligation and responsibility. I'm not going to bind myself to some ridiculous vow and then regret ever making it." Stepping back, I sheathed my daggers, grinning at him all the while. "I just want you to remember, I haven't forgotten, prince. So, you had better watch your back. This thing isn't over yet."

Ash said nothing. He just watched me, his expression unreadable. With a final sneer, I turned and left the gardens, heading back into the palace.

I could feel his gaze on me the entire way.

Back in the guest quarters, I went to my personal room and wandered onto the balcony, gazing out over the city below. In the shadowy twilight, Mag Tuiredh glimmered like a valley of fireflies, glowing with streetlamps, vehicles, even the Iron fey themselves. Leaning against the railing, I watched the sun set over the city of the Iron fey and thought back to my last conversation in the courtyard, when I basically told my best friend we were still enemies, and he'd better watch his back.

What the hell is wrong with me?

I wasn't born yesterday. I'd been through enough curses to know I wasn't acting like myself. Ever since the fight with the big bad, I'd been sliding further into my nasty, more primal nature. So, I knew this situation wasn't normal, that whatever the monster did, it had awakened something I'd thought was buried. But the anger I'd felt toward Ash was real. I couldn't just shut it away and pretend it wasn't there. Puck might've been able to do that, for friendship's sake. But I wasn't him any longer. I was Robin Goodfellow, and right now, a bit of old-fashioned retribution sounded like a lot of fun.

After we'd killed this monster. I could be patient until then.

"Admiring the view?"

I jumped and whirled around. "Geez, Nyx! Don't do that to me." I shook my head at the cloaked Forgotten who had some-how *poofed* onto the balcony with me. Not even shadows and wraiths had an easy time sneaking up on yours truly; a lifetime of playing pranks had made me somewhat paranoid of retalia-tion. "Is that your personal brand of assassination, then?" I asked the faintly smirking Forgotten. "The heart attack special? If you ever want to give up the assassin thing, you'd be a natural at surprise parties."

"Generally, I find a dagger is a much better alternative to stopping someone's heart than a surprise party," was the wry response. "There's far less of a chance they'll stab you back."

"That's your answer for everything, isn't it? Stab it in the heart."

"It hasn't failed me yet." Her eyes narrowed, and suddenly, everything about her turned dangerous. "Especially when some-one I know is about to start a fight with the prince consort of the Iron Realm, and I'm wondering if I'm going to have to stab him myself."

My grin faded. "You saw that, did you?"

"Once the sun went down, I ventured out to let you know I was all right. I figured I'd find you outside, probably in the courtyard or gardens, so I headed there." Nyx's voice was hard, her golden eyes cold in the shadow of her hood. "Imagine my concern when I saw you pull your daggers on none other than the Iron Queen's husband. If anyone else saw that, you could have been killed."

"Very doubtful." I grinned at her, waving away the concern. "No one would dare attack Robin Goodfellow here. Besides, Ash and I have gone at it so many times, if we *don't* threaten each other occasionally people will wonder what's wrong."

"I saw the look in your eyes, Puck." Nyx's lethal expression didn't change. "I heard what you said. That was not the look of a faery who was joking."

"I wasn't," I told her, sobering for the moment. "I meant what I said. This thing with me and ice-boy, it goes way back. Before Meghan, before the Iron Kingdom, before the rise of the Lady and the Forgotten. It's not exactly a secret, nearly everyone knows the history between us." Leaning back, I cocked my head, regarding the Forgotten across from me. "But I'm sort of struggling with why you should care."

Nyx's eyes gleamed dangerously. "We're on an important mission," she reminded me. "In case you've forgotten, the monster we're chasing nearly killed us both the last time we encountered it. We need powerful allies if we want to have any hope of defeating this threat. The prince consort of the Iron Realm is one of those powerful allies. Furthermore…" She hesitated, a shadow crossing her face as she stared me down. "Keirran is my king. I swore an oath to protect him, his kingdom, and his kin for as long as I am able to do so. If you raise your weapon against Keirran's father, Puck, I will have no choice but to cut you down."

"That easy, is it?" I smirked at her, trying to ignore the instant flare of vindictive defiance. "Do you know how many times I've heard those exact words, Miss Assassin? Do you know how many times something has tried to kill Robin Goodfellow? More times than I can count. But I'm still here, and if you want to try, I'm afraid you're going to have to get in line."

"I don't know that Robin Goodfellow," Nyx said flatly. "His name does not inspire the fear that it does in others. You would just be another target, Puck."

I clenched my jaw. It felt like she had taken one of her moon-blades and driven it straight into my heart. Meeting her eyes, I forced a hard smile. "Well then, I aspire to surprise and disappoint you. No promises, but I think you're going to find Robin Goodfellow your most difficult target yet."

Nyx didn't flinch. "Don't make me your enemy, Puck," she warned. "We're on the same side in this. We want the same thing. If you are going to take your vengeance on Keirran's father, at least wait until after we've killed this monster. Surely you can see that eliminating this threat takes precedence over any plans for revenge."

"Oh, don't worry, Miss Assassin." I leaned back against the railing with a shrug. "I know what's at stake, and I told ice-boy the same thing. Taking care of the big nasty comes first. I fully intend to indulge in some good old-fashioned Robin Goodfellow pranks, but only after I've carved this thing into tiny pieces and danced a jig on them." I crossed my arms and stared her down. "So, you can relax. I'm not going to slip a dozen vipers into ice-boy's mattress. Not today, at least."

The Forgotten considered me without expression. "Is this the side that everyone is afraid of?" she wondered. "The faery with the reputation? Is this the true nature of Robin Goodfellow?"

"What if it is?"

Nyx shook her head and took a step back. "I liked Puck better," she said softly, right before she shimmered into moonlight and disappeared.

Alone on the balcony, I turned and leaned against the railing, gazing down on the glittering lights of Mag Tuiredh. And I wondered if I would just keep pushing everyone away until I was, truly, all alone.

PART

III

TIR NA NOG

A few centuries ago

It was possibly not the best idea I'd ever had, but I'd never let that stop me.

It was the name that piqued my interest: The Lost City of Frozen Skull Forest. I mean, how could you not be curious? Lost cities typically had all manner of ancient treasures, and all manner of ancient beasties, traps, and guardians to overcome. Never mind that it was deep in Unseelie territory, in a tangled, frigid wood that I discovered was also home to some very cranky ice trolls who didn't take kindly to me stomping through their hunting grounds. I was, of course, not supposed to be there. I was part of the Summer Court, and this was Winter's territory; if Mab or any of the Unseelie discovered I was trespassing, it was within their rights to have me killed.

Again, not that I ever let that stop me.

"Well, that was fun," I muttered, dusting snow off my hands and gazing around. The bodies of the three ice trolls that attacked me had already turned to stone, which was what happened when you tried to ambush Robin Goodfellow. I had nothing against trolls, but if you were going to pop out of your little ice hole to try to shove a claw through my face, expect me to do some stabbing in return. "Sorry about your luck, guys. Though I do appreciate the knowledge that there are troll holes in the world. That alone is worth it. Now…where the heck is this lost city?"

Turning from the bodies, I scanned the forest, shielding my eyes from the glimmer of sunlight on the snow. It was suddenly very quiet.

I paused a moment, listening to the forest, then smiled.

"You're awfully good," I called to the empty air. "I can't get a bearing on where you are, so congratulations for that. But you might as well come out. Unless you plan on staying in a troll hole all afternoon. There's no reason to hide, I don't bite. Hard."

For a few heartbeats, there was only silence. Then a ripple of glamour went through the air, and a dark form stepped out from behind a cluster of trees. Tall and lean, like most gentry, he was dressed completely in black, with a cape that rippled behind him and a glittering blue sword at his side.

My eyebrows arched as the faery prowled forward and stopped at the edge of the circle, watching me with eyes like silver coins. "Well, don't I feel important," I announced, smirking in the face of that cold, hostile stare. "If it isn't Mab's favorite son. What was your name again, princeling, something with a tree, right? Prince Dogwood, Prince Huckleberry? Tell me if I'm getting close. Prince Crabapple?"

"You don't need to know my name," the Winter faery replied. "It won't matter for much longer. I know who *you* are, Robin Goodfellow."

"You and the rest of the Nevernever, princeling," I drawled. "Not much of a mystery, there. Everyone knows who I am."

"I also know that you're trespassing."

"Wow, nothing escapes you, does it?" I grinned at his annoyed look. "Well, Your Highness, guess I'll just have to call you ice-boy until you actually grace me with your name."

I knew his name, of course. He'd been to several Elysiums now, and one did not forget the sons of Mab. I'd crossed paths, and blades, with his two brothers before. Sage was a competent swordsman, and sometimes hunted the woods of the Never-never, but as the heir of the Winter Queen, he was almost always surrounded by warriors and gentry of the Unseelie Court. We had dueled a few times, but I got the feeling that Sage was almost bored with the hassle of it all, and the only reason we were fighting was that it was expected of us. I couldn't stand the other brother, Rowan; he reminded me of a grinning viper that would bite you as soon as your back was turned. He, too, was a competent swordsman, but I very rarely saw him outside of the court and Elysium. From what I'd observed, he probably didn't like getting his fancy clothes all dirty. Though I had to admit, it took talent to pull off white on white.

So, how would Ash, the youngest son of Mab, stack up to his brothers?

Ash took several steps forward, prowling like a panther over the snowy ground. He certainly moved like a fighter, graceful and sure-footed. His sword pulsed blue against the pale backdrop as he stared at me with a cold, flat expression. "You're trespassing in Unseelie lands, Robin Goodfellow," he told me in an icy voice. "No one from the Summer Court may cross into Tir Na Nog without the queen's permission. According to ancient law, I could kill you on sight for this transgression."

"Not going to happen, ice-boy," I said breezily. "But you could certainly *try*—whoop!"

The words were barely out of my mouth when Ash gestured, and a flurry of glittering ice daggers sped toward me out of no-where. I dodged and twisted, and the frozen projectiles went hissing into the woods, sticking in tree trunks and pinging off rocks. Grinning, I looked back at the Winter prince, who looked slightly annoyed that I wasn't peppered with ice shards.

"Oho, that was a sneaky move, princeling." Pulling my daggers, I twirled them once and shook my head at the still impassive Winter faery. "You almost had me. I was sure you were going to spend at least the first half of the fight monologuing like your brother." Raising my chin, I looked down my nose at him while striking a ridiculously imperious pose. "'Well, well, well, what have we here?'" I drawled in my best nasal voice. "'A lost Seelie dog, come sniffing around where he doesn't belong. Oh wait, not a dog, but a vermin. A Summer vermin, in the land of Winter. How do you want me to dispatch you, vermin? Let me regale you with the ways,' blah blah blah." I rolled my eyes. "Makes you want to stab yourself just to get him to stop talking."

One corner of the prince's mouth twitched, as if he was fighting to not smile. "I'm not Rowan," he said. "I don't see the point in talking when we should be fighting. If I'm going to duel someone, it's to hone my skills, not to listen to a speech." He looked like he, too, was on the verge of rolling his eyes, before he caught himself. Setting his jaw, he raised his sword and pointed it in my direction. "But that is a prince of Winter you're disparaging, Summer fey. I should cut out your tongue for such mockery."

I smiled. "You and everyone else in the Nevernever, princeling," I said cheerfully, and raised my own weapons, feeling glamour swirl around me. "Well, shall we get on with it, then? Though I can't promise not to creatively insult you while we're trying to kill each other. That's just part of the fun."

Ash returned the smile, though his was rather grim. "That will be difficult once your tongue is missing," he said, and lunged at me.

We met in the center of the clearing, blades flashing and snow twirling around us. To no one's surprise, the youngest son of Mab was a skilled swordsman. He wasn't as viciously sneaky as Rowan or as formal as Sage, but he was quite graceful, and faster than either of them. I found myself working hard to avoid or counter his blows, which was both surprising and delightful. It had been so long since I'd had a decent challenge. I think I liked this kid enough to *really* play with him.

"Not bad, ice-boy, not bad," I taunted, leaping back from a stab to the chest. He gestured sharply, and I ducked the ice daggers that came at my head, snatching a few dead leaves from the ground as I rose. "I hope you're having as much fun as I am. In fact, I'm having so much fun, I think I need to invite my friends to the party."

I tossed the leaves into the air, and they exploded into three identical Pucks, grinning widely as they surrounded the prince. Ash jerked back, momentarily startled, as all four of us Pucks laughed, our voices ringing over the treetops.

"My brothers said you were devious and didn't fight fair." Ash parried a dagger thrust at him but immediately had to step back as another Puck pressed close, swiping at his head. "I see that they were right."

"You're not telling me anything I don't already know, ice-boy," I said, leaning back and watching him dance around the clearing with the copies. "But if you already know so much about me, you should have predicted this. And if you knew it was going to happen, you should have already been prepared for it."

The prince snarled. "I am."

Leaping back, Ash raised his sword, then thrust it point down into the snow. I felt the ripple of glamour spread over the ground in an icy wave, and quickly leaped into the air, changing into a raven midjump. Below me, there was a flash of blue, and a layer of ice instantly coated everything, freezing the duplicate Pucks and turning them into rime-covered statues.

Whoa, that was a lot of glamour. Well, congratulations, prince, I am officially impressed.

Swooping down, I landed on one Puck's head, pecking curiously at his hair. The duplicate radiated cold, his face frozen into a permanent startled expression.

A few paces away, the Winter prince still knelt against the icy ground with his sword driven into the earth. Gazing at the frozen trio, a faint smirk crossed his face, until he spotted me perched atop one's head. I let out a loud caw, flapping my wings at him, and his eyes narrowed.

Standing, he yanked out his blade, and the statue below me, along with the ice covering everything, shattered. The three Pucks instantly dissolved into nothing with the icy explosion, and I launched myself off the statue before I could be shredded by crystal shrapnel. Wheeling around, I circled the prince's head once with an indignant caw, before swooping up and changing into my normal self.

Dropping to the ground, I shot a wide grin at the Winter prince, who was breathing slightly harder from the use of so much glamour at once. "You're looking a bit tired there, ice-boy," I observed. "Not much of a partygoer, then? Is this too much fun for you to handle?"

"I'll show you fun," the Winter prince said, and raised his sword. Smirking, I drew my weapons again as the ice faery stalked forward, and as he did, the ground shivered, a tremor going through the earth below us. For a split second, I could feel the cracks in the earth, the unstable crust of rocks and snow under my boots, like a layer of rotten, too-thin ice over a fathomless lake.

Uh-oh.

With a roar, the ground under our feet gave way. Rocks, dirt, and chunks of ice surrounded me as I plummeted, raising my arms and trying to keep debris from bouncing off my head. For a moment, I thought of turning into a raven and flying back up, but with the vast amount of rocks and ice chunks tumbling around me, I couldn't get a bearing on anything.

Glancing down, I saw a glimmer of black water rushing up at me and braced myself.

Dammit, this is going to be cold.

I hit the water, and unsurprisingly, it was really, *really* cold. I stifled the urge to gasp as I went under, the frigid water closing over my head. I floundered to the surface and looked for the shore. Rocks, dirt, and ice rained around me, plunking into the water, chunks of ice bobbing to the surface again.

Looking behind me, I gave a start, seeing a massive arm rising out of the water. After a momentary heart attack, I realized both the arm and the hand attached to it were made of stone and jutting out of the water at an odd angle. Gazing around, I saw other structures poking through the surface as well; broken stone walls and the tops of roofs. The massive head of a stone statue peered out of the water at me, only its eyes and the top of its skull visible. Part of its face was gone, but from what I could see, the statue itself had been massive.

Ash's dark head broke the surface several feet away. Flinging his hair back, the Unseelie prince gazed around as I had, before his glittering silver gaze landed on me.

I shot him a grin, treading water, though the absolute cold made it hard to move my limbs freely. "Oh hey, princeling. What a surprise. Fancy meeting you here." I forced my teeth not to chatter through sheer application of will. The fey of the Summer Court were not terribly fond of the cold, especially *this* fey. "You, uh, wouldn't happen to have a boat in your pocket, would you?"

He stared at me, and then a smirk crossed his face. Raising an arm, he gestured to the lake, and with sharp crinkling sounds, a portion of the water froze, thickened, and became a floating plank of ice bobbing on the surface. The Winter prince heaved himself out of the water onto the plank, gave me a smug smile, and raised his arm. An icy wind blew in out of nowhere, taking the boat, and the Winter prince standing on it, toward the far side of the lake.

Well, I suppose I deserved that.

With nothing else to do, I began swimming.

I followed the Ice Prince, stroking through the ridiculously cold water until I finally reached the shore, a stretch of silver-gray sand surrounded by a sheer wall of rock stretching up into the darkness. Shivering, I hauled myself out of the water and staggered onto dry land, gazing around to get my bearings. The cavern that we had plummeted into was very large and mostly covered in water, though there were a few dry patches along the edges of the lake. Luminescent blue-and-white toadstools grew along the walls and on pieces of driftwood poking out of the sand, casting the entire chamber in an eerie glow.

Gazing up, I searched for the hole that we had fallen through, but saw only a ceiling of rock, with just a few tiny slivers of light peeking through the stone. Apparently, we wouldn't be getting out the way we came in.

I looked around and saw the Winter prince a few yards up the beach, taking off his cloak and draping it over a twisted branch poking out of the sand. Wrinkling my nose, I started toward him, pausing to gather twigs and pieces of driftwood that were scattered about the beach.

He gave me a cool stare as I joined him, dumping the armful of wood in the sand between us. "What are you doing, Good-fellow?" he asked as I knelt and began scooping out a pit. "Do you wish to fight right here? I am ready to continue."

"Well, you're just going to have to discover your patience, princeling," I muttered, not looking up as I arranged the twigs and sticks into a pyramid. "I know you Winter fey don't feel it, but right now I am cold, I am wet, and I am generally un-comfortable. Also, I make it a habit not to fight duels in soaked undergarments. I hate it when I start to chafe." Holding a hand over the wood, I sent out a pulse of glamour, and a tiny flame flickered to life, slowly creeping up the twigs. "If you want to be helpful, prince, you could try finding us a way out of here. Otherwise, you're just going to have to wait until I'm dry to start any more duels."

He gave me a flat stare, then turned away, gazing out over the water. His stare lingered on a domed roof a few yards away, covered in glowing fungi that gave off a soft green light. "I don't recognize this place," he muttered. "I wasn't aware that there was once a city down here. I wonder what happened."

I peered up at him, frowning. "What? You've never heard of the Lost City of Frozen Skull Forest? What kind of Unseelie are you, prince?"

"The Lost City of Frozen Skull Forest vanished centuries ago," the Winter prince said, a bit defensively. "No one knows what happened to it. There are no stories that claim it sank into the earth. This might not be the same place."

"Frozen Skull Forest is right above us, ice-boy," I pointed out. "I'd say the mystery is solved, unless you have evidence that the lost city somehow grew wings and flew away."

He glared at me but didn't say anything to dispute my claim.

I grinned and returned to poking the fire. "So, who lived here, anyway?" I asked, adding a few driftwood sticks to the growing flame. The dry branches ignited almost immediately, but when the flames reached the lichen growing along the wood, they sputtered and flickered blue and green for a moment. "I've never heard of a city in Winter territory that wasn't Tir Na Nog, have you, princeling?"

Ash shook his head. "No. But there were fey who existed in the Nevernever before us," he said thoughtfully. "Before the courts, at least according to legends. Though almost nothing is known of them."

"Well, maybe we should remedy that."

"What are you talking about?"

I waved a hand at the massive stone arm coming out of the water. "There is a lost city all around us, prince! One that hasn't been seen since before the formation of the courts. Aren't you curious? I think we should do a little exploration. Who knows what treasures are buried down here?"

For a moment, I could see the spark of intrigue in his eyes. He was curious, just as curious as me. That thirst for excitement, to explore and uncover new things, to push himself and see what was really out there, was even stronger than his hatred for all Summer fey. I sensed a kindred spirit, a fellow adventurer, even as his eyes clouded over and he turned a sneer in my direction.

"I have a better idea, Goodfellow. Why don't I kill you right here, and then take all the treasure back to the Winter Court, where it belongs?"

"Well, that's just impractical, ice-boy. How are you going to carry it all yourself?"

A splash echoed somewhere out in the water.

We both stopped talking. When I glanced back toward the lake, a chill that had nothing to do with temperature skittered up my spine.

A pale, unearthly form hauled itself out of the black waters a few yards away and rose, staring at us with empty, glowing green eyes. It might have been a dwarf once; it had a tangled beard that was full of algae, and it was shorter than either of us by several feet. Much like the rock dwarves of the mountains or even the deep dwarves that lived far below the earth and hated sunlight. But there was one massive difference between them and the figure staring at us now.

It had no skin. Or organs, or blood. A skeleton stared at us from the edge of the black waters, clad in a dented breastplate with a rusty helm perched on its skull. A decaying battle-ax, clutched in one bony hand, scraped over the pebbles as the creature took a few shambling steps forward, its eyes burning with malevolent green fire.

Ash drew his sword with a flash of blue light, and I leaped to my feet, pulling my daggers. "There's your answer, Good-fellow," the Ice Prince snapped as the skeleton let out a chattering noise that raised the hair on the back of my neck. "If you want to stay and explore the city, you're welcome to it. I don't think you're going to get very far."

Behind the shambling creature, the waters rippled and more skeletons began lurching out of the blackness. "Oh look, ice-boy," I said as we retreated up the beach, putting our backs to the cliff wall. "The whole city has come out to greet us. Don't you feel important?"

He shot me a sideways glare and raised his weapon. "If we get out of this," he growled as the first wave of skeletons reached us, "I'm going to kill you."

"Pfft, bet you'll never say that again, ice-boy."

The undead hordes were endless. I lost track of how long we stood there, side by side, fighting the skeletons that crawled out of the lake. There were hundreds of them, maybe more, and they came at us with single-minded purpose, unflinching and unswayable. They swung at us with rusty swords and axes, poked at us with broken spears, or sometimes just grabbed at us with clawed, bony hands. That they could shamble at us from only one direction made it possible to stand our ground, but there were still so many of them. If it wasn't for the solid rock wall at our back, we would've been swarmed in seconds. But even with our combined skills and magic, there was no end to the horde rising from the lake.

"I think a tactical retreat is in order, ice-boy!" I panted, blocking the broken haft of a spear thrust at my face. The skeleton wielding it rattled its skull at me, and I kicked it in its bony chest, shattering the rib cage and flinging it back. "Personally, I'd rather not stand here and fight the entire city, if it's all the same to you."

Ash swatted aside a double-bladed battle-ax, then returned with a quick swipe across the skeleton's neck, cutting the skull from its body. "There is no visible way out, Goodfellow," he snapped, slicing another undead in two with the snapping of bones. "Where do you think we can go?"

"Well, I would suggest up." Something flew by my face, hitting the rocks with a clink and leaving a stinging gash across my cheek. "Ow, dammit, now they're shooting arrows. We should leave now, ice-boy! Just keep them off me for two seconds and I'll find us a way out of here."

Ash snarled. Taking a step back, he gestured sharply and with a flare of glamour, a wall of ice rose from the ground between us and the undead. Immediately, the skeletons on the other side began clawing and hacking at the frozen barrier.

Ash, standing with his arm raised and his jaw set with concentration, shot me a split-second glare. "I can't keep this up for long, Goodfellow," he warned.

"And yet, you still have the strength for talking." Turning to the cliff wall, I put a hand against the cold, damp rock and closed my eyes, calling up my glamour and searching for what I needed. Even in the cold, hostile lands of Winter, I could still find aid with my Summer magic.

Hello, trees, roots, plants. Would you mind doing us a favor?

Buried deep in the earth, the roots of the forest above responded sluggishly, frozen in eternal hibernation. I poured my glamour into the land, trying to thaw it with the warmth, thinking of sunlight and crackling fire and hot tea, everything not cold.

"Puck!" Ash's voice rang out behind me, though it seemed to come from a great distance away. "They're breaking through!"

Sorry, trees, I can't be polite anymore. I need you to respond now.

I pulled, and with rumbles and the cracking of stone, roots and vines broke through the cliff wall. They slithered and curled into view, forming handholds and a ladder of sorts all the way up the rock face.

"Let's go, prince," I called, but as the rumbles of shifting rock faded away, a new tremor shook the ground beneath us.

The water parted, and a massive head rose from the dark surface, looming high in the air. An enormous reptilian skull with horns and spikes and teeth the size of your boots, but as skinless and skeletal as the undead around us. Rearing up, the undead dragon opened its jaws and roared, green flames blazing to life in its eye sockets, before turning a terrifying gaze on us.

"Okay, it is *really* time to go, prince!"

Ash didn't argue. He turned, flinging himself at the cliff face, just as the wall behind him shattered. Undead poured in, and we fled up the roots, scrambling for handholds and branches. The skeleton army followed, swarming the rock wall like ants, using their own bodies and numbers to start the climb. The horrible undead dragon heaved itself onto the beach, water and algae dripping from stark white bones, and began a slow, ponderous walk toward the cliff face.

"Keep going, ice-boy!"

We kept climbing, grabbing for whatever exposed roots and vines we could, ascending higher and higher until, at last, the stone-and-ice ceiling loomed above us.

"Goodfellow." Ash glared down at me, and several bits of dirt showered me in the face. "There is still no way out. We're still trapped down here."

"What did I say about discovering your patience, princeling?" I sent one final pulse of glamour into the air, and overhead, the rocks began to shudder and crack. Gnarled roots broke through the ceiling of ice and stone, coiling about like snakes, and shafts of sunlight pierced the clinging darkness.

A bony hand clamped onto my heel. I yelped and kicked the skeleton clinging to me in the face, sending it clattering back down the cliff. But there were more behind it, a swarm of pale ants moving toward us up the rock face. "Move, prince!" I snarled, and the Winter faery grabbed onto the roots above him, pulling himself up through the hole. I followed on his boot heels, wriggling through dirt and stone, until my head broke the surface and a blast of fresh, cold air hit me in the face.

On our knees, we both turned and peered down into the hole, but quickly jerked back as a bony arm reached up and latched on to the edge.

"Seal it, Goodfellow!" Ash's voice rang in my ears, sharp with authority.

"I can't do that, prince!" I scowled at him. "I can talk to plants and cajole trees into doing a little jig. I can't move solid rock."

"Then I'll take care of it. Keep them from reaching the hole."

As one, we knelt and pressed our hands to the icy ground, ripples of both Summer and Winter glamour going through the earth beneath us. On the cliff wall, the horde of undead had nearly reached the ceiling when a shudder went through the rock, and all the vines, roots, and branches that had poked through the stone suddenly began flailing and whipping about like maddened tentacles. They flung the skeletons away, smashing them from the cliff wall, and the bony attackers went clattering to the ground in waves. At the same time, a layer of ice spread from the edges of the hole, crawling over the ceiling and down the cliff face, turning everything slick and treacherous. Even more skeletons lost their grip on the ice and fell, bouncing off stone and their fellow undead, before smashing to pieces at the bottom.

I looked down, and a chill went through me as I stared into the glowing eyes of the undead dragon, peering up at us from the ground. As skeletons rained around it, shattering into bone shards, it opened its jaws, and a baleful green glow ignited between its fangs.

"Uh, prince?" I glanced at the Unseelie; he still knelt in the snow, eyes closed in concentration as he worked his Winter magic. "Not to rush you, but if you're going to seal this thing, now would be a good time."

The dead dragon roared, and a column of green fire exploded from its jaws, racing up the cliff face. Where it touched the plants, instead of bursting into flame, the vines, roots, and branches instantly withered and died, blackening into shriveled husks. As the fire came at us, I tensed, ready to leap back and drag the Winter prince with me if I had to. True, he was the enemy, and we still had a duel on the horizon, but I would much rather face Ash the Unseelie prince, not Ash the undead monstrosity.

But just before the column of flame reached us, just before I was ready to tackle the Winter prince, there was a final flare of glamour, and a thick layer of ice appeared, plugging the hole and freezing the snow we were kneeling in. There was a flash as the dragon's baleful green flames hit the ice in a flare of dark glamour, causing the earth beneath us to tremble. Then there was silence, and an eerie calm descended on the woods, as suddenly as if someone had dropped a blanket over it.

Ash and I both fell backward, landing on our backs in the snow, panting in relief and from the intense amount of glamour we'd spent. Far below us, through the snow and rock and layers of ice, I thought I could just make out a roar of frustration, and I hoped the bony reptile and all his little friends would return to their nice black lake and go back to sleep. They wouldn't be disturbed by me, that was for certain.

"Well, that was...fun," I gasped. "Nothing like running from a horde of cursed undead to make you appreciate being alive, right, ice-boy?"

"I...am going to kill you," Ash panted in return.

I laughed and pushed myself upright, brushing snow, dirt, and ice flecks out of everything, then grinned at the Winter prince as he rose.

"Not today, princeling. No offense, but I've officially gotten tired of snow and ice and anything colder than a spring breeze. I think I need a month in the steam caverns just to thaw out." I rubbed my hands together, blowing on frozen fingers, before shaking myself and giving the Winter prince a mocking salute. "See you around, princeling," I announced. "And don't worry about that rematch, I'm sure we'll run into each other again." I grinned at his glowering expression. "*But* if you ever get bored and want to do something exciting, come find me. I know lots of places just begging for the two of us to come knocking on their doors."

Ash narrowed his eyes. "If I see you again, Summer jester, it will be to run a sword through your heart," he warned as I started walking away. "Don't think this makes us even, Goodfellow. We can't be anything more than enemies. Our next meeting will be the last."

Suffice to say, that wasn't true.

14

YET ANOTHER PROPHECY

Coaleater was already in the courtyard, leaning against a trunk with his arms crossed, his eyes glowing red in the shadow of the tree. Meghan and ice-boy hadn't arrived yet, and I didn't see Grimalkin around, though knowing the cait sith, he could have been anywhere. The same could be said of Nyx, who was also missing. Or at least, not visible at the moment. I wondered if she was hiding in the trees or behind a lamppost, waiting to stab me if I wandered by.

The Iron faery glanced up, then pushed himself off the tree, stretching his massive shoulders. I grimaced as he bent his head to each side with the grinding of what sounded like metal against metal.

"Geez, tin can, how long have you been standing there? Need a little oil between the ears so you don't rust in place?"

"I am eager to get started," Coaleater replied calmly, rolling his shoulders back. "If this beast is what is causing the disturbance to the Obsidian Plains, I wish to dispose of it as quickly as possible. That I will be fighting alongside the Iron Queen once more is a great honor. I did not want to cause her any doubt by being late."

"Yeah," I muttered, gazing around. "So, where is everyone else? You haven't seen Nyx hiding in a potted fern or something, have you?"

"Potted ferns are impractical," said a voice behind me.

I turned to see Nyx step out from behind a tree, where I was certain nothing had been a few seconds ago. Her hood was up, but her eyes shone brightly as she met my gaze, raising a quizzical silver brow. "They make too much noise, and I don't like all the dirt in my hair. Topiaries work much better, or vases will do in a pinch."

I wasn't sure if the Forgotten was joking or not, but at that moment I felt a ripple of power go through the air as the rulers of the Iron Court walked toward us, followed by a very anxious-looking Fix. The Iron Queen was dressed for travel in black jeans, boots, and a coat, her steel sword at her waist. Ash looked the same as he always did, dark and dangerous, his ice blade throwing off a cold blue aura that left tendrils of mist behind him.

Our eyes met over the yard, and for the barest of heartbeats, I could see the question in his eyes. The briefest flicker of hope that we might be okay, that I was back to my normal, goofy, annoying self. That I hadn't meant what I told him on this very spot, earlier this evening.

I gave him a hard smile and saw that hope vanish instantly, replaced with the blank mask he used to shield his emotions from everyone. Nobody saw it, not even Meghan, who, by the distinct lack of worried or angry glares shot my way, was not aware of our conversation, either. For the moment, it seemed Ash was keeping what went on between us private, which was fine with me. Better that Meghan not become involved; she had enough to worry about. This was just between ice-boy and Robin Goodfellow.

"Is everyone here?" Meghan asked, striding to the center of

the group. Her gaze went to Nyx, waiting quietly at my side, and a smile crossed her face. "Nyx. I'm glad to see you on your feet. Are you feeling better?"

The Forgotten bowed her head. "Yes, Your Majesty," she replied. "I apologize for the worry I caused this afternoon. It won't happen again, I assure you."

"No apologies necessary," Meghan said. "Any friend of Puck and Keirran's is family here. If you need anything at all, don't hesitate to ask."

Nyx gave a solemn nod, which Meghan returned. And for just a moment, I felt a weird ripple of...something...go through me. Meghan and Nyx. The woman I'd loved once and lost, and the assassin who had threatened to kill me but was somehow always in my thoughts. I could see shadows of Meghan in Nyx, and vice versa, that same strength, courage, and determination, though they were two vastly different people.

I've seen that look before, Ash had told me earlier. *Not often, but enough. You're falling for her.*

No. No way. Nope, nope, nope, I wasn't going to do this again. It hurt way too much the last time.

"So, to paraphrase a certain cat, are we going to get started or not?" I wondered loudly. "The wyldwood isn't getting any closer. I take it that, since we're not perched on the very tippy top of the palace roof, we're not using gliders this time."

Gliders were the Iron Realm's special mode of transportation. Basically, they were giant metal dragonflies that you rode on the wind currents, but not in a normal way that you would ride say, a horse. Nope, these things carried you in their creepy metal insect legs, kind of like a living hang glider, and you yanked on said insect legs to steer them in the direction you wanted to go. They were huge and disturbing and buzzed in your ear the entire time, and I hated using them even more than I hated the spider carriages.

"No, we're not using the gliders," Meghan said to my immense relief. "There's a rather steep learning curve to fly them properly, and I suspect Coaleater will be too big for them to carry." She gave the Iron horse a respectful nod; he only shrugged. "I've sent for a pair of carriages," the Iron Queen went on. "They'll take us to the edge of the wyldwood. From there, I trust Grimalkin will lead us the rest of the way."

I still didn't see Grimalkin, but I had no doubt he was around, listening to us. Meghan knew it, too. We had dealt with the cait sith often enough to know he would pop up when he was needed and not before.

"Oh goodie," I sighed. "Carriages. What will these be, I wonder? Giant spiders or those enormous beetles the size of a blimp?"

Meghan gave a weird little smile. "No bugs this time, Puck." She raised her head to the wind, as if hearing something we could not, and the smile got wider. "They're coming. Everyone might want to take a few steps back."

I frowned, but then the hairs on my arms started to rise. The air turned sharp, like the energy before a storm, and a flicker of lightning from the clear night sky made my hair stand up the rest of the way. I took several steps back, as did everyone else, as a blinding flash of blue-white energy struck the center of the courtyard, making me flinch and shield my eyes.

When I looked up, two carriages glowed and flickered in the spot I had been standing moments before. They had no wheels and seemed to float in the air, two giant coppery spheres hovering several inches off the ground. They were pulled by a pair of white, deerlike creatures with horns that spiraled into the air like corkscrews. Their eyes were electric blue, and strands of lightning crawled along their hides and over their slim bodies, snapping in the air around them.

"These," Meghan announced into the shocked—haha, see what I did there—silence that followed, "are volt hinds, and they are the fastest way to get around the Iron Realm. It should only take us a couple hours to reach the edge of the wyldwood." Her gaze met mine, a knowing smile crossing her lips. "For those of you who dislike taking the normal carriages."

"Oh, that's great," I said cheerfully. "So, instead of getting eaten by giant spiders, we can now be electrocuted by static goats. I like this *so* much better. Can they charge your phone while you ride as well?"

The Iron Queen shook her head. "Grimalkin," she called, ignoring my last question, "are you ready? Do you want to ride with us, or shall we meet you there?"

With a yawn, the gray cat raised his head from where he'd been lying very close to the first carriage. I was quite certain he hadn't been there two seconds ago. "I was waiting for the rest of the party, Iron Queen," he stated, rising lazily to his feet. "I do applaud you for deciding to take the volt carriages. We will need their speed if we are ever going to get anything done tonight. Shall we go, then? The night is not getting any longer."

Meghan nodded, glancing at the rest of us. "We'll see you in the wyldwood," she said, and walked toward the first carriage with Ash beside her. The driver, a skinny faery with wires for hair and a whip made of lightning, reached down and opened the door of the floating carriage, and the Iron Queen stepped inside, followed by Grimalkin. Ash didn't glance at me as he trailed Meghan and the cat into the carriage, ducking through the frame, and the driver shut the door behind him.

It was, I expected, a much tighter fit with Coaleater in the carriage with us. The big Iron faery hunched his shoulders and tried to make himself small in the corner, but he filled nearly the entire seat. Nyx and I sat on the opposite side, trying to avoid his knees, and glancing out the window, I could swear the floating sphere hovered a little lower than before. The driver gave Coaleater a dubious look as he shut the door, and the Iron faery grimaced.

"This is going to be a long ride," he muttered.

"The Iron Queen said it would take only a couple hours to

reach the wyldwood," Nyx replied, gazing past me out the window. She shifted, and I suddenly was hyperaware of her body next to me, her slim leg brushing my shaggy one.

Coaleater gave a snort. "Not to contradict the Iron Queen, but I am not sure how that is possible," he rumbled. "Mag Tuiredh lies very deep in the Iron Realm, days from any border. The fastest way to reach the city is by train, and even then—"

There was a sudden crackle of energy around us, the lights outside flickered, and the carriage suddenly lunged into motion. I was flung back and pressed into the wall of the carriage, and Coaleater was nearly yanked out of his seat by the force. Only his enormous mass, weight, and strength kept him from face planting into Nyx's lap.

After only a few seconds, though, the carriage came to a stop, again so suddenly that I had to brace myself from flying into the opposite seat. I smelled ozone, like the air after a lightning strike, and there was a faint ringing in my ears. Glancing at Nyx, I saw her silver hair standing on end, like she'd jammed a finger in a socket. I couldn't help but snicker, and she arched a brow at me.

"Don't laugh too hard, Goodfellow. You look like a lightning gnome just stuck its thumb up your arse."

Before I could reply, the carriage jolted forward again, and my clever comeback was yanked from my lips and lost in the buzzing of static.

It continued this way for I don't know how long, short frantic bursts of speed followed by a jarring, sudden stop. Just long enough to draw in a quick breath before the carriage shot into motion again. The few times I thought to look out the window, I had no idea where we were. One time we seemed to be on a street corner, the next we were on an open plain with the moonlight blazing down on us, the next we seemed to be in a forest surrounded by trees.

I felt like I was inside a pinball machine, bouncing wildly from place to place with no time to stop, breathe, or think. Coaleater huddled in the corner with his arms crossed and his jaw clenched, looking straight ahead and waiting for it to be over. Nyx had drawn into her hood and closed her eyes as she leaned back, the picture of calm except for the tight press of her lips and the flexing of her fingers each time the carriage changed direction.

Finally, the ride came to another instant, jarring stop, but this time, it didn't immediately surge forward. After a few seconds of waiting, bracing myself for another burst of motion, I gradually relaxed, letting my jaw, arms, knees, fingers, and other muscles uncoil. My butt cheeks were clenched so tightly they would feel like rocks for several days.

"Okay," I breathed as my two companions slowly uncoiled as well, "that settles it. No more complaining about giant spider carriages. I didn't think there could be anything worse, but apparently I can still be wrong every century or so."

"That was...interesting," Nyx mused, trying in vain to smooth down her hair. I reached up to feel my own and found it standing on end like a dandelion puff. Sparks snapped at my fingers as I withdrew my hand. "Where are we now, I wonder?"

"Let's find out," Coaleater rumbled, and shoved back the door, letting in a cool breeze that dispersed the charged air of the carriage.

My relief at being out of the carriage was short-lived as I hopped from the doorframe, dropped a few feet, and landed in a pool of standing water up to my knees. My hooves sank into the mud and with a yelp, I leaped for the nearest patch of land, only to find the nice, dry-looking spot of grass I'd aimed for was waterlogged as well. Finding a stump, I perched gingerly atop the wood, shaking out my hooves and surveying our surroundings.

Apparently, we had landed in the middle of a swamp. Pools of black, still water surrounded tiny islands of dry land, dead trees and long cattails poking out of the mud. A few feet away, the carriage floated above the offending water, the two hinds that carried it perched daintily on a rock. The driver, gazing down at me with a half-amused, half-apologetic look, shook his head.

"Forgive me, Master Goodfellow," he called. "If you had waited a moment, I would have opened the door and also warned you to watch your step."

"Oh, no worries." I turned and gave him a wide, toothy grin. "It's not like I can craft an elaborate prank where every time you venture outside you step in mud for the rest of your life. That's not something a normal faery could do, right?"

His face blanched, losing the amused look as he stammered a much more heartfelt apology.

I felt a tiny prick of gleeful satisfaction. There was so much I hadn't done in many, many years; maybe it was time to remind everyone, Iron fey included, why Robin Goodfellow was a faery you did not want to cross.

With a splash, Coaleater dropped from the carriage into the pool of water, not seeming to notice or care about the wet soaking his boots. Nyx was right behind him, only she leaped gracefully from the edge and landed on a mound of dry earth a few feet away. A gust of wind pushed her hood back and caught her silver hair, tossing it around her. My heart twisted, torn between smiling wistfully and hurling a mudball at her.

I looked around and saw the second carriage a few paces away, glowing against the darkness. Unlike our carriage, it had chosen to touch down on a patch of dry land, small but large enough for two people to stand on. Ash was helping Meghan out of the carriage, and Grimalkin sat a couple feet away on a rock, busily washing his tail. For just a second, I thought the cat's fur looked twice its normal size, poofed out like the feline had just gone through the spin cycle in a dryer. But I blinked, or maybe the moonlight shifted, and the cat was back to normal.

With a crackle of energy, the two carriages sprang into the air, trailing sparks and light, and flashed their way across the swamp.

Bouncing from rock to rock, they zipped across the ground like twin balls of lightning. In seconds, they had disappeared.

The three of us sloshed our way toward the rulers of the Iron Realm and their small, dry island in the center of the swamp. "Well, this is a lovely place," I commented as Coaleater and I splashed up. The fur on my legs was already drenched; I saw no point in trying to pick my way across the dry spots. Unlike Nyx, who somehow did just that. "I take it we're still in the Iron Realm?"

"Yes," Meghan replied. "This place is called the Glowing Swamp, and it sits close to the spot where we'll find the oracle, according to Grim. We'll have to cross into the wyldwood first, but the border isn't far. We just might have to get our feet a little wet."

Beside her on an old log, Grimalkin sniffed. "Speak for yourself, Iron Queen," he muttered, and hopped off the stump onto a nearby rock. "This way to the oracle," he called back, trotting into the swamp with his plumed tail held high. "Do try to keep up, and do *not* think to 'accidentally' splash water at me if you wish to reach your destination at all, Goodfellow."

I snickered. "You wound me, Furball," I scoffed as the five of us headed into the marsh after the cat. "Why would I use water when mud is so much more entertaining?"

The marsh was still as we followed the cat over puddles and small bits of dry ground, but it was hardly silent. Insects buzzed, a constant drone in our ears, and birds trilled somewhere in the reeds. Every so often, there was a nearby splash as some creature vanished into the dark waters, always gone before I could see it clearly.

Nyx glided along beside me, as graceful and silent as a shadow. A few paces ahead, Meghan and ice-boy led the way, and Coaleater sloshed tirelessly through the mud, steam curling from his nose and mouth to drift away on the breeze. I felt a twinge of nostalgia, of familiarity; how many times had I done this—

me and my two closest friends, following an annoying cait sith toward an unknown destination? Circumstances would be different, and our allies would change, but somehow, it was always us four—me, Meghan, Ash, and Grimalkin, on a quest to save the Nevernever once again.

And yet, if that was the case, why did this time feel so different? Maybe because *I* was different now. Maybe because the happy-go-lucky, smile-even-when-it-hurts, has-a-joke-for-everything goofball was gone, and the faery left behind made everyone slightly uncomfortable. Even me.

An orange glow suddenly lit the darkness, and we came upon a narrow wooden walkway stretching out over the swamp. A lantern hung from one of the posts, swaying gently and filling the air with a high-pitched creaking sound.

"This is the edge of the Iron Realm," Meghan announced, stepping onto the boardwalk with an expression of relief. Mud clung to her knee-high boots, but the rest of her had escaped mostly unscathed, unlike myself and Coaleater, whose bottom halves looked like we had sloshed out from the set of *Swamp Thing*. No one doubted or questioned her claim. Like all rulers of Faery, she was strongest while within her own realm and knew instantly when she had left her territory. "Where did you say the oracle lived, Grim?"

Grimalkin leaped atop one of the wooden posts and vigorously shook one back leg, looking indignant that it had dared get wet. Only after he'd sat down and licked it furiously several times did he deign to answer.

"The oracle lives deep in the Black Marsh, whose edge we have only now reached," the cat replied, rising with a yawn and a wave of his tail. "It is not too far, but it is not terribly close, either."

"Vague as always, Furball."

"Does anything else live out here?" Nyx wondered, stepping easily onto the planks. She had managed to keep herself bone-dry through the entire trek, and I both admired her grace and envied her lack of soggy socks.

Meghan nodded, stepping back as the rest of us clambered atop the narrow boardwalk. "There are a few species of fey that call this swamp home," she told the Forgotten. "But they're shy and keep mostly to themselves. It's likely we won't see anyone until we get out of the marsh."

After a few minutes, the dry land disappeared, the small islands vanishing beneath the muck, until it was a solid pool of black water and dead trees stretching away into the night. Colored fireflies appeared, bobbing over the surface like tiny Christmas lights, flashing red, green, blue, and pink against the pitch-black water. It was very quiet. Save for the tiny floating lights, nothing moved out in the swamp, no splashes of frogs or fish or startled turtles echoed around us. The surface was as still as a giant black mirror under the stars.

"I feel like we're being watched," Nyx murmured beside me.

A grimace crossed my face. "You, too, huh? Oh good. And here I thought I was the only one being paranoid—"

Something flew at me from the water. I spun, catching sight of a long spear, the tip curved in a nasty, serrated barb, flying right at my head. I twisted aside, and the projectile sailed past me into the water.

"Uh, princess?" I called, as all around us, the water started to move. "I don't think the locals are as shy as you first let on."

We all spun, glamour flaring and weapons unsheathed, to face the churning waters. I pulled both daggers, watching as a few dozen or so heads broke the surface of the swamp, rising from the muck like zombies. They looked like some sort of merfolk or fish creatures; fins sprouted from their cheeks and ran down their backs, and their taloned fingers were webbed. Rubbery, dark blue skin blinked with dozens of tiny luminescent lights scattered down their arms and shoulders, and a glowing bulb dangled from the top of their skulls like a huge angler fish. Enormous white eyes fixed on us hungrily, and their mouths opened to show rows of gleaming, sharklike teeth.

With furious hisses, the mob of fishmen raised their spears and swarmed toward us.

I tensed, but before anyone could do anything, a massive jolt of power went through the air. A streak of lightning descended from the sky, striking the upraised hand of the Iron Queen with a dazzling flash and a boom that rocked the planks and sent waves through the surface of the swamp. Meghan stood there a moment, strands of blue-white energy flickering around her, making the air crackle with power.

Unsurprisingly, everyone, fish and friend included, went rigid and stared at her.

Lowering her arm, the Iron Queen gazed calmly at the mob of luminescent fishfolk surrounding us. "You know who I am," she said, and though her voice wasn't loud, the planks trembled under our feet, and ripples spread through the water. "This does not have to end in violence. Depart in peace, and we will do the same. But attack my companions, and I will have no choice but to defend them."

For a few heartbeats, the creatures stared at us, baleful hunger battling the obvious fear of the Iron Queen standing in the center of the walkway. Ash stood at Meghan's side, his posture calm, but his hand resting close to his sword hilt, ready to defend her if needed. I could feel Nyx at my back and caught the shimmer of light from the blades in her hands, back to her full power. For which I was very relieved. And yes, a tiny bit worried, but mostly relieved. Coaleater faced the mob with his arms crossed and his head raised, almost daring them to take one step forward. Grimalkin, of course, was nowhere to be seen.

Then one of the fish creatures hissed softly and drew away, sinking back into the water. As the blackness closed over its head, the rest of the swarm began to follow, sinking into the muck and vanishing from sight, their glowing angler bulbs the final things to be swallowed by the darkness. Within moments, they had all disappeared, and the waters were perfectly still once more.

Meghan slumped, as the power swirling around her flickered once and died, taking the steely Iron Queen persona with it. "What was that about?" she whispered, gazing around the now quiet marshland, her blue eyes narrowed in concern. "The merfolk have never been aggressive. What is going on here?"

"It is the same in the Obsidian Plains," Coaleater rumbled from the back. "Tensions are rising between fey that have always been peaceful. There is…an anger that I have never felt before. It is why I am here now. And I assume it is why we are going to the oracle."

"That monster's influence couldn't have reached this far," Nyx began, but before she could finish, a shudder went through the planks at our feet. I looked down through the cracks just in time to see a glowing bulb vanish beneath the water.

"Uh-oh."

There was a lurch, an earsplitting crack, and then the entire walkway collapsed, plunging us all into waist-deep swamp water.

The waters boiled, and fish creatures surged out of the depths, surrounding us. Clutching spears and baring jagged fangs, they swarmed us like piranhas, stabbing and biting. I dodged a spear thrust at my head, then floundered back as a pair of snapping jaws followed me. Reaching down, I snatched a piece of the broken walkway and shoved it between the nasty set of chompers coming for my face. Serrated fangs snapped shut on the wood, and the fishman gargled in fury.

Coaleater bellowed as a group of fishmen pounced on him, clawing and biting only to recoil with shrieks of pain from a mouthful of iron. His huge fists lashed out, sending several of them flying into the water, though more piled on him as soon as they were gone. A flurry of ice daggers sang through the air in an arc, courtesy of the Ice Prince himself, and the fishmen burbled as they fell back, recoiling from the storm of frozen shards.

I twisted to avoid a pair of spears thrust at my face, feeling the sharpened tips barely graze my skin, and the fury in me roared. *Okay, fishies, you wanna play with Robin Goodfellow? Let's see how you like this little trick.* Sloshing back, giving myself a little room, I glanced around at the cluster of fishmen and their spears and smiled. *You really shouldn't run with sharp things. You might poke your eyes out.*

With a pulse of glamour, the ring of spears surrounding me began sprouting with vines and flowers, growing rapidly as they bloomed from the wooden shafts, causing the fishmen to pause and stare at their spears in confusion and alarm. A few of them began shaking the spears, trying to remove the blossoms, and I grinned.

Just wait. You haven't seen anything yet.

Long black thorns shot abruptly from the wood, piercing hands, arms, eyes, and throats, impaling the fishmen on their own spears. A couple of them howled, trying in vain to drop their suddenly spiky weapons, but the thorns had pierced their hands and fingers, and they couldn't drop it even as the spines continued to grow. They shrieked as the barbs reached their faces and chests, desperately trying to arch away, but their voices were cut off as the thorns slid through their bodies and silenced them. The rest, the ones lucky enough to die quickly, let out choked gurgles and slumped beneath the water, sinking from view.

I felt a brief stab of disgust with myself and quickly squashed it; that was another particularly nasty trick I'd stopped using, but Meghan had given these slimy bastards the chance to run and they'd ambushed us instead. Really, they'd brought this on themselves; I refused to be turned into Goodfellow sushi for a bunch of garbling fishmen.

In the breath of stillness that followed, I looked around to see Nyx slice through a trio of fishmen who had stupidly gotten too close to her, and Coaleater give a bellow of annoyance as his body erupted with flame. The fishpeople clinging to him let out hisses and shrieks as they leaped off the blazing faery into the water. They didn't surface again.

Silence fell. I glanced around at the others and saw Meghan and Ash standing back to back, swords in hand, surrounded by a ring of dead, scaly bodies. The Iron Queen hadn't used any of her glamour, but then again, she hadn't needed it. Meghan was quite the competent swordswoman now, having been trained by one of the best. With a sigh, she lowered her blade and sheathed it at her side as the last few fishpeople decided this wasn't worth it after all and fled. They slipped beneath the water as suddenly as they had appeared, and we were alone in the swamp once again.

"Well," I commented, smirking and gazing around at the carnage left behind. "That was fun." The frozen, charred, stabbed, and dismembered bodies of the fishmen wriggled as they suddenly turned into piles of leeches and lampreys, and I wrinkled my nose as they slithered into the black waters and vanished. "Not very nice of them, collapsing the bridge like that. Although I suppose if I were an unreasonably hostile fishperson, I wouldn't want a fair fight, either."

"It was more than that," Ash said, sheathing his own blade. "This wasn't just an ambush that would give them the advantage in the water. They knew Meghan wouldn't be able to use her full power, not without hurting the rest of us."

I remembered the lightning Meghan had called down from the sky and knew Ash was right; if she had used it against the fishmen while we were all submerged, everyone's hair would be standing on end right now.

"That they would attack us at all is concerning," Nyx broke in. She stood chest deep in swampy black water, silver hair floating around her, and looked faintly annoyed that she was now submerged with the rest of us. "Unless things have changed drastically since I've been gone, no fey, even mobs of fey, would dare attack the Lady. Are the rules different now?"

"No," Coaleater said, billowing indignantly in the water,

steam rising off him in clouds. "They are not. No fey would attack the ruler of a court. It's blasphemous to even think such a thing."

"I wish I knew what was happening," Meghan said, sounding frustrated. "This isn't normal behavior for any of them. They didn't have to die." She sighed, rubbing her forehead, then gazed behind her at the edge of the boardwalk that hadn't been submerged in water. "Get us to the oracle, Grim," she ordered. "I need answers, and I need them now."

The cat peered down from the edge of the broken walkway, curling his whiskers at us all. "I am doing my best, Iron Queen," he said in a put-upon voice. "Perhaps if you would all stop playing with fish, we would arrive a lot sooner. Just an observation." He turned, flicked his tail, and leaped to the edge of the shattered boardwalk. "This way, if you would."

"Ugh," Nyx muttered as she hopped gracefully onto the walkway again. "Now I smell like a bog. It's going to take forever for my boots to dry."

Coaleater tossed his head, choosing to walk alongside the narrow planks instead of atop them, which was good, as his huge iron body would likely collapse the rest of the walk. Steam billowed off his skin where the water touched the superheated metal. "I could dry them for you," he said seriously, and snorted a cloud of flame and smoke into the air. "If you don't mind a few singed spots."

Nyx grimaced. "I think my soggy boots will be fine."

The swamp continued, the walkway snaking over water and through fields of cattails and dead trees, colored fireflies bobbing lazily through the air. Gradually, the marshland began to change, the trees growing larger, more twisted and gnarled. The streetlamps jutting out of the water disappeared, and curtains of moss began appearing in the branches overhead, draped like lacy green curtains over the walkway.

"We must be close to the center of the marsh by now," Meghan mused from up ahead. "How far is it to the oracle, Grim?"

"Not far. In fact…" The cat paused, raising his head, his ears pricked to the breeze. "We are here."

We stopped. Up ahead, the trees thinned out a little, revealing a small island in the center of a black pond. A wooden cottage sat in the middle of the island, surrounded by a pair of enormous, moss-covered trees, the roots snaking up the walls and curling over the thatched roof like grasping fingers. A pair of naked skulls sat atop the posts at the edge of the island, and a black cauldron huddled in the ashes of a large firepit just outside the door. A flickering orange glow spilled through the single round window in the wall, as inviting as the light coming from the mouth of a dragon.

"Oh," I commented. "That's great. This couldn't scream 'witch's house' any louder if the walls were made of gingerbread."

Nyx frowned at me. "All the witches' houses I knew of were made of stone. Or sometimes bones. What is this strange magic where the walls are made of bread?"

"I'll tell you the story later."

The wooden door creaked open. A figure emerged from the hut, standing for a moment in the doorframe. From this distance, it was hard to see it clearly; it wore a tattered green cloak or dress, but that was all I could make out. It stood in the frame a moment, gazing right at us, before it lifted an arm in a wave, turned, and went back inside.

"And we're expected," I went on. "This just gets better and better." No one answered me, and I grinned. "Welp, no use standing around here. Shall we go and see what's for dinner? Hopefully it won't be us."

Cautiously, we followed the winding planks toward the island in the center of the pond, hearing the boards creak under our feet. Bullfrogs croaked out in the marsh, and hanging vines dripped warm water onto our heads.

Meghan walked up to the door and raised an arm to tap on it, but a quiet voice echoed through the wood before she made contact.

"It is open, Iron Queen."

Meghan pushed the door open. It swung back with a groan, revealing a small, cozy room, a fireplace crackling on the far wall. Crystals, bones, and other, stranger things hung on strings from the ceiling, dangling throughout the room and catching the firelight. I ducked a pair of bird feet as I stepped through the door, the tiny claws withered and dry as they spun on the twine.

A chair sat before the fireplace, its back to us. It was occupied, but all I could see was a slender hand and forearm, and the hem of a ragged green cloak. As everyone but Coaleater stepped into the room, the arm lifted in a vague greeting, accompanied by the same voice.

"I knew you were coming, Iron Queen. Come in, come in. Though, be informed, the floor will collapse if the Iron creature steps in any farther. That I have seen."

Coaleater blew out a breath of steam and tossed his head. "I will wait outside," he informed us, and wandered away toward the edge of the island, presumably to keep watch. The rest of us crowded inside, ducking trinkets and paraphernalia, until we were all clustered together in the small room.

The figure in the chair rose, turning to face us. My brows arched. I'd been expecting a withered hag, a hunchbacked old crone with crooked talons and dental problems. Like the previous oracle. I was not expecting a young, beautiful faery with perfectly manicured nails and long raven hair without a strand of gray in it. She stood tall, unbowed, though her gaze seemed to stare right through us at the opposite wall. It seemed rather odd, until I noticed her eyes. They had been blue once, but were now hazy and clouded over, the pupils focusing on nothing. She was blind.

"It is not polite to stare, Robin Goodfellow," the faery said without looking at me. "My eyes may not work, but I see more than you could ever imagine."

"I dunno about that," I said, just to be contrary. "I can imagine a lot."

Meghan stepped forward before I could say anything else. "You are the oracle, I presume."

"Am I?" The faery put a hand to her eyes, peering out between her fingers. "I suppose that's right," she muttered. "Hard to claim otherwise. When you see these things, you are either an oracle or delirious."

"Or both," I put in. "Both is always an option, I've found."

Meghan shot me a look that said, *How is this helping?* before turning back to the oracle. "We need your help, Oracle," she went on, getting right to the point. "I will be brief, because there might not be much time. There is some sort of terrible creature plaguing the Nevernever. It radiates negative emotions, is immune to glamour, and has the power to change faeries into crueler versions of themselves. We need to know what it is, and where it might be now."

The oracle's already pale face went even whiter, her cloudy eyes getting huge and round. "No," she whispered, turning violently away. "It cannot be that time. It is too soon. Too soon, too soon. Evenfall comes. All is emptiness, and darkness, and nothing."

"What is?" Meghan stepped forward, and the oracle cringed back, hands flying to her face. "What are you talking about?"

"I do not know."

"You are the oracle," Ash put in, stepping up beside Meghan. "You must know. What have you seen that is causing you such distress?"

The oracle sobbed, spinning away, her arms gesturing uselessly at nothing. "I do not know!" she wailed. "I cannot see. There are pieces of me that are gone. Missing. The thieves who stole them left only holes behind." The oracle whirled back, clutching at her face. "Can't you see? I cannot remember! Those memories are gone, and I cannot remember the memories that were stolen."

"Someone stole your memories?" I snorted, which made Meghan frown. Years ago, when Meghan had first come to the Nevernever, she had traded one of her own memories to the previous oracle to get answers. "Well, ignoring that bit of delicious irony," I went on, smiling gleefully, "how did that happen?"

The new oracle trembled, then slumped to her chair, still covering her face. "I died," she whispered. "Or the one who was oracle before me died. Her memories are supposed to be mine, or I am supposed to remember her visions of before, but when I came back, I was not whole. Pieces of me, of her, missing. Pieces stolen away, gone forever."

"The Forgotten," Meghan said, making Nyx straighten. The assassin had been standing quietly in the corner, watching the proceedings with her arms crossed, but at Meghan's statement she immediately raised her head. The Iron Queen regarded the distraught oracle, her face grim in the firelight. "Ethan told me he was there when the previous oracle died," she murmured. "A group of Forgotten drained her of all her glamour so that she Faded away." She turned to find Nyx, meeting the Forgotten's gaze. "Could they be the thieves she's talking about?"

"Perhaps," Nyx said softly. "The Forgotten don't just drain glamour. They can steal emotion and memory as well. If these Forgotten were responsible for her death, it is possible that they would possess bits of the oracle's memories."

"Or in this case, her visions," Ash muttered.

"Hold on a second." I held up a hand. "Let me see if I have this right. So, are you telling me we have to go track down these Forgotten who stole your memories several years ago, not knowing where they are or if they're even still alive, to ask them about these visions they probably don't even understand?"

"I could…feel them," the oracle whispered. "Like tiny embers, flickering, flickering. Most have already flickered out. The others…are terrified. That's all I can sense from them now. Fear. There were several once. Now there is only one."

"Where?" Ash questioned.

The oracle scrunched up her forehead, as if thinking hard or trying to remember something difficult. "I…I saw… a castle," she finally whispered, the words dragged out of her. "Surrounded by thorns and roses, filled with broken statues. Something watches from the window of the highest keep. A fountain in the middle of the courtyard, still spewing clear water. A curse of sorrow and regret holds everything captive."

"I know that place."

Grimalkin. I had forgotten he was still there. We all turned to the cat, who was sitting calmly on an end table with his tail curled around his feet, watching us.

"Yes," he announced. "Before you ask, I can take you there." His tail gave a few agitated thumps against the end table before he went on. "However, I will warn you, it is a place of misfortune. Of nightmares come to life. There is a powerful curse worked into the very stones, and the keeper of the castle does not take kindly to visitors."

"Nothing in the Briars takes kindly to visitors, Grim," Meghan said, and I nodded in agreement. "If you know where this place is, we need to go and find this Forgotten. It sounds like this monster, whatever it is, has been part of the oracle's visions. All the more reason to learn as much about it as we can."

"The light flickers," the oracle murmured. "A darkness is approaching, seeking to swallow it whole. To snuff it out. Closer, closer." She paused, and then her whole body slumped as she sank to the floor, her voice a ragged whisper. "Gone."

I shivered at the deadness in her tone, as if she had just lost something that could never be recovered. The Iron Queen took one step forward and knelt in front of the oracle, her voice and expression gentle as she placed a hand on her arm. "Will you be all right here, Oracle?"

"I am broken," was the flat reply. "I am a shell, missing pieces scattered to the wind. My Sight gazes into the darkness, searching for fragments of the future, and sees nothing. Is it my eyes that are empty? Or is it because there is nothing to see?"

A violent spasm rocked her thin body, and she toppled forward out of the chair. Meghan caught her, holding her steady, as Ash stepped forward in concern. She gave him a quick look, shaking her head, and the Ice Prince halted, though he continued to watch them both.

"I saw him," the oracle whispered as Meghan gazed at her, her features grim. "For just a moment, I saw his face. The bright one. He shone against the darkness, and the darkness swallowed him whole." She blinked and looked up at Meghan, a spark of lucidity returning to her face. "Evenfall comes, Iron Queen," she said. "The darkness sleeps now, but I can feel it stirring, deep beneath Faery. I feel the ripples as it shifts and moves, growing more conscious of the world above. I fear we are close to the end."

"The end of what?"

"Everything."

And with that, the oracle slumped in Meghan's arms with a soft moan, and none of the Iron Queen's gentle prodding drew any response.

"Okay, on that cheerful note, maybe we should go," I offered. "Places to be, Briars to hack through, cursed castles to assault, that sort of thing. You ready to get us out of here, Furball?"

Grimalkin yawned. "As soon as the Iron Queen is finished."

Meghan stood, drawing the oracle to her feet, and helped her back into her chair. The faery slumped against the side, mumbling, her eyes glazed once again, and the Iron Queen stepped back.

"We're done here," she murmured, turning around. For a moment, the stern persona of the Iron Queen shone through, steely-eyed and terrible. But she shook herself and glanced at the rest of us. "Let's go, everyone. Grim? Take us into the Briars."

"As you wish."

15

A NIGHT OF CONFESSIONS

"What do you think she meant?" Nyx asked, her voice grave as we made our way through the wyldwood, following the cat once more. "Do you really think she believed it is soon to be the end...of everything?"

I shrugged. "Oracles are like sphinxes," I said. "At least the ones I've met. Always talking in riddles and metaphors, and that's when they're *not* completely raving and delirious. Besides—" I snorted "—do you know how many End of the World prophecies I've heard in the past few centuries? It's never as bad as they make it out to be. Hell, Keirran was part of one of those doomsday prophecies himself. Poor kid was 'fated to destroy the Nevernever' from the get-go. But we're all still here, and thankfully he got over his Destroyer of All Things phase." Nyx raised a brow, and I grinned at her. "I think we're gonna be fine."

I saw Ash glance back at me, narrowing his eyes, and realized he had heard my comment about Keirran. For a second, guilt prickled. The pain of having to exile their son from the Nevernever was still raw for the rulers of the Iron Realm.

I knew they would much rather have him home, but Faery law was Faery law. Keirran had betrayed the courts; his only choices were banishment or death, and the Forgotten did need someone to look after them in the Between. Keirran was proving to be a good king and a competent ruler, but that was small comfort to his parents, who I'm sure missed him and hated the fact that he couldn't come home.

Ash brought this on himself, that evil part of me whispered. *It was his stubborn quest to be with Meghan that sent us through Phaed where the Lady was sleeping. His fault that she woke up. If he had just let Meghan go, none of this would have happened.*

"Do you still love her?"

Ice flooded my whole body. For a second, I didn't think I was hearing correctly. I blinked and glanced at Nyx, who was watching me with a grim look on her face.

"Sorry, what was that?" Tilting my head, I stuck a finger in my ear and wiggled it around. "A fly or something must've flown down my earhole, because I was almost sure I heard you imply that I was in love with the Iron Queen."

The Forgotten didn't smile. "I've been around a long time, Puck," she said. "Part of the reason I'm so good at my job is that I'm observant. And I know that in Faery, grudges never go away. They can fester for years, sometimes without our knowledge, until they finally consume us. Because we are fey, and we can't let anything go. You were in love with the Iron Queen." Nyx stated this calmly, glancing ahead to where Ash and Meghan walked side by side. "And she chose him. Simple as that."

"You wanna rub the salt in a little deeper? I don't think you've ground it in far enough."

"I know vengeance, Puck." Nyx glanced at me again, her golden eyes both sympathetic and cautious. "I know it all too well. Revenge was something the Lady specialized in, and I was often the one she used to carry it out. But my question to you is this... This desire for revenge against the prince consort—

is it because you're still in love with the Iron Queen, or is it because you lost?"

I scoffed. "I don't lose well, lady assassin," I told her. "It happens so rarely. But you know nothing of the years, the *centuries*, of the time ice-boy kept trying to kill me. Over a girl. So, don't think you understand what's happening between the two of us. It would take an oracle to untangle all those threads."

Nyx gave me an unreadable look and seemed about to say something more, but at that moment Meghan paused and turned around, raising a hand to bring the group to a halt.

"We'll stop here for the night," she announced as I realized we had reached the banks of a greenish-black lake, mossy trees with twisted branches rising out of the water like grasping claws. "Grim says that the entrance to the Briars is on the other side of the lake, but since this is also lindwurm territory, I don't want to attempt to cross it in the dark. I hope none of you object to making camp for the evening."

No one did, and sometime later, a cheerful fire crackled in the pit, and several large lake eels sat cooking on sticks close to the flames. I would've preferred fish, but hey, you took what you could catch in the wyldwood. Judging from the eels' size and rather large teeth, I'd say that they were at least partially responsible for the severe lack of fish in the water.

I lounged against the log Coaleater and I had dragged close to the firepit, while Nyx perched on the end, drawn into her hood and watching the dancing flames. On the opposite side of the pit, Meghan sat on the ground with her legs crossed and her sword resting on her knees. Ash sat behind her on a rock, his arms resting lightly on her shoulders, and I still had no idea how he managed to look completely at ease and insanely protective at the same time. Coaleater had wandered down to the lake, and Grimalkin had vanished in that obnoxious feline way of his, so it was just the four of us, sitting around a campfire. Except for Nyx, it was just like old times.

Only, it really wasn't.

Meghan let out a long sigh and leaned back against Ash, resting her head on his knees. "It's nice to get out of the palace every once in a while," she murmured, looking less like a queen and more like a normal girl again. "Even if it is for another catastrophe. I hope Fix doesn't have a nervous breakdown while we're away."

"Glitch will be there," Ash assured her. "Between the two of them, they should be able to handle most emergencies. And they'll send a gremlin if something truly disastrous comes up."

"I suppose you're right." Meghan raised her head, glancing at the Forgotten across the firepit. "You came from the Between, is that right, Nyx?" she asked, and the Forgotten's hood lifted as she met the Iron Queen's gaze. "From Touchstone? How is Keirran faring nowadays?"

"He is a good ruler," Nyx replied immediately. "A fair king. He cares for his people, that much is obvious. Although…" She paused, drumming her fingers on her knee in thought. Meghan watched and waited patiently as the Forgotten struggled with what to say.

"He…carries a great deal of guilt with him," Nyx finally said, and Meghan closed her eyes. "He blames himself for events of the past, and that can sometimes cloud his judgment, make him question himself. He can also be…reckless with his own safety, if it means protecting the Forgotten and the Between. It has made my job more difficult, when the king insists on standing between his subjects and every creature that means them harm."

A tiny smile crossed Ash's face, and he shook his head.

Nyx paused again, contemplating her next words, before she continued in a soft voice. "He wants very badly to redeem himself for past mistakes, but he doesn't believe he will ever be forgiven." She grimaced then, giving the rulers of the Iron Realm an apologetic look. "I'm sorry, I've spoken out of turn. Please excuse my forwardness, Your Majesty."

"Don't apologize." Meghan opened her eyes, giving the Forgotten an appraising look. "I asked a question, and you answered truthfully. I appreciate your insight, Nyx. I know Keirran can be reckless. I'm glad he has someone like you watching out for him. Especially since that creature showed up in Phaed. And now that we have a bit of time..." She glanced at me, her blue eyes suddenly sharp. "I would like to know more about this creature you fought. You were both there with Keirran—you experienced its attack. If the oracle's thief can't tell us anything, we might have only your knowledge to go on. What happened that night?"

I shrugged. "Not much to tell, princess. We fought the thing, it kicked us around like soccer balls and then hightailed it into the Nevernever as soon as the way opened. All the magic and glamour we hurled its way didn't even phase the thing. Even Keirran's Iron glamour didn't put a scratch on it."

"Maybe the answer isn't magic, then," Ash mused. "Maybe the solution is a solid blade through its heart."

"What a brilliant plan, ice-boy. Why didn't I think of that?" I sneered. "I'm telling you, this thing isn't like any monster we've faced before. Nothing seems to hurt it or slow it down. We stabbed it, poked it, blasted it with Summer, Winter, and Iron magic, and the thing barely sneezed. But by all means..." I waved a hand at him. "Feel free to shove your sword up its butt. The last time I tried poking it with the sharp end of my knives, I ended up with a few extra appendages." I tapped my forehead, smirking at him. "This is what happened to me, ice-boy. Just think of what the former Unseelie prince could become if it got its claws into *you*."

Ash stiffened at that, and Meghan's jaw tightened as a somber air descended around the campfire. We all knew, to varying degrees, what Ash was capable of should he turn, well... evil. Yeah, Robin Goodfellow was a dangerous menace that you didn't want to cross, and his pranks were a bit on the cruel side, but he wasn't a murder-hobo. I'd seen a glimpse of a—thankfully avoided—future where the son of Mab had basically flattened the entire Nevernever in a war that decimated all the courts and left all Faery a frozen wonderland. Oh yeah, and in that vision, he'd also killed me. Not something I wanted to undergo in real life.

Ash's expression darkened; I could tell he was starting to fall into that melancholy that sometimes overtook him when he remembered certain things about his past. But Meghan reached back, placing her hand on his forearm and squeezing gently. "That's not going to happen," she said. "Not with all of us here, supporting each other. There are rules in Faery. Nothing is completely indestructible."

"That is true, Iron Queen," came Grimalkin's voice near the firepit. The cat was curled up on a flat rock, as close to the flames as one could get without catching fire. How the cait sith's wispy gray fur hadn't spontaneously combusted yet was a mystery. "The Nevernever ensures that there is always something to exploit," the feline went on in a sage voice. "Some small weakness, no matter how slight or insignificant. A tiny hole in the dragon's armor, just big enough for an arrow." His gold eyes narrowed, and the claws on one foot flexed, scratching the rock. "Although, from what I have heard, I fear this beast might be different. I do not think it is fey, or anything that is part of the Nevernever."

"What is it, then?" Ash wondered. "If it's not part of Faery, what are we dealing with?"

The cat gave him an impatient look and thumped his tail. "If I knew that, prince," he said, "we would not be here in the Briars, chasing down a group of Forgotten to ask *them* what it is."

"You're a plague, Goodfellow."

I turned. Ash stood several yards away, his face shrouded in darkness from the canopy overhead, his features hidden. Only the neon-blue glow of his ice sword shone clearly through the gloom.

I grinned, showing all my teeth. "A plague, you say? I'm flattered, ice-boy. That sounds impressive." Drawing my knives, I twirled them in my hands and struck a pose, still smiling. "Let me show you the other thing I'm impressive at."

I lunged at him. He met me in the center of the clearing, sweeping down with his blade, as we began the dance we were both familiar with. Round and round we went, hacking, dodging, parrying, while indistinct faces appeared at the edges of the shadows and watched.

"You infect everything you touch," the prince spat at me as our blades flashed and clanged off one another's. "You're alone in the world because, sooner or later, everyone realizes you can't be trusted. That's why Meghan chose me. That's why Nyx will never want you."

"You know, I don't remember you being so obnoxious."

Ash stepped back, his blade falling to his side, to stare me down with cold silver eyes. I glared back, one corner of my mouth twisted in a sneer, as around us the figures silently watched and judged.

"Why are you still fighting me, Goodfellow?" Ash wondered, a smirk of his own creeping across his face. It transformed him into something ugly and hateful, and I squeezed my daggers until the hilts bit into my palm. "You lost. Meghan loves me, and nothing will change that. I've already won."

"I wouldn't celebrate just yet, prince." I stalked toward him, feeling hate and glamour swirl around me like a whirlwind. "You could still lose everything. After all, I'm still alive."

I lunged at him, stabbing my daggers right for his offensively pretty face...and the world disappeared.

I opened my eyes. The fire in the pit had burned low, and the sky was still pitch-black through the trees. Carefully, I sat up, gazing around for the others. Grimalkin was gone, typical for him, but I could see the red glow of Coaleater under a tree several yards away, equine head bent low as he slept standing upright. I wondered when he had changed into horse form, and also if he found sleeping upright more comfortable. I didn't see Nyx anywhere, but I wasn't too worried about the assassin; if she was on watch, she was probably stalking the woods around the camp, silent and unseen and looking for things to stab.

Across the fire, Meghan dozed in Ash's arms, with the Ice Prince leaning against a tree and both their swords out and within easy reach. And though ice-boy looked like he was sleeping soundly, I knew that was often a lie. All it would take was one twig to snap and he'd be on his feet, already slashing at whatever had made the noise. Years of trying to sneak up on him had taught me to be wary even when I thought he was unconscious.

But it had also taught me the difference between the times he was conscious and those brief moments when he was truly asleep.

Like now.

Memories of the dream trickled back to me, seeping anger and resentment into my veins. I felt a slow smile stretch across my face as I rose, gazing down at them, at the slumbering Ice Prince in particular.

Well, don't you look comfortable, ice-boy. I don't think you're taking me very seriously, to be so relaxed. Maybe it's time I did something about that...

"Can't sleep, Goodfellow?"

I jumped, nearly falling into the firepit. "Geez, Nyx," I whispered, turning to find her crouched silently on a rock a few feet away, crescent blades held loosely in her fingers, eyes glowing yellow in the darkness. "Not that I mind the whole guardian-angel-of-death thing you've got going on, but could you not loom so menacingly?"

"Why not? I'm very good at it."

"No argument there." I scrubbed a hand over my chin as the assassin continued to watch me, unblinking. "But it's still a few hours till dawn, and now that I'm up I might as well take watch. Maybe you should try to get some sleep?"

She gave me a faint, knowing smile. "I can't," she said simply, keeping her voice barely above a whisper. "I'm a nocturnal fey, Puck. I don't sleep at night. I'm not even sure I could if I wanted to."

"Really? That's unfortunate. Sleeping is one of my favorite things to do, after all. And all the activities that come before sleeping as well."

Whoops, did I just say that out loud? I eyed the Forgotten, wondering if she would take offense, ready to leap back should she hurl a moonlight shuriken at me. She gave a weird little smirk beneath the hood and rose, brushing the cowl back so that the light spilled over her silver hair.

"I, too, enjoy the activities that come before sleeping," she said. "Quite a lot, in fact. Come find me, and I'll show you what they are."

And before my eyes, she shimmered, like a beam of moonlight across a glass window, and disappeared.

"O-kaaaaaaay." I shot a look at Meghan and Ash, still dozing against the trunk. Despite my earlier feelings, I didn't exactly want something to jump them while they were asleep. If I went prancing off into the woods without explanation, they might be cross if some big nasty ambushed them while I was gone. Though honestly, those two would be fine. Meghan was the Iron Queen, and Ash was Ash. They didn't need me watching over them.

The glint of a single golden eye pierced the darkness as I stood there, debating with myself. From an overhead branch, Grimalkin gave me a bored look, then closed his eye again, curling his tail around his nose.

That decided it. If Furball was unconcerned, then there was

no danger. I turned my back on the sleeping pair and slipped away, into the woods where I hoped the shadowy Forgotten had vanished to.

Turns out, I didn't have to search far. Making my way into a tiny grove surrounded by shadowy pine, I paused as, with a shimmer from the corner of my eye, Nyx slid from the shadows like a ghost. She wasn't smiling, her eyes were hard, and those lethal crescent blades glimmered in the darkness as she circled me like a beautiful, dangerous phantom.

I swallowed, resisting the urge to draw my own weapons as she stalked closer, moving with liquid grace over the ground. "Um, okay, then. Obviously, we were thinking of vastly different things. Is this how your Order starts everything off, then? With a ritual stabbing?"

She didn't stop, continuing to glide toward me, and nothing in her gaze or stance said she was playing around. She looked entirely serious about stabbing me.

I backpedaled a few steps, but my hoof caught on an uneven root and nearly dumped me on my backside. "Nyx, wait," I said as the Forgotten closed in. "Hold up. Can you just stop for a second, please?" I raised my empty hands in the universal gesture of *I don't want to fight you*, and the assassin finally halted. "I will admit, I'm a little confused as to what's happening here," I said, holding her gaze. "If you've brought me out here to kill me, you could've just stabbed me in my sleep and saved yourself the trouble."

For a few seconds, the Forgotten stared at me, her expression flat and dangerous in the moonlight. For a second, I thought I might have to defend myself from a deadly, highly efficient killer who was just as fast as me, whom I did not want to fight for many reasons. Finally, though, she let out a small, slightly frustrated sigh and lowered her weapons, allowing me to breathe again.

"I can't figure you out, Goodfellow." Nyx glared at me across the clearing, her gaze both angry and conflicted. "I want to believe you're honorable, that you're loyal to your friends, that you're someone I can trust. But then, I see *him*..." she gestured to my forehead with the hilt of her blade "...and it makes me wonder who you really are. It makes me wonder if I can trust anything about you."

I smirked, unable to stop the flippancy that came from my mouth even now. "You and everyone else in the Nevernever."

"That is not reassuring, Puck." Nyx narrowed her eyes, un-amused. "I'm a Forgotten," she went on. "I feel the glamour auras around me more keenly than most. And yours is...fright-ening. There is a viciousness inside you that is fighting to get out, and once it does, I'm afraid of what it might do. And what *I* might be forced to do in return."

"I know." I scrubbed my fingers through my hair, wincing as they hit my horns. "You're not really seeing me at my best," I told her. "This..." I raised my arms in a helpless gesture. "I haven't been this guy in a long time. I honestly thought I got rid of him. Turns out he was always there, just buried."

Nyx circled closer, a graceful predator with glowing yellow eyes. "What changed?"

"It's a rather long, boring story. Do you really want to get into it right here?"

"Well, it's either that or keep wondering if I should kill you or not."

"Always with the stabbing." I sighed. "Fine. Sit down, get some popcorn, and I'll tell you the sordid tale of how Robin Goodfellow grew a conscience."

"A long time ago," I began in a grand voice, "in a galaxy far, far away... Wait, hold up. Wrong story. Lemme try that again."

"A long time ago," I went on, ignoring the impatient look from Nyx, "Oberon banished me from the Nevernever. It was the first time he had ever banished me, but no one was surprised. For years, Titania had demanded that he exile me from the court, but it was Mab who finally convinced him. Basically, she gave him the choice—either banish me, kill me, or go to war with Winter. I…uh…might've really pissed her off that year. I won't go into details, but there was a high and mighty Winter noble who chased a Summer faery into a cavern and somehow got himself eaten by a dire weasel. Unfortunately, unknown to the Summer faery, that noble was the Winter Queen's current boy toy. And she was not at all happy about his sudden demise, accidental as it was."

Nyx shook her head, a faint smile quirking one side of her mouth, but she didn't say anything.

"Anyway," I went on, "that was too much for Mab to handle, and since Oberon didn't want a war with the Unseelie right then, he exiled me from Faery. Forever."

"Forever," Nyx repeated, and shook her head. "Didn't seem to take."

"Yeah, you noticed that, did you?" I shrugged. "Eventually, Oberon rescinded the exile, but we'll get to that in a minute. Point is, this was the first time I'd ever been banished from Faery. I really did think it might be forever."

"What did you do?"

"Wandered for a bit. Several years, actually. I traveled the human world, hung around a few places for a while, but I always moved on. I traveled, played pranks, inspired a few folk legends and horror stories, and generally tried to keep myself entertained. Those first few years were actually kind of freeing… I wasn't part of the Summer Court any longer. Oberon wasn't looming over my shoulder, ordering me around. True, there was always the danger of Fading, but back then mortals still believed in magic and the fey, and technology hadn't taken off yet, so the risk of Fading wasn't quite so severe. I can't lie and say I didn't miss the Nevernever and the Summer Court, but for the first time, I was actually free."

A shadow crossed the Forgotten's face; the notion of freedom, or the distinct lack of it, was all too familiar for her. The difference between us was Nyx never questioned her service to the Lady, never deliberately defied her orders just to prove that she could. Guess I was just a rebel at heart.

"Eventually," I went on, "I ended up near this tiny village in Wales. I don't remember exactly where, but I was in the forest one day, not really doing anything, when this little kid wandered through. She couldn't have been more than five or six, and was obviously very lost. She was wailing like a bean sidhe, and also attracting every goblin and bugbear in the area. I was, admittedly, a bastard back then, but even I didn't really want to watch a kid get eaten alive by a bugbear, so I introduced myself and offered to take her home."

"A human child," Nyx repeated. "That young, they can still See us as we are. The Mist has no effect on them yet."

"Yep. She called me Funny Goat Man the entire way home." I chuckled at the memory. It had been so long ago, another lifetime, really. But I still remembered that girl's smile, her small fingers clinging tightly to my own. "Her name was Drysi, and when she was safely back at her cottage, she asked if I would come play with her and her friends the next day. Naturally, I told her I would."

Nyx nodded in understanding. Children, especially young kids, were irresistible to faeries, and don't take that the wrong way. They had the brightest glamour aura, and young kids could still see the hidden world and the creatures that were invisible to adults. They believed in faeries, magic, and monsters under the bed. And while there were always goblins, witches, and ogres who would love nothing more than to eat a lost, wandering child, there were many of us who delighted in playing with a human who could See us and wasn't afraid. Ever known a kid who had an imaginary friend? More than likely, that friend was a faery.

"I went back the next day," I went on. "And the next. And the day after that. I hung around that village for nearly fifteen years. And I watched that kid grow up. When it got to the point where she couldn't See me anymore, I glamoured myself to look like a human boy, just so we could keep being friends. And after a while, I became part of that village, too. Drysi was..." I sighed, shaking my head. "She was an incredible mortal. Strong and fearless, but always wanting to take care of others. When the village was attacked by raiders, she was right there on the front lines, swinging a staff without any regard for herself." I gave a wicked smirk. "Course, I might've taught her how to fight, and Drysi wanted to learn, despite being forbidden to do so by the elders of the village. She didn't have a sword, but we would sneak out to the sheep pasture and practice with staffs and staves, until she was a match for any human. Those raiders certainly got a shock when they tried manhandling her. And they didn't know the village was under the protection of Robin Goodfellow." My grin turned vicious as I remembered the carnage, the screams, and the terror of the attackers. "It was not a good day to be a raider.

"I was going to kill them all," I went on, "but Drysi stopped me. By that time, most of them were running away. I was going to make sure they never came back, but she begged me to be merciful. She said that taking a life, no matter whose it was or what they had done, was a stain upon your soul. Not terribly concerning to me, since the fey don't have souls. But hey, who was I to deny a pretty face? She didn't want me to kill them, so I let them go."

Nyx cocked her head, regarding me in that intense, appraising way of hers. "Were you in love with this mortal?" she asked.

"No." I shook my head. "I was fond of her, and she was the first human I considered a friend, but I wasn't in love with her. I was still a bit too fey for that, if you know what I mean.

"Unfortunately," I went on, "I couldn't say the same for Drysi.

One night, a few months after the attack on the village, she confessed that she loved me."

Nyx's gaze narrowed. "And what did you do with this revelation?" she asked.

I sighed. "I was going to give her what she wanted," I began. "I was fey, and there was this pretty girl who admitted to being in love with me. Any normal faery would've taken advantage of that. But..." I frowned, shaking my head. "I couldn't go through with it. For the first time, I felt guilty about what I was doing. Even though I had no idea what this strange new sensation was, I didn't want to hurt her.

"I left the next morning," I continued. "Turned my back on the village and disappeared into the forest again. It was better that way. I couldn't be around Drysi anymore, not with what I knew. A human falling in love with a faery never ends well. And I couldn't give her what she wanted. So, it was best that I moved on."

"And the human?"

"I made sure she wouldn't remember me," I said. "The rest of the village was easy. When you're fey, humans tend to forget you were ever there. The memory of the human boy who had appeared out of nowhere one day would just fade from everyone's minds. Drysi was a little harder... She loved me, and that tends to make forgetting difficult. I did end up using glamour to make her forget. I didn't want her to spend the rest of her days pining after the boy who disappeared with no warning or explanation. I wanted her to be free. Frankly, it ended up being the best decision. A few months later, Oberon called me back into the Nevernever. My exile was over, and I had to return to Faery and the Summer Court.

"But when I came back..." I raised both arms in a shrug. "I wasn't the same Robin Goodfellow. I had changed. I started calling myself Puck, to further separate myself from the faery I was before. The name stuck, though most of the Nevernever still treats them as one and the same. I know the difference, though, even if the rest of Faery never lets you forget what you did in the past."

"And what happened to the girl? Did you ever see her again?"

"I did, actually. As soon as I could get away from Oberon, I went back to the mortal world, to the village I left behind. I thought it had been a couple years, but time flows differently in the Nevernever. Drysi was a grandmother by then, a village elder, with a horde of children and grandkids frolicking around her. She had definitely moved on.

"So, that's my tale." I crossed my arms, giving the Forgotten a challenging look. "How Robin Goodfellow went from being a jackass to a less egregious jackass. All because of a mortal, and the power of *loooove*." I snorted and rolled my eyes. "I haven't told that little story to anyone, you realize. Not even Meghan and ice-boy. I'd appreciate it if you didn't mention it to anyone, either. Sometimes it's a good thing the rest of the Nevernever doesn't realize that Puck has a conscience.

"So," I continued, watching the other faery's reaction. Nyx hadn't moved any closer, though the moonlight blades in her hands had not disappeared. "What's the verdict, Miss Stoic Assassin? Kill me now for the threat Robin Goodfellow represents, or take a chance with Puck?"

Nyx considered me, her face unreadable...before she shimmered into moonlight and disappeared. I had about a second to be surprised before a curved, shining blade was pressed against my throat from behind.

A soft chuckle escaped me. "Wow, I can't believe I fell for that," I muttered, feeling the Forgotten's presence at my back. The sword edge hovered against my skin, cold and razor sharp for being made of light. "Well, Miss Assassin? I'm still waiting. What's it to be?"

"It depends." Nyx leaned closer, bringing her lips to my ear, her breath cool on my skin. "Can I trust you, Puck?"

"I don't know." I wanted to shrug, but that was kind of hard with a sword at my throat. "Honestly, I don't really trust myself right now. I'm not completely *him*, though. Not yet."

"Not much of an assurance, Goodfellow."

"Here's one more, then." My hands shot up, striking her elbow and forcing the blade from my throat. At the same time, I twisted in her grasp, sliding out and grabbing her wrist. A half second later, it was Nyx backed against a tree with my dagger over her heart. "I'm not going to do anything to jeopardize this mission," I told her as she froze. "I fully intend to find this monster and stick it with knives until it dies properly this time. And if that changes me back, then so be it. Truthfully, that's probably the best outcome. No one likes a horny Robin Goodfellow."

"I wouldn't go that far." Nyx stepped closer, the faint smile and the look on her face making my heart pound. Her hand reached up, long fingers caressing the wrist that held the dagger...before she grabbed it and spun with preternatural speed, tripping me and tossing me to the forest floor. With a grunt, I hit the ground on my back, the assassin straddling my chest and my own blade at my neck.

Smirking, I gazed up at the Forgotten, who stared back with a cool, triumphant look on her face. "Are we going to do this dance all night, then?"

"Is there something else you would like to do all night?"

"I can think of a few things."

One more time, I flipped her, pinning the Forgotten to her back and reclaiming my dagger. The knife once more hovered at her throat as I pressed her down. "Unless you're ready to admit defeat."

She smiled at me, and I realized her hands were not empty, after all. I suddenly caught the glimmer of a moonblade, pointed at a part of me that I really did not want it to be pointed at. Nyx's grin was wicked as she met my gaze. "Don't be so smug,

Goodfellow. If I have to admit defeat, I'm at least taking a trophy with me."

"Okay, okay." With a grimace, I dropped the dagger, raising both hands in surrender. "I concede. You win, though that was a dirty cheater move, Miss Assassin."

"This from the one they call the Great Prankster." Nyx shifted to get more comfortable, though she did not release the blade in her hand. "Aren't dirty cheater moves your specialty?"

"That doesn't mean they should be done to *me*," I protested, making her snort. "One, some things are sacred. And two, I notice you're not making the sharp stabby thing go away."

"Just want to ensure your continued good behavior," Nyx replied easily. "I know you have another weapon on you, Goodfellow. If I make this disappear, how will I know you won't immediately try something sneaky?"

"Because I really want to kiss you now," I replied softly, suddenly very aware of my pounding heartbeat, my stomach tying itself into knots. "And having a knife in your groin makes it very difficult." It was useless trying to ignore this, to deny that the Forgotten hadn't wriggled her way under my skin. I was done trying to fight it. "If you don't want me to kiss you," I went on, "just say the word. But if you do, I'm going to be very distracted unless that stabby thing points somewhere else."

The Forgotten's gaze was suddenly hungry, golden eyes shining like a predator's. But she still hesitated, her voice turning grave. "Didn't you just say you weren't certain that I could trust you?"

"I did," I husked out. "And you probably shouldn't. I will fully admit that my head is screwed up and I'm not the person I was. Say the word, and we can go back to camp and have Furball shoot us smug looks all night. But I thought… I was hoping I wasn't alone in this."

Nyx hesitated. I held my breath, counting my heartbeats, feeling my stomach coil and twist like an agitated snake. The faery's expression was haunted, fighting an inner battle with herself. Then, without warning, she sat up, shoved me in the chest, and toppled me backward. I hit the ground on my back again, my wrists pinned to the forest floor and her lips pressed against mine.

I groaned, all my nerve endings standing at attention. The Forgotten was not timid; her lips caressed mine a few moments before moving down my neck, making me gasp and arch my head back. I finally freed my hands and slid them up her arms, burying my fingers in her silver hair and pulling her closer. Her palms traced down my chest, slender fingers leaving trails of icy heat, making me shiver where they passed.

Abruptly, the Forgotten sat up, straddling my waist, her hands resting lightly on my stomach. I gazed up at her, watching her hair spill around her shoulders like a silvery veil, her lithe body perched above me. Her expression was hungry but conflicted, golden eyes shadowed as they met mine.

"Nyx." My voice came out as a whisper. "You okay? Having second thoughts?"

She shook her head, and her voice, when she answered, was barely audible in the stillness. "Just…promise me one thing, Puck. Tell me this doesn't mean anything to you."

Stunned, I stared at her, my mind spinning in confusion. Not what I had been expecting, or really wanted to hear. "Is that what you think of me?" I asked. "That this is just a game?"

"We are fey, Puck." Nyx's voice was unapologetic. "This is what we do, no emotions, no attachments involved. One night of fun, and we can move on. We can forget it ever happened."

My stomach clenched. That had been true, once. There had been a time, before I'd met Drysi, when Robin Goodfellow could seduce anything that moved. I knew I was good-looking; by most standards, some might say I'm irresistible. Species, gender, human, fey, it didn't matter. All I had to do was turn up the charm, put a little smolder in my gaze, and I'd be golden.

But that was the old Robin Goodfellow, the carefree faery

without a conscience. I wasn't like that now. Which meant I hadn't turned into him completely, that there was still a bit of Puck left inside.

Before I could answer, Nyx closed her eyes, and a tiny shiver went through her. "I shouldn't be here," she murmured, making my insides tie themselves into a knot. "I swore I wouldn't let emotions get in the way of my work again."

"Again?" I repeated softly, making her wince. "I take it this has happened before?"

"Once," she began, and sighed. "A long time ago. But since this seems to be the night of confessions…" She shifted off my chest, settling beside me in the dirt with her legs crossed. Taking a deep breath, she let it out slowly. "I was in love with someone, once," she murmured. "He died." She hesitated, looking uncertain and ashamed for the first time I had known her. "By my own hand."

My mouth went dry. "Nyx. You don't have to tell me this if you don't want to."

"No." The Forgotten raised her head, her face grim. "No, before we go any further, this is something you need to hear. His name was Varyn, and he was a member of my Order, a moon elf like me. We did a few missions together, we killed when we were called upon, and we protected the Lady like all members of the Order. He was utterly loyal to her. We both were. We would've given our lives for our queen without hesitation.

"One night," Nyx went on, "we were returning to court after a successful mission, when were attacked by a…a…" Her brow furrowed. "I don't remember its name. Which probably means it doesn't exist anymore. But it was big and fast, and since we were still fighting it when the sun came up, it nearly killed us both. Varyn was badly wounded, and after we finally defeated it, we took shelter in a cave to wait out the sun. And…things happened.

"That was the beginning," Nyx went on. "After that, we

started spending more time together. He was an amazing warrior, like you." She paused, the faintest of smiles crossing her face. "Though he had a much better sense of humor."

"What?" I exclaimed. "Impossible. Those are fighting words, I'll have you know."

The smile faded. "After a time," she went on, "it just seemed natural that he was always there, always a part of me. We were each other's shadows. Where one was, the other wasn't far, watching from the darkness. We really should have known better.

"I told you the Lady was a jealous ruler," Nyx continued, and a very uncomfortable prickle ran down my spine as it began to dawn on me where this was going. "After a while, she didn't approve of me and Varyn spending so much time together. She disliked having our attention and loyalties split. So, one night, she called Varyn before her and told him that his next target… was me."

I bit my cheek, anger, horror, and sympathy a raging storm in my head. "Damn," I breathed. "I knew I hated her for a reason. Did he…?"

"Varyn was loyal to his queen to the end." The Forgotten's voice was matter-of-fact, though her eyes were faraway, lost in memory. "He tried to end it quickly, but I wasn't quite ready to die just yet. We fought for nearly the whole night. I pleaded with him to stop, begged him that we could find another way, but he had his orders, and he couldn't disobey the Lady.

"In the end…" Despite herself, Nyx's voice trembled. She clenched a fist, taking a breath to compose herself. "In the end, one of us had to die. Varyn was skilled but…I had always been the better killer. It was quick at least. He didn't suffer. But right before he died, he told me he was sorry, that he loved me but he couldn't betray the queen. And I understood that."

Nyx paused, that unruffled mask falling into place again as she glanced up. "I told myself then I wouldn't make the same mistake," she said. "Love and emotion...they have no place in the life of an assassin. That's what I've been telling myself ever since I met you. That's why it would be better if you didn't feel anything."

"Too late." My insides wouldn't stop twisting around. Carefully, I sat up, bracing myself with one arm, to be eye level with Nyx. Reaching out, I brushed a strand of hair from her eyes, tucking it behind one pointed ear. She gazed at me, looking unexpectedly vulnerable, and my heart gave that weird little flutter I'd felt only a few years ago. "Dammit," I sighed. "Last time I said something like this, I got burned pretty bad, but... I *can't* say that this means nothing to me. And if I end up with a sword through my middle, well, that's a chance I'm willing to take. If you are."

"This isn't going to end well." Nyx eyed me warily but didn't pull back. "I don't want to have to kill you, Puck. I don't want to go through that again."

I gently put a hand on her cheek, making her blink at me. "I'm not Varyn," I murmured. "And the Lady isn't here anymore. No one, Keirran especially, is going to order you to take a life, I can assure you of that. And if it gets to the point where you feel you have to kill me yourself, then I probably deserved it." I attempted a wry smile that she didn't return. "This is mostly your fault, you know," I went on, stroking her skin with my thumb. "You can't be completely beautiful and funny and amazing and expect me not to notice. I'll make you a deal, though."

Surprise and caution flickered across her face. You couldn't say the words *deal*, *price*, or *bargain* around a faery without raising red flags. Or without provoking an instinctive curiosity. "What kind of a deal?"

I rose, pulling her up with me. "We put this on hold for now," I said. "Until you decide what you want to do. I don't like it, but I have been known to have patience if pressed hard enough." She blinked, gazing at me with those solemn gold eyes, and I stifled the urge to kiss her again. "Nyx, if you're not comfortable with me, or any of this, then I'll wait. Robin Goodfellow isn't a complete barbarian all the time. I want you to decide that it's worth it, after all."

"I want to trust you, Puck," Nyx said quietly. "But everything is so uncertain. I'm not sure if I can trust myself, much less anyone else. Maybe when this is over, when Keirran and the Forgotten are safe, when we finally kill that monster, maybe then we can travel the Nevernever and see all the things you talked about." She paused, and then a small smile spread across her face. Looping her arms around my neck, she gave me that intense, appraising look that made my stomach squirm. "So, I guess you have a deal, Robin Goodfellow. Maybe I won't end up killing you after all."

"That is the plan," I said, sliding my arms around her waist. "Not getting killed by beautiful assassins is something I aspire to every day. Right after not getting eaten by a dragon and not letting Titania turn me into a rosebush."

A small chuckle escaped her. "I find it amusing that turning into a rosebush happens more often than assassination attempts on your life."

"Believe me, she tries it at least once a year. I end up pulling thorns and rose petals out of my hair for a month afterward."

The Forgotten laughed again. Standing on her toes, she leaned up and kissed me, turning my insides into a dancing pretzel party. I closed my eyes, putting my life in her hands, and let the Lady's assassin do with me what she would.

16

THORN SISTERS AND CRANKY TREES

There were many in the Nevernever who, despite living in the wyldwood their entire life, had never seen the Briars, didn't even know what they looked like. Which I found absolutely hilarious, because once you saw them, the Briars were impossible to miss. It was hard to see an endless wall of writhing, slithering brambles looming fifty feet in the air with bright red thorns longer than your arm and think, *Oh, that's normal.*

Beside me, Coaleater stared up at the shifting wall of thorns and let out a snort. "So, these are the infamous Briars," he muttered. "As I understand it, Ironhorse went through them once with you and the Iron Queen, Goodfellow."

"Yep," I answered. "Fun times, that. If you like running into things like dragons, murderous piskie swarms, and hedge wolves. Oh, and spiders the size of Volkswagens, those are always fun."

Nyx frowned. "What is a Volkswagen?"

Her voice sent my stomach into a mess of squirming knots again. My senses were still buzzing from last night's kiss, and the dark confessions we'd both shared. I still didn't know if I would actually survive a relationship with the Forgotten Queen's former assassin, but I did know that I was done trying to fight it. I might have my heart broken, by a literal dagger this time, but what was life without a bit of risk?

"It's a car," Meghan replied, appearing in front of us. "A type of vehicle from the mortal world. And thank you, Puck, for reminding me of that." Her nose wrinkled with the memory. I grinned. For all her bravery, wisdom, and incredible power, the Iron Queen was still a half mortal named Meghan Chase who disliked spiders almost as much as I did.

"Anytime, princess. Wouldn't want you forgetting all the fun times we had in the thorns, would we?"

She grimaced, mirroring my own thoughts. Truthfully, I was not really looking forward to this. Not because the Briars were one of the most stupidly dangerous places in the Nevernever, but they had an alarming concentration of creepy, skittery things with more than four legs. I had been through the thorns more times than I could count, and I still did not relish the thought of tromping through them once more.

Ash prowled up behind Meghan and softly touched her shoulder. Briefly, his gaze met mine, solemn with memory, and my stomach twisted. I knew, suddenly, what he was thinking. The last time I had been through the Briars, it had been with Ash on his quest to get a soul. We had traveled all the way through the thorns, and beyond the Briars we had found the End of the World, where the shadowy Guardian had put Ash through a series of impossible tests. Or at least, they were supposed to be impossible. No fey had succeeded in overcoming them. But Ash had survived, passing all the trials the Guardian threw at him, and in the end, became the first faery to ever earn his soul, all so he could be with Meghan in the Iron Realm.

Ash had gone to the End of the World to be with Meghan. But I had gone to the End of the World for her, too. Because I'd loved her and I wanted her to be happy, even if it wasn't with me. And the most ironic part? Ash was strong, but he wouldn't have made it to the End of the World on his own. If I hadn't been there, the Winter prince probably would have died.

Turns out, Fate has a pretty twisted sense of humor.

I smirked at Ash, earning a wary frown from the former Ice Prince. "What about you, ice-boy?" I challenged. "We've had some good times in the Briars, haven't we? Hey, remember that time we stumbled into the spider queen's nest, and you ended up webbed and wrapped up on the ceiling?"

"That was both of us, Puck." Ash's voice was unamused. "And we only ended up that way because you had to grab that sword stuck in the webbing, which alerted the entire nest."

"Fascinating as this is," came Grimalkin's bored voice near our feet, "we are not here to recount amusing tales of large arachnids. If you would follow me, the castle should not be too far from here. As always, though I do not know why I continue to repeat myself as it never seems to take, I would advise caution and stealth while traveling through the thorns. Generally, giant spiders and all their kind should be avoided, I think we can all agree upon that."

"Yep, and if the cat poofs out on us, then we know something dangerous is coming to eat our faces," I added as Grimalkin turned and padded toward the wall of thorns. "It's not like we haven't done this a million times before, Furball."

As usual, Grimalkin pretended not to hear.

The Briars loomed over our heads, waving and rustling menacingly, bloodred thorns looking sharp enough to punch through an Iron knight's breastplate like it was made of Bubble Wrap. Grimalkin ducked beneath a tendril and vanished like a living cloud of smoke, but as we stepped closer, the branches shivered and began peeling back, revealing a long, narrow tunnel through the thorns and brambles.

The Briars were expecting us.

We stepped into the passage, and the entrance slithered shut behind us, plunging the corridor into shadows. Grimalkin's eyes seemed to float in the tunnel ahead, his furry body barely visible in the gloom. "This way. And do try not to get lost."

Coaleater snorted, filling the air with the tang of sulfur as we trailed after the cat. "Ironhorse traveled these very Briars with the Iron Queen even before she took the throne," he mused, gazing at the bristling walls on either side of us. "I cannot believe I am walking the same path as our progenitor, in the company of the queen and the very heroes of the last war." He tossed his head, the iron cables of his mane clanking against his neck and shoulders. "Let the giant spiders come. I will protect our queen with my life."

Meghan glanced over her shoulder with a smile, blue eyes affectionate as they settled on the Iron faery. "Hopefully there won't be any spiders this time," she said, one hand resting easily on her sword hilt. "We've learned a lot since then. When I first came through here with Ironhorse, I was younger, and much more..." She paused.

"Reckless?" Ash said quietly beside her.

"Impulsive," Grimalkin added up front without turning around.

"Prone to shrieking?" I put in, not about to be left out.

The Iron Queen glared at us all. "All those things, I suppose," she said in a flat voice that hinted at retribution later on. I would've been mildly alarmed, if it wasn't for Ash's almost-there smile. Coaleater looked uncomfortable, as if needling the queen of the Iron fey was something he wouldn't have dared try, but Nyx had a slight grin on her face.

The Iron Queen rolled her eyes. "So, yes, I was much younger then," she continued. "And we did run into several creatures that might have required a strategic retreat."

"You mean the piskie swarm, the giant spider, and the pissed-off dragon?" I snickered. "That's a fancy way of saying we ran away screaming like bean sidhes."

"Please keep the screaming like bean sidhes to a minimum," Grimalkin sighed from up ahead. "It alerts everything in a five-mile radius to our presence, which is something we are trying to avoid."

The Briars continued, an endless wall of thorns that were never still. You would think that after a while, the constant slithering, snapping, rustling sounds would just become white noise, but that was the special thing about the Briars: they never got to the point where you were comfortable. Every snapped twig, every moving branch or vibrating leaf reminded you that things lurked just out of sight in the darkness. And if you let down your guard for just a moment, something would reach through the brambles and drag you into the thorns.

As we moved deeper into said thorns, the tunnel suddenly opened up. We stepped from a tight, claustrophobic passage into a vast forest of vines. Huge, twisted branches, caught somewhere between a thornbush and a tree, rose up until they joined the interlocking web of briars far overhead. Thin streams of sunlight barely pierced the canopy, ribbons of light slicing down through the hanging darkness and casting mottled patches of gold over the ground. Monstrous vines, some of them in bloom, dangled from tree limbs, filling the air with the scent of rotting flowers, and the forest floor was carpeted in a blanket of moss several inches thick. Everything was tinted green, and in the cool, dim stillness, you could almost hear things growing.

Cautiously, we moved through the grove, feeling the ancientness of the place surround us. The ground under my hooves was spongy and thick, like we were walking on a giant angel cake, muffling our footsteps and absorbing all sound.

"So, anyone else have a craving for sponge cake?" I asked. And even though I kept my voice soft, it still seemed to reverberate through the grove, a too-loud intruder definitely out of place. Which, of course, just made me want to talk more.

Ash and Grimalkin gave me exasperated looks. "Do be aware

that we have entered Thorn Sister territory, Goodfellow," the cat chided, his tail flicking agitatedly back and forth. "They are not very tolerant of intruders and have been known to shoot first, ask questions later. Perhaps we should not risk attracting their—"

He didn't finish the sentence. One second, the cat was there, trotting over the ground, the next, he passed beneath a low hanging branch and vanished.

I groaned. "Looks like we already did."

Ash stopped and drew his sword. Meghan and I followed suit, as around us, figures seemed to melt out of the undergrowth like they were part of the brambles themselves. A dozen or so riders on the backs of very green, spiky deer with antlers resembling thorn branches. They looked like part of the Briars had come to life and twisted themselves into creatures resembling stags, draped with moss and bristling with thorns. The riders themselves were the same color as their mounts, thin and spindly elves with moss green hair and spiky black thorn armor. They were all female.

The deer surrounded us, the riders peering down with hard black eyes, arrows nocked but not pointed at us—not yet, anyway. They didn't say anything, either to threaten or ask questions, but the aura of silent menace that came from the group was obvious.

Meghan stepped forward, the persona of the Iron Queen settling over her like a mantle. Raising her head, she faced the warriors without a hint of fear. "I am Meghan Chase, queen of the Iron Realm," she announced in a clear, confident voice. "We want no trouble. My companions and I are simply passing through the Briars. If we have trespassed into your territory, I apologize, but I do ask that you move aside and let us through."

A soundless murmur went through the riders surrounding us, and the deer shifted nervously. Then, the largest of the stags, the one with a truly impressive rack of thorny antlers, stepped forward, parting the others before it. The rider atop the stag wore a headpiece that looked like it was made of brambles and bone, and a mossy green cape fluttered behind her.

For a moment, she gazed down at Meghan, who faced her calmly. Though Ash was a tightly coiled spring at Meghan's back, ready to explode into action if needed.

Then, in a surprisingly quick motion, the rider dismounted, took one step forward, and sank to a knee before the queen, bowing her head. I took a furtive breath, releasing the grip on my daggers as the tension, both in the riders and the rest of us, abated instantly.

"Iron Queen." The kneeling figure's voice was soft but raspy, like two branches slithering over one another. "The Thorn Sisters recognize your sovereignty and welcome you to our hunting grounds. You and your companions are free to come and go as you please. You will face no repercussions from us or the rest of our tribe.

"However," the Thorn Sister went on, and bowed a little lower, pressing both hands to the mossy floor, "we have a favor to ask of you, Iron Queen. We felt your approach on the wind. The thorns themselves spoke of your coming. We are hoping you will be able to help us."

"I can make no promises," Meghan replied gently. "But I will at least hear you. What is it you need of me?"

"A great shadow has come to our territory," the Thorn elf went on. "We share our hunting grounds with many creatures... With the hedge wolves and living mounds and the Stingfly piskie clan. Occasionally, our paths will cross, but we are all predators, and we respect each other's strengths, so there are few conflicts. But recently, something has changed. The treants, once our most peaceful neighbors, have become aggressive and violent. They wander through the Briars, attacking and killing anything they come across, and several of our warriors have fallen to their unprovoked attacks. We do not have the power or the numbers to survive a war with the treants, even if we wanted one. We were hoping they would listen to a queen of Faery."

"Treants are attacking people unprovoked?" Meghan echoed, frowning. "That's not like them at all. Have they given any reason for these assaults?"

"No, Your Highness." The Thorn Sister shook her head. "We don't know why they are so angry... They rebuff any of our attempts to speak with them peacefully. The only things they say, over and over again, are 'leave' and 'unclean.'"

"That is weird," I agreed.

The treants, enormous living, walking, sentient trees, were notorious for being nonviolent and peaceful, almost to the point of pacifism. Of course, being walking, talking trees, they didn't have many natural enemies unless the Briars were plagued by an infestation of giant beavers. Only the most depraved or callous could provoke a treant's wrath, but when they did become angry, oh boy, just get out of their way and let them do their thing, or risk being swatted like a mosquito. Fighting a treant was right up there with doing battle with an ancient dragon; it could be done, but it was going to be a long, difficult slog fest figuring out how to actually hurt the thing. Turns out, swords and daggers are not very effective in cutting down trees. Treants also had really, *really* long memories, and had been known to bide their time for centuries until they finally took their revenge, sometimes eons later.

In short, not something you wanted to piss off.

Meghan looked troubled. With a sigh, she turned to the rest of us. "I know we have to reach the castle quickly and find the Forgotten," she began, "but I feel this isn't something we can ignore, especially if people are dying."

"I agree," Ash said. "The treants should not be this hostile. Something is wrong, and we should get to the bottom of it, before it goes any further."

"Any objections from the rest of you?" Meghan asked, glancing at me.

I shrugged. "No arguments here, princess. I was *just* thinking it was nearly time for the 'something huge is trying to squish you' part of my day. Hey, did ice-boy ever tell you about the time we raced each other to the top of a tree, only to have that tree try to scratch us off once we got there?"

"Completely unprovoked, I'm sure," Meghan deadpanned, and turned to Nyx and Coaleater. "Are you two still with us?" she asked. "I won't force anyone to come. Treants can be dangerous when they're not being hostile. You can remain here, or I can send you on to the castle with Grimalkin."

"I am with you, Your Majesty," Coaleater said, almost before she finished speaking. "Whatever you must do, whatever needs to be done, I am here to aid you in all your decisions. That has always been the Iron herd's promise."

Nyx bowed her head but shot a quick glance at me before she did so. "I stand with the Iron Queen," was all she said.

"Where are the treants coming from?" Meghan asked, turning back to the Thorn Sister. Guess that meant we were going to chop down some talking trees. Or at least try to have a friendly conversation with them. Fine by me, I'd been wondering when the Briars would start getting interesting.

"Many of them have gathered in the Green Darkness," the elf replied, pointing a long finger in a random direction. "It is a pocket of wood that is deeper and more tangled than most, and lately the very land has started turning against us. We don't dare venture close anymore. Sometimes the treants wander as far as the borders of our camp, but most of them seem to return to that area."

"All right," Meghan said, stepping back. "We'll go check it out, see what has the treants so agitated. Until we can, I would have your people avoid the Green Darkness. With any luck, we can turn things back to normal soon."

"We appreciate it, Your Majesty." Rising, the Thorn Sister bowed again, then turned and swung atop her stag mount. "You have the gratitude of the Thorns. May the ground under your feet be clear, may the brambles never hinder your path, and may all your hunts be fruitful."

Meghan nodded. At a word from the leader, the group of mounted elves turned and leaped silently into the brambles, passing through the thorns as easily as a fish tossed back into the river. With the faintest of rustles, the briars closed behind them, and they were gone.

"Okay," I announced into the sudden silence. "Marching into hostile tree territory, nothing we haven't done before. Though I feel like I'm going to need an ax. A magic one preferably. Anyone have one of those lying around? They're usually gold, with a nice leather handle, and sometimes they sing."

"The treants should not be this hostile," Ash said with a slight frown, ignoring me. "Not without reason."

"Yes," Meghan agreed. "If something has angered them, then we need to find out what it is. That means we're going to try talking to them first. And let's hope they'll be interested in answering our questions, because I don't feel like fighting a mob of giant trees in the middle of the Briars."

"They will not attack the Iron Queen," Coaleater said, frowning at me but sounding a bit confused as well. "Even I have heard of the treants... They are among the oldest and wisest denizens of the Nevernever and have always recognized the kings and queens of Faery. To even think of threatening the queen is profane. It would be akin to the Summer knights turning on King Oberon or Queen Titania. Unless we are at war, Faery does not raise its hand to the rulers of the courts."

"Sorry, Rusty, but I think the fishpeople in the swamp would disagree with you. That might've been true before, but it seems all bets are off now."

"Yes," Meghan said gravely. "Which means we need to be very careful."

"Yep," I said. "But I still want an ax, just in case they're not interested in talking. Then I can really 'ax' them a question." I grinned and looked around at the somber faces, before rolling my eyes. "Really? Nothing? You guys suck."

"Have you noticed all these dark, tangled places have very nearly the same names?" I asked as we made our way deeper into the Briars, following the path the Thorn Sister had pointed out. "The Green Darkness, the Deep Tangled, the Dark Tangled Woods of Everdark and Gloomy? We never get to go to the Friendly Briars or the Cheery Tanglewood. Although, now that I think about it, that might be even scarier than the Dark Tangled Woods of Everlasting Doom."

"Goodfellow," Grimalkin sighed from up ahead. The cat had appeared once the stag riders had disappeared, announcing that he knew the way to the Green Darkness, because of course he did. "Must you make noise simply for the sake of making noise? How is any of this relevant?"

"Oh, come on. Where would you rather plunk down a nice cabin, the Dark Tanglewood or the Smiling Forest of Too Many Butterflies—"

Of course, that was when one of the many enormous trees we were passing beneath reached out and swung at me.

The party scattered, leaping back as a huge, moss-covered limb came crashing down right in the center of us all. It rose as the giant creature it was attached to stepped out of its perfectly camouflaged hiding spot and towered over us, thirty feet of gnarled, moss-covered tree person with clawlike hands and hollow eyes peering out of a lined, walnut-colored face.

"Leeeeeaaaave," it rumbled, glowering down at us. Its legs made the ground shake as it took a step forward, looming over us and blocking out the sky. "Leeeaaave, or I will crush you alllll."

"Forest guardian, stop!"

Meghan stepped forward, power snapping around her like lightning. "We are not your enemies," she called up to the living tree. "We are not here to hurt the forest or disturb any of your charges. If something has angered you, we want to set things right. Please, tell us what is wrong."

The treant's lined, gnarled face twisted in a grimace of disgust and rage.

"Unclean," it rumbled. "Infected. Flesh pods. Spreading your filth. Destroying all that is green." It swept a tree trunk limb into the air menacingly. "Leave this place. Leave. *Leeeeeeeeeeeeave.*"

The limb came crashing down toward Meghan, who threw up a hand as Ash tensed to spring at it. Summer glamour swirled around her, causing flowers to sprout and grass to grow at her feet. The treant's giant arm slowed, then came to a shuddering halt in midair. Its beady eyes bulged, and it strained against the magic holding it back, but it seemed to have hit an invisible wall. Or the magic of the Seelie King's daughter. The only being more powerful than Meghan when it came to Summer magic was Oberon himself.

"I don't want to hurt you," Meghan said, her voice slightly strained. "Please, stop this. We only wish to talk."

The treant roared. Dark purple-black thorns erupted from its back and shoulders, and its beady eyes turned red. Reeling back, it sank spiny fingers into the ground, and the earth around Meghan erupted with thick black briars that curled over her like a giant fist. I caught a split-second glimpse of Meghan throwing out her hands, and Ash going for his sword, before the spiky branches clenched shut and they disappeared beneath.

"Okay, peace talk's over!" I drew my blades as Coaleater let out an angry bellow and charged, fire streaming behind him. I felt my glamour surge to life, felt my body dissolve into dozens of tiny, feathery bodies that spiraled into the air and flapped angrily toward the tree man.

The treant turned toward us, red eyes blazing, and howled. One giant limb swooshed toward me, but the swarm of my bird selves veered aside. The few that did get caught exploded into small clouds of black feathers that drifted lazily toward the ground. The rest of them came on, cawing angrily as they swooped around its head.

From the bramble knot on the ground, there was a pulse of frigid blue light, a moment before the branches turned to ice, then shattered. Splinters and frozen thorns flew into the air, and an angry Ice Prince stepped from the frozen rubble, sword glowing blue in his hand. Behind him, Meghan shook brambles from her hair, brushing away leaves and twigs as she followed.

I dove from the rest of the flock and swooped toward them, changing to my regular self in a poof of feathers as I landed. "Princess, you okay?"

"Yes." Her voice was calm but resigned as she moved beside Ash, gazing up at the raging treant.

Coaleater stampeded around its gnarled ankles, kicking and breathing flames, while Nyx was a quicksilver shadow scrambling over its head and shoulders, moonlight blades flashing.

"It's not going to stop," Meghan sighed, watching the treant as it thrashed and bellowed in rage. One of its flailing limbs caught another tree, sending it crashing to the ground, and Meghan winced. "Dammit. I don't want to, but if we must do this, let's do it quickly." She glanced at us, her expression now resolved. "I'll need the treant to be completely still for a moment," she told us. "Not long, but it cannot move for at least five seconds. Can you and the others handle that?"

"Easy." Ash's smile was grim. Gripping his blade, he looked in my direction, raising an eyebrow. "Ready, Goodfellow?"

I felt a tiny flutter of vindictive defiance and squashed it down. "Just try to keep up, ice-boy."

We sprinted toward the giant, flailing tree in the center of the clearing. Coaleater had managed to set part of its foot on fire, and the treant was *not* happy with that little development. It howled and lashed out with a gnarled limb, finally catching the Iron faery in the shoulder and smacking him into the thorns. I heard an angry bugle over the crashing and snapping of branches, and figured the iron-encased horse was more annoyed than hurt.

"Oy, big ugly!" I bellowed. Ash paused, and I felt a pulse of Winter glamour go through the air as I continued to charge forward. "Look this way!"

The treant turned toward me, eyes blazing. With a roar, it sank its fingers into the earth, and thick black briars erupted from the ground, curling toward me like talons. I skidded to a stop, dodged a spiny branch that swiped at my head, and leaped through a knot of thorns that tried closing around me. More brambles surged into the air, and I grimaced. "Hey, ice-boy, you can help out anytime."

Through the writhing branches, I saw Ash drop to one knee and sink his blade point down into the earth. A ripple of freezing glamour spread out from the point of the sword, but directed underground instead of on the surface. Suddenly, the thrashing, flailing brambles and thorns surrounding me slowed, then stopped moving as a thick layer of ice crept up the stalks, freezing them in place with sharp crinkling sounds.

The treant gave a bellow of surprise and rage and tried pulling back, but his fingers were frozen solid now, and he couldn't break free of the ice.

I grinned viciously. "What's the matter, spiky? Got a bit of the frostbite on the ol' fingers, there?" Ducking beneath the ice-covered brambles, I raced up to the giant and leaped onto a gnarled leg. Now that the treant wasn't thrashing around, it was much easier to balance on the giant tree without being tossed about like a ship in a storm.

Nyx dropped beside me, golden eyes glittering with a dangerous light. Her moonblades were in her hands, and bits of twigs and leaves were caught in her hair as she shook her head, glaring up at the monster tree. "I can't reach its heart. It's too well protected."

I smiled, strangely proud that she knew that. One of the only reliable ways to kill a treant was to stab it in the heart, which, if you could reach it, was oodles easier than chopping or hacking at the monster tree until it died or squished you like a bug. Unfortunately, treants hid their hearts in weird places, like the soles of their feet or their armpits, and protected them behind layers of bark and thick wooden skin. You had to literally peel back their armor to get to the heart, and no treant was going to sit still and let you do that.

Fortunately, we had a few tricks up our sleeve, too.

"Worry not, Miss Assassin," I told the dubious Forgotten beside me. "This overgrown topiary is already chopped, it just doesn't know it yet."

I reached for my Summer glamour, sent it deep into the ground and felt the earth respond. Leafy vines erupted from the dirt, slithering up the treant's legs. They coiled around its ankles and wrapped around its limbs, anchoring it to the ground. If the treant hadn't already been occupied, such a trick wouldn't have worked, but the monster tree was a little distracted with a very bad case of frostbite, so the vines continued their journey until they reached the thing's chest, then continued to slither up toward its head.

"That's not going hold it for long," Nyx said calmly, watching the creeper vines coil around the massive tree.

I grinned. "We don't need long," I told her, and raised a dagger with a wink. "Just long enough for this."

Across the clearing, another ripple of magic went through the air, only much more powerful. The Iron Queen, wielding the glamour of both Summer and Iron, blending them together in the way only she was capable of. The magic raced across the ground and sank into the vines tangling the treant, and the little creeper vines swelled into thick brambles, ropy and flexible but tough as steel. The treant gave a roar as it was suddenly encased in a knot of trunks and branches. It thrashed, rocking its huge body from side to side, making the brambles shake and creak violently, but it wasn't going anywhere.

I grinned at Nyx, who was watching all this unfold with a stunned look on her face. "Things are a little different when you've got a queen behind you. So, where did you say its heart was, again?"

She blinked and shook herself, then pointed a moonblade toward the treant's chest. "Under the left shoulder," she replied, "right below where the collarbone would be, if treants had bones."

I tipped an imaginary hat to the Forgotten and leaped onto an overhead branch, making my way up to the top. The treant's shiny black eyes suddenly fixed on me, and its lined face contorted with loathing.

"Filth," it rumbled. "Flesh pods, destroying everything you touch. Kill you all. Crush your bones, turn you to rot, feed you to the roots."

"Sorry, big guy." I hauled myself up the final branch, so that I was right below the monster tree's face, looking at the spot Nyx had pointed out. It was covered with thick wooden plates, but between the cracks, I could see a faint pulse of greenish light. "Afraid you're not going to be crushing anyone's bones today."

"Insects," the treant howled as I took a step toward the pulsing light. "Filthy destroyers of all that is green. Kill you all! Return you to the earth. Feed your tainted blood to the worms and saplings. The Mother wishes it."

The Mother wishes it? I felt a chill crawl down my back as I raised a hand, Summer glamour flaring to life once more. *Okay, that's not good. It's definitely time to end this.* Closing my eyes, I felt the connection to the magic and everything it touched, the earth, the forest, even the treant beneath me. The monster tree was strong, but it was still a tree, and I was Robin Goodfellow. The forest, and every living flower, sprout, and tree within it, bent to *my* will.

The plates covering the green light shuddered, then peeled back like a flower opening. A cloud of darkness billowed out of the crack, smelling of rot and decay and anger. It buzzed around my head like flies, and the onslaught of rage, loathing, and hatred that accompanied it made my head spin.

With a splintering crash, the ice covering the brambles shattered. The treant wrenched its arms free, surging up with a roar, and I lost my footing on the narrow branch. As I fell backward, I saw the treant's arm, spiny claws gleaming like polished wood, coming right at me, and I changed into a raven just before the thorny talons sliced the air overhead.

Wheeling around, I ducked the other arm and flapped over its head, intending to spin around and finish the job. There was no need. Nyx leaped off its shoulder, swung on a vine, and drove her blade through the glowing hole I'd opened in the treant's chest.

An ear-piercing wail rang out. The treant staggered, curling its arms around itself, and swayed in place for a half second. Quickly, I swooped to a branch, changing into my normal self as Nyx vaulted off the treant into the boughs of a tree and Ash scrambled out of the way.

"Timber!" I called as the monstrous tree crashed face-first to the ground with a rumble that shook the forest floor.

We waited until the dust settled and the forest was still again before dropping to the ground and warily approaching the fallen giant. The treant's face was turned toward us, but the light had gone from its eyes, the magic that had sustained its life missing. It looked like a huge, vaguely man-shaped pile of moss and branches, rotting in the dirt.

A somberness descended as Meghan and Ash joined us in staring at the dead treant. This wasn't like slaying a dragon or some vicious monster that had tried to swallow you whole. The treants were near immortal, or they might as well be with how long they lived. Regardless of age, they had always been revered as the wise, peaceful guardians of the forest. Killing one felt like an affront to Faery itself.

The Iron Queen let out a long sigh, a pained look crossing her face as she gazed at the once living tree. "I'm sorry," she murmured. "I wish we could have spoken, but I had no choice." Her mouth thinned before she glanced around at the rest of us. "Is everyone all right? Any injuries?"

"Only my pride," Coaleater muttered, shaking leaves from his mane as he stomped up, swishing his tail in an irritated fashion. Twigs and branches jutted from the chinks in his metal hide, and he had a few dents that weren't there before, but seemed fine otherwise. With a snort that singed a stubborn leaf to ashes, he gazed up at the fallen treant and pinned his ears. "My apologies for not being able to aid you in battle. A pity the creature is dead, but it should have known better than to attack a queen of Faery."

"Something was wrong with it," Nyx said quietly. "When I stabbed it, the heart felt...tainted." She shot a glance at me. "Not unlike those Forgotten we battled in Phaed."

"Yeah," I agreed. "You don't think the big ugly himself is *here*, do you?"

"If it is," Meghan said, "it would save us the time of finding it. Though if it's powerful enough to corrupt a treant in such a short time, it's even more dangerous than we thought."

"Worse than that, I think," Ash broke in, sounding grim. He nodded to the motionless treant. "Did you hear what it said? *The Mother wishes it.*" He shook his head. "If that is true, then things are more serious than we know."

"I am unfamiliar with this 'Mother,'" Coaleater announced, tossing his mane. "I was not aware trees had such things."

"It's referring to the Mother Tree," Nyx replied gravely. "The oldest tree in the forest. The Mother Tree is responsible for the birth of all sentient plant fey—dryads, treants, even a few of the piskie tribes. The treants are connected to her, as are most of the trees in the area. If the Mother Tree perishes, the forest will wither, the treants will all die, and the land will turn barren and lifeless. It would be a death sentence to the Briars, or at least, this part of it, for miles around."

"Oh," Coaleater said in a much more subdued voice. "That is…very troubling."

"Very much so." Meghan rubbed a hand across her eyes. "I think we need to find the Mother Tree," she announced, earning a nod from both Ash and Nyx. "If she is in danger, then the whole forest is at risk. And if the Mother Tree is the one inciting the treants to attack…" She trailed off, as if she couldn't bear to think about the repercussions. "Grimalkin, can you take us to the grove of the Mother Tree?"

"I can, Iron Queen." The cat appeared on a fallen branch, like he had been there the whole conversation. "It is not far, though I would advise caution while traveling through the territory of the walking trees. There are likely more treants surrounding the grove of the Mother, and fighting a pair of them, or more, would be most inadvisable. I realize it is difficult for certain members of the party to restrain themselves…" He paused and looked directly at me. "But I would suggest keeping the noise level to a minimum. Do give it your best attempt at least, hmm?"

17

GROVE OF THE MOTHER TREE

We didn't run into any more hostile trees, though not for lack of them trying. If you think a giant, murderous tree stomping around is easy enough to avoid, you'd be wrong. Turns out, treants are very good at looking like...well, like trees. Normal, nonhostile trees that will not come to life and try to squish you for passing in front of them. Fortunately for us, both Furball and Nyx were experts at spotting which trees were trees and which trees were looking to step on our heads. Following the two masters of stealth, we managed to sneak around the half-dozen or so treants on our way to the grove without being spotted by any of them. Even Coaleater.

Finally, the briars and trees opened up, and we stood at the edge of a small clearing. I say *small*, but only because there wasn't a lot of space left, due to the biggest tree you'd ever seen in your life sitting smack in the center. I didn't even know what kind of tree it was, just that it was huge, dwarfing even the biggest treant. It would probably take a hundred or so people to stretch their arms around the gnarled trunk, and its branches soared up until they disappeared into the canopy overhead, spreading out like a leafy ceiling. Moss, mushrooms, creeper vines and toadstools grew from the trunk and around the massive roots, and a continuous rain of leaves drifted from the branches above, spiraling to the ground like feathers.

"I take it this is the Mother Tree," Coaleater remarked, craning his neck up to stare at it. Pinning his ears, he snorted and tossed his head. "Let's hope it isn't hostile, because it would take a very long time to chop down."

"You cannot chop down the Mother Tree," Nyx said, sounding faintly horrified. "The forest would die, as would all the treants and dryads attached to her. This tree has been here longer than any of us."

Coaleater blew a puff of smoke into the air. "Then perhaps we should ask the Mother Tree why she has been sending her children to kill everyone else."

Warily, we stepped into the clearing. There were no explosions, no twiggy hands surging out of the earth to grab at us, so we started walking. Toward the huge tree in the center of the grove.

"Puck." Beside me, Nyx shuddered, causing all my alarm bells to go off. "Can you feel it?" she whispered.

I gave a slight frown. "What are you—?"

And then I felt it.

A taint on the air, in the earth and trees and rocks surrounding us. The same malevolent, roiling glamour we'd felt in Phaed. Disgust and loathing, and a deep, pulsing rage toward the insignificant fleshy creatures who defiled the forest and used her children for their own gain. The flesh creatures did nothing but exploit and waste and destroy, and it was the forest that suffered the most. Perhaps it was time that the trees rose up to do a little damage of their own.

Oh boy. This was going to be interesting.

"Mother Tree," Meghan called, taking a few steps toward

the massive trunk. A root as thick as she was curled back as she approached, like a snake getting ready to strike, but the Iron Queen didn't flinch. Ash, however, slid his body between it and Meghan, one hand on the hilt of his sword.

"I am Meghan Chase, Queen of the Iron Realm," Meghan went on, facing the giant trunk. "I bring no trouble, Mother Tree, to you or your children. I wish only to talk. Will you speak with us?"

"Insects."

The branches overhead rattled, shaking the canopy and sending a shower of leaves hissing to the ground. In the center of the trunk, the gnarled bark shifted, moving around like wax, forming the vague impression of a face. A pair of eyes emerged, shiny and black, and a slash formed in the trunk as words spilled forth, slow and rusty, as if they had not been spoken in centuries.

"Parasites," the voice whispered, though it still caused the ground to shake and the branches above us to tremble. "Weevils and termites, digging into my flesh, burrowing through my blood. Carrying your diseases, leaving nothing behind. What do you want? Haven't you already taken enough?"

"Mother Tree." Meghan stepped forward. "My friends and I have taken nothing, from you or this forest. We wish only to pass through in peace. Likewise, the Thorn Sisters have great respect for you and the woods in which they hunt. Why do you send your children to attack them? Have they offended you in some way?"

"Offended me?" The Mother Tree didn't sound amused. She sounded disgusted—as disgusted as an ancient tree could sound, anyway. "Their entire existence is an offense to the forest," she rasped. "They, and all the other flesh creatures who take and take and take and give nothing back. They have become as greedy and destructive as the humans in the mortal realm, who raze the trees and destroy the earth with no thought or regret, unable to hear how the land screams out in pain."

"Surely that isn't true, Mother Tree," Meghan reasoned. "At least, not here. I've seen no signs of destruction. No swaths of cleared forest or chopped trees. Perhaps your anger at mankind is what's driving this, but the fey who live in the Briars are not deserving of your wrath."

"You think not, flesh queen?" Oh, this wasn't going well. The Mother Tree's voice had turned icy, which caused Ash to step closer to Meghan, every muscle in his body coiled to react. "How many trees have they felled to build their homes?" the Mother Tree went on. "How many saplings have they uprooted to craft their bows, spears, and weapons of death? How many branches have they ripped asunder and burned in their firepits?"

"That is just basic survival," Ash broke in. "The fey of this world have always depended on the forest for their homes and tools. This is nothing new, Mother Tree."

"The wolves do not uproot my trees to hunt," was the uncompromising reply. "The deer do not build fires to keep themselves warm. The bears do not need bows to fell their prey. Only the fleshy two-legs must continuously destroy to survive. Like a colony of termites, eating, eating, eating, until the tree they depend on for their home is consumed and chewed to nothing. Then they simply move on and find another tree to kill." Branches rattled, and all around us, the roots of the tree coiled beneath the ground like giant worms. "You...you are an infestation, all of you. Why should we not take offense to this?"

Meghan's voice was hard, as if she realized talking to this fanatical, overgrown shrub was getting her nowhere. "Is that why you sent the treants to kill the fey who live here?"

"I did not send my children to do anything," the Mother Tree said. "I do not order or give commands. The younglings simply realized the stain and took it upon themselves to remove it from the forest. They act without my guidance, but their actions do not displease me."

"Mother Tree." Ash stepped forward. "The fey here depend

on the forest for their survival. If you continue to allow your children to kill, there will be a war. And then more trees will die."

"The earth is tainted," the Mother Tree went on. "You do not understand. I feel it, in the ground under your feet. I stretch my roots out, and…"

Suddenly, she shuddered, and the earth shuddered with her. Leaves spiraled to the ground, and flocks of birds took to the air, as the ground literally rumbled and shook, causing us all to brace ourselves. The face in the tree contorted, warping into an expression of rage and agony, before it went slack.

"Um, okay," I said as the tremors finally stopped. "That was weird. Did the old shrub just throw a temper tantrum and go home? What the hell is going on here?"

The Mother Tree still stood there with her eyes shut, unmoving. We all shared a glance, and Meghan stepped forward when the trunk stirred, shedding leaves, and the eyes opened.

Oh crap. A fist made of ice dropped into the pit of my stomach and stayed there, freezing me in place. I stared at the Mother Tree, or rather, at the face in the trunk of the Mother Tree. Because the gaze pinning me in place was not the angry, unreasonable forest guardian we had been speaking with until now.

It was *him*. Or it. Whatever it was. The presence I'd felt before, staring at me from the eyes of the monster in Phaed, trying to figure me out. Curious and intrigued, but somehow…sleepy, as if it wasn't quite awake yet. I felt it again, that same cold curiosity, mingled with the edge of frustration. Frustration that it wasn't quite conscious, as if its thoughts weren't entirely clear yet.

It lasted only a moment. One split-second glance. Then, the Mother Tree blinked, and the other presence was gone.

I shivered, all the way down to my toes. Around me, I could see the others were feeling the same; grim and shaken by what they'd seen, even if they couldn't quite understand it.

"What was that?" Coaleater muttered behind me.

The Mother Tree shuddered again. Opening her eyes, her face twisted, warping even further into a mask of horror and rage. I felt a ripple go through the earth at my feet, as if the roots of the great tree were writhing around, trying to escape a predator.

"Aaaaauuugh," the ancient tree groaned. "Too deep. Too deep, I can feel it. Roots cold, burning. Something…beneath the earth. Can't pull back."

Meghan looked at the ground, her expression pale with understanding. "Something beneath," she whispered. Stretching a hand over the earth, she closed her eyes, and glamour began swirling around her. I felt the pulse of Summer magic, felt it following the roots of the great tree down into the darkness. I saw her frown, a furrow creasing her brow, as she sent the magic deeper, deeper…

Suddenly she gasped, and her eyes flew open as she recoiled, nearly falling backward. Ash lunged forward and caught her, holding her steady as she regained her balance. Above us, the Mother Tree wailed, an unearthly cry of rage and despair, sending ripples through the entire forest.

Heart pounding, I looked at Meghan, who clutched Ash tightly, her face white. She was shaking, breathing hard, as if we had just fled the Briars with that pissed-off dragon behind us.

"Meghan." Ash's voice was low, concerned. He didn't move, just continued to hold her, but his entire posture was tight. "What happened?"

"There is something down there," Meghan whispered. "I don't know what it is, but I could sense its presence. I've never felt anything so…"

"Angry?" I supplied in a soft voice. "Hateful? Like it wants to burn down the world and every living thing in it?"

She nodded, pale and shaken, then glanced up at the Mother Tree and took a quiet breath. "Whatever it is," she whispered in a steely voice, "I can't let this continue. Her roots are too close."

She raised her head and drew away from Ash, standing tall on her own. "I'm going to try to pull her out."

The Mother Tree wailed again, her voice scraping like bark against my ears, and turned a furious gaze on us. "Insects," she almost snarled. "Parasites. You will not touch me with your rotten flesh digits, your tainted glamour." Her trunk shook, and her voice seemed to echo through the forest, reverberating through the trees. "Leave my grove," she ordered. "I give you this one chance to depart peacefully, flesh pods. Leave my forest, or we will crush your bones, rend your disgusting flesh, and let the earth drink your poisoned blood."

Meghan ignored her. Stepping forward, she stretched out her hand again, and glamour began rising once more. I felt the pull of magic, as she seemed to call on the forest itself to aid her, and the Summer glamour was quick to respond, flowing into the Iron Queen and filling her with power.

The Mother Tree hissed, her voice turning ugly and guttural. "I gave you the chance to leave, insects!" she snarled. "But you never listen, you continue to consume and slaughter and destroy. Very well, we will not stand for it a moment longer. The forest will tear your blight from the earth, and your bones will be food for the saplings for years to come."

A rumble went through the earth. Overhead and all around us, the Mother Tree's huge branches rattled, hissing with the sound of a million shaking leaves. And then I noticed *all* the plants—grass, brambles, bushes, toadstools—were shaking and writhing madly, causing a chill to slide up my back.

"Uh, princess? I think we're about to be assaulted by the entire freaking forest. Perhaps a tactical retreat is in order?"

"No." Meghan's voice was strained but unyielding. The Iron Queen hadn't moved, though a furrow creased her brow as she struggled to draw glamour against the very forest fighting against her. "This has to be done. Try to keep everything back. I just need a few seconds—"

With a crack and a piercing groan, a huge branch swung toward Meghan, moving with unnatural speed. Instantly, Ash snatched the queen around the waist and yanked her back, and the branch barely missed them both as it swept by. Meghan winced, losing hold of her glamour for a moment, but she didn't even open her eyes. Ash drew his sword and stepped in front of her, placing himself between the Iron Queen and the giant trunk of the Mother Tree.

"Protect the queen," he snapped at the rest of us, as with eerie hisses, creaks, groans, and scrapes, the forest floor rose up and started reaching for us. Grass covered my boots, vines tried slithering around my ankles, brambles clawed at me with spiky talons. I cut myself free of vegetation and had to duck as a branch swooped by with the groan of splitting wood.

"Dammit, ice-boy!" I sprang toward Meghan and Ash, trying to get to Meghan's other side, but the surging roots and vines clawed at my feet, slowing me down. "Do you know how hard it's going to be to fight the entire forest?"

A trio of spinning light crescents flew by my ear, slicing into a tangle of bramble rearing up to impale me, and cutting the shrub into pieces. I glanced back to see Nyx cut a sapling in two as Coaleater reared up and stomped a log into charred, smoking pieces, then blasted a coiling vine into a withered husk. Nyx sprang onto Coaleater's back, then leaped gracefully off the Iron faery, soared over my head, and landed next to Meghan, cutting through a root reaching up to grab her. Together, the four of us surrounded the Iron Queen, a living barrier between her and the madness swirling around us.

"Insects!" the Mother Tree cried, making my ears ring. "Blight bringers! Destroyers! Crush them! Impale their diseased flesh! Grind their bones to dust! Rise up, my children, and swallow them whole."

Around us, beyond our protective ring, the forest was crawling toward us like a steady, unstoppable tide. A sea of brambles, thorns, vines, and roots, seeking to bury us beneath a flood of angry plants.

Nyx hurled light blades into the approaching wall, and Coaleater blasted nearby offending plants with flame, but the sea of vegetation continued to creep closer, a constant hiss in our ears.

"Puck!" Slashing through a swiping branch, Ash turned to glare at me. "Slow it down, Goodfellow," he ordered, jerking his head toward the wall of plants. "Meghan has to concentrate. She can't do anything right now, but you can. Put that Summer magic to work before it's too late."

"Don't ask for much, do you, ice-boy?" I snapped, but dropped to a knee in the writhing grass and pressed a palm into the ground. Sending my own glamour into the forest around me, I could feel the anger pulsing beneath my skin, the rage and loathing for all of us fleshy creatures who continuously destroyed the forest. The Mother Tree's despair pressed down on me, heavy and suffocating.

Gritting my teeth, I extended my will into the thrashing forest, into the roots and branches spread through the dirt. Sweat beaded on my forehead, running into my eyes as I fought the ancient and supremely powerful will of the Mother Tree and tried to hold back the entire forest.

The crawling plants slowed, and a headache began pounding behind my eyes with the effort. I clenched my jaw and kept pouring will and glamour into the forest around me, silently begging the Iron Queen to hurry up. I could feel her glamour suddenly, the alien sensation of Iron mixed with Summer magic, descending into the earth, into the roots of the Mother Tree herself.

A bramble curled around my arm, digging spiny thorns into my flesh as it tried yanking me away. I winced, but there was the flash of a blade that severed the branch, and Nyx stepped in front of me with her light blades out. From the corner of my eyes, I saw the forest reaching for us, twiggy hands, coiling vines, thorny claws just a few breaths away. Despite my attempts to slow it down, another few heartbeats and we'd be buried.

Another thorny vine coiled around my arm, leaving threads of blood against my skin. A root slithered into my pant leg, and something sharp and twiggy touched my neck. At that moment, I felt the strange, steely glamour of the Iron Queen yank on the roots of the Mother Tree, pulling them up, up, and out, spreading them to different corners of the forest.

The Mother Tree screamed, and the forest went wild. The wall of vegetation recoiled, writhing and thrashing, roots and branches flailing about like the ends of whips. Gradually, however, they stilled, sinking back and returning to normal.

Panting, I slumped, letting my glamour drop as around us, the vicious sounds of branches, grass, and leaves faded away, and all was quiet once more.

Lowering her arms, Meghan swayed on her feet, then collapsed into Ash's arms.

The Ice Prince scooped her up, holding her close, as overhead, the Mother Tree gave a final wail and collapsed into herself. Her eyes shut, and her lined, wrinkled face disappeared, seeming to melt into the bark of the trunk, until a huge but nonsentient-looking tree sat in the center of the now silent grove.

"I did…as much as I could," Meghan whispered between breaths. "I pulled up the roots…sent them in different directions. They won't stay that way for long but…at least for now… they're out of that thing's influence. This is a temporary fix at best. I wish I could have done more."

"It is all you could have done, Iron Queen," said Grimalkin's voice, as the cat looked up from where he sat on a root. He curled his whiskers, gazing up at the Mother Tree's empty trunk. "This is the root of the treant's corruption. Had you not acted, they and all the other sentient plants would continue to attack the fey and perhaps all living creatures in the Briars. But you are correct. Though the treants' hostility will fade and they will eventually revert to their former selves, it is likely not permanent. Unless you sever the corruption at the source."

"You did everything you could," Ash told Meghan gently. "Rest now. We're getting out of here. Goodfellow…" He shot a glance at me, and I couldn't tell if he was relieved or annoyed that I was still there. "Can you stand?"

I forced a tired smirk. "Sure, everyone, go check on the Iron Queen. Pay no attention to the guy that actually slowed down the entire forest." I pushed myself upright, and Nyx stepped forward, letting me lean on her for support. I would've told her not to worry, but my legs were shaking, my arms felt like they were made of noodles, and I was feeling unreasonably cranky at the moment. "Don't pretend that you care, ice-boy," I told him. "Let's get out of here. Right now, I don't feel like fighting anything meaner than a butterfly."

Meghan sighed. Leaning her head on Ash's shoulder, she gazed up tiredly at the Mother Tree, her features pinched with concern. "I'm sorry," she whispered. "I hope we've at least brought you some measure of peace."

There was no reply from the Mother Tree. The trunk remained blank, empty of face or expression.

Grimalkin hopped down from the root, waved his tail once, and padded out of the clearing without making any comments. With Ash still carrying Meghan, we followed, and the grove of the Mother Tree faded behind us.

18

CURSES AND ROSES

That night, we made camp in the center of a small ruin, surrounded by crumbling walls and gargoyles being choked by thick black bramble. A shattered fountain that might've been a mermaid once but was now nothing but a tail and a pair of arms stood desolately in the center of the room.

Nyx leaned against the lip of the fountain with her legs crossed and her blades in hand, staring at the tunnel we had come in, making certain no nasty bug or giant centipede slithered into the room with us. Coaleater, too, had taken up guard duty, planting his large body in the doorway, so that if said giant centipede tried squeezing in, they'd get an angry Iron horse to the face.

(One might think all these centipede precautions were going a bit overboard, except we'd all seen the big ugly bastard as we slipped back into the Briars tunnels, a fifteen-foot monster making its merry way through the thorns, bright yellow antennas waving. And since I liked bugs as much as I liked a rousing kick to the gonads, I thought being overprepared was better than waking up with a centipede trying to eat my eyeball.)

I glanced at the lovebirds, who had claimed one of the far corners. The Iron Queen sat with her back against the stone wall, with Ash crouched in front of her, his silver gaze intense. Meghan still looked pale and exhausted, which was prompting Ash to be even more protective and overbearing than normal. He looked like he wanted to scoop her up and take her back to the Iron Realm, which Meghan would never allow and would likely kick his ass for attempting, but that didn't stop him from wanting to.

"I'm fine, Ash," she told the hovering Ice Prince, for the second or third time, I was guessing. "I told you, I'm just tired." Raising a hand before her, she gave a rueful smile. "Probably shouldn't have expended all my glamour at once, but it had to be done. Just give me an hour or two of sleep, and I'll be ready to go." Ash started to say something, and she glared at him. "Unless I don't get any rest from the constant hovering of an overprotective Winter faery who is worried that I'm not getting enough rest."

Ash slumped in defeat. "Fine," I heard him say. "As you wish, my queen. But if you pass out or fall asleep during the fight with the big monster, I get to be 'unbearably overprotective' for the next month."

Meghan yawned. "And that is different from everyday life, how?" she murmured, leaning back and closing her eyes.

Ash snorted, placed a kiss atop her head and rose, black coat and protective glamour aura falling around him. He caught me watching them, and one brow lifted before he turned and started making his way in my direction.

I stiffened, angry memories stirring to life once more, even as I tried shoving them down. "Ice-boy," I greeted, smiling coldly as he came up. "That's quite the talent you've got. Even after all this time, you can still make me want to stab my eyeballs out."

He didn't say anything at first, just leaned back against the lip of the fountain next to me, crossing his arms. For a moment, we didn't speak, gazing silently over the ruined courtyard, an icy barrier radiating between us.

"How long?" Ash wondered at last. Puzzled, I glanced at him, frowning, and his jaw tightened. "How long have you felt this way, Puck?"

"Always, ice-boy," I answered softly. "From the moment I saw you and Meghan dancing at Elysium. Oh, I got over it, but it's always been there. You know better than anyone that I've always been kind of a sore loser."

Ash briefly closed his eyes. "I don't want this, Goodfellow," he murmured. "I thought we were done with this feud. I don't want to have to fight you again."

"Well, that's too bad, ice-boy. 'Cause we don't always get what we want." I sneered at him, making his eyes narrow. "I didn't want to have to fight you for countless years over an oath. I didn't want to watch Meghan fall in love with you, when I was at her side the entire time. I didn't want to get smacked down by a big ugly bastard who brought all these lovely memories right back to the surface again. But I did, and now we all have to live with it, whether we want to or not."

I crossed my arms, imitating his pose, and gave him a challenging smirk. "Just be glad my good old-fashioned talent for revenge has a bigger priority right now than you. Once this is over, get ready to meet the real Robin Goodfellow. And like your brothers, you'll find out he was an even bigger bastard than anyone realized."

"Puck." Ash pushed himself off the lip of the fountain, not looking at me any longer. A flash of pain crossed his face before he could hide it. "I can't fault you for wanting revenge, not after my oath with Ariella, but…" He paused, as if struggling with himself, then said, very quietly, "Rowan and Sage are gone. You…are the only brother I have left."

He turned and walked away before I could reply, striding back toward the now sleeping Meghan, leaving me staring after him.

From the corner of my eye, I saw Nyx at the mouth of the bramble tunnel, her golden eyes shining in the gloom as she watched us. And I knew that she had heard every word I'd said.

Dammit. I slumped against the stones, putting a hand over my eyes, and teetered between planning the most cruel, horrible prank in the history of the Nevernever and hoping no one saw the water trickling slowly between my fingers.

I woke up to the smell of...roses?

Opening my eyes, I gave a start. Once black, stark, and empty, the thorns and brambles that covered the walls and stones of the ruins now blazed with color. Roses in red, white, black, blue, yellow, and purple had sprouted everywhere among the thorns, filling the air with the scent of flowers and a riot of pigment.

"Ohhh-kaaaaaaay." Cautiously, I rose, seeing everyone else gazing around with their hands close to their weapons, too. "Who ordered the wedding setup? Or is the Queen of Hearts attempting to smother us with rosebushes?"

"No idea," Coaleater said, stamping a hoof that sparked against the stone floor. "They just bloomed out of nowhere a few seconds ago." His nostrils flared, as if he was contemplating setting fire to the lot of them. "I don't know what this means, but I don't like it."

Meghan stood up. She looked stronger now, almost back to normal. "They don't feel hostile," she mused, touching a fingertip to a yellow rose petal. It stirred at her touch, almost like a cat waking up to someone petting it. "I don't think they're here as a warning or a threat."

"It is the castle." Grimalkin peered down from atop the broken fountain, golden cat eyes seeming to float in the gloom. "It knows we are coming."

Nyx appeared beside me. I could feel her presence with every fiber of my being, but I couldn't bring myself to look at her right then. I didn't want to see anger in those moon-colored eyes, or worse, disappointment. Because she had seen the real Robin Goodfellow again and knew he could never be trusted.

"If it knows we are coming," Nyx said softly, "then I see no reason to keep it waiting."

The roses continued through the Briars, forming a passage of color and scent. We didn't need Furball to guide the way anymore, as it was obvious which direction we needed to go. Following the trail of flowers, we pushed our way through the Briars tunnels until they opened up once again, and we stepped into a massive courtyard.

"Well," Meghan commented as we all stared at what awaited us at the end of the road. "I'd say we found it."

Silhouetted against the sky, an enormous stone castle rose from the brambles and thorn bushes, towering over us in ominous, medieval glory. Multiple towers and turrets rose into the air, pointed roofs stabbing at the clouds, and dozens of stone gargoyles peered down at us, their faces twisted into frozen snarls and leers. Black, thorny vines slithered their way up the stone walls, curling around railings and gargoyles and making the entire castle bloom with roses. The courtyard was covered with them, too, tangled in the trees and coiled around crumbling pillars, the smell of ash and dust mingling with the scent of flowers. A full moon, glowing bright overhead, cast an eerie silver luminance over everything.

My gaze went to Nyx. Unlike everyone else staring up at the waiting castle, she stood with her eyes closed and her face slightly turned to the sky, basking in the glow of the moon. Her hood had fallen back, and her hair, rippling softly in the breeze, looked like liquid silver in the darkness.

She was absolutely beautiful.

And I didn't deserve her. Not for a second.

The cat took the lead again, and we followed him, walking carefully across the courtyard that, for some reason, had a light dusting of snow covering it. More brambles split the flagstones and coiled around statues of twisted beasts scattered through the yard.

I peered closely at one and wrinkled my nose. It looked like an ambitious sculptor had tried chiseling out a horse, but half-way through had either forgotten what a horse looked like or decided to switch to a bear or some other shaggy thing. The result was a warped amalgamation of animal parts that definitely should not have gone together. The statue beside it didn't look much better and had actually covered its face with both gro-tesquely long arms, as if embarrassed to be seen like this. I shook my head in sympathy.

"Man, who's the landscaper here? I think we need to have a talk, unless 'creepily ominous' was the vibe they were going for—oh." I paused, seeing a crooked sign bearing the words Keep Out! and No Trespassing! poking from the brambles. "Or, 'stay the hell away,' that would work, too. Anyone else get the feeling we're not really welcome here?"

"It doesn't matter," Meghan said quietly from up ahead. She turned down a path that led straight to the castle, contorted statues of unnamed beasties lining either side. "The oracle said the Forgotten with her memories is hiding here. We need to find it, and see what they know about this monster."

"Monster?"

One of the statues moved. Something huge and shaggy, with massive shoulders, horns, and a muzzle bristling with fangs, stepped from the shadows into the middle of the path. With a growl, it rose onto two legs, looming over us, enormous clawed hands opening at its side. Cold blue eyes, slitted like a cat's, glared down with feral intelligence.

"You want a monster, trespassers?" the creature said in a low, gravelly voice. "Here I am."

Meghan held up a hand, stopping Ash from pulling his sword, as the rest of us tensed behind her. "We mean no harm," she told the shaggy beast blocking our way. "I apologize for trespassing, but we wish only to talk. Will you allow us to speak to your master?"

The creature curled a lip. "*I* am the master of this castle," it growled through its fangs. It took a step forward, causing Ash to drop a hand to his weapon and Coaleater to give a warning snort. From the corner of my eye, I saw Nyx's cloak ripple, and knew she had called her blades to her hands.

The monster eyed them warily before turning to Meghan again. "You speak to the lord of this land now. Who are you, and what do you want?"

"I am Meghan Chase, Queen of the Iron Realm," Meghan replied, and the monster's blue eyes widened a fraction. "These are my friends and companions. We're looking for a faery who supposedly fled here and is hiding in your castle. Do you know anything about this?"

"Iron Queen." The creature's guttural voice turned flat. It gave a snort of its own and backed off, shaking its shaggy head as if the matter was done. "So, you are the queen of the poisoned realm," it growled. "The one the shadow fey won't stop talking about."

"Oh, look at that, princess," I said into the surprised silence. "We *are* expected, after all."

Meghan took a step forward. "It is here, then."

The monster curled a lip. "I caught the creature lurking about my gardens," he said. "It was deranged, screaming and crying about things that made no sense. I tried driving it out, back into the Briars, but it refused to leave. Said something was after it, and it would rather die than risk whatever was coming. So, I offered it a room in my tower cell, where it could wail and sob in peace." The creature made a disgusted gesture with one huge claw. "It is still there, if you think you can get any sense out of it, Iron Queen."

Meghan exchanged a glance with Ash, then nodded. "If you

JULIE KAGAWA

would let us speak to this Forgotten," Meghan said, "we would very much appreciate it."

The creature snorted again. "Iron Queen, if you can actually get it to stop squealing like a tortured pig or babbling like a fool, you would have my eternal gratitude. This way." It raised a hairy forepaw and turned, beckoning us forward. "Follow me."

Dropping to all fours, it lumbered toward the castle, and we trailed bemusedly after.

The inside of the castle was elegant and surprisingly clean, though I wondered where the servants were. I didn't see anyone, and I was certain our hairy guide didn't do all the sweeping, cooking and cleaning himself. I had a quick mental image of the enormous shaggy creature in a white apron, sweeping the furniture with a tiny feather duster, and snickered out loud.

Ash shot me a warning look, as if he knew what I was thinking, and the monster glanced at me over its wide hairy shoulders. "Something funny, Goodfellow?"

"Oh, nothing important," I said, grinning back. "But you know who I am, that's good to hear." I smiled wider and glanced at Nyx. "See, even cursed, lonely beasts know me. Everyone knows me."

Nyx only rolled her eyes, but the creature gave a disgusted growl. "I've lived here for a while, Goodfellow," he rumbled. "I've heard the stories, same as everyone else. I would ask that you kindly keep your hands to yourself. I would hate to have to rip them off your arms."

We continued, following the creature up a flight of cracked marble stairs, down a long hallway with soaring arched windows that looked out on the courtyard, and up a spiraling staircase to the highest tower. Coaleater was forced to change into his more human form to fit inside the claustrophobic staircase, but other than letting out an exasperated sigh that filled the doorway with smoke, he did so without complaint.

About halfway up the staircase, the babbling started.

We all stopped, listening to the low, constant murmuring that drifted down the steps. The voice was too soft and faraway to make out, but I caught a few choice words like *death* and *futile* and *it's coming*.

"Oh," I remarked. "Good. That's the type of thing you wanna hear. Those are the words of a completely rational faery. I can't wait to have a perfectly ordinary conversation with him."

The monster shook his shaggy head, curling a lip at the sounds floating down the stairwell. "Now you know why everyone avoids this part of the castle," he growled. "When the shrieking starts, you can hear it all the way out in the halls."

Meghan's brow creased in sympathy. "Have you been able to understand him at all?" she asked the monster, who snorted.

"A few words. I don't really listen. He screams 'it's coming' a lot. Considering that he's hiding here and refusing to leave, I'm guessing he thinks something is after him."

"Or something is really after him," Nyx put in.

The monster shrugged. "It would have to find this place first, and then it would have to get past me. Not that I care what happens to him one way or another, but I don't take kindly to trespassers." A shriek rang out somewhere overhead, and he winced. "Ugh, it's starting again. This way, Iron Queen. Once the wailing really starts, you won't be able to get two coherent words out of him."

He turned and started padding up the stairs, and we followed him to a small stone landing with a thick wooden door set into the wall. Sobbing and nonsensical mutterings echoed through the door, filling the small enclosure, buzzing in my ears like really whiny mosquitos.

"The door isn't locked," the monster told us, gesturing to the handle with a huge hairy paw. "You can just open it…" He pushed on the wood, but was met with a clunk, and the door stayed firmly shut. The monster sighed. "Unless he's barred it from the inside again."

"If you'll allow me." Meghan stepped forward, and the creature moved aside with a shrug. Stepping up to the door, the Iron Queen put her hand against the wood and closed her eyes. Glamour flickered around her, and something on the other side of the barrier clicked, then dropped away.

She pushed the door open, and a howl immediately echoed through the chamber as something came hurtling through the doorframe. Meghan ducked, and Ash's sword flashed out, striking the small clay bowl and shattering it into a dozen pieces.

"Noooooo!" shrieked a voice that seemed to come from nowhere. "I'm not here! Not here, you won't take me!"

We all peered into the room. At first, I couldn't see anything but shadows. Dank stone floors met dank stone walls, with the only light coming from the door and a tiny barred window near the top of the room. The back of the cell was nearly pitch-black, and nothing seemed to move in the darkness.

Then, a glimmer of yellow light winked into existence, followed by another, like a pair of round golden fireflies. After a second, I realized the two floating lights were actually eyes, belonging to the shadowy form of a Forgotten crouched in the corner of the room. Unlike Nyx, this one looked like the Forgotten I was used to: jet-black and featureless, like a shadow come to life.

I squinted against the darkness, trying to see it better, but it was like trying to spot an ink stain on a black carpet at midnight. And the extra bright glowing eyes, huge and round like car headlights, were not helping.

"Nooooo." The Forgotten's voice slithered out of the cell again. It wasn't loud, but it still caused the hairs on my neck to rise. "No, not yet. Not yet, it isn't time. The dream is not over. It sleeps still, not time yet."

"Calm down." Meghan's quiet, soothing voice cut through the rising tension. "We're not here to hurt you. We just want to talk."

"The queen." Even though I couldn't see him clearly, the Forgotten was clearly talking to himself. "The queen has come. The end is nigh."

Meghan straightened at that, and Ash pressed closer to her, crowding the door. I scowled and stood on tiptoes to peer over his shoulder, as from the corner, a piece of the darkness slid away from the rest, coming into the light.

A thin silhouette of a humanoid faery, meaning it had two arms, two legs, and one head. Its ears were long and pointed, and it didn't seem to have any extra limbs, wings, or tails. But that was all I could say for certain, as the Forgotten really did look like a shadow had stepped off the floor and come to life. It might've been beautiful, terrifyingly hideous, or covered in bright orange feathers; we would never know.

"Iron Queen," the Forgotten whispered. "You have come." It trembled, then like an ooze of ink running down a wall, sank to the floor. "She is here," it moaned. "It comes. It comes with her. The end has started at last."

Meghan stepped into the cell. The rest of us, even Ash, hovered in the doorway, watching as the Iron Queen walked to the faery's side and knelt, gazing at the undistinguishable lump on the floor. "You've seen the oracle's memories," she said, and the Forgotten moaned, curling in on itself, looking even more like a blob of oil spread over the floor. "What are you talking about? What's coming? Do you mean the creature that's stalking the Nevernever? The one that can transform fey by touching them?"

"It comes," moaned the Forgotten. "It comes. For me. For you. For us. For the world. The surface breaks and shatters, and the darkness beneath rises to swallow us all. You cannot stop it. No one can stop it. The world will fray apart and drown in hate. The harbinger will find us. You cannot hide, cannot run, cannot will it away. It…"

The Forgotten stopped. Grew very still. For a second, it was a motionless dark lump on the stones of the cell. Then, a giggle escaped it. And another. Rising, it threw back its head and laughed, high-pitched and frantic, making the hairs on my arms stand up to join the ones on my neck.

Ash's hand slid to his sword hilt, but Meghan remained calm in the face of the Forgotten's laughing fit; she even reached out to steady the faery when it seemed in danger of collapsing again.

Behind us, the beast let out a disgusted growl, the hackles on his neck and shoulders standing up like spines. "This is what I mean, Iron Queen," he said over the shrieking laughter of the faery in the cell. "The creature is inconsolable when he gets like this. Want me to knock him senseless and give us all a little peace and quiet?"

I was tempted to say yes, but the Forgotten then stopped, as suddenly as flipping a light switch.

"No." He panted, a few hysterical chuckles slipping out, and shook his head. "No, you do not understand. Iron Queen…" He clutched at her arm, though Meghan did nothing to shove him away. "You're too late," the faery whispered. "Too late. It comes. For me. For you. For us all. I have seen it. It will not stop, it is unstoppable. It…"

He raised his head, a chilling, terrifying light sliding across his vision. The realization of something that could not be taken back. "It is here."

A baleful, familiar howl rang out somewhere in the night.

19

ANOTHER LAST STAND

It's here.

Cold flooded my veins, as my insides immediately turned themselves into a tangle of knots. I looked at Nyx, who remained very still as the echo of the howl reverberated through the walls and floors of the castle. On the floor, the Forgotten collapsed into soft but incessant giggles, covering its glowing eyes with both hands.

With a growl, our shaggy host turned and gazed out one of the tiny barred windows in the wall. "What is that?" he asked as the echoes died away. "Is something coming onto my land? Intruders will not be tolerated. Stay here," he told us. And before we could stop him, he lowered his head, shouldered his way to the stairwell, and vanished through the frame.

"Wait!" Meghan rose swiftly, but the beast was already gone, his thunderous footsteps fading down the stairs. The Iron Queen gave an exasperated sigh and stepped out of the cell, her gaze falling on me as she came through the doorframe. "Puck? You've faced this creature before. Is it...?"

I gave a solemn nod. "It's him, princess." The way my insides were churning, the sudden rage and dread coursing through my veins…it couldn't be anything else. My voice was shaking, and I couldn't tell if it was from fear or a sudden, gleeful anticipation. "The big bastard has either tracked us down, or is after our giggly friend."

Meghan returned the nod. "Then it looks like we have no choice but to face it." Her blue eyes continued to gaze at me, worry and concern shining through. "Puck…are you going to be all right? You don't have to fight now. The rest of us can take care of it—"

"Not a chance, princess." My words sounded strange; cold and flat, even as I felt a big, toothy grin stretch my face. "I owe that bastard a little retribution, so if you think I'm gonna sit this one out, I'm afraid I won't be doing that." Raising my daggers, I gave them all a hard smile. "It brought out the old Robin Goodfellow. Let's see how it likes dealing with him now."

I could see the worry on the faces of both Meghan and Ash, and felt Nyx's steady presence beside me. The howl came again, closer this time, and a chill crept through the air, coating the stones with frost for a split second before it melted away. I shivered and blinked ice crystals from my lashes, as the Forgotten in the cell curled into itself, making hopeless, nonsensical sounds. Fragmented bits of "it's here, it's here," drifted out between giggles.

Meghan closed her eyes. "All right," she said, and her voice turned steely. Opening her eyes, she gazed at all of us. "Let's do this. Be careful. Watch out for each other. We don't know the extent of what this thing is capable of."

Ash drew his sword, and Nyx called her light blades to her hands. "We're ready, Your Majesty," she said. "We follow you."

"You can't stop it," the Forgotten moaned as we turned to leave. "No one can stop it. The end approaches. Evenfall has come. The world will crack, and the abyss will swallow us whole."

And on that cheerful note, we walked down the stairs, back through the castle, and into the courtyard, where a monstrous shadow appeared at the edge of the Briars.

I took a deep breath, forcing back the fear, the rage, and all the other emotions that came rushing to the surface. It was him, all right. The big bad himself. The monster with a capital M.

It towered over the wall, a horrible conglomeration of animal parts twisted together into the ugliest mofo that ever walked the Nevernever. It was even bigger than last time, and the shadowy tendrils on its back and shoulders were everywhere now, making it look part squid as well. It stepped over the wall, and as it did, black tentacles sprouted from the ground and stones around it, writhing and snapping at the air.

A challenging roar rang out as we reached the edge of the courtyard, not coming from the big Monster, but from the shaggy beast we'd met earlier. The lord of the castle stomped forward, bristling, the spiky hair on his back and shoulders standing straight up. "Intruder," he snarled. "You are not welcome here, creature! Leave my castle, or I will be forced to tear you apart!"

The Monster turned its antlered head toward the smaller beast, pinning it with that cold, blank-eyed stare. Raising its head, it howled, making my gut contract and the tentacles surrounding it thrash wildly.

The beast gave a roar of his own, dropped to all fours, and charged the Monster.

"That's not good," I muttered.

The Monster also dropped to all fours as the beast came in and leaped fearlessly for its head with its claws and fangs bared. The Monster didn't move, but the tendrils rose up, a black tide that intercepted the lunging beast, wrapping around him and dragging him from the air. The beast gave a snarl, fighting and ripping several tentacles from the ground, but the Monster continued to lift him, and he eventually vanished beneath a tangle of darkness.

"That's also not good," I said as we all hurried forward.

Another roar echoed over the courtyard, and the beast burst from the knot of tentacles, landing on all fours in front of the Monster. He was bigger now, his horns longer, his paws huge and tipped with massive talons. Growling, he swung a thick, blocky head toward us, fangs curling from his muzzle, his eyes empty of reason.

"Trespassers," he rumbled, ribbons of saliva dripping from his fangs to the ground. "Kill you. Kill you all!"

"Oh, that's *really* not good!" I said as the beast growled and sprang toward us, huge jaws gaping wide.

With a bellow of flame, Coaleater reared up into his stallion form. "Nyx," he cried, and Nyx immediately leaped onto his back. "Stop the creature," the Iron faery told us. "We will deal with the beast."

Nyx met my gaze, her golden eyes shining with several emotions I couldn't place. "Be careful, Puck," she said firmly. "Don't lose yourself completely. I still want to see the Nevernever when this is all over."

I swallowed the sudden lump in my throat and grinned back. "Count on it."

Coaleater whirled and galloped straight for the beast bounding over the courtyard toward us. I watched them go, feeling my heart leave with the silver-haired faery assassin, my insides a tangled mess. Coaleater charged at the beast, swerving aside at the last minute, and Nyx's swords lashed out, scoring the shaggy hide. The beast roared in fury and whirled, chasing them toward another section of the courtyard, away from the rest of us.

I breathed deep, trusting my assassin would come through this just fine, and turned toward the real problem at the edge of the Briars.

The Monster let out a bellow and prowled forward, and the

carpet of tentacles began creeping toward us as well. The closer they got, the colder the air became, and the more my own stomach churned with fear and anger. I could feel the taint now, the roiling mire of rage and hate, emanating from the Monster and seeping into the ground. The ruthlessness in me stirred, responding to the glamour aura, as unwelcome thoughts and memories began flickering through my head.

"Nothing to say, Goodfellow?"

I blinked and glanced at Ash, walking beside me with his sword at his side. He shot me a look, then turned his attention back to the Monster prowling ever closer. "This is the quietest I've ever heard you before a fight. You're usually taunting our opponent or making ridiculous comments by now. Don't tell me you're scared."

I sneered at him. "Me? Scared? Who do you think you're talking to, ice-boy? Is this the face of someone who's afraid of the big bad monster?"

He shot me another glance, his brow furrowed. And I knew I couldn't hide it. Not from him. I was afraid. My hands were shaking, and the phantom wound I had taken before was throbbing, an icy cold pulse right below my ribs. But I was also furious, shaking with anger and hate for this Monster. This thing that dared make me, Puck, feel real terror for the first time in eons, who had twisted my world around and turned me into something I loathed. The Robin Goodfellow everyone had despised for his cruelty and vicious pranks. Who held grudges, played with human emotions, and crafted elaborate schemes of revenge. The faery who was contemplating becoming an enemy to his best friend once more.

So, yeah, I wasn't feeling very jolly at the moment. I felt less like making jokes and more like carving this bastard's ugly head from its neck. Though I knew it wasn't going to be easy, even with the Ice Prince and the Iron Queen at my side.

"What is this thing?" Meghan whispered, as the silhouette of the creature grew even larger, huge antlers framing the moon. "The amount of negative glamour it's putting out...is frightening."

"Yeah," I growled. "Whatever you do, don't let those tentacles touch you. It's not fun, and you might end up...a little different than before. I found that out the hard way." I spared a glance at the direction Nyx and Coaleater had fled but couldn't see either of them among the forest of statues.

Ash raised his sword, letting the icy blue light wash over us all. For just a moment, in the chilly glow of the blade, the prince's face was pale. "Then let's kill it quickly, before it does any more damage," he said, and plunged the blade down, sinking it into the earth.

With a rush of glamour, ice spread out from the tip of the sword, coating the ground in a frigid wave. It covered the stones, the walls, the twisted statues scattered throughout the courtyard. The writhing carpet of tentacles froze as they were encased in ice, then shattered into thousands of tiny shards, creating a crystalline blizzard in their wake.

That was our cue. I sprang forward with a snarl, daggers in both hands, racing across the frozen ground toward the Monster. Ash was right beside me, throwing out a flurry of frozen knives that spun through the air right at the creature's ugly face.

The Monster lowered its head, and the dozens of tendrils on its back and shoulders flailed, striking the darts from the air. By that time, though, Ash and I were right beneath it, darting to the left and right as it lashed out, curved talons slamming into the flagstones and shattering them with a roar.

Fear suffocated me. This close to the Monster, it was hard to breathe without gasping in terror. I shoved down the dread and latched on to the rage that came bubbling to the surface, anger toward the Monster, toward Ash, toward Oberon, Titania, and the entire Nevernever. I channeled that rage into a knifepoint and with a snarl of my own, slammed my daggers deep into the

Monster's side. At the same time, I felt the chill from Ash's sword as the ice blade came slashing down, hitting the creature from the other side and probably severing something vital.

Beneath my dagger hilts, the creature's dark, leathery hide rippled like shadow, almost insubstantial. The Monster itself barely made a sound. No howl of pain, no roars of anger or agony; my blow didn't even seem to register. I yanked my blades free, and a spray of darkness followed, writhing and thrashing as it solidified into a long black tendril, grabbing at me as I danced away.

Despair and anger rose up, even as I shoved them back. Same thing as before; I couldn't hurt the bastard, and even worse, my strikes seemed to be making it stronger. On the Monster's other side, I saw Ash dodge a vicious swipe and lash out with his blade, cutting deep into the hairy arm. It should've severed the limb completely, or at the very least opened a huge gash in the flesh. I'd seen him do it before, on things that were just as big. But there was nothing. No blood, no reaction from the creature; only those wisps of darkness that turned into more of those damned tentacles.

The Monster lashed out with its other arm, and Ash rolled away, just barely avoiding the claws that raked deep gouges in the stone. I darted in while it was distracted with Ash, leaped off a thigh, and drove my weapons into the base of its spine as hard as I could, putting all my anger and hate for this thing into the blow.

It jerked up with a snarl, blank white eyes rolling back to glare at me, giving Ash just enough time to slide beneath it and jam the full length of his sword into its chest, far enough that the very tip erupted through the skin of its back.

Panting, we circled around to its front, watching as it spun to follow us with that horrible, surprising grace. Its movements were slow and smooth, not hampered in the slightest. Though three feet of superchilled metal right through their rib cage would've killed most monsters, all we had done to this one was annoy it.

Ash shook his head with a frustrated noise. "This isn't working, Goodfellow."

"Oh, you think, ice-boy?" I curled a lip at him. "What was your first inkling?"

He glanced at me, and his eyes narrowed, anger sparking to life within. My gut twisted as I recognized that glare. The same look I'd faced when Ash had been out to kill me.

And then, the skies flashed, and a bolt of lightning streaked down to hit the Monster in the skull. It roared, the first sound of pain I'd heard from it tonight, and it staggered back, baleful white eyes snapping to the figure behind us.

Meghan stood a few paces away, sword drawn and shining beside her, one arm outstretched toward the Monster. She blazed with power, her blue eyes hard as she stared at the creature, and for just a moment, my heart swelled with hope.

Then the Monster threw back its head and roared, and the ground at our feet erupted. I scrambled back as dark tendrils rose into the air, writhing and lashing out at everything. They spread over the whole courtyard, until no part of the ground was left uncovered.

I dodged a pair of tentacles, leaped through another, then felt one snake around my waist, burning with cold as it pulled me down. Images flooded my head again, unwanted and unwelcome, and rage flared. Snarling, I freed my arm and sliced through the coils around my waist, seeing Meghan and Ash also entangled in the darkness. The ones surrounding Ash had frozen solid, but more were rising to take their place, and a couple had managed to coil around the prince's legs and sword arm. With a flash of glamour, they stiffened and iced over, and the prince tore himself free with sharp crinkling sounds.

Just as a massive claw snatched him up, lifted him into the air, and slammed him into the stones with a sickening crack.

My heart stopped beating. The Monster gave a howl of fury and triumph as it pounded Ash into the ground again, then lifted him up with a roar, jaws gaping to bite off the prince's head.

"*NO!*" Meghan raised her hand, and a pulse of electricity rippled through the ground, centered on her.

The writhing carpet of tentacles jerked, snapping wildly, then vanished into coils of darkness on the wind. With a yell, the queen flung out her other arm, lightning streaking from her fingers to slam into the Monster's chest. The creature snarled, dropped a bloody Ash to the stones, and went stumbling back a few steps, shielding its face.

With lightning sizzling around her, the queen strode forward, grabbing Ash as he struggled to his feet. The Ice Prince's long coat was tattered, blood streaming down one side of his face, but he still turned and gestured weakly at the Monster, and ice spears sprang up from the ground, surrounding them both in a protective ring of frozen crystal.

"Ash." Meghan's voice was breathless, her normal calm shattered. She sounded terrified now, kneeling on the flagstones with her Ice Prince, clutching his shoulders. Her fear echoed over the wind, carried on the wisps of darkness till fading around us. "Talk to me. We have to get you out of here."

"I'm fine," Ash gritted out. He didn't sound fine; he was obviously hurt, and the tightness of his voice showed how bad it was. Like Nyx, the stoic Ice Prince never let on how badly he was wounded. His free hand came up, covering Meghan's, as he met her gaze. "I'm fine, Meghan," he rasped again. "I can still fight."

Above them, the Monster reared onto its hind legs and roared, dark tendrils flailing, and more rose from the ground, surrounding the pair in the circle of ice. Meghan gestured toward it, and the skies flashed as another lightning bolt slammed into its skull, but this time it didn't even flinch.

Watching them, I had a sudden, strangely calming realization. We were going to die here. The prophecy, fragmented and incomplete as it was, already said this Monster was unkillable. That no one could stop it. If even the Iron Queen's magic couldn't give this Monster pause, there was nothing we could do.

I was going to lose them both.

A hollow pit opened inside me. A world without Meghan and Ash? I couldn't imagine it. What would I do if they were suddenly gone? If I could never again tease Meghan or get under ice-boy's skin? If we never fought side by side together, explored new and hidden places in Faery, or saved the Nevernever one more time? And suddenly, all that resentment and jealousy I'd been carrying around seemed petty in comparison. Why had I been so angry? Why had this Monster been able to bring out the absolute worst side of Robin Goodfellow?

Nyx's voice came back to me, soft and damning. *This desire for revenge against the prince consort—is it because you're still in love with the Iron Queen, or is it simply because you lost?*

I hadn't replied, not truthfully, because deep down, I already knew the answer. It was the reason Nyx had become so intriguing, the reason the Lady's assassin was constantly on my mind and in my thoughts. Because…I *had* moved on. I didn't love Meghan that way anymore, not romantically.

But if I had moved on, then the reason for my anger and resentment was because I had lost to Ash. Because I had been too proud, stubborn, or defiant to admit that, after everything, after all the fighting, grief, and hell we put each other through, he was the one who had come out on top. He had won his soul, gotten the girl. And worst of all, he'd been able to forgive us both and put all that anger and hate behind him.

My throat closed at the realization. Ash had forgiven me for Ariella, and he had forgiven himself for all those bad years between us, but I had never done the same. This feeling of bitterness and rage… I had carried it around for years, never airing it, burying it under laughter and sarcasm, letting it fester without even knowing it was there. The Monster hadn't changed me into something I wasn't, it just brought all those feelings to the surface again.

And now, I would never have the chance to set things right. *What? No, screw that!*

Deep inside, a tiny spark of defiance flared, a bit of Puck surging to life. Give up now? Was I really going to sit here and watch my best friends get stomped into paste by some random big nasty? I'd never surrendered without a fight before. And even if the prophecy was true, even if this thing *was* unkillable, was I going to let that stop me? Or I was I going to look it in the eye and laugh in its ugly face?

The Nevernever could be crumbling under our feet, echoed a voice in my head, Grimalkin's, a memory from not so very long ago, *and you would make a joke about it.*

Well, duh. It would be my last chance to. If I'm going to stare Death in the face, I'm gonna do it laughing at him.

Oh yeah. *That* was who I was. In all this chaos, I had somehow forgotten.

I took a deep breath. Welp, no time like the present to make up for it. Especially since we were probably all going to die. Bending down, I picked up my daggers, twirling them in my hands as I rose. Gazing at the Monster, at the creature who was very likely going to kill me, I grinned.

Ash had struggled to his feet, and now he and Meghan stood side by side, facing the Monster who towered over them, silhouetted against the moon. Surrounded by a shrinking island in a sea of black, the Ice Prince brandished his sword, and the Iron Queen raised a hand, lightning snapping at her fingertips.

The Monster roared, rearing onto its hind legs, talons spread and horrible jaws gaping, to tear them apart once and for all.

With a cry and the flapping of wings, a flock of screaming ravens flew right into its face. Shrieking and cawing, they swirled around its head, tearing at tentacles, pecking at eyes and skin and everything they could reach. The Monster bellowed and staggered back, swiping madly at the screaming cloud of birds, ripping them from the air. A few ravens fell, exploding into puffs of black feathers as they hit the ground, but the rest continued to shriek and flap around its head.

Cawing, the ravens swirled together, forming a whirlwind of feathers, wings, and talons right above the Monster's skull. With a final raucous caw, the flock scattered, flying away in different directions, and with a loud whoop, I dropped from the mass of feathers onto the Monster's head.

"Hey, ugly! Guess who it is!"

The Monster jerked, throwing its head back. I grabbed one of its antler tines and waved at the eye that rolled back to glare at me. "Oh hey, fancy running into you here. I was in the area and thought I'd drop in to say hello. You don't mind, do you?"

It snarled, and the tentacles on its neck and shoulders flailed, lashing out at me. I dodged one, swiped at another, and scrambled farther up the Monster's bony skull, away from the writhing shadows. "Whoops, guess I came at a bad time, then. No, no! Bad tentacle, no touchie!" I spun and danced on the Monster's head, avoiding the lashing tendrils while sparing a split-second glance at the figures below. "Hey, ice-boy, not that I don't enjoy monster-skull tap dancing by myself, but feel free to jump in anytime!"

With a howl, the Monster lowered its head and charged a pair of statues standing together against a corner of the courtyard wall. I saw what it was intending and leaped off its head with a yelp, just as the Monster's bony skull slammed into the figures and shattered them into tiny marble fragments. The tentacle-covered ground rushed up at me, but there was a pulse of static filled glamour that sent lightning coils across the ground, and the carpet of black vanished into mist.

I hit the flagstones with a grunt and immediately scrambled back as the Monster's claws smashed into the ground where I'd just been. The creature lunged at me with a roar that made the ground shake, and more shadowy tendrils erupted all around me. I could feel the rage and hatred pulsing from them, from the Monster, from the dark corners of my own heart. I could feel the fear rising again, seeking to drag me under, to suffocate me.

I laughed instead, and a strange thing happened. The tendrils reaching for me drew back, just slightly, as if recoiling from my presence. Of course, that didn't stop the Monster's talons, which came scything down with the force of a missile. I ducked beneath them, wincing as flagstone chips peppered my back.

"You know, for a big, scary monster, you're awfully clingy," I called up to the creature, who curled a lip at the sound of my voice. "Do you want to kill us, or do you just want a hug? I'm getting mixed messages here."

It smashed a fist at me. I leaped back, grinning. "Okay, so not a hug. Maybe you just need a friend? Are you a lonely monster who's just misunderstood?"

With a roar, the creature barreled right at me, coming in shockingly fast. I scrambled back, but with no room to move aside, my choices were either leap into the tentacles or get stomped by the Monster. I saw its gaping, fang-filled mouth coming at me, gripped my dagger, and leaped straight up.

The creature's bony head hit me square in the chest, driving all the air from my lungs, but I raised my dagger and stabbed it into one blazing white eye, before the force of the blow hurled me back several feet. As I flew into the air, I heard the Monster let out a scream of pain at last.

I hit the ground on my back and felt the tendrils latch on, coiling around my waist, arms, legs, and chest. Cold burned my skin, images and emotions flooding my mind, even as I tried blocking them out. Rage. Betrayal. Despair. I felt the darkness rising again, trying to drown every good emotion and memory I had.

Nope, not this time, big ugly. With a deep breath, I closed my eyes, summoning the courage for what I should have done a long time ago. *Are you listening, then? I forgive Ash. I forgive Ash, and myself, for everything that happened between us. I forgive myself for that thing with Ariella, I forgive Meghan for not loving me, hell, I'll even forgive Oberon for being such a jackass all these centuries. Let's start over, clean slate, blank everything. Free love for everyone, whaddya think about that!*

The coils around my limbs vanished, and the bleak emotions trying to suffocate me disappeared. Panting, I struggled to my elbows, then looked up into a pair of familiar silver eyes. Ash gazed down at me, glowing blue sword unsheathed, his face shadowed with concern.

I grinned up at him. "A little late there, ice-boy. Why do you *always* have to wait until the last dramatic moment?"

A relieved expression crossed his face, and he held out a hand. I grabbed it and let him pull me upright, meeting Meghan's worried gaze as she joined us. Several yards away, the Monster was howling and thrashing about, crushing the stones and the statues around it with its tantrum.

"Puck, are you all right?"

"Never better, princess." I offered a real smile, which startled her for a moment. "Just had to find a little piece of me that was lost for a while. I'm good now. I'm back, and I'm here to stay."

"You hurt it." Ash sounded surprised, but there was something else in his voice that wasn't there before. Hope. "It didn't ignore it like last time."

"Yep, I did, didn't I? It looks like the invincible monster isn't quite as invincible as it would have us believe." Still grinning, I turned to look at the Monster, who had lowered its arm and was now glaring at us with the coldest hate, its ruined eye now an empty black hole. "You know, I think I've figured this thing out," I said, smiling with the realization. "I believe our big ugly friend feeds on negative emotion. That's why we couldn't hurt it, and that's why it tries to evoke those emotions whenever it can. Things like rage, fear, and despair only make it stronger."

"So, the answer is not to feel anything?" Ash wondered.

"Not necessarily." I shot him a challenging grin. "If rage and hate make it stronger, then we should do the opposite. Maybe you should try smiling, ice-boy. Oh, and laugh a little, I think that really pisses it off."

The Ice Prince gave me a pained, weary look. "What are you talking about?"

Some distance away, the Monster bared its fangs, then reared up with its loudest, most terrifying roar yet. I looked at Ash, who had a dire, determined look on his face as he grimly raised his sword. I watched him steel himself for battle, him and Meghan both, and a wicked idea floated to mind. A ridiculous, inappropriate, completely Puckish idea.

"Hold on, ice-boy." Reaching back, I plucked something from my hair and held it up: two jet-black feathers that fluttered in the breeze. "Before we start again, we have to set the mood. This could be our last stand, after all. And what's a last stand without some cool battle music?"

I tossed the feathers into the air, sending a pulse of glamour after them. There was a soundless explosion of smoke and feathers, and two more Pucks stood a few feet away, watching us with twin smirks. One held a lute, the other clutched a pan-pipe under his lips, ready to play. As Meghan blinked in astonishment and Ash frowned, I regarded the duplicates critically a moment, then shook my head.

"Huh, something is missing," I mused.

Across the courtyard, the Monster snarled again and prowled forward. Its steps were measured and unhurried, and tentacles sprang up once more, creeping toward us as it came. Meghan and Ash gave it wary looks, but I ignored it, tapping a finger to my chin as I pondered.

"What is it, what is it? Oh, I know!" While he was distracted by the Monster, I slipped behind Ash, grabbed a single strand of jet-black hair, and tugged it free.

"Ow." The Ice Prince stepped back and glared at me. Not long ago, that sort of action would've required me to dodge a swat from his sword or an ice dagger hurled at my head. Now he just gave me a look of resigned exasperation. "What are you doing, Goodfellow?" he snapped.

"Help me out, ice-boy." With a grin, I raised the strand of hair between my fingers. "Remember that period of time where you were trying to learn a new skill?" I went on and watched his brow furrow in confusion. "I think it was to impress Ariella? You spent an entire summer trying to perfect it. Did you ever tell Meghan about that?"

For a second, he continued to frown in confusion. Then his eyes widened, and his face took on an expression of alarm. "Goodfellow, don't you dare—"

I released the strand with a little nudge of glamour. It soared over to the pair of Pucks, and with a poof of smoke, a second Ash appeared between them. He was a bit younger than the Ash standing beside me, dressed in a fine suit with tails, his hair pulled back, and in one hand he held an elegant white-and-gold violin.

Meghan's eyes went huge, and she clapped both hands over her mouth in both amazement and utter delight, forgetting, for the moment, the huge creature still stalking toward us.

I chuckled and looked at Ash. "I seem to remember you played quite well, ice-boy," I said, grinning as the Ash double expertly raised the instrument and placed it under his chin, touching the bow to the strings. "Why don't you start the final battle, then?"

Ash glowered a moment longer, then let his head fall back with a long sigh, raising an arm toward the trio of musicians waiting off to the side. "Goodfellow, I am going to kill you for this," he muttered, and snapped his fingers.

Music filled the air, haunting violin chords that soared up and around us, followed by the sounds of lute and panpipes. The melody swirled around us, rising toward a crescendo that pulled at your emotions, dramatic and exciting and completely epic. It drowned out the snarls of the approaching Monster and made my heart soar in response.

I laughed and looked at Ash again; the Ice Prince stood there glaring at me, but there was the faintest of smirks hiding behind that silver gaze, and Meghan was smiling broadly.

"There now, ice-boy, who said you can't have any fun?"

With a roar, the Monster descended on us, smashing its claws into the middle of our little party, and we scattered. The musicians leaped back, filling the air with a rousing chorus, even as the Monster howled and slashed at them. The two Puck musicians danced as they circled the Ash in the center, eyes closed as he deftly sawed at the strings. The whole thing was so ridiculously wonderful that I laughed out loud, even as I ducked beneath a pair of flailing tentacles and darted close to the flailing Monster.

"And this little piggy went 'ow!'" I said, stabbing my dagger point into one big, hairy toe. The Monster jerked, pulling his foot back like he had just stepped on a hairpin. I danced away, grinning at Ash who was circling around the creature with his sword raised. The Monster's head followed me, eyes blazing with fury, and I shot Ash a gleeful look.

"Come on, ice-boy, I can't be the only one doing all the work. So far, the score is two–zero in my favor."

He gave me a brief, half-annoyed smile as glamour started swirling around him. "Stubbing its toe counts for nothing, Goodfellow," he returned.

I dodged a swat from a giant talon that swooshed over my head. The musicians danced around us, continuing to fill the air with song, the melody rising to fever pitch. "Well, it's better than you're doing, prince!" I challenged, and pirouetted away from the second swat. "I'm still waiting to be impressed. When are you going to start stabbing things?"

"Right now."

The creature bellowed. Tendrils rose up, surrounding me in an inky black forest, but the air turned frigid a moment before ice froze them all in place. The Monster smashed down with its claws, and I danced out of the way as the blows shattered the tentacle forest into tiny pieces.

I grinned, seeing ice-boy on the Monster's other side, hand outstretched as his glamour turned the air frigid. There was a streak of white, and Meghan darted past him, sword upraised. She sprinted at the monster, and with a gesture from the Ice Prince, a series of frozen pillars appeared in front of the Iron Queen, each taller than the last. Meghan bounded up these icy steps, leaped at the Monster just as it was starting to turn, and brought her sword slashing down across its face.

The Monster screamed and reeled back, one hand going to its eyes. Unlike the wisps of shadow from before, dark liquid oozed between its fingers and dripped to the ground. The Iron Queen landed and rolled away as the creature's claw hammered down, shattering flagstones and sending ice chips flying.

"Ooh, nice one, princess!" I grinned as the Monster growled and turned on Meghan, its one remaining eye blazing in fury. "Okay, fine, that was impressive, you two. Now, let's see if you can bring it home."

The Monster took a menacing step toward the Iron Queen. I darted behind it, drew my arm back, and stabbed the point of my dagger into its rear haunch, right below its buttocks.

"Oh, that wasn't nice of me, was it?" I grinned as it whirled with a yelp. "You know, there's still time to work this out— sit down, have a cup of tea, cry on each other's shoulders. No? How about a dance, then?" I danced a little jig, dodging a couple vicious swats, as all the while, the music continued to play, filling the air with emotion and triumph. I laughed again, just because I felt like it, hearing my voice echo over the battlefield and join the rising music.

"You know," I told the creature, smiling as I backed up and

it loomed over me, baring its fangs, "you may be one scary mofo, but you're not very bright. Anyone of average intelligence would know that I'm very clearly the obnoxious decoy, and you're about to get your ass handed to you by the real powers. So, yeah, have fun with that."

For just a second, it seemed to understand my words, for it paused and turned its head to where Meghan and Ash had stopped a few yards away. The Iron Queen stood with her eyes half-closed, palms turned up and glamour swirling around her like a whirlwind. Behind her, Ash stood with his hands on her shoulders, adding his own icy power to the mix, and the storm of magic around them caused the air to flicker and frost to spread out over the ground.

The Monster gave a snarl of what almost sounded like alarm and turned, intending to charge the pair, just as the sharp clatter of hooves over stone rang over the courtyard.

With Nyx on his back, Coaleater charged around a broken wall, barreled toward the Monster, and slammed his powerful iron body into a thick hairy leg. The was a crack, and the fiend staggered with a roar, as Nyx leaped from the Iron faery, vaulted off the Monster's thigh, and brought both moonblades slashing down across its neck. The Monster gave a shriek, flailing wildly, and Nyx sprang away from the lashing tentacles, landing on Coaleater's back like they had practiced this move for decades.

I grinned as my heart soared with relief and pride. "When did you guys decide to join the party?" I called as Coaleater spotted me and galloped over, snorting steam. On his back, Nyx smiled down at me.

"About the time the music started," she replied. "We were letting our host chase us around the courtyard, but when the music started playing, it was like he remembered who he was again. Or at least, the Monster's influence started to fade."

"Where is he now?"

A massive shadow leaped to the top of the courtyard wall,

eyes blazing. With a roar, the beast sprang at the Monster, landing with his full weight atop its back and driving it to its knees.
And at that moment, the rulers of Iron unleashed their glamour.

The ground trembled, and enormous roots erupted from
the earth, breaking through flagstone and shattering the stones
around them. The roots coiled around the Monster, thickening
and tightening, becoming as gnarled and tough as tree trunks.
They also radiated cold. Even from my perch, I could feel the
icy waves, see the tendrils of mist and frost in the air as the roots
continued to coil around the Monster like massive pythons. The
creature snarled and thrashed, raking the ground and causing
several roots to snap, but with a shimmer of glamour, the roots
turned to steel cables and the cold grew even sharper.

A coating of frost crept up the Monster's legs, turning to ice
as it rose higher. Ice covered its bottom half, freezing it in place,
and continued to climb with sharp crinkling sounds.

I saw what was happening, and an evil, Puckish grin spread
over my face.

"Puck." Nyx saw my expression and immediately held out a
hand. I grabbed it, and she pulled me up behind her, balanced
on the Iron faery's broad metal back. "Where to?"

"Right at it," I answered. "As close as you can get."

We charged. Coaleater's hooves rang against the stone as he
cantered toward the looming mountain of Monster, still thrashing against the web of ice and iron holding him down. Snorting
fire, the Iron faery dodged a flailing claw and swerved close,
leaping over the tangle of tentacles sprouting around the Monster. At the peak of his jump, I sprang off his back, landing on
the slippery, ice-covered slope of the fiend's shoulders.

Farther up the back, the beast turned and gave me a look
as I sprinted toward him, dodging the final few tentacles as I
reached its head.

"Hey, beastman, give me a lift!"

He scowled in confusion for half a second, before understanding dawned in those blue eyes and he crouched, opening his paws for me to step into. I sprang onto his palms, and he rose, hurling me straight into the air and over the Monster's head.

Throwing back its muzzle, the Monster let out a final bellow of fury before the growing layer of ice reached its skull, flowing over its head, covering its antlers. And suddenly there was an enormous frozen statue standing in the center of the courtyard. Right underneath me.

Pulling my daggers, I grinned down at it. "Checkmate, big ugly."

I plunged toward the Monster, bringing both daggers point down on its skull, and the creature shattered.

With the sound of a million china cups crashing to the floor, the fiend that had terrorized Phaed and the Nevernever, turned me into an evil bastard, and had very nearly killed us all exploded into thousands of glistening crystal shards that scattered throughout the courtyard. There was a rush of wind, a howl that curled my insides, and a choking cloud of darkness emerged through the falling ice, fraying apart as it spiraled up and vanished into the night.

I landed on the broken flagstones, covering my head as frozen bits rained down around me, stinging exposed flesh and plinking off the stones. Sharp bits of hail struck my arms and bounced off my head, but it was ice and nothing else. No blood, bones, or frozen creature parts. The Monster had vanished, as if it never was.

As the rain of crystal shards came to an end, I straightened and looked around for the rest of the party. A few paces away, Coaleater tossed his head, then reared onto his hind legs with a bugle of triumph, pawing the air. At the edge of the shattered flagstones, Meghan let out a sigh and leaned backward into Ash, whose arms came up to support her tightly. And the beast stalked through the glittering remains, nodding his horned head and looking pleased.

I turned, looking around for Nyx, then felt the cool edge of a moonblade against my throat from behind. "Sloppy again, Goodfellow," the Forgotten murmured in my ear. "Even after a victory, you shouldn't let down your guard."

I grinned, shaking my head. "Is this how it's going to be, then?" I asked, as the blade dropped away and Nyx slid around to face me fully. "Knives to my throat after every major occasion? Is that how your Order said happy birthday or congratulations, you just saved the world?"

"Typically not," Nyx replied. "It's just more fun with you." Her eyes went to my forehead, and cool fingers brushed my hair back. "You're not horny anymore."

I chuckled, relieved beyond common sense that I was finally back to normal. I could see my regular, nonhorned reflection in her eyes, feel the lack of fur beneath my pants, and grinned at the Forgotten in front of me. "I could go sooo many places with that."

She rolled her eyes. "Yes, well, it's getting rather old, so let me stop you right there."

And she kissed me.

I closed my eyes, wrapping my arms around her slim waist as her arms circled my neck. For a few seconds, there was only Nyx, her body against mine, and the sweet feeling of triumph, elation, and relief sweeping through us both.

Suddenly, I became aware of the music, of the sweet, haunting notes of a violin mixed with the melody of a lute and the sound of panpipes. Opening my eyes, I saw the three conjured musicians surrounding us, the Ash double out in front, playing, unless I was mistaken, the theme song from *Lady and the Tramp*.

Which I certainly hadn't told them to play.

I jerked my head up and saw Ash, standing with his arms around Meghan, smirking at me over her shoulder. I felt my face heat, even as a laugh crawled up my throat and burst free, even as Nyx gazed at us both in confusion. The lingering anger and resentment that had been buried deep inside me was finally gone; for the first time in centuries, I felt truly free.

"Oh touché, ice-boy. Happy to see you finally grew a sense of humor."

He smiled. Meghan chuckled and leaned against her husband, resting her head against him with a sigh. "Well, this was an ordeal," she said, letting a hint of weariness creep into her voice along with the relief. "Everyone, you have our gratitude, and the appreciation of the Iron Realm. That you would stay and fight, even when things looked hopeless…" Her blue eyes flicked to me, her smile a thank-you without words. "I'm grateful."

"It was an honor to fight with you, Your Majesty," Coaleater said in a solemn voice. "The Iron herd will always stand ready to defend the realm and its queen, from any threat. I am just glad that it's over."

"I would not celebrate just yet."

Everyone turned. Grimalkin sat a few feet away, his back to us, his gaze pointed toward the beast's huge castle. But his attention wasn't on the castle itself. The Forgotten we'd left in the tower had come forward, staggering like a drunk across the courtyard, staring at us with its yellow headlamp eyes.

"Not over," it whispered, taking a few shaky steps forward. "It's not over yet." It paused, staring at the place the Monster had vanished, at the smashed stones and broken statues, and gave a violent shudder. "No, this…this was just a fragment, a stray thread of consciousness that escaped from the whole. It sleeps still, barely aware of the world above. But it is starting to awaken. It is starting to become aware, and when it does, the world will crack, and we will all plunge into the abyss."

It turned huge, maddened eyes on us, raising an arm toward the horizon. "The end has begun," it whispered. "You cannot stop it. No one can stop it. Evenfall is coming. Faery, and every living creature that exists under the sun, is doomed."

And before we could do anything, it reached down and drew

a dagger out of nowhere, from the shadows that made up its whole form. The blade was obsidian black, seeming to draw in the light rather than reflect it. I jumped as, with a cry, the Forgotten raised its arm and plunged that inky blade into his own chest. He jerked once, twitched twice, and then seemed to fray apart into tendrils of shadow that coiled into the air and faded on the wind.

In the stunned quiet that followed, Meghan took a shaky breath and stepped away from Ash, her expression grave as she faced us all. "All right," the Iron Queen said, and her voice was steely, preparing for what was to come. "I think it's time to go home."

EPILOGUE

The world certainly didn't *feel* like it was on the brink of the End of All Things when we left the Briars and returned to the wyldwood. Everything looked and felt normal; from the piskies that dropped pine cones on my head as they zipped by in the trees, to the large redcap motley that tried ambushing us near the border…until they realized we had the Iron Queen in our party and became very sniveling very quickly.

I myself was feeling rather cheerful, back to my old Puckish self. My horns were gone, and my bottom half didn't look like I'd done terrible things to a goat. We had just defeated the big bad threatening the Nevernever, I had survived, and all of my friends were alive and well. Best scenario I could've hoped for.

But most of all, my senses were still buzzing from the kiss of a certain Forgotten. I could feel her beside me, an elegant, funny, dangerous, beautiful shadow, and holy balls I was in deep, wasn't I? I hadn't felt this way since…well, since a half-human princess had broken my heart all those years ago.

Would Nyx do the same, I wondered? Was I in even more

danger now? Because not only could she crush my tender feelings, she could also very easily slice my throat from behind, and I'd never see it coming. I didn't know, but at the moment, I was willing to take that chance. After all, my name was Robin Goodfellow. Flirting with danger was something I was very familiar with.

But even though I was feeling rather optimistic about my life in general, a shadow lingered over my thoughts. The Monster was just a fragment of something bigger, the nameless Forgotten had said, a thread of a consciousness just starting to wake up.

How much bigger, I wondered. Were we talking mountain giant, ancient dragon, or Godzilla? Or something even bigger than that? I remembered the grove of the Mother Tree, how Meghan had recoiled when she'd followed the roots down into the earth. Was that our big nasty? A darkness sleeping under the Nevernever, slowly corrupting everything it touched?

I shivered. Well, whatever it was, when it did decide to wake up and claw its way to the surface, bent on chaos and destruction, it would find all of us waiting for it. I gazed around at the people walking back with me: Meghan and Ash, Nyx, Coaleater, and Grimalkin. We wouldn't stand by and do nothing, even in the face of prophecy. When the time came, futile or not, we would fight with everything we had. And just like today, if we stood together, we might just turn that prophecy on its head and win.

That was my plan, anyway.

At the edge of the Iron Kingdom's border, a carriage stood, apparently waiting to take the rulers of Iron back to Mag Tuiredh. Turning, the Iron Queen gave us all a weary smile.

"I must return to the city," she said, with the tired relief of a queen who knew her people were safe, at least for the moment. "We accomplished what we came to do, which was to kill the threat to the Nevernever and Faery. But I fear this isn't the end of it. Something is coming. Both the oracle and the Forgotten mentioned it."

"Evenfall."

The word came from Grimalkin, and I felt a chill run from the top of my spine all the way to my nonhairy feet. "The onset of evening," the cat went on. "The coming of dusk. When everything falls to twilight. I have not heard this prophecy before, which means it is either very new, or older than the Nevernever. I do not like the implications of either."

"Whatever it means," Meghan continued, "something *is* coming. And I want us to be ready for it when it finally appears. That means we need to warn the other courts of what we saw tonight. Puck," she went on, glancing at me, "I need you to go back to Arcadia. Let Oberon know what is happening. Ash will do the same with Mab. Coaleater, return to the plains and inform Spikerail of what is going on. Let him know that I might need to call on the Iron herd before this is all over."

"I will, Iron Queen." The Iron faery straightened and put his fist over his heart. "The Iron herd will stand ready to aid you whenever you need us."

Meghan nodded, then glanced at the Forgotten beside me. "Nyx..."

Nyx gave a solemn bow. "I will return to the Between and tell Keirran what has happened here, Your Majesty," she said. Raising her head, she gave the Iron Queen an understanding look. "And whatever else you wish to tell him."

I stifled a sigh. Yeah, I knew that had to happen, but it was still mildly annoying. Now, instead of relaxing and traveling the Nevernever in the company of a beautiful assassin, I was going to have to deal with this newest problem. Stupid End of the World prophecies, always popping up at the most inconvenient times.

Meghan smiled, but at that moment, movement near the border caught my attention. A trio of figures slipped around the carriage and came striding toward us, the sunlight flashing off their metal armor. I saw flickers of purple lightning and saw that Glitch was in front, his face intense as he walked straight for Meghan.

"Your Majesty!"

Meghan turned as the first lieutenant bowed and the two knights went down on a knee before her and Ash. "Glitch," Ash acknowledged. "What's wrong? Why are you here, away from Mag Tuiredh?"

"Your Highnesses." Glitch rose, his expression grave and his already pale face nearly white. In that moment, a chill went through my stomach. I knew, somehow, that whatever news the first lieutenant had to deliver was not going to be good.

"I'm sorry, my queen," Glitch said into the sudden tense silence. "But we received a message today…from the Between. Touchstone, the capital of the Forgotten, is no more. Prince Keirran, King of the Forgotten, has vanished."

★ ★ ★ ★ ★

We hope you enjoyed this journey into the
magical and perilous world of Faery!
Look for book 2 of The Iron Fey: Evenfall trilogy,

The Iron Sword.

Only from Julie Kagawa and HQ!

ONE PLACE. MANY STORIES

Bold, innovative and
empowering publishing.

FOLLOW US ON:

@HQStories